PRAISE FOR *TH*

"*The Hike* just works. It's like early,
Magary underhands a twist in at the end that hits you like a
sharp jab at the bell... It's just that good." — NPR.org

"Magary even nails the ending with a *Twilight Zone* twist that
would have Rod Serling nodding with approval."
— Kirkus Reviews

"*The Hike* is Cormac McCarthy's *Alice in Wonderland*."
— Jeffrey Cranor, bestselling co-author of *Welcome to Nightvale*

PRAISE FOR *THE POSTMORTAL*

"A must-read for fans of postmodern dystopia in the vein of
Margaret Atwood, Chuck Palahniuk, and Neil Gaiman." —
Library Journal

"Magary's vision of future technology and science is eerily
realistic... By the time you finish, you'll want to hold your
loved ones close and stockpile bottles of water. If all else fails,
you could potentially make a living selling them a few decades
from now." — The New York Press

Point B
(a teleportation love story)

Drew Magary

This one goes out to all you crazy kids out there

Once you give the gift away
There's nothing you can do about it
Nothing that you do or say
Can change the way I feel about it
-Sugar, 1995

Terms and Conditions

PORTPHONE8 TERMS AND CONDITIONS: SECTION II, PARAGRAPH 38(g)

The PortSys Operating System (pOS) is based on the antihydrogen porting method,
which includes the following restrictions:

1. Porting is limited to the surface of Earth and any manmade structures on it, as tracked by the PortSys GPS system.

2. Porting cannot be done in groups.

3. Users cannot port into solid matter.

4. Only living humans can port, plus two additional kilograms of inanimate mass with them in transit. (YOU PLUS TWO™)

**By accepting these terms and conditions, you agree that PortSys cannot be held liable for any damages
incurred in the porting process, or at any point thereafter.**

☐ I have read and agree to the terms and conditions

AGREE AND CONTINUE

PROLOGUE—ROCKVILLE, MD

Sarah Huff needed a gun. A gun of her own. She wouldn't tell her mom about it. She wouldn't tell Anna about it. If they knew she had a gun, they would just freak out and make the whole situation worse. She went to a strung-out 22-year-old named Bryce, who loitered around the same abandoned corner in the free zones of Rockville every day, selling black market shit to anyone who needed it. Bryce had weed. Bryce had pills. Bryce had prepaid PortPhones. And, upon special request, Bryce could get you a weapon if you agreed to re-connect with him at a secondary pin of his choice.

So that's what Sarah did. She found Bryce hanging out by the railroad crossing and asked him for help.

"What kind of help?" Bryce asked her.

"Someone's harassing me," she told him.

"Someone you know?"

"I'd rather not say."

"So just port away from him."

"No matter where I port, he can find me. Even behind a good portwall."

"That's not possible, kiddo."

"It is for him," Sarah told Bryce, "and I'm the one who should be calling *you* kiddo. Can you help or not? I got fifty bucks."

"I can get you a piece of shit for that much."

"Do you have something nicer that's still a decent price?"

"You've never bought a gun before, have you?"

"No."

"Well, any gun you buy for fifty bucks is gonna be a piece of shit, but I can get you a piece of shit."

"Deal."

He took out his phone and sent her a pinned location.

"Go here at 3:55 and I'll give you the goods," he told her.

She spent the rest of that day sweating the clock. After getting the gun, she would have to port home to stash it, and then port to San Francisco to punch in to her hostessing job at 4:30pm sharp. It was gonna be tight. When the clock finally hit 3:55pm, she took out her phone, hit PORT, took a step, and felt the shiver.

1

Now she was in Houghton, MI. The Upper Peninsula. A tiny peninsula *on* that peninsula, naked to the violent winds sweeping in from Lake Superior. She was standing in a small, beached cove along the lake's canal, water so clear and clean that you could see twenty feet to the bottom. You could even drink it straight. Bryce was waiting for her with a paper bag.

"Is this where you always do pickups?" she asked him.

"I have favorite drop spots. Other dealers always pick Tahiti or some other tropical joint. I pride myself on being a bit smarter than that."

"It's nice here."

"Who cares. Where's the money?"

She handed Bryce the cash. By the time she opened the bag, he was already gone, sending himself wherever his whims felt like taking him. Inside the bag she saw a pistol so old and rusty, it looked like it belonged on a mantelpiece. Then she realized what she had forgotten.

"There are no bullets in this thing!" she texted Bryce.

"Bullets are $20 each. :)"

"You bastard."

She ported home and scrounged up the extra money. One slow night's worth of hostessing tips was enough for two lousy bullets. She ported home with the loaded pistol and scoured her room for a place to hide it. Her mom, Sandy, liked tidying up the house whenever the girls were out, so Sarah stashed the gun on the top shelf of her closet, behind a red fleece blanket that hadn't moved from its spot in over eight years, remarkably avoiding Sandy's more fastidious tendencies. There was no telling if Mrs. Huff would, in a fit of inspiration, go rummaging through that closet one day, hunting for new items to donate to Goodwill. But as hiding spots went, it was the best Sarah could do for now. Sandy Huff had a gun, but only she was allowed to wield it. Her daughters weren't supposed to have one.

That night, after Sarah had finished her shift the at MyClub in San Francisco, she came home to Maryland, brushed her teeth, put on her t-shirt and shorts, slowly opened the closet door (it creaked;

2

doors always betrayed her like that) and felt around that top shelf in the dark. Anna, Sarah's little sister, was fast asleep in the room next door with their mom. At last, Sarah felt her hand wrap around the duct-taped butt of the pistol, and carefully slipped it under her pillow. She wasn't comfortable with it so close by. Then again, it had been a long while since she had been comfortable at all.

There was no telling when the man would port into her bedroom. Sometimes he came every night. Sometimes he'd let a whole week pass before appearing, a tall dark shroud at the foot of her bed with his hair parted down the center, clad in khaki pants and a black t-shirt with a crude emblem on the front:

Sarah had tinkered over and over with improving her mom's portwall, moving the router around to help keep the signal clear, but it was no use. It wasn't like the portwall they had at work. If you wanted a decent portwall, you had to pay WallTech for one, and they didn't build them for just anybody. And this ghoul could slither past any of them, even the good ones. Even when Sarah spent the night elsewhere, there he was again.

In a way, Sarah preferred the nights when the man showed up. Once he came and went, she knew he wouldn't be back for the rest of the night. She could trust the silence again. She hated the silence before his arrival, knowing it was mere prelude. Anna and her mom rarely woke up from the portclap because, like everyone else living in the free zones, they wore earplugs at night. On the nights the man didn't show up, Sarah would just lie there, dreading his arrival until the sun rose. She felt him, at all times. Even if he was on the other side of the Earth, she knew he was but a push of a touch screen away. His presence permeated the room like a lingering scent.

Tonight, she had the alarm clock turned away from her on the nightstand, so that she wouldn't be tempted to sneak a peek. It didn't matter. Every time she felt a coming wave of dreams, she would think of the man and be jerked back into consciousness, like a dog on a leash. He occupied her headspace fully. The best she could do was idle herself by manufacturing distracting thoughts: mental chew toys for her brain to go fetch. Tonight she thought about friends, and about Anna, and about music, and about movies, and about the gigantic, AI-enabled smartwall that the government was supposedly trying (and failing) to build around the contiguous forty-eight states. But she was only able to hold her brain off for so long before the man was back inside her.

Finally, after Sarah had been trapped in an insomniac's purgatory for hours, the troll ported into her room, the blowback from his arrival sweeping over her in an angry gust. He loomed over her bed. She could hear him breathing. God, she hated that sound. It filled the bedroom with a kind of awful hunger. As with every other visit, he was carrying a butcher knife on him, hewn from a single piece of reinforced steel. He had never used it on her. She figured he enjoyed the threat of the knife more than actually stabbing people with it, although maybe he'd change his mind about that sometime. The man also never touched Sarah when he ported in, but he may as well have. He may as well have taken a bit drill and bored a hole clean through her body.

He held out his free hand and whispered, "You know the drill."

She tossed her PortPhone to him.

"If you have any other cameras on right now, I'll know."

"I know," Sarah told him.

"Good, then we can begin. You're a pig. Kill yourself." That was the central message of every visit. *Kill yourself.*

She sat up and pointed the gun at him.

"What is that?" he asked.

"You leave me alone and never come back."

"Awwww, little piggy's got a gun, does she? Tell you what, sweetheart: Kill yourself with that. Be free."

"I'll shoot you, I swear to God."

"And then what? Then you go to jail forever, and then you kill yourself anyway. Save yourself the headache."

"Why are you doing this to me?"

"Why not? The world would be better off if you died and went to Pig Heaven."

"I'll port somewhere new and you'll never find me."

"Sure I will. I'll always find you."

"LEAVE ME ALONE!"

Even when she screamed, no one could hear her. The rest of the world was entirely at peace, regardless of her torment. She was all alone with her demon.

The man locked the bedroom door, then turned and stood in front of Sarah defiantly.

"Do it," he commanded. He was staying longer than usual. The gun only seemed to please him. He was so unfazed by its presence that he set his butcher knife down on her desk and gave it a spin, for kicks. "Go on."

Sarah began to cry. "Please just leave me alone."

"There's only one way to ensure that I will," he said calmly. "Pull the trigger and you won't remember I existed. You won't even remember *you* existed. Don't you want that freedom, dear? When you die you'll be untouchable: the god you were always meant to be. People will say only the best things about you once you're gone. It'll be so much nicer than what they say about you now."

"I'LL FUCKING KILL YOU!"

"Sarah?"

That was Sarah's mom, stirring next door. But by now it was too late. The man was right. She'd never be free of him, no matter what she did or where she went. He'd always know where she was, and he could slip past any portwall. How could he do that? No one else could. And if she killed him, well then he'd *really* be with her

5

forever now, wouldn't he? You couldn't escape anyone anymore. Not in this world.

"Mom," Sarah shouted calmly. "Mom and Anna, I love you both so much."

"SARAH?!"

She put the gun to her chin.

ONE YEAR LATER

DRUSKIN GATE

Anna Huff wasn't going anywhere. She ported in next to the gargantuan Penske truck that was parked outside Druskin Gate, grabbed her suitcase—a stubborn, lumbering thing that froze in place whenever it came into contact with any uneven surface—from the back, and tugged it down the loading ramp. Sandy, smothering her daughter properly, ported in barely an inch away from Anna, the force from the blowback of displaced air nearly knocking Anna over in front of everyone.

"Mom."

"Sorry."

Sandy Huff dutifully followed Anna toward the gate, still too close, spitting out a stream of reminders so long that Anna couldn't even remember which reminder came first.

"Now, you have to check in before you can go to your room."

"I know, mom."

"Are you hungry? We could eat before we go in. There's a pizza place nearby that is getting absolute raves. We could even go hog wild and skip over to Italy for a minute. We've still got our passports out."

"I'm not hungry."

"Let me take a picture of you."

"Please God, no."

There were a handful of armed troops standing around on the street to patrol this first day of school, checking everyone who ported in to make sure they were wearing their passport card lanyards. One of the soldiers—seemingly young enough to be a Druskin student—flipped Anna's over using the barrel of his rifle. She hated when they did that.

"I'm a U.S. citizen," Anna insisted.

"Sorry ma'am, but we do have to check."

"With your gun? You have hands, don't you? Or are you just so in love with that thing you gotta stroke it all day long?"

Her mom intervened.

"Oh my goodness sir, I'm so sorry for my daughter."

"Why are you apologizing to him?" Anna demanded to know.

9

"Because he has a gun. Can you wait until we've been here for longer than thirty seconds to start being a pain in the tushie?"

She yanked Anna away from the guard. There was a slipstream of other kids flowing through Druskin Gate. They were part of Anna's porting group, each group scheduled to arrive in 15-minute intervals on Orientation Day. If anyone ported in earlier, Druskin officials would smile passive-aggressively and make them port right back to where they came from. *Oh, you seem to be mistaken as to when you were supposed to port in, aren't you?* They were fun like that.

Anna's mom wasn't about to let her join the procession through the gate just yet, nor did she seem to care that every other student in their porting group was going to reach check-in before them. She was perfectly content to hold Anna hostage. The longer the two of them stood out there, the more self-conscious Anna became. Yep, she was the one with the overbearing mother. *Everyone have a good look.*

"Can we please go?" she begged Sandy.

"Let me just get one more photo of us together."

"Fine."

Anna posed for the selfie but didn't smile. She had the sullen 17-year-old look down, and she was quite proud of it. The world had never seen such dramatic indifference.

"Oh, Anna. That was awful. Let's do it again."

"You said one."

"One *good* one."

"How do you know that wasn't good?"

Sandy had heard enough.

"You know Anna, you agreed to come here. You agreed to be held back a year to enroll. I never forced this on you. You know what a fantastic opportunity this is. Look around you. This place is flawless."

Even with the pallid skies, it was true. Beyond the wrought iron gate Anna could see a table of cheery Orientation leaders, and past them a gentle hill sloping down to a perfectly manicured quad crisscrossed with paths, like stripes on the Union Jack. Weeds were nonexistent. It already felt more stable at Druskin than anywhere else Anna went. Grounded. It was nice to know she wouldn't be sleeping in a new ShareSpace every six weeks. She remembered the day she got into this place, when admissions chair Mr. Glenn ported directly to their ShareSpace to give Anna the news in person, and to present her with a formal acceptance letter that she swore to keep forever.

"Mom, I really do appreciate this."

"Do you?" asked Mrs. Huff. "It's safe here."

"I get it. But I don't know if I wanna be safe."

"Yes, you do."

"What do you want me to say? Do you want me to set off sparklers and have a party?"

"No. I want you to recognize hope when you see it."

Anna sighed and turned back to the gate, which was flanked with Druskin's own security guards—all of them equipped with enough firearms to raid an aircraft carrier—and had a big sign that cried out STUDENTS AND FACULTY ONLY BEYOND THIS POINT. Port marketers blew in for a last-second chance to hawk supplies, music subscriptions, and OTC stimulants to incoming students and their harried families.

There was a bin twenty yards to the left of the gate, where students were expected to drop their PortPhones off for the entirety of their stay on campus grounds. Behind the bin was a brick wall that stretched twenty feet high and ran the entire perimeter of Druskin campus, over 600 acres. It was a gorgeous structure, in its own daunting way. The bricks were spotless, like they had been scrubbed daily with a toothbrush. Druskin brochures boasted that the school's portwall cost $1 billion and was utterly impenetrable. The physical wall itself probably cost them nothing by comparison.

Sandy walked next to the PortPhone deposit bin. "Are you ready?"

Anna saw other students walking to that box like they were going to view a corpse at a wake. But Anna was ready. They could take her phone, but she'd still sort out a way to go where she wanted, yes she would.

Just then, a coterie of adults blew by the Huffs. They were dressed in fine Italian clothing, all of it custom-tailored, all of it fitting with subatomic precision. Other grownups ported in around the mob: family members, friends, even a TV cameraman or two. They were like popcorn popping, the blowback from porting jostling them all around, like they were all trapped in a scrum with a gang of invisible hooligans. Anna tried to make out the center of the mob but could only spot a sharp bob of black hair. A teenage boy holding a bouquet of tulips that each suffered from bad posture ported in and desperately tried to muscle his way into the mob, shouting, "Lara! LARA!" He seemed desperate and miserable, clutching the flowers so hard he may as well have been strangling them. Seeing that pitiful boy was the first time all day that Anna smiled.

Once the horde reached the portwall, POP POP POP they went, leaving quick as they came with nothing but rude thunderclaps in their wake. Now Anna could see the object of their affections: a girl her age, with an ink-black bob that looked like it had been cut with a diamond laser. The girl took a look back from the gate and Anna could see her in full: all polished cheeks and green eyes. Now Anna wasn't in such a dickish mood. She could have sworn she had seen this Lara girl before, but couldn't quite place her. Regardless, now she wanted to go through Druskin Gate very much. She wanted to go wherever that Lara was going.

The girl slipped through the gate without a word and her suitor was left alone and ignored. Grief-stricken. He threw his flowers against the brick wall and yelled "Bitch!" before taking out his phone and porting away. Another rude thunderclap.

"What was that all about?" her mom asked.

"I don't know, but I hope that kid ports into an open volcano."

"Anna."

"I'm joking. I meant that I hope he ports in front of a locomotive."

"Anna."

"I didn't say it had to be *moving*."

"Drop your phone in and let's get on with this."

12

Anna joined her mom at the bin and took out the PortPhone. It still felt great to hold it in her palm. She had a thick case for it in the shape of a bulldog, and she called the phone Dougie when no one else was around. What a miracle the thing was. You could take it out of your pocket, hit PORT, feel the shiver, and then be anywhere you wanted, albeit still stuck on this chaotic shithole of a planet. The PortPhone was a key to every door, and Anna loved Dougie as much as everyone else loved their PortPhones, no matter how much misery owning one brought her, nor how much misery she could carry with it.

She took the bulldog cover off and saved it. Now it was just some phone. Now it would be easier to abandon.

"Anna."

"I'm ready."

She held the phone over the bin and dropped it down.

"How'd that feel?" her mom asked.

"Like the cell door just slammed shut," Anna answered. She was faking that particular bit of drama. It didn't feel *that* bad.

"They give you laptops and tablets and smartphones, you know. You'll still be able to scratch a lot of your itches."

"You still have *your* PortPhone, don't you?"

Her mom sighed. "I know, I'm a hypocrite."

"It's all right. I get it. I'd be a hypocrite about it too if I were you."

"You're gonna be all right here."

"I know that. What about you, mom?"

Her mom began to cry. "Oh, Anna. Anna, I'll never be all right."

They wrapped their arms around each other. Whenever Anna was away from home, she had terrible visions of Sandy dead from suicide. She could picture Sandy slipping away from one of her two dishwashing jobs and doing it with a gun, or with a razorblade, or porting to a scenic cliff and taking a swan dive off of it. Anna didn't want to picture any of that, but her imagination possessed an inward cruelty that she couldn't purge no matter how hard she tried.

They kept hugging. Every time they embraced, the angst would bleed out of Anna and leave her refreshed and renewed. And yet, how often did she and her old lady hug each other? Once a month? Why didn't they always hug like this? It was like both of them *wanted* to be stiff with tension all the time. Like they both knew instinctively that relaxing, in this world, was a lousy idea.

"Port to Hawaii for a little bit," Anna whispered. "Get some sun."

"Hawaii is an ant farm these days," Sandy said. "Everyone ports there."

"Then go where the people aren't. Send pictures."

"Your tuition here may be paid for but your room and board isn't, and your father has never written me a child support check. I have work to do."

"Just take care of yourself."

"There's no point in that. You're all that matters, Anna." She pointed at her watch. "Every Wednesday, at 5pm, I'll port right here so you can see me. That okay?"

"Of course."

"You don't even have to come out to say hi if you're not in the mood. I'll never smother you."

"Too late!"

"But I'll never stop worrying."

"I don't think anyone stops worrying anymore."

"I guess not."

It was time for Sandy to go, but of course there had to be an awkward bit of lingering. There had to be an all-too-noticeable moment where Mrs. Huff didn't want to leave, and Anna felt too guilty to actively push her mom away. The port group after Anna's started popping in, the portwinds blowing harsh against the Huffs.

"Mom, you should probably let me go."

"Can you blame me if I don't want to?" Sandy asked.

"Of course not."

"But you're right. I guess it's time. But remember: Wednesday at 5pm."

"Got it."

"And I love you."

"Me too."

Her mom took out her PortPhone and hit PORT. Another portclap. That was it. Sandy Huff was back in Maryland already. It took nothing to leave, and nothing to be forgotten.

SEWELL HALL

"Welcome to Druskin!"

That was Orientation leader Brendan McClear. Anna knew his full name because it was right there on his name tag, in handwriting far too neat for a boy his age. Brendan McClear handed Anna five different forms.

"You're gonna have to sign these," Brendan McClear told her.

"What are they?" she asked.

"Just some silly forms. Oh, and here's your name tag."

"I don't want a name tag."

"But—"

"No," Anna insisted. "I hate name tags."

"Everyone has one today. Plus you can take your passport lanyard off as long as you're on campus! Don't you want everyone to know your name?"

"Not really."

"Oh." Brendan McClear was crushed. The flop of blonde hair on top of his preppy little head wilted at her reply. Brendan McClear couldn't comprehend a world where people didn't want to wear a name tag. Anna half-expected to see tiny gears and flywheels come popping out of his head. "You should just keep the name tag handy in case you change your mind."

"I won't."

Brendan McClear remained undeterred. "Now, I've got your room assignment and your transponder."

"Transponder?"

"Yes!" He fished a clear plastic band out from a basket. "It goes around your ankle. Very light. You don't even notice it's there after a day or two."

"What does it do?"

"It alerts them if you cross the Harkness Wall, that's all. Please note that Druskin would never sell your personal information to a third party or use your location for financial gain."

"I'm not wearing that. They use those in prisons."

"I'm sorry but it's compulsory."

"You're not sorry."

She took the transponder and strapped it around her ankle. Brendan McClear wasn't smiling anymore. He was now deterred. He'd had enough of dealing with someone so rude.

"It monitors your vitals," he reminded her, "So if you take it off, they know."

"Well now, if they know so much, it makes you wonder why I'd ever need a name tag, then."

"It's not for them, it's for your fellow classmates."

"Who is 'them', anyway?" Anna asked.

"Student Services."

"That's a pleasant name," Anna cocked an eyebrow, "for a bunch of *spies*."

Brendan McClear took out a map of campus and circled one of the buildings, then slipped the paper her way. "You're in Sewell Hall, room 24. I can walk you there if you'd like, although I bet you'd prefer to find it on your own."

"That I would, Brendan McClear." She waltzed away from the Orientation kiosk and toward Sewell Hall: a boxy, red-bricked edifice that looked like a giant board game piece. Its metal front door was propped open with a rock that had been painted over many, many times. The freshest coat had WELCOME JUNIOR CLASS OF 2032 spelled out in deep maroon strokes. Next to the door was a ceremonial cornerstone with the inscription SEWELL HALL, 1920.

No one was there to greet the new Sewell girls as they lugged their rollerboards over a threshold that jutted up from the doorway with nasty intent. All of the seniors were due later that day. Anna passed through the entrance and into a damp, airless hallway. All hard surfaces: brick pillars, iron window frames, thick linoleum flooring. The spirit of 1920 had clearly never left this place. It was an architectural curiosity of a dump. The hall made a T at the end and split off to both sides. Anna got to the split and looked through a wide glass partition down to a sad little common room below.

This wasn't in the catalog.

At both ends of the T hallway were cold, dark stairwells that wound up to the top of the dorm, like twin freight shafts. Anna searched in vain for a working elevator—that charming relic of years past—but it was already clear that she was gonna have to hoof it. Every quarter-turn of the west stairwell brought her to an even-numbered room, each door colorfully festooned with the names of its residents, with new girls giggling and yammering away behind it. Like they all already knew each other. Like they had instantly figured out who was whose best friend before Anna had even entered the fray. As always, her best one-liners would be reserved for an audience of herself and no one else.

Three full flights and she was only at Room 12.

"Jesus."

She could dive like a champ, so she was in much better shape at the moment to fall than to climb. By the time she made it to the top, her back was a waterfall.

Her first assembly was in less than thirty minutes. She walked into the room and was greeted by blank white walls and a bed (a cot, really) with a thin mattress and a nasty iron frame that was a close relative of chain link fencing. There was a cheap particle board desk, upon which rested a school-issued laptop already plugged in and network-enabled. Five sad brown cardboard boxes were stacked in the center: all the crap that Anna and her mother had shipped to school in advance of her arrival, all in boxes carried along dilapidated highways by trucks that now ruled the roads in grim solitude. On top of the boxes was a laminated piece of orange construction paper that blared ANNA HUFF in all caps, with little stars and flowers surrounding her name. The kind of nameplate that would decorate a preschool coat hook. She took it and threw it in the trash can.

There was a mini-fridge and Anna prayed it would be fully stocked. She swung open the little brown door and saw nothing but fluorescent light and barren, off-white grates. Right away she decided this fridge would be for sugar-free energy drinks and nothing else. No food. If there were food in there, it would leak and stink and take up too much room and she would eat it at unhealthy hours. Instead, she would stock this fridge exclusively with bullet-shaped cans adorned in green lightning bolts and flaming skulls, with twenty-four ounces of liquid taurine packed tight inside.

If you could just port, you could get an energy drink. Why can't we just port to get some goddamn drinks?

The room was a double and Anna could hear rustling coming from behind the door of the inner room. She was terrified of knocking. God only knew what kind of fresh awkward hell awaited her behind that door. She was gonna put off the discovery of her new roommate for as long as possible. Instead, she went over to her new bed and opened up the drawstring of the thin white laundry bag sitting on top of it. Inside she found a towel, a fitted sheet, a starched top sheet, a blanket, and a generic toilet kit. All of it was mummified in shrink wrap. A bugle played "Reveille" in her mind while she stared at the package.

Suddenly, there were voices coming from the inner room. Anna turned and stared at the door.

"Mom, what are you doing here? You can't just port in."

"Is this where they put you? In a double?"

"It's fine. Be cool about it."

"Unacceptable. I'll be talking to Dean Vick about this arrangement."

The door swung open and Anna saw a massive shadow creep across the threshold: the silhouette of a woman six feet tall. Anna always noticed the shadows of people first. A tall woman emerged in front of Anna, clad in a royal blue pantsuit, with all manner of chunky blue-and-gold costume jewelry hanging off her wrists and ears and neck, like spoils of victory. Her hair was ink-black and aggressively curly, like a Slinky you twist and twist some more until it's on the verge of lashing out at you. On her left wrist, between her solid gold bangle bracelets, was a platinum watch encrusted with enough precious gems to fill a throne room. Anna recognized her instantly.

"You're Emilia Kirsch," Anna said.

Kirsch glanced at Anna but didn't bother to address her directly. "This is the roommate?" she said curtly to the inner bedroom. "This is unacceptable. We're being treated very shabbily here."

"Mom, it's fine." Now here was Lara Kirsch coming out of the room to tame her own mother. Sleek black bob with bangs. Green eyes. Neon blue eyeshadow. Bright clear lip gloss. Jean vest. Black tank top. Neon bangle bracelets. She was the girl at the gate. No wonder Anna thought she had recognized her. It was Lara Kirsch, for shit's sake. The CEO of PortSys was in Anna's room, and now her kid was Anna's roommate. Anna had seen Lara on the Internet dozens of times, photographed out in the wild with male and female paramours alike. Anna always paused on those photos for just a second to get a better look at Lara. Now they were face-to-face. In person, Lara Kirsch was even more magnetic to behold.

"Everything is fine, mom," said Lara. She looked at Anna with a wink. "She's cool. You're Anna, right?" Lara's voice was low and smoky enough to unlock muscle knots.

"Yeah," said Anna.

"I'm Lara." She ran a finger across her name tag. "You didn't get a name tag?"

"I didn't want one."

"Man, I should have been smart enough to turn mine down, too."

"Well it's a completely absurd arrangement," said the elder Kirsch. "After all I've given to this school."

"I really don't mind, mom."

"Well I do," Now Emilia gave Anna a scan. "Lara, you were not supposed to have a roommate, much less one who seems so… pedestrian."

"How do you know I'm not a superstar?" Anna asked Kirsch. Lara held back a guffaw when she heard it. For Anna, that made mouthing off to Kirsch worth whatever came next.

But Kirsch didn't bother returning the volley. Instead, she took out her PortPhone and queued up Maps.

"How can you port from inside the wall?" Anna asked.

"Donate $50 million to this school and you'll have the answer. I somehow doubt you'll ever attain the privilege, dear."

Kirsch evaporated with a pop, leaving the two girls alone in Room 24. Anna stared at her new roommate. She couldn't help it. She wanted another laugh out of Lara. A full one. She wanted to pull endless laughs from her.

"I really hope she went to buy us drinks," Anna cracked. Lara's eyes crinkled as she broke into a spasm of giggles. One laugh down.

"I can't believe you talked shit to Emilia. No one does that. You're my hero, Roomie."

"Really?" Now Anna wanted Kirsch to port back in so she could get off a few more potshots.

"I'm sorry about her," Lara said.

"She clearly loves you," Anna replied.

"Love takes on a lot forms, but I haven't figured out what form hers takes just yet. You're gonna get me in trouble with her if you're always that proud of a wiseass."

"I'm not." Not always.

"You all right if I take the inner room? It's more private and protected for me. But it's also a touch smaller, so it's a fair tradeoff."

"It's fine. Who was that boy?"

"What boy?"

"The boy hounding you at Druskin Gate."

It took a second for Lara to remember. Anna wished the boy could have seen how easily she had forgotten him. "Oh! Oh, him. He's just some boy."

"He seemed fond of you."

"Kiss them once and they expect the world."

Anna nodded, even though she had never been kissed, nor she did ever talk about the fact that she had never been kissed. One time a boy tried to kiss her in eighth grade, but that didn't count because boys were disgusting. True kisses had thus far eluded her. She kept that morsel of personal information wrapped in thick, impenetrable layers of brute snark.

"You going to the assembly?" Anna asked.

"I don't think we have much choice. Wanna go together?"

YES. "Sure."

"Then I'm gonna get settled and then we can head over, provided ol' Emilia doesn't port back in." Lara walked up close to Anna and, for a brief moment, stopped smiling. It was like the whole room went dark. "For real though, Anna: be careful around my mom. You don't want her eyes on you."

21

"Okay."

That was it. Whatever black veil fell over Lara as she spoke urgently about her mother was gone, and she radiated joy yet again.

Another girl, blonde and tan and vivacious, came up the stairwell and leaned through the doorway.

"Lara!" The girl shouted Lara's name like she knew her well. Anna already hated her. "Lara, you hitting assembly?"

"Yeah!" said Lara. "Cool if my roommate comes?"

The girl in the doorway looked at Anna and took a split-second longer to approve the request than Anna would have liked. *That girl should be asking* us *if it's cool for* her *to come along.*

"Yeah, sure," the girl said. She was not nearly enthusiastic enough for Anna's taste.

"We'll see you there, then," said Lara.

"See you!"

Once the interloper was gone, Anna slyly nudged the door closed. Judging by the mob outside of Druskin Gate, Lara Kirsch was not the sort of girl who was left alone very often. Already, Anna was angling to preserve whatever solitary moments she could get with her.

"So," Anna said, "You're from New York, huh?"

"I am but I hate it there."

"Why?"

"You mean, apart from the obvious?" Lara gave Anna a flawless impression of her mother's scowl. Almost *too* good. *"This is unacceptable, Lara. We're being treated very shabbily here."*

Now, it was Anna's turn to laugh. They already had a little code: a glossary of inside jokes they were compiling.

Lara went over and sat on the edge of Anna's bed. "I remember before porting, when I was a kid. We had a nanny. Don't judge me for having a nanny."

"I won't."

"She was cool. Her name was Valeria and she would take me on the subway every day. Emilia would rather die than set foot in a subway station, but Valeria knew the subway and every part of the city. So she would have me a pick a different stop each weekend and we would just go exploring. We could sit on a train for ten minutes and walk up the stairs and BOOM! Whole new world. I mean, the subway may have been busted as shit, but it was like porting before porting. Anyway, my mom fired Valeria because she fires everyone. Then she started PortSys and the subways died. Then the neighborhoods died. I mean, people still port into Manhattan for work but by nightfall a lot of them are gone. You been lately?"

"Only at Christmas," Anna confessed.

"That doesn't count. You go any other night, walk away from the big spots in midtown, and it's like walking through the end of the world. And so many PINE troops with guns. Gun after gun, like the whole agency is on a duck hunt or something. You know how many port immigrants I've seen shot? Those PINE assholes shoot them and leave them there. I port out every chance I get."

"Where do you go?"

"Anywhere. Anywhere people are happy. People don't get how punk happiness is. Sometimes I look at my mom and I can tell how much it pisses her off that *I'm* not pissed off."

She opened up her jean vest, a vape pen discreetly poking out of the inside pocket. Anna got a peek at Lara's bare shoulder. A smattering of freckles, one of them adorned with a miniature *B* tattoo. Anna wanted to connect the freckles with her finger, with that Point B as the final dot.

"It's fun to know she can't rattle me," Lara said.

"I bet it is."

"You want a hit?" Lara pulled the pen out and took a long, smooth hit. "It makes all the lights go soft."

"I'd love to, but sometimes it messes with my head."

"This is good stuff, though. One of the perks of having a mother worth thirteen figures. She can't keep track of *every* dollar. And it's a light pen, so you can port with it."

One time, when she got a rare invite to a house party in Maryland, Anna took a puff off a joint—a legit, old-school joint—and coughed so hard that she threw up on the back deck in front of everyone, her vomit quickly leaking between the gaps in the Trex boards. She didn't care to repeat the mistake with Lara.

23

"I'm cool for now. Maybe later."

Lara put the pen away. "What about you? You got a favorite pin?"

"It's boring," Anna told her.

"No, come on. Tell it."

"We used to port out to Lucerne, in Switzerland. To the top of Mt. Pilatus."

Lara gasped. Might've been a fake gasp. Anna knew how skilled other girls were at acting surprised. "Oh my God, I love it there."

"You do?"

"Yeah!"

"They have a gondola you can still ride up to the top," Anna told her, "but that would make me shit my pants. So we'd cheat and skip that part."

"Same here. Gotta watch your ears when you port right to the top, though. They pop like a motherfucker!"

That was the exact sensation Anna remembered having as well. Lara wasn't faking that little gasp at all. They shared Lucerne now. Anna was ready to share more.

"So we'd port to the summit and stare out," she told Lara. She could see the view from Pilatus in her mind: with Lake Lucerne resting calmly in the distance, surrounded by countryside that was predictably Swiss in its meticulousness. Everything sharp and clear and tranquil. Like the whole scene had been painted upon the landscape.

"You said 'we'?" Lara asked.

Anna felt a quick jab of panic. It was Sarah who had showed her Lucerne. It was Sarah who always went there with her to take in the pastiche. In fact, Lucerne was the last place they had ported together.

Anna wasn't ready to explain all that. "Just me and a few buds," she told Lara.

"We can go there."

"For real?"

"Uh huh. I know where else we can go," Lara said slyly. "My mom, she bought Lily Beach in the Maldives. The whole resort. When she and my brother aren't there, it's all mine. I have the run of the place. It has a ring of water villas sitting right out in the Indian Ocean. Each villa has its own infinity pool, its own hot tub, everything. I can port to the resort and chill in whichever one I want."

"Holy shit."

"That's right. Holy shit. Most of the time, I like to get high and walk through the water from bungalow to bungalow. At night, the staff lines the walkways above the water with votive candles and I love to watch the flames soften. Then morning comes and I smoke up again. I get high in my fingers and my toes. I love being stoned in the heat. I love feeling the sun come off my skin. I want everyone to feel how good that feels."

Lara sharpened her look at Anna, a look as intense as Emilia's scowl but suffused with an innate warmth that the CEO of PortSys lacked. "I want *you* to feel that. You wanna to go there with me sometime? It's got a good portwall. No one else gets to come to this place. Emilia doesn't even let friends use it when she's not around. It would just be us."

No one, and certainly no one this cool, had ever offered Anna a chance to bypass every velvet curtain left in an otherwise open world; to see what wealthy porters were frantically try to keep cordoned off from everyone else; to bask in the tropical candlelight with her new roommate. Alone.

"I would," Anna said. There wasn't time for a more poetic reply. Managing the tone and speed of "I would" had proven tricky enough.

"Awesome," said Lara. "I can't wait. Maybe after that and after Lucerne I'll take you to my absolute favorite place. My favorite-est place."

"Where's that?"

"I'm not high enough yet to give that one away," Lara said.

"Take another hit off that pen, then."

"You're funny."

"I like your bracelets," Anna told her.

"You want one?"

"No no no! I wasn't trying to *have* one."

Lara giggled again. "They cost a buck each at Duane Reade. Here." She took a rose pink bangle off and gently slipped it onto her Anna's arm. Anna turned her wrist back and forth, watching the bracelet hula hoop around. *You shouldn't wear this all the time, because then you'll look like a follower.* And yet, somehow Lara had made that cheap-ass bracelet cool. Her coolness was contagious. It could spread to things, to people, to Anna Huff. She was suddenly feeling confident. Sweet Jesus, did it feel good to feel confident.

"It looks good on you," Lara told Anna.

"Thank you so much for this."

"What about you? You got a mom?"

"No, no mom. I was raised by apes."

"Apes can be cute."

"I have a real mom. Sandy's fine."

"Dad?"

"He left. I mean, sometimes he would come back. Then he didn't."

"God, that sucks."

"It's better he left, honestly. All he did was make things worse. My mom always said that if you give a man a chance to get out of something, he'll always take it. You know your dad?"

"Only through the gossip feeds. You probably could have guessed this, but ol' Emilia enjoys getting divorced a lot more than she enjoys getting married. Siblings?"

Anna had a rehearsed answer for this question, hewed down to a crisp block of text that did the job with maximum efficiency. But before she could deploy it, Emilia Kirsch ported in a second time.

"Well, they won't move you," Kirsch said to Lara, exasperated.

"Mom, it's all right."

"Imbeciles. Just monstrously incompetent, these people." She looked at Anna. "And you, Anna Huff."

"Yes?" said Anna.

"I've done background on you, my dear. I know things about you now." At this, Kirsch smiled for the first time. "It's fun to know things, don't you think?"

Anna stared down at the floor. Lara was right about Emilia. Kirsch's hound dog eyes were on Anna and she could feel the woman undressing her psyche will malicious intent. *What did she know? She probably knows all the basics, but God, the basics are awful enough, aren't they?*

Kirsch's smile grew broader. "No tart comeback this time, eh? You may test well, Anna Huff. But that wit of yours will have to get quicker under duress."

She got ready to port, but took a second to zero in on Anna's new bracelet. She barked at Lara, "You *gave* her something?"

"Relax already! Jesus!" Lara said.

"Stop giving her things. Everybody wants things for free in this world. It's disgusting." Then Kirsch cast a withering stare at Anna's worn-out mary janes.

"Young lady, if you want me to take you seriously, wear different shoes the next time I visit here. That pair is hideous."

She ported out with an imperious boom. The clap was always louder when people ported indoors. This one shook the door of the room and danced along the walls, burrowing deep into Anna's tender ears: Kirsch's way of leaving her something to think about.

THE ACADEMY BUILDING

Anna cursed herself for being stuck on a video call with her mom as Lara rushed off for assembly without her. By the time she managed to disengage herself from Sandy and race to the Academy Building, the orchestra section of the assembly hall was already packed with new arrivals, with Lara sitting in the dead center and wreathed by girls who either wanted to be her friend or perhaps already were. Anna prowled along the rows of seats—all upholstered in deep maroon, the fabric as threadbare and scratchy as burlap— looking for an open spot and hoping to catch Lara's eye. After a few awful seconds, Lara spotted her deserted roommate and smiled at her. Lara's smile had a way of wiping away any trace of angst or misery. Seeing her was like arriving home after a long time away.

"Anna!"

Anna gave a weak wave, her new bracelet jangling around her arm, and silently mouthed a *hey*. Lara picked up her jean vest, which she had left next to her, and patted the open spot. But there were a good two dozen students in the row blocking the way: a gauntlet of turned heads and boys spreading their legs across hemispheres. Anna couldn't find the courage to blaze a trail through all that, not on her first day. But God, she wanted to. Anna had known Lara for barely an hour and already the sight of her was making her body feed blood to other parts of her body.

Hey, you know what would be nice? If you could port to that seat.

"It's okay," she said to Lara.

Lara looked disappointed. "Really?"

Anna nodded and Lara gave her a fluttering wave before the row condensed and the saved seat disappeared, the entire orchestra section now full. Anna had lost this round of musical chairs. Lara had all the friends. Lara had everyone. She was the sun. What was that like? What was it like to be able to *choose* your friends? That had never been a luxury for Anna. She wasn't a dork. She wasn't an outcast. She just never registered with other kids. She had her small pursuits and she had diving and she had Sarah. *Had* her. But she lacked the motivation and the precious teenage confidence to venture much further beyond that. She took whatever friends life gave her, and life was stingy with them. Who knew how long Lara would treat her as a special friend, perhaps as more, before picking out a new muse from hundreds of willing candidates?

Anna stood in place in the filling assembly hall for nearly a minute, feeling like a hired usher. Then she felt a hand on her shoulder and turned around to see a boy who was easily 6'4". He looked like he could scrape the ceiling. He was dressed in a yellow suit festooned with bluebirds and had a wild, craggly beard. He smelled like meat. Anna was so stunned by the sight of him that she didn't even think to recoil.

"The balcony," he told her in a low drawl.

"What?"

"The balcony looks closed, because no one is sitting up there. But it's not. Now isn't that a little bit of sunshine on your doorstep? Everyone rushing in just so they can claim the worst seats."

He walked through the entryway toward the grand staircase and beckoned to Anna.

"Well, come on now. Someone else'll figure out the secret eventually."

Anna followed the big yellow suit out of the entryway and up the stairs. He led her down to the front row overlooking the orchestra section. The perch was their domain exclusively. Everyone stared up at them. Well, at *him*. Anna spotted Lara. Lara winked at her and there went all that blood rushing everywhere again.

"You're blushing," said the boy.

"I'm hot," Anna said. "There's no air-conditioning in here." The assembly hall had all the ventilation of a satin casket. Its ceiling went to the sky, but that did nothing for the air flow. The walls around the kids were lined with immense oil portraits of every dean in Druskin history: a succession of sour, humorless men and women. All frowning. All gazing upon the hall with stoic disapproval.

"Air conditioning is for the weak," the very large boy said. He pointed to a name tag that read J. PAUL BAMERT and then extended his hand. "I'm sorry I never formally introduced myself. I'm Bamert."

29

"It's that what everyone calls you?"

"People have a *lot* of different names for me, most of them unkind."

"Well, you do kinda stick out."

"If you're gonna stick out, don't half-ass it. That's what I say." Bamert drew a pocket square from his jacket and mopped his brow. "And your name? I see you were too cool for a name tag."

"I'm Anna Huff."

He shook her hand. "And how are you today, Anna Huff?"

"Christ, I don't know."

Bamert laughed loud enough for everyone down below to crane their necks again. Anna was beginning to regret being within a ten-foot radius of him. It was like sitting next to a lit Roman candle.

"That sounds about accurate for here. What's your dorm?" he asked her.

"Sewell."

"Oh, Sewell is a true shithole."

"A lot of stairs."

"Well, that's good. With stairs, every day is Leg Day." He slapped his own beefy thigh. "I'm on only the second floor of Kirkland. It'll do nothing for these quads."

"Bamert?"

"Yes?"

"Are you always like this?"

"Only when I'm awake. Now, why was Lara Kirsch waving at you?"

"You know Lara Kirsch?" Anna asked him.

"Everyone knows Lara *Kush*," he said, pantomiming a bong hit. "She's the princess of porting. More intriguing is that she seems to know *you*."

"She's my roommate."

"She's your roommate? My goodness."

"Shhhh!"

"She's a dash of pepper, that one. She give you that bracelet? It's a winning little accessory."

Anna rubbed the bangle nervously. "Maybe."

"Did Lara's mom port into Sewer Hall, too? Did you meet Emilia Dearest?"

"Yeah! How did you know she could do that?"

Bamert snorted. "She built that wall. It stands to reason that she's free to walk right through it."

"I bet I could find out her password," Anna said.

"She probably didn't just write in on the inside of her palm, you know."

"That's true. But if the key exists, that means it can be found."

"Aren't you so bold, Anna Huff?"

"What's your deal, Bamert? Why do you look like you're 30?"

He stroked his whiskers. "I am gifted in the follicle department. Also, I'm a new senior."

"As in senior citizen?"

He grinned. "Oh, isn't that so fiendishly clever of you."

"Are you a postgrad?"

Bamert howled with laughter. "I assure you: If I had already graduated from high school, this'd be the *last* place I'd hang. I'm just a regular senior. I'm also a physicist. Or at least, I will be. Normally I just apply what I know to the science of barbecue, but I do know a thing or two about porting."

"You know exactly how it works?"

"Okay, I don't know quite *that* much. PortSys keeps the recipe locked down tight. But you and I, Anna Huff, maybe we could collaborate. I am an open source gentleman, happy to tell you everything I know about this port life."

"Will it take long to explain?"

"Oh, I'm sorry," he deadpanned. "Were you going somewhere more important? Do you have an appointment at the Vatican?"

Anna smiled. "I don't. I guess it'd be cool to work together."

"This is a very promising development, Anna. Because once we know how Kirsch beats the Harkness Wall..."

Dean Vick stood up on stage and cleared his throat into the microphone. Bamert finished with a whisper that could still be heard from Ontario.

"Maybe *we* can figure how to beat it, too." He opened his suit coat to reveal a pocket flask. "Until then, this is the only teleportation device that will work for us."

"Am I the only person who *didn't* smuggle booze and weed into this school?" she asked.

"Probably. You should have done your homework. Weed is legal everywhere now anyway."

"Not here."

"Well, nothing's legal here. That's the fun of it."

Dean Vick shushed the kids into submission with a sharp, angry hiss. The man had wispy salt-and-pepper hair that ran halfway down the back of his neck, and he possessed a near-lipless mouth that went in a straight line. A strong hissing mouth. Vick was gonna fit right in on that wall of musty paintings one day. He took out a stack of notes and Anna groaned at the thickness of them.

"Okay," said the dean. "So, welcome to the Druskin class of 2032." He had a thin, reedy voice that was perfectly tailored for humorless bureaucracy.

The boys and girls whooped. Vick raised one corner of his coin slot mouth half a centimeter. It was as mirthful as the man got. He was raised in a single-room house in Unadilla, Georgia, sent out to work in the pecan orchards at age eight, and hadn't taken a day off since. Fun was not a necessity for the man. Fun was a horrible distraction. The crowd settled.

"We sent you an information packet prior to you arriving here. But we find that students don't typically read through the materials, so I will give you a brief topline. The most important thing we have here at Druskin is Druskin itself: the grounds, the buildings, the faculty, and most important of all: you, our students. It is our haven and it is well protected by the Wall System. The portwall and the red brick Harkness Wall are there to safeguard you. That is why we ask that you never leave campus without prior authorization. Do not expect securing that authorization to be automatic. Circumstances must be urgent. Any student caught porting outside of campus or attempting to breach the wall will be subject to expulsion. For any field trip or sporting event that takes place off campus, you will travel by chartered bus."

The entire audience groaned. Vick ignored them. He was used to students groaning.

"We want you to *want* to be here. I know that this transition won't be easy for many of you. It will take a certain period to adjust to the fact that you are no longer porting on a regular basis. Those who adjust, excel. Those who do not"—the dean cast a look toward the balcony—"do not."

"Seems uncalled for," Bamert whispered.

"Shut up, man," Anna said.

"By now, you've all been outfitted with a transponder that tracks your movements in a benign fashion. It does not spy on you, except to see who you are texting."

There was silence.

"That was a light joke," Vick said.

That caused Bamert to let out an ironic "Ha haaaa!" from the gallery, which in turn caused the whole audience to roar in genuine laughter. Vick stared darts at Bamert, but Bamert was too satisfied with the result of his joke to worry about it. Anna liked him immensely.

"Please do not tamper with your transponder. Anyone caught tampering will be summarily put up for disciplinary measures. And that's that. Whether you know it or not, you are about to become part of something very important. Something beyond you. When you commit yourself to a larger cause, *you* yourself become larger. Everything in this world is so transient now. But Druskin has remained right here the whole time, in this place, and it will always remain here. It is sacred ground. One day, you will have a profound appreciation of that fact. This is only a two-year preparatory school, but these will be the most vital two years of your life: years you'll recall with great clarity for the rest of your days."

Bamert turned away from the stage, dipped a tiny straw into his flask, and took a sip.

"When Elias Druskin founded this school in 1794, he saw it as Grand Experiment. He saw this school as a great living organism: a place that would not only influence those who pass through its halls, but would itself be equally influenced by those same, extraordinary students. You will have the opportunity to leave your mark here, and those who choose to excel will find that the marks they leave last far longer than anything you could spray paint onto a wall or carve into a tree."

"Now there's an idea," said Bamert.

"You are now part of that Grand Experiment. Open yourself to Druskin, and you will find—"

"LARA!"

There was a commotion coming from the entrance to the hall. Bamert and Anna peered over the balustrade so they could get a look underneath.

It was the boy from Druskin Gate. He was still clutching his flowers, only now his leg was broken. He staggered into the hall dragging the lower half of that leg behind him. It was bent in places where legs should not bend. Anna looked at Lara, who seemed just as shocked at the boy's emergence as Anna was. Dean Vick's head condensed with rage.

"I climbed the Harkness Wall for you!" the boy shouted. "It was worth falling that far for you, baby! I'll always fall for you."

"Holy shit, that's the corniest line I've ever heard," Anna said.

"That's how you know he means it," Bamert said.

The boy was clearly hoping Lara would respond, but the entirety of Druskin's security force had other ideas. They swallowed him up and by the time they dispersed, the boy was gone. Not in cuffs. Not dead. Gone. Anna was dumbfounded. The orchestra section quivered with nervous giggles, Lara included.

"Wait," said Anna. "How did they—"

"Now that's a trick, isn't it?" said Bamert. "The media and PortSys say it's impossible to port anyone but yourself. And yet."

He gestured to the empty spot on the hall floor where the failed Romeo had vanished.

"Quite the Grand Experiment they have going on here, no?"

SEWELL HALL

Lara was nowhere to be seen after assembly. Anna trudged back to Sewell and lounged on her new bed, skimming through the assigned common read. It would have taken her less time to eat the pages than to read them in full. She instantly forgot each sentence by the time she had moved on to the next. The book's only saving grace was a smooth matte cover that Anna liked to run her hands across. Her hands were always moving, always taking in new information. She would have been a fabulous blind person.

She eyed the door for Lara every few minutes. She took a break by going down to the common room, only to encounter a tight circle of girls that was impossible to breach. When they turned her way, she would let out a weak, "Hey guys," and then realized she had nothing else to add. She headed back upstairs and flirted with the book again, drawing pentagrams in the margins to keep herself interested. To diversify her procrastination methods, she hopped on the laptop. But the school's Internet firewall proved just as feisty as its other walls. She'd have to sort a way past it if she wanted to do her standard online snooping. There was someone out in the ether that she still needed to find.

As night fell, there came a knock on the door. Anna sprung up in glee before realizing that her roommate probably wouldn't bother to knock before entering.

"Come in."

A middle-aged woman with thick, owl-eyed glasses and a dome of straight red hair came in, carrying a tray of oatmeal chocolate chip cookies.

"Hmmmm, let me guess: Anna Huff." She had a German lilt and pronounced Anna's last name like *hoof*. "Sorry, my dear."

Did something happen to Lara? "Sorry for what?"

"That I wasn't here. You must be thinking *what the shit*, yeah? I'm Mrs. Ludwig. Cookie?"

Anna wolfed down two before realizing she was in dire need of supplemental fluid. "Do youf haf anyfing to drink?"

"Oh. Oh, that would have been a good idea. *Scheisse.* Yes, let me get that right away."

"Ith's fine."

"No no no, stay there. I get it for you." She set the tray on a box and rushed downstairs. Anna took two more cookies and stuck them in the fridge, violating her No Food rule within hours of imposing it upon herself. When Mrs. Ludwig returned, she was carrying a new tray with tea service: bags, pots, mugs, creamer, and six different kinds of sugar.

"Tea?"

"Thanths." Anna awkwardly grabbed the teapot and a cup from the tray as Mrs. Ludwig tried to keep it balanced.

"Now, I must again apologize for not being here. Our cat, it died this morning. Run over by a truck." She set the tray down and clapped her hands together. "Squashed it, just like this."

"Oh my God. That's so sad!"

"Not really. It only had two legs. It'll go to cat heaven, yeah? We have two dozen more anyway."

"Oh."

"Anyway, we can't have a dead cat out on the grounds on your first day, but this school has a big stupid process thing." Mrs. Ludwig started making yapping gestures with both hands. "I had to fill out four separate forms, all for this goddamn cat here. Can you believe that?"

"That's a lot of forms."

"All longhand. My back hurts now. Are you hot? It's too damn hot in this place." Mrs. Ludwig took off her cardigan. Her top was drenched in sweat.

"I'm fine," said Anna.

"Well good. You're here now, and all settled in. This is very nice."

"Have you seen my roommate?"

"Lara Kirsch, yeah? She had to go to tutoring."

"But school hasn't even started."

"Yes well, when Emilia Kirsch wants extra tutoring for her daughter, she gets it. Now, who are you?"

"I'm Anna. You already knew that."

"Yes, but who *ahhhhhhh* you? You're more than a name, Anna Hoof. For example, I know from your background that you play piano, and it said that you're quite the diver."

Anna squinted. "Lotta people digging around my background today. What else do you know about me?"

Mrs. Ludwig squirmed. "Oh, nothing! Just school records and what not. That's why I'm here, *schatz*. I wanted to get to know you, and perhaps tell you about myself if you wanted such a thing."

Anna let Mrs. Ludwig twist a moment before finally letting her off the hook. "Ah. Okay."

"So how has your day been?" Mrs. Ludwig asked her.

"Boring," she lied. Standard teenager reflex.

"Well now, that can be good or bad now, can't it? I like a day that's somewhat eventful, but not too, too dramatic."

"The Wi-Fi here is spotty."

"Oh, it's shit. They're always onto the next thing before perfecting the last thing."

"The firewall blocks a lot of sites I need for my, uh, studies."

"Did you try the school's intranet? They say there are over seven trillion volumes archived in the virtual Helton Library, although I haven't looked at any of them. Books, ugh."

"Okay, but what if I still need more?"

"Then you're a better reader than I am. You can always file a request with IT. You kids are nifty with that little machine there. Always a good skill for anyone to have, yeah?"

"Sometimes. Other times I wanna throw my laptop out a window and then flatten it with a steamroller." Mrs. Ludwig fidgeted. Anna gave her a wink. "See now, I thought you'd know from checking my background that I'm a bit of dick."

Mrs. Ludwig smiled. "I knew you were very clever, Anna Hoof. That's for certain."

"Why are you here?" Anna asked her.

"Pardon?"

"Why are you here? I mean, I know why *I* gotta be here: learning, college prep, personal growth, yada yada. But what about you? What makes you wanna babysit 40 girls all year long?"

37

Mrs. Ludwig put a hand on Anna's shoulder. Her fingers were crooked from rheumatoid arthritis, but her palms were as soft as fur.

"Anna Hoof, you're not the only one with a background, see."

"You said you would tell me about yourself."

"Some of it, *schatz*. But not all of it."

"Oh."

"My door is open anytime. And if you like a nice Sunday drive, I can get you permission to leave Druskin Gate with me and go out for a spin. I have a vintage Shelby Cobra. You can buy one for practically nothing these days, did you know this? Mine goes very fast. At 120mph, most of the girls turn shit white." She picked up the tea tray again. "Don't forget about the Welcome mixer at 8pm at Dunbar. There's music. Food. Kids. Big party, ooh."

"I don't think I'm gonna go."

"Well," said Mrs. Ludwig, trying to suppress a cackle, "if you just sit here, maybe you really *ahh* a 'dick,' yeah?"

"Okay, you're right. I should probably go."

"Only so you can complain to me about it afterward. This is the fun part of things."

"That's a deal."

Mrs. Ludwig backed out with the tray and Anna slipped on her busted mary janes. Before she hit the welcome mixer, she had to go to the bathroom, so she clambered up to the dingy bathroom near the summit of the stairwell. Inside the toilet stall was a worn-out spiral notebook with an index card taped to the front that read:

The Shit Memoirs

Anna cracked the tome open and found scribbles in blue ink, red ink, pencil, and black Sharpie. The front pages dated all the way back to 2028. Each page had its own collage of stains from presumably nasty fluids. The copy inside the notebook was just as rude. Anna tore through each page and marveled at the volume and ferocity of the gossip. The book named names. Colleen Mulwray was a bitch. Jessie Stimes was a *super* bitch with fat legs. Cady Douglas had sex with Mr. Highland's teaching assistant. Jenny Hall

was nicknamed Squirrel because "she loves nuts in her mouth."
Anna wanted to learn who each girl mentioned was, so that she could
better appreciate every bit of invective. When the copy wasn't
vituperative, it was downright surreal. One page had BIG HAIR IS
BIG FUN written in orange marker, and nothing else.

On the back of one of the pages, she found an anonymous entry
written in glittery purple ink. It was only three words long:

My roommate's
weird

DUNBAR HALL/FIELDS

The party was lame as shit, but Anna knew that would be the deal going in. The Orientation Committee had banquet tables with cookies and punch set up outside the dorm while Brendan McClear manned the Sonos and subjected everyone to his own personally curated playlist. All the kids were drinking out of Solo cups that they all direly wished had beer in them. When Brendan McClear looked up and saw Anna milling around the lawn nearby, she sensed his gaze and locked eyes on him. Sometimes, when Anna wanted to freak people out, she could turn feline on command: zeroing in with an unwarranted, accusing glare until they were forced to look away. It always worked. Brendan McClear looked back down.

She scanned the throng of kids for Lara and saw nothing but boys with unkempt hair and girls with deep tan legs. Ever since middle school, Anna figured that she could look cool and important if she was seen looking around for cool, important friends. It was not a canny strategy.

A hickory-scented mitt landed on her shoulder. Here was Bamert, clad in a whole new suit. This one was bright red with little geckos all over it.

"You're not wearing a tie," she told him.

"It's a casual affair. Who were you looking for just now?"

"No one."

"Well you were sure looking hard for no one."

"Don't push it, Bamert."

"Okay, all right."

Another boy sidled up next to Bamert, wearing an argyle sweater vest and crisp trousers. He looked deeply annoyed.

"What kind of sound system is this?" the boy asked, seemingly to no one in particular. "They must have fished those speakers out of landfill. The array is off center line. You'd get better sound quality aiming your phone at a sheet of foil. Am I the only one who cares how tinny this is?"

"Burton, I can assure you that you are. Anna, this is Jamie Burton: also new but a junior, like you. He's from my hometown of

Richmond, Virginia and is also, without question, the most annoying person you will meet here."

"Why is he saying you're annoying?" Anna asked Burton.

"I have no idea what Bamert's talking about," Burton said. "He's the one who's louder than a jet engine and dresses like he's hosting a murder mystery."

"Anna, after five minutes of being exposed to Burton, I promise you'll know what I'm talking about. Now, as to this party…"

Bamert surveyed the scene. From his lofty view, he could make out every face in the crowd: all the reticent newbies and all the android Orientation leaders trying to coax enthusiasm out of them. A box of *Twister* loomed ominously under the DJ table.

"I can declare, with a near pathological certainty, that this party blows," he said.

"It's a school party," said Anna. "What do you expect? A party thrown by some school isn't a party at all."

"That's true. This is why I suggest we create a soiree of our own." Bamert opened his jacket to again reveal his hip flask.

"I don't drink," Anna said.

"Neither do I," said Burton.

"Yes, but that's immaterial to me."

"You're really gonna get thrown out before you've taken a single class," Burton said to Bamert.

"If I try hard enough. Follow me."

He led them away from Dunbar and down High Street, past the school's brutalist concrete gym and onto a vast, darkened plain of playing fields. Anna looked past the infield diamonds and took in the silhouettes of trees soaring over the Harkness Wall in the distance. Her lungs opened like valves, clear and full. She felt as if she could inhale the sky. There was something different about Druskin, something she couldn't quite get at until she ran her hands over the front of her pants and realized there was no PortPhone on her. There was nothing on her that gave her that nagging itch to be someplace else. *Is this what normal feels like?*

"Now, isn't this lovely?" Bamert asked.

41

"They've planted tall fescue here," Burton said. "Poor grass. It'll be taken over by crab grass if they get anywhere near the standard amount of rainfall next summer."

"Once again, dear Burton, you have taken us sideways. How do you always manage it?"

"I hate to ask," said Anna, "But are you two, you know…"

Bamert and Burton looked at each other. Bamert let out a mighty roar. "Anna my dear, I regret to inform you that Burton and I are heterosexual in ways that would both disappoint and appall you."

"Well you're really good at not liking each other."

"Comes with practice," Bamert said. "You'll get the hang of it."

He took a swig from his flask. Anna pointed to a stone bridge that skipped over a small river on the way to the school football stadium.

"What's that bridge?" she asked.

"It's just a bridge," Bamert said. "Charming that there's still a place in the world where a person might need to cross one on foot, no? Come with me."

Bamert led Burton and Anna across the soft, wet fields, past a bronze plaque honoring dead football coach Barty Kissel, and over to the bridge, a rusty NO JUMPING/LOW WATER CONDITIONS sign dangling off its parapet. He led them to the center of the arch. There, set in the concrete, was a placard that read, "Gift of the class of 1948."

Bamert held his stomach, like he was a touch nauseous. "Ugh, this is awfully high up for my tastes. Now look down. I'm gonna keep looking up for my constitution but you two look at the water."

Anna leaned over the parapet and down at the cool moonlight glazing the river below. A tickling breeze troubled the water and the surface came alive, shimmering and pulsing and rippling to the banks.

"You see the light?" Bamert asked her.

"I do."

"Now, moonlight exists above and below the surface of that water, but the reflected light—the captured light—is what you see most clearly. Imagine the world you live in IS that light on the surface."

"This isn't an accurate analogy at all," said Burton.

"Shut up, Burton. Anna, there are levels to the universe— membranes—above and below us that are invisible to the undressed eye. Think of our world as 2D and the universe as 3D. Porting, you see, is the act of diving into that water, swimming under the light on the surface, and popping back up somewhere new."

Burton butted in once more. "You're making this far too simplistic."

"I really wish you drank alcohol. Anyway, faithful Anna, let's say we all port by swimming a foot under the water, but the Harkness Wall has put a big ol' barracuda there, with sharp fangs, and it's hungry for *man*."

"Kirsch has a password to make the barracuda go away," Anna said.

"Maybe. Or who says we only need to swim a foot down? What if we swam *two* feet down?"

"Or three!" said Anna.

"Well if we go three feet down, a black hole condenses us down to a neutrino that's a trillionth of a trillionth the size of a single atom, so let's not. Now, Portsys's network takes the biometrics mapped by your PortPhone, learns your spatial intent, and then opens up a beautiful little wormhole for you to step into. But Kirsch, wily ol' coot that she is, may have access to another level, another 'brane, that she can use that is *not* patrolled and renders the Firewall irrelevant. Her own private network."

"So then it's a matter of finding it and busting into it. I can do that."

"Can you now?"

"I once convinced my middle school principal over a dummy email address that I was his wife and that I was leaving him. Then he drove home midday to smooth things out and she really *did* leave him."

"That was funny right up until the part where you left him in ruins," Bamert said.

"He was a creep. The point is, I can find whatever password or dark network she uses." She took in the now reservoir-still river and surrounding countryside. "I'm good at finding odd things."

"I believe you, Anna Huff."

"But what then?" asked Burton. "You're here so that you *don't* port, so that you're safe from all the garbage out there. Anna, why come here at all if you just want to leave?"

"I *do* wanna be here, but I'm also looking for someone," Anna said.

"Who?" Burton asked her.

"Piss off, that's who."

"I don't know how you plan on finding them with that little helper wrapped around your leg."

Anna looked down at the transponder anklet. It was so inconspicuous—no thicker than a hair tie—that she had forgotten about it already. It freaked her out how easily she had adjusted to it being on her body.

"You can trick it," Anna said.

"How?" Burton asked.

"Well, in Bamert's case, you could just strap it to a brisket."

"Oh, don't talk to me about fine meats right now," Bamert said. "They served pot roast in the dining hall tonight. Or, at least, it was supposedly pot roast. I'd have been better off eating my own belt."

"These anklets are garbage," Anna explained. "They're made by a company called Blackheel. The CEO scored a $500 million contract to make them for the U.S. prison system, and then he pocketed at least half for himself. They're cheap and buggy."

"How do you know all that?" Burton said.

"From that dude Erick Martin's feed."

"He's batshit."

"Everyone is batshit," Anna said. "You just have to have good radar for when they occasionally make sense. You can trick this anklet somehow."

"You'd have to match it with something that had your exact same biometrics," said Burton. "Heart rate, blood temp, everything. You're not that clever."

"No?" Anna gave Burton the same look she gave Brendan McClear.

Bamert whistled. "Goodness me, Burton. Don't test this girl."

Burton was unfazed. "You can't fake anatomy."

"Ah, but it's heavenly to think about figuring it out somehow, isn't it?" Bamert asked. He took a long drag from his hip flask. The whiskey dribbled into his considerable beard and he lapped at the runoff like a retriever.

"Do you always drink this much?" Anna asked him.

"He does," Burton said.

"Why?" she asked.

Bamert smiled. Anna Huff was not the only kid at Druskin with a rehearsed reply on hand for pointed lines of inquiry. "My father, who has all the warmth and charm of a dead snake, sent me to Deerbrook for middle school, deep in rural Massachusetts. Awful state, even worse than this one. Terrible food. And when one of the eighth graders there gave me a beer, it was an epiphany to me. I fucking hated that school. But the beer made there feel like *not* there. That was a wonderful trick to me."

"Did it ever occur to you that you'd be better off actually uncovering and addressing the real sources of your unhappiness instead of drinking?" she asked him.

"Maybe," he said, rubbing his thumb over and over across the silver coat of arms on the flask. "Or maybe there's a black curtain around me. Maybe there's this darkness so thick you could reach out and tug on it. You ever feel that curtain go in front of your eyes?"

"Every day," Anna said.

"Ah well then, I guess you know how hard it is to get rid of. This tastes better than therapy."

"You'll get booted."

"My darling Anna, that'll never happen."

"Why not?" she asked.

"He thinks he's bulletproof here because his family is loaded." Burton said.

Bamert nodded. "What he said."

"But he's wrong."

"You can shut up again now, Burton."

Just then, they heard giggling. Anna turned and saw a whip of black hair in the moonlight. It was Lara, in a loose paisley minidress with just the right amount of flow and bounce to it, cinched with a thick brown leather belt. She had the girl from Sewell—Anna's freshly minted nemesis—with her. Bamert, ever the gentleman, knew when to take his cue.

"Well now Burton, I think it's time for us to retire for the evening."

"Speak for yourself. I have a million things to do. I have to attend a pre-band meeting, record the Tri-Nation cricket test, fix three out of the four computer monitors I brought with me, walk Mr. DeMarco's dog—"

"Oooh, is it a bulldog?" Anna asked, suddenly excited.

"No."

"You know, I'd ask *how* you ended up needing to do all those things," said Bamert, "but then I'd have to refill this flask."

"You will anyway because you're a big alkie."

"I am an *enthusiast*. Let's go. This bridge is making me queasy. I don't like heights over water. Let's leave Anna Huff to more genteel company."

"Oh!" said Burton, "Is this girl coming now the girl Anna's into?"

"Shut it," Anna hissed at him. *Goddamn those two.*

"What?" asked Burton.

Anna gave Burton The Look. "Funny how rumors about girls always spread faster than rumors about boys."

Bamert stepped in between them to cool off the tension. "I assure you, my dear, that Burton is too distracted by his own idiotic musings to compromise you on this." He gave her a reassuring pat on the shoulder and whispered in her ear. He smelled like witch hazel. "Good luck. Make sure that when you pursue her, you pursue her with ethics."

"What on Earth does that mean?"

But Bamert didn't bother to elaborate. The two boys walked past Lara and her friend on their way back to campus. Bamert mimed tipping a cap to them, but they either didn't notice or didn't care. When Lara saw Anna, her giggles got even louder.

You're weird. She thinks you're weird. She and that girl were somewhere talking in private about how weird you are.

They moseyed onto the bridge, both stoned. Lara threw her arms around Anna and squeezed her tight and now Anna could smell her: all fresh cotton and sweet shampoo. She could have buried her face in Lara's neck and made a little home there, but it was too soon. Everything about today felt too soon. It was like she had ported directly into her own future.

"ROOMIE!" Lara cried.

"Oh right, this is your roommate!" the other girl said. Her wrists her bare. Lara hadn't given her one of *her* bracelets. *Only you were worthy of the bracelet. Only you were worthy of Lily Beach.*

"I'm Anna," Anna said to the girl, flat and cold.

"I'm Jubilee."

"You are not."

Jubilee laughed. "You're lucky Lara let me hit that vape because normally I get all pissy when people joke about my name."

"If you're not pissy about it right now, then I can joke about it more."

Jubilee gasped. "Where did you *find* this girl?" she asked Lara.

"Roomie's cool," Lara said. "Roomie'll talk shit to anyone, even Emilia. Isn't that right?"

"It's all I've got," Anna said.

"You got a bathing suit, too?" Lara asked, gesturing over the parapet. The moon-slicked river beckoned. Rumor was you could only jump off one side of the bridge because the school used the opposite side for illegal dumping: old tackling sleds, ripped-out bleachers, etc. Anna looked down at the water and thought about all of the potential, dangerous wreckage waiting just beneath the glimmering surface. She pictured herself stupidly impaling herself on a javelin, the entire student body rushing to the bridge the next morning to gawk at a grisly Anna-kebab. The Low Water warning sign cultivated an additional, alternate shade of fear.

"We gotta jump," Jubilee said. Jubilee was not interested in negotiating this. She stripped down to her sports bra and underwear and leapt up onto the stone parapet, positively bouncing with excitement. She didn't even wait for Lara and Anna to follow suit. Then she cried out "BITCHES!!!" and leaped over. Anna rushed to look, secretly hoping Jubilee had broken her leg on an old lacrosse goal. But no, Jubilee splashed down into the silvery water and screamed with laughter.

"Omigod COLD!"

Lara smiled at Anna. "I guess we have no choice."

Lara stripped down to her underwear. Now Anna knew she'd have to jump into that river, if only to cool off the rest of her own body. She kicked out of her mary janes and pulled off her jeans, but made an executive decision to leave her shirt on for the jump. Then she got up on the parapet with Lara and locked eyes with her as Jubilee cavorted down below. In the distance, another petal-soft breeze had the treetops exchanging high fives.

"It's nice out here, isn't it?" Lara asked Anna.

"Yeah. I like it. I mean, I'm sure it's no Lily Beach."

"You're gonna love it when I take you there." *When*, not if.

"I know I will," Anna said back. "Better than going to assembly."

"True."

"But it's definitely pleasant around here. Almost too pleasant."

"I know what you mean."

"I like that it's dark out here, though. I always liked the dark parts of places."

"Me too. Who were those two boys you were with?" Lara asked her.

"Bamert and Burton. They're just friends."

"That's what boys are best left as. What were you guys talking about?"

"How to break out of here," said Anna, matter-of-factly.

Lara's green eyes swelled. "Ooh, I want in. I wanna break out, too."

"You do?"

"Yeah," said Lara. "Let's do it. Let's be everywhere. Lucerne, Buenos Aires, Lily Beach."

"The Seychelles," said Anna.

"Hokkaido!" said Lara.

"Berlin!" said Anna.

"Amsterdam!" said Lara.

"Wichita!" said Anna. Lara busted out laughing at that one.

She's flirting with you. She likes you.

"You're weird, Anna Huff."

Or not.

Flirting time was over. "I'm sorry. I didn't mean to be weird."

"No, it's cool. Everyone's weird." She took Anna's hand and their bracelets clanked together. No one, outside of relatives and teachers, had taken Anna's hand before. This was a first for her. *Hands. Hands, then lips. Hands, then lips, then bodies.* She was detonating inside: a romantic neophyte desperate for the ability to tell if vibes were vibes. She wanted to touch Lara more than she was already touching her.

"Weird is good," Lara assured her. "*You're* good. I like you, Anna. There's something true about you. We'll be okay here, I promise."

"You do?"

"They can tell us what to do, but that doesn't mean we have to listen. Right?"

"Right."

"Life is about getting away with everything you can get away with. We'll get away with it all. We'll show them how punk it is to be happy. We'll bust out of here and then we'll go everywhere the shitty people aren't, and they won't ever be able to find us. Will you come? Will you come with me?"

I mean, breaking out was your idea first but… "I will."

"Look up for a second," Lara told her. The stars were out and giddy. She pointed to the brightest dot halfway between them and the horizon. "That's Jupiter, right there."

"We can't port to Jupiter."

"No, not yet," Lara laughed. "But maybe one day. Sometimes I think about how enormous it is, how enormous *everything* is, and I can't stand it. You know Jupiter made us?"

"Made us?"

"I read all about it. I'm smart. Don't tell Emilia. That would just fucking ruin it."

"I won't."

"I like books about UFOs. I like to read all the cool shit they never assign. Jupiter's got this electromagnetism, see. Kept all the bad shit away when we were just a baby planet. But it's got a lot of gravity, too. All of the gravity. So one day, it'll crash into the sun and bring us along with it. And then what made us will break us."

"That's pretty dark."

"It is." She leaned into Anna and whispered, "But for now, we're here. And we've got a little gravity of our own." Her lips were close to Anna's ear, her breath sweetly cradling it. Anna scrambled to cut the anticipation. To fill dead air.

But Jubilee did the job for Anna by screaming, "GET YOUR ASSES DOWN HERE!"

"Are you ready to jump?" Lara asked.

"I'm gonna jump on that girl's head," Anna said.

"Don't do that. Big breath!"

Lara jumped a split second before Anna did. They had to release hands in midair to keep from ripping each other's shoulders out. Anna boomed down into the frigid water and felt for the bottom. The low water sign had been a lie: a fruitless deterrent. Seven feet down, she grabbed a fistful of muck. Not sand. Just dead, fetid crap. She shook her hand clean and frog-kicked an extra ten yards along the decaying riverbed.

When she resurfaced, there was a bright light. Not the moon. No, this was something more pointed. Almost like…

A flashlight. Oh crap.

Lara and Jubilee were already sprinting out of the water and grabbing for their clothes and shoes.

"Anna, run!" her roommate cried.

Anna swam for the banks as the other two ran from the growing, accusing light. No time for her to grab her shoes or her shirt.

"Hey, you three!" cried a voice. Male. Dopey.

Anna was not in any condition to break into a sprint at the moment. She was sopping wet and already worn out from the dreaded Sewell stairwell. She could swim. She could dive (in fact, she was hoping to dazzle Lara with a back tuck off the bridge). But she hated running. A mess of overgrowth along the banks nipped at her ankles as she fled from the bridge. She scampered across the playing fields only to be tripped up by a divot housing an in-ground sprinkler. Her ankle collapsed. By the time she was back up and hobbling away, the security guard was closing in.

"Freeze right there!"

Lara and Jubilee were now fifty yards ahead of Anna. They were gonna escape, but she was fading. Her ankle felt like it was made of gravel. Every step she took was like a knife to her lower leg. The light grew brighter behind her, her lumbering shadow growing more pronounced in the fields, until she could sense the security guard within striking distance.

"Stop!"

She did as she was told.

JEREMIAH GOREN HALL

Dean Vick's office was easily twice the size of any anodyne ShareSpace that Anna and her mother routinely split out in the free zones. There was a chandelier dangling from the ceiling that looked like it hadn't been dusted in eight decades. In the center of the room was a large round table haphazardly littered with stacks of books: books that Anna presumed were put there for show. Behind the table was an equally massive desk. Behind the desk was a wall of degrees. Anna also spotted a framed, decades-old photo of the extended Vick family. No one was smiling in it. The only thing in the office that offered a hint of personality was a tiny figurine on Vick's desk of a bulldog made out of crushed pecan shells and lacquered a deep brown. Anna was dying to steal it.

Vick, clad in jeans and a light blue polo, was waiting for her at the table. She hadn't even stepped foot in a classroom yet before being sent to the dean's office.

She was still damp. The rent-a-cop hadn't bothered to offer her a towel. He had marched her directly to Goren Hall, barefoot and pantsless. She could smell herself. She smelled like she lived at the bottom of that stupid river.

Vick gestured for her to sit, browsing through a file with her name on it.

"Annie, is that right?"

"Anna." *Your name is right on the file. He botched it on purpose.*

"This is an unfortunate situation, Annie. As dean of students, it's my job to keep all of you safe. It's a responsibility that I take very seriously. So when something like this happens, the first question I ask is: *what could Druskin have done better? Have we done enough to prevent this sort of behavior?* Then I remember the preventive measures that I, along with the administration, have put in place here: measures that I know have served us well for some time. And so then I have to consider other factors." There was that reedy voice again, making her flesh peel.

"All we did was jump into a creek."

"Ah, see. I find it interesting that you said 'we'. Wade, our head of security, says there were two other girls with you."

"I'm not selling anyone out."

"He also said he smelled scented cannabis oil. Marijuana."

"There's no way your boy Wade could smell a thing with that much aftershave on him."

She laughed at her own joke to sell it, but that only made Vick angrier. He frightened her with his grimness. He seemed to bleed hate. Looking at him was like looking into the mouth of a very dark cave and knowing, instinctively, that you should avoid it. Somehow this was going even worse than she had pictured it.

He pointed an angry finger at her. One of his eyes was perpetually jaundiced and cloudy, as if he had been bitten by the undead. Such a dour, hideous man. She couldn't feel a soul anywhere inside of him.

"You're not as funny as you think you are," Vick said. "I find myself disheartened that a student such as you, on her first day no less, would have such a cavalier attitude toward such things. You know there's no swimming in the Hobscott. You know there's no drug use allowed on campus."

"I didn't smoke any weed. Gimme a blood test if you want."

"That isn't necessary, so long as you give me the names of your other two friends."

"It's my first day. I don't know *anyone*. People were just out there."

"You were holding hands with a girl when you jumped."

For a brief moment, Anna let herself remember what it was like to hold Lara's hand and jump off together. It was just one moment, but it seemed to promise so many more. Lily Beach. Private villas. Candlelit boardwalks. Indian Ocean sunsets. They were gonna be everywhere. They had a plan. A scheme. She had never been part of a real scheme before, and she'd never felt cooler. She closed her eyes to get a better look at the memory and found herself grief-stricken—sick to death at the thought that her time with Lara might be ending just as it was beginning. She'd had crushes before—minor league infatuations with Danni Pullen in eighth grade and then Emma Chance in ninth grade, both of which went unrequited—but she had never run into this sensation, where every single thought of love (oh god, that word) just blows up inside you. Love becoming grief, grief becoming love. Adults didn't understand this. They did at one point in their lives, but it was almost as if they had all forgotten how much love went into first love. Like they had never loved anyone at all.

"It was nobody," she told Vick.

"Was it Lara Kirsch?" he asked, eyeing the rose pink bracelet.

"No."

"As I said, this is all very unfortunate. You've put me in an awkward position where I feel compelled to call your mother—"

"Please don't do that."

"—to discuss reducing your financial aid package, which appears to be far too generous."

That got her. Anna fell apart. She tried desperately to fight back the tears, but they found their way out regardless. A lone corner of Vick's mouth turned up slightly and she felt a murderous rage toward him, all hot and primal. She could see herself wrapping her hands around Vick's throat and making his tight veins go tighter, smashing his head against the desk over and over until his temporal bones collapsed and his head was nothing but a mound of blood and loose bone shards and jellied brain parts and unidentifiable gristle.

They can try to tell us what to do, but that doesn't mean we have to listen. That's what Lara told Anna out on the bridge. She sniffed up whatever tears and snot she could, and then spat a final shot of courage at him: "I'm sorry, Dean. But I can't help you."

Vick took out his phone.

"Well then, I guess I'll have to make this call."

She couldn't bear the thought of Sandy getting a call and hearing the news that her own daughter had submarined her Druskin career before it had even started. More tears came pouring out of her as she grasped for a solution, any solution. Her lips were hot and puffy. Vick was an impenetrable as the wall around Druskin, and all it took was three minutes for her to realize it. There was no use trying to find a soul in there.

She weakened. A branch bent too far.

"Wait," she told him. "There must be some other way."

He stopped and pocketed the phone. The moment the offer left Anna's mouth, she regretted it.

SEWELL HALL

When Anna got back to Sewell and dragged herself up to Room 24, she glanced at the threshold under Lara's bedroom door and saw nothing but blackness. She stripped off her wet clothes, stuffed them into the white laundry bag, and then jammed wads of old newspaper into the soaked mary janes that Wade had left in the dorm's lobby along with the rest of her unadorned wardrobe. She sat on the bed and went back to messy crying. The harder she tried to purge Vick from her brain, the more forcefully his vile, stone face came roaring back at her. It was like Vick *knew* he could take her brain hostage in addition to her body, and delighted in it. Before she was allowed to leave his office, he had given her a very specific directive:

You are to report to my house on Wednesday evening at 7pm. You will dress lightly. You will not carry anything on you. You will tell no one, or else you'll be expelled and the record will show it was due to you committing hate crimes. Do you understand?

The instructions horrified her. She fought against the shame and the fear with all her might, along with the nagging voice inside her crowing that she deserved whatever consequences Vick had planned for her, because she had been such a fool. No. No, she would not accept that shame. She would only accept the anger. She was good at anger. She could hang with her anger all night, because it was so deserved and so righteous.

In the meantime, she cried some more. Half of her wanted to see Lara open that door and come out to comfort her. The other half knew that her face currently looked like a tomato someone had dragged across a cheese grater.

You should shower.

She went to grab her bathroom kit but then heard Lara's doorknob twist.

Shit.

Quickly, she went to bureau and grabbed a loose robe, cinching its belt so tight that it nearly cut her in half. The door swung open and Lara came over.

"Are you all right?"

"I'm okay," said Anna.

"What did they do?"

"They took me to Vick's office." Just saying his name brought her to an elevated state of rage that was impossible to keep disguised. His hateful stare remained tattooed onto her brain.

"What was he like?" Lara asked.

Anna played it off. "He was a dick."

"I bet he was."

"I didn't say anything though."

"It's not fair that we put you through that. I'm sorry."

"It's all right. Better me than all three of us."

"You were crying, though."

"Today was a lot," Anna said. "More than I could handle. I wish I had someone to talk to about it."

"You can talk to me."

"I can?"

"You can tell me anything, Roomie."

"You don't know what that means to me. Because I used to have someone I could vent to, but…" *I have a sister but I don't see her much anymore. I have a sister but I don't see her much anymore. I have a sister but I don't see her much anymore. I have a sister but I don't see her much anymore.* "She died."

"Anna?"

"My sister, Sarah. I could tell her anything, but now I can't."

"Oh god," Lara said. "I'm so sorry."

"Don't feel bad. No one else does."

"*I* do. What happened to her?"

Don't talk about it. All that does it make the hurt come back. "Someone killed Sarah, but I don't know who. They ported into our house one night and disappeared and I don't know who it was. I was asleep until the gun went off. I'm so sorry I'm unloading this on you."

Lara took Anna's hand. That she was willing to hold hands with Anna so often felt like dumb luck: a thoughtless tic Lara might cut out the second she realized she was doing it. "Is that why you wanna break out of here?"

"Yeah, but I don't know if I want to find out what I might find out. Getting away to the Maldives with you seemed more pleasant."

"We can still go there."

"You have to mean it."

"I mean it," Lara promised. "And I also mean it when I say that I can help you find whoever killed your sister, too."

"How?"

"Emilia owns the company. I can figure out who ported in that night. When you port you leave a signature. I know how to find those."

"PortSys isn't supposed to keep porting histories if people don't give them permission."

"PortSys isn't supposed to do a lot of shit. But I'll help, I swear."

If Lara Kirsch meant it, she was a rare find, indeed. Everyone else the Huffs enlisted to help track down the intruder that killed Sarah proved worthless. Sarah's bosses were worthless. Her friends were worthless. No one ever believed the Huffs. The police were the worst of the bunch. They were so profoundly useless when Sarah died, as if the only reason they showed up to Anna's house the next day was to torture the Huff family with their boundless capacity for indifference.

Anna was catatonic in the living room when they arrived on the scene. When she first saw Sarah's body, she noticed an orange rope bracelet sitting on the nightstand, and the bracelet continued flashing through her mind while she was trying to process her shock. She remembered seeing her mother on the floor of Sarah's room, clutching her sister's lifeless body, her screams turning to loud heaves. There was so much dried blood that it had flecked off everywhere. The room was a haven of blood dust. The cops didn't care. They ruled the death a simple suicide, and when Sandy insisted someone else had ported out of the house that night, they laughed at her. Could she identify the stranger? No, Sandy could not. Did Sandy have any idea who might have broken in? No, she did not. Did Sandy know her daughter owned a gun? No, Sandy did not. They told her that she had imagined the portclap, then laughed in her face for being such a comically oblivious parent. These cops weren't gonna spend one extra minute to determine if this was one of the thousands of port break-ins that happened on a daily basis in the free zones. They had no interest in *work*, especially when that work didn't involve the chance to fire a gun at somebody.

The cops didn't even bother talking to Anna. She was just a piece of furniture to them. All they did was crack wise about how Sarah was "probably a real looker," and then they swiped a couple of croissants off the kitchen counter before porting out. Anna said nothing. Did nothing. There are those really big events in life where people stand idly by and stare in shocked disbelief as the tragedy rushes by them like a rampaging locomotive. They don't react. They don't say anything. They just freeze in place, unable to absorb it all. *That's what you did. You sat there by your sister's corpse and let her death whizz right past.*

And now here was Lara Kirsch, offering a hand in every conceivable form. It was so wonderful, so *easy*, that it felt like it could all come undone at any second.

"Thank you, Lara."

"You know it, Roomie."

"Your mom probably knows my sister is dead. That's what she was getting at when she met me that first time."

"Fuck her. Whatever Emilia thinks she knows about you isn't as important as what *I* know about you now." She lowered her voice to a conspiratorial whisper, "The key is Network Z."

"Network Z?" Anna asked.

"Network Z."

"What is that?"

"I can't explain it right now, but you might be able find out about it if you look hard enough."

"Thanks. I'm sorry I mentioned it to you," Anna said. "I just miss having someone to talk to."

"I never had anyone to talk to," Lara said.

"I don't buy that."

"Look at me." Anna looked up from the floor and into Lara's verdant green eyes. When Lara looked at you with those eyes, it felt like you were the only thing she wanted to look at. They were a truth serum. "I never had anyone to talk to. I swear. Please believe me." For Anna, believing Lara took no effort whatsoever. "People talk to me because I'm a Kirsch or whatever, but they're not really interested. Know what I mean?"

"I do." All too well. Both Lara and Anna were demoralized from living in a time when it was nearly impossible to get other people to give a shit. They might *pretend to* give a shit by posting the occasional earnest WorldGram message when tragedy struck. But getting them to care to the point where they might act on that compassion, outside of them porting to an organized vigil to hold a candle for five minutes, was so fruitless that both girls had grown disillusioned: too numb to even *attempt* to get people to care about anything of consequence.

Until this moment. There Anna and Lara were, face to face, eager to truly matter to one another.

"Everyone lies to me," Lara said. "All the time. Even the people who are trying to be nice."

"I'll never lie to you."

"I'm just decoration to a lot of people, Emilia and Jason included," Lara went on, wrapping her hands around her own arms and swaying. "My family doesn't care about me, but they don't understand the damage that I can do."

"What do you mean?"

"You'll see when we bust out of here. I know some things about those two, and I'll show you them."

"I think I can figure out how to get past that portwall."

"I bet you can. I believe in you," Lara told her. "Shit being how it is right now, people don't make any effort to know my soul. But you can. You can help take me away from the parts of me I wish didn't exist." Lara had no clue how mutual that feeling was.

"So we can talk then? To each other?"

"Anytime, Roomie. I'll talk to you all night. I told I liked you and I meant it."

She likes you. Lara was pulling that black curtain away, letting sunlight into Anna's mind for the first time in well over a year. Anna was still crying but the tears were almost joyful now. "Thank you. I stink. I really oughtta shower."

Lara grabbed Anna and hugged her tight, her neon bracelets jangling behind Anna's neck. Charles Vick beat a hasty retreat from Anna's thoughts. Her robe belt cut deeper into her waist, but she could barely feel it now because love was unloading on her so quickly. *I like you. Will you come away with me? I'll talk to you all night.* Love everywhere. Love in Lara's velveteen black hair. Love in her soft, freckly shoulders. Love in her cute little crab shorts. Love in her tiny stud earrings. Love in those green eyes. It was all hot, fast, *relentless* love porting directly into Anna. It was built on scraps: moments of unsolicited kindness and brief intense encounters and clandestine plots, but it was love all the same: a feeling of total freedom, a lack of encumbrance that bordered on the mystical.

Druskin told every student on campus that they were exceptional. And Anna's mother always insisted that her little girl was special. But with Lara, Anna at last *felt* exceptional: treated as extraordinary by someone who had no obligation to do so. Once Lara had asked Anna to come away, and to help avenge Sarah, the world rebooted for her. Every city and continent and island held new potential, new daydreams, new *culprits* to apprehend. Love made everything feel new. She had no idea what to do with this love. It was embarrassing. She was *that* roommate now: the obsessive, psycho roommate. *Awesome. Just fucking awesome. Don't hug back too hard. Don't push it, girl. You smell, remember. You are wet and in your robe. Don't say anything dumb. Do not say anything dumb.*

"I'm glad you're my roommate." Anna whispered to her. *Dumb.*

"Me too. You have no idea. I don't even know why I'm at this school, really. But at least we found each other, right?"

"Yeah." Anna sensed their faces were drawing closer. She was ready to close her eyes and tilt her head ever so slightly, to accelerate something that was already moving at warp speed.

Instead, Lara let her go. "Okay you really do stink," she joked. That was it for hugs, for now. "But I owe you one. Got any favors you need done?"

A few, yes. "Yeah, don't tell anyone I smell this bad."

Lara laughed. "I won't." She walked over to Anna's desk and scribbled down a 917 phone number. "Here: I'm gonna give you my PortPhone number so that you always have it."

Holy shit, you got her contact.

Anna wrote her own contact info down for Lara, then grabbed her toilet kit and trudged upstairs to the hallway bathroom. In the shower stall, she pressed both hands against the grimy white tiles and aimed the crown of her head at the hot spray. She closed her eyes and saw Vick's face staring back at her with his clouded, undead eye: pulsing with fury. She jacked up the hot water until it burned.

When Anna got out and dried off, she looked under the stall door and saw the Shit Memoirs laying there. She was about to snatch it from the floor when suddenly, she heard shouting. She put on her robe, grabbed her kit, and went out to the stairwell. It was clear that the shouting was coming from her and Lara's room. Though it was muffled behind a gauntlet of closed doors, she could still make out Emilia Kirsch's curt voice.

Oh no.

She tiptoed back to Room 24. Down the stairwell shaft, her dorm-mates cracked their doors and stuck their heads out over the railing for a peek upward at the commotion. Anna tried the turn the knob as gently as she could, but it was a hilarious failure. The door squealed like it had an alarm attached to it. She kept up the self-delusion that she was being discreet and eased into the room, still hoping to be unheard. When she closed the door, it squealed again. She may as well have brought a live seal into the room with her.

Anna leapt into bed and cracked open the common read, then flipped the pages every time the alarm clock moved a minute ahead. She didn't read a word. This was as subtle as her eavesdropping got.

"Your first day," Kirsch bellowed from behind the door. "Your very first day and I've already got Dean Vick calling me."

"Mom, it's no big deal."

"Nothing's a big deal to you because nothing HAS to be. You're an average child, and you've never aspired to be anything more than that. It's disappointing. You lack anything resembling your brother's ambition and intellect."

"He's an asshole," Lara said.

"And what are you?" Emilia asked. "You are a distraction."

"That's not fair."

"Maybe I should have Jason pay you a visit."

"Don't you dare."

"Well then, you'd best get your act together. If you're gonna smoke drugs all day, I can have you do that at a public school for free, with the rest of the welfare kids who get ported in from the ghettoes and shitholes."

"I wasn't smoking anything."

"Lara, I spend my entire work day arguing with elite minds and defeating them, your brother included. Do you really expect to win this fight? This is a demo argument. You're a remedial thinker, and now I'm concerned that you'll stay that way even if I leave you here."

"You didn't send me here to make be better. You sent me here to be rid of me."

"Who can blame me? And yet, you get here and instantly manage to cry for attention. Shape up, and stop hanging out with your loser of a roommate."

"I'll hang out with anyone I want to," Lara snapped back. "That goes for Anna especially. Maybe I'm not the genius you were hoping to raise. But I trust my soul, and I know you sure as hell don't. And I know exactly how much gin you need to forget that every night."

Anna heard a sharp smack and Lara crying out in pain. Then, another smack, this one signaling Kirsch's abrupt exit. Now there was nothing coming from behind the door but stifled crying. Anna turned in her bed and buried her face against the wall. She wanted to blend into the plaster and become nothing but a great white blank, forever unnoticed and unseen by anyone ever again.

She felt homesick now, but for what home? For the past year, she and Sandy had lived in one crummy ShareSpace after another—Rockville, Columbus, Munich, Hartford, São Paulo, Brisbane, Budapest, Denver—all the while keeping their crap in a locked, windowless trailer pod in Rockville, a mile away from the house that Sandy had abandoned in both grief and in crippling debt. Like the rest of the Newmads (as ShareSpace affectionately dubbed their customers), they would shuffle back to their locker over and over for clothes and toiletries, and then they would emerge in some other ShareSpace assigned to them, rootless and jaded.

Like everyone else, they kept hoping the next place they ported to would be better than the last, only to immediately begin searching for new ground once they arrived. Whatever elements of home they once had—rooms, possessions, neighbors—all of those had been forcibly split up and consigned to new, separate economies. Home was an illusion. Home was broken.

Even when they ported away for a night to somewhere cool, they invariably ended up in yet another ShareSpace. The subscription was all that Sandy Huff could afford, and so they'd trudge into yet another glorified hostel, with a room of their own and a common area and kitchen stocked with plain potato chips and even plainer neo-gypsies: old folks, tourists, vagrants, chirpy young professionals banging away at chrome laptops. They were comfortable places to stay, but vacancies filled quickly. They were never yours, and they never felt safe. There was nothing that was the Huff family's own anymore. So Anna was crying not because she was homesick, but because she was lost, and she had never realized HOW lost she had been until just now.

This was the first night she'd spent alone in a room in years: without her mom sleeping in the bed next to her and without a gun tucked under Sandy's pillow. She wouldn't need earplugs to sleep at Druskin. She wouldn't need melatonin to ward off port lag, which always hit whenever she ported around too much and her body clock went schizo. She couldn't sneak away and foolishly port somewhere lethal, the way that one kid did on Mount Everest. She could close her eyes this night and hear the world in full: crickets and swaying oak branches and very distant portclaps coming from behind the Harkness Wall. It was all so terribly pleasant, and yet here Anna was, warding off trauma coming on from all new fronts.

Lara's door flew open and she stormed over to Anna's bed. One side of her face had a long, thin welt from where Emilia had slapped her. She grabbed Anna's shoulder and yanked her away from the wall, then jabbed a finger at her. Two angry fingers in one night.

"You told."

"I didn't, I swear!"

"I don't know if I can believe you." Oh, and the words were so sharp. They cleaved Anna right in half. Lara was definitely her mother's daughter. The scowl she borrowed from Emilia was real this time, and no less formidable.

"Lara, if you had *any* idea what I just agreed to keep quiet."

Lara started pulling her own hair. "God, this place is so fucked. *Every* place is fucked now! I needed someone. I needed *you*. I needed you so much more than you understand. I wish things could have stayed real between us. I wish we could have gotten away."

"I. Didn't. Say. Anything."

"I can't take this. I can't. I'm sorry I put you in the middle of my bullshit."

She stormed back into her room and slammed the door shut. Slammed Anna's whole world shut.

The next morning, Anna was shocked awake by two distinct claps coming from Lara's bedroom. When she gathered up the courage to get up and crack the door, she discovered that Lara Kirsch was gone.

SEWELL/PHILLIPS HALL

Lara's bedroom was cleaned out from corner to corner. Save for a fluorescent light buzzing overhead, it was as empty as a hole. Anna surveyed the barrenness, dried tears crusted around her eyelids. You never got to watch anyone leave anymore. Everyone just vanished. Anna walked over to the window and looked out at the hill leading down from the dorm, a little patch of grass with lounge chairs that all the girls christened Sewell Beach even though it wasn't a beach of any sort. Lara and Anna could have hung out on Sewell Beach. Could have. She opened Lara's desk drawer and found a Post-it note, with a single word written in glittery purple ink:

Roomie

Anna slipped off the rose pink bracelet and tucked it, along with the Post-it, into her pillowcase for safekeeping. The only person who spoke to Anna that morning was a kindly Mrs. Ludwig, waiting in the common room with a basket of fresh milk rolls and a tray of chicken drumsticks slathered in sticky sweet barbecue sauce for all the girls. When she saw Anna looking despondent, she stopped munching on a drumstick, wiped her hands, and then hugged Anna tight as one of her cats came by and nibbled away at the pastries.

"I know you got in some trouble there, but everything will be fine, just fine."

"Where's Lara?"

"Anna Hoof, I'm not important enough to know the answer to that."

Everyone else in Sewell Hall gave Anna the silent treatment. When she said "hey" to the dreaded Jubilee in the bathroom, there

66

was no "hey" back. When she went to the bathroom, she cracked open the Shit Memoirs and, against her better judgment, gobbled up the new entries.

"Anna Huff is a fucking rat."

Fucking sweet. Great to hear.

"There's a stupid diver who got Lara Kush put up on the first night of school."

That's not quite accurate.

"Paul Bamert goes here. Everyone knows <u>he's</u> a sack of shit."

Hey! Lay off!

A couple of girls averted their gaze when they saw Anna on the stairwell. Along the fresh asphalt path down the hill to Phillips Hall for English class, more students did likewise, while a handful of others did the opposite and delivered withering stares. Everyone knew. Everyone knew *this* was the girl who fucked up and drove Lara Kirsch away from Druskin. Maybe they knew how Anna felt about Lara to boot. She wanted control over that particular bit of information, but she learned long ago that she lived in a world where everyone knew you better than you knew yourself. She kept her head down and bulldozed through the fog of rushed judgments. Meanwhile, PINE choppers crisscrossed overhead, snipers eager for more port immigrants to gun down.

She walked into Phillips Hall and climbed a wide Carrara marble staircase that was so worn down from decades of student footfalls that the lip of each step was half as thick in the center as it was at either end. Like the Academy Building, the entire hall predated modern air conditioning. The airflow inside this dump hadn't re-circulated since 1926. This was air that had dimensions to it like a runny cheese: damp, rusty, and thick.

When Anna opened the door to Mr. Nolan's classroom, Bamert was waiting for her, clad in a lime green suit and matching bowtie, sitting at the head of the giant mahogany table in the center of the class. His head seemed to fill the entire room. He patted the open seat between him and Burton, like it was a prize for her to claim. She trudged over. Through the grimy windows she saw the old brick dorms framing the manicured quad, eager preps damn near skipping along its smooth paths. They all had so much more to look forward to than her. So much promise. Her time here at Druskin was already over. From now until whenever she left, she would be the campus undead. She dreaded the idea of seeing Vick ever again.

"And how was your rendezvous last evening?" Bamert said.

"I don't wanna talk about it," she whispered. The more kids filled the classroom, the lower her whisper went.

"Everyone else would, though."

"Everyone else can piss off," she told him.

"Yes, well as you mourn your social life, you should be aware that our little Burton may or may not have had a breakthrough last night."

She turned to Burton, "Really?"

"Do you realize that the dining hall doesn't serve *any* cashew milk? What am I supposed to put on my cereal?" Burton asked.

Anna glowered at Bamert. "*That's* his breakthrough?"

"No, he's just being a moron. Burton, tell her about the thing."

"I'm not gonna tell her about the thing," Burton said. "There are people here."

"Well, that thing better be a good thing because I've had ten hours of nothing but bad things," said Anna.

"Anna, do you really think you're the only kid on this campus right now who feels angst?" Burton asked her. "We're here because we're *all* anxious. I take Ambien to sleep at night, and Ambien is for sixty-year-old ladies and shithead jocks who can't get their hands on other drugs."

"Listen to Young Burton," said Bamert. "I have the blood pressure of a sitting President. We are not a healthy lot."

"Especially if the dining hall is giving us *those* milk options."

"H. Christ, enough about the milk already. Dairy cows were put on this Earth to give man epicurean pleasure, Burton. Meanwhile, you're in the dining hall bitching for nut water."

"I need both of you two to shut up right now," said Anna. "Whatever good advice you think you have for me, I promise: you don't have it."

Just then, Mr. Nolan rolled into the class in a wheelchair, sporting a bowtie of his own. He was an ancient man. Sickly looking. The bags under his eyes weighed his whole face down and kept the bottom of his eyelids permanently ajar. You could see the pink flesh gleaming under his eyeballs. Anna wanted to hook up an IV to him.

Nolan had presided over this classroom since 1990. An assortment of books and tchotchkes littered the room and served as living artifacts of the man: a musty globe, a red clay pot, a stuffed squirrel, forty years worth of framed portraits of the English faculty at Druskin with Nolan wearing an equally dorky bowtie in each of them. There were also multiple editions of the same Joyce book on the shelves, purchased over and over because Nolan would mark up the old ones and run out of room. He was the first unarmed teacher Anna had seen since the first grade.

Nolan rolled up to the table and took out a book from a leather valise he kept on his lap. When he scratched his face, Anna was afraid his whole cheek would fall off.

"You've all had a chance to complete the common read." He got a smattering of timid grunts in affirmation. "What'd you think of it? What did you think of *Portrait of the Artist As A Young Man?*"

The entire class went mute, except for Burton. Burton held his copy up and let it flop open. The binding was split. Two of the pages fell out.

"Why did they have us buy such cheap copies?" Burton asked.

"Come again?" Nolan asked.

"This isn't reinforced binding. They may as well have just given us a Xerox of the book. There was a Vintage edition of this that was the same price from port retailers, and it uses animal protein glue binding. This is thermal. Thermal is downright shoddy. There'll be a family of silverfish crawling through this thing by next week."

"Does anyone else have thoughts on the book?" Mr. Nolan asked aloud.

"If I may," said Bamert, "I believe my compatriot here, in a very roundabout and annoying way, has pointed out the physical

69

flimsiness of this tome as a way of also condemning its *intellectual* flimsiness."

"That's not what I was doing at all."

"Shut up, Burton."

"Go on," said Nolan.

"It's an indulgent book. A relic. I think you would agree with me that Joyce doesn't actually care much for Steven Dedalus, right?"

Nolan smiled. Suddenly he didn't look so dead after all. "Maybe."

"Definitely! He's a weenie!" The rest of the class laughed. Bamert had them all now. "This book is a classic, but only by assignation. It is self-indulgent and dated. *Masturbatory*. Why *not* let the pages fall out of it?"

Nolan turned to Anna. "Do you agree with this?"

"Honestly, Mr. Nolan, I didn't like it because I didn't understand any of it. And I don't think the author cared much if *anyone* did."

"That's Joyce for you now, isn't it?" Nolan joked. "What is your name?"

"Anna Huff."

"Anna Huff, do you think that, when you're older, you might understand this book more?"

"Probably."

"Do you think, when you're older, that you might view your younger self with similar contempt, as Joyce does?"

"I don't need to age another day for that."

Other kids pepped up and the class breezed by. When Nolan excused the kids at the top of the hour, he rolled over and gave Anna a soft tap on her waist.

"Would you mind staying for a moment?" he asked her. She nodded and Nolan closed the door behind a nosy Bamert and Burton, both of them loitering next to the doorway to eavesdrop.

"You were placed on 'stricts last night," Nolan said to her.

"I was."

"You'll learn a lot here, Anna Huff. I saw your records before today and it's clear you have a swift learning curve."

"Not when it comes to that book."

"Yes, Joyce'll stymie even the quickest of minds. Regardless, perhaps the vital thing you'll need to learn here is how to properly get into trouble."

"I don't suppose there's a class for that."

"There isn't, but I'm certain you'll get the hang of it. And with great speed!"

Anna was staring at Nolan's wheelchair. *You're staring too long. Stop doing that. Why are you still staring? You're the fucking worst. Don't ask him.*

"Can I ask you something?" *Idiot.*

"Of course," said Nolan.

"How do you—"

"I can't. Not without great difficulty. PortSys didn't devise their little gadgets with someone like me in mind."

"So you're just here, all the time?"

"Do you think that's so terrible?"

"Oh my god, no. No. I'm sorry, I didn't mean to imply—"

"No one ever means to." He gestured to the shelves in his classroom. "I have my books and that is all the transport I need. Besides, why port when *I* can be the destination that others seek, hmm? I have students like you come to me, Anna Huff. You're good and interesting kids, and I needn't bother zapping myself everywhere to have the pleasure of meeting you all. Isn't that grand? Tell me, where was the last place you ported before you ported here?"

She couldn't remember the last place she ported. She couldn't even remember the *first* place she ported. It might have been Baltimore.

"I think I was in Denver," she told him. A pointless lie that could easily be sniffed out.

"For what purpose? Fun? Work?"

She sighed. "I don't remember, sir. I don't remember anything about anywhere."

"Well, if it comforts you, you are now in a place that will almost certainly remember. In the meantime, read more carefully. You never know what good things you might have missed."

71

Anna pointed to the stuffed squirrel in the corner of the room. "What's with the squirrel?"

"Oh, Fred? I keep my classroom open at all hours, so that my students can study here if they feel like it. You're welcome to do so as well. If I'm not around, I have Fred there to keep an eye on you."

She squinted, trying to see if there was a hidden camera inside Fred.

"I don't mean that literally," Nolan said.

"Oh."

"The door is open any time. And follow me on WorldGram. I take excellent photos of Salton Boathouse, you know."

That was all Anna needed to hear. She had a classroom to work with now, and the Internet in Phillips Hall was far less restrictive than it was in the dorms. She had a base of operations: a place where she could figure out Kirsch's porting secrets and then find the opening in time and space that would bring her back to Lara, back to the dazzling moments they started from.

She felt something that first night with Lara, and now she wanted that something back. *I needed you.* No one apart from family members had ever needed Anna Huff before. Anna would find her. She would find everything that she was looking for: Lara, this Network Z, her sister's killer, all of it. She would prove to Lara that she was *right* to need her. Together, they would seize justice for Sarah, and then they would hold hands and jump off once more through the welcoming moonlight and into a world turned gold. And no billionaire mom or psychotic dean or annoying third wheel or donut-humping security guard would ever get between them again.

THE BOY ON THE MOUNTAINTOP
By Katy Wagner, GizPo
9/21/2030

(COOS BAY, OR) — Melanie Greenberg has a plan for what to do if she ever meets the Kirsch family. She's rehearsed her speech in the mirror for over a year now. Late at night, when she's mired in the private hell of insomnia, she'll jot down tweaks to her working script, each word chosen carefully for maximum impact. She's learned to write legibly in darkness; rarely does she misspell a word or write one word over another despite writing blind. She can feel the pages for indentations from where she's put pen to paper, so she can locate free white space beneath. And she has sharpened the words down to a blade, so that when she sticks them into a Kirsch, they'll leave a mark.

Can you tell me what you plan on saying?

"The words 'you killed my son' will be in there somewhere."

You think they killed him.

"I know they did. Emilia Kirsch runs the company. Jason Kirsch invented the technology. Tell me who else would be responsible."

Do you want to physically harm Emilia and Jason?

"Yes, but I know I can't. I've convinced myself it's the wrong idea anyway. I want them to live with the hell of being themselves. Emilia and Jason can stay rich. They can stay free. But they'll always have to live inside their hateful bodies, and I want that to hurt them."

It wasn't always easy to get to Coos Bay. You used to have to drive here from Portland, taking the 5 South down to Route 38 and then across to 101, a tattered ribbon of a country highway that would test even a cast-iron stomach. That slim passageway through the wild, coupled with eternally damp weather, was enough to keep Coos Bay relatively isolated in the beginning of the century, especially as shipping jobs began to dry up and drugs took hold over this otherwise anonymous bit of Oregon shoreline.

"We'd have campers and tweakers," says Greenberg. "But now you get these clusters of surfers and fishermen, all zapping in together at exact times and making a goddamn mess before zapping right back out again. And, of course, we have a few port refugees from here and there."

But the greater impact that porting has had on Coos Bay hasn't come from people bypassing the endless roads to come here, but rather its original residents *leaving*. When the world opened up, the youth of Coos Bay fled in droves. So many kids have dropped out of nearby Marchfield High that the school has been forced to shutter entirely.

One of the kids who dropped out was Melanie's son, Jeffrey. If you're conjuring the stereotype in your head of what a high school dropout might look like these days—lazy, disaffected, porting at random, addicted to black market opioids, etc.—Jeffrey's story will alter that image drastically. He was a straight-A student. He was lead trumpet in the school marching band. He never drank or smoked. A sophomore at Marchfield during the advent of porting, he was already receiving letters from prominent Pac-12 schools with hints of scholarship money in the offing.

"I think, in some ways, porting has been worse for the smart kids," Melanie tells me. I'm in her house right now. It's a split-level abode nestled deep in the woods. This is an area that gets little port traffic, although that hasn't stopped Melanie from keeping dozens of guns handy to fend off aggressive trespassers and would-be squatters. She makes me a fresh pot of coffee but, in a moment of absent-mindedness, forgets to put a filter in the coffeemaker. Hot water and loose grounds spurt all over the kitchen counter.

"Jeffrey wanted to leave Coos Bay, and I don't blame him. I mean, this place was a meth hole. He was excited to get out and see the world, and I was excited for it, too. I just think you have to be *ready*, you know? No one was ready for it."

She held off buying Jeffrey a PortPhone for as long as she could, but after he saved up hundreds from his own personal landscaping business, she couldn't fend him off any longer.

"I remember where he ported to first," Melanie says to me as she rinses the soaked coffee grounds out of her pot and puts in a fresh filter. "It was Cancun, which is predictable for a 16-year-old. I made him promise only to go for a couple of minutes. So he zaps out, and

I'm waiting, and waiting, and I've got half a mind to go to his pin and thrash him in front of all of Mexico. Then he finally came back."

And what was that like?

"He wouldn't stop laughing. That ever happen to you? You're so happy you start laughing, and you don't know why? It was that. And I saw that look of joy from him and..." she begins to cry, "I'm a mom, you know? When you see your kid happy, you want them to stay that way forever. It's like when you give a small child candy, and they go crazy for it. It makes you want to give them more. To spoil them. Because it's so *easy*. Spoiling them makes them happy. But you know you can't spoil them always because if you keep giving candy to them, it'll..." She can't finish the thought. She presses her hands against the counter and lets out a long exhale.

Jeffrey began porting every weekend, and then every night. Once PortSys began offering unlimited plans, Melanie felt powerless to stop him. He always managed to talk his way out of having the phone confiscated. Sometimes they would port together places, but more often it would be Jeffrey out in the world on his own, Melanie dying a little inside every time he vanished.

"Everything was different overnight, and I needed more time to adjust to that. We all did. We all still do! But PortSys? They never gave a shit. They weren't careful. They didn't bother preparing anyone for this kind of world. They charged ahead because they knew no one would ever have the courage to stop them."

One Sunday in May, Jeffrey told his mom he was going to Los Angeles with fellow bandmate Paul Gallagher. They had an agreement that he would share his pin with her anytime he went somewhere. This day, the destination was the Santa Monica Pier. Melanie watched Jeffrey port out, then ported to Atlanta herself to visit a friend before coming home to wait for him.

But Jeffrey never showed. Melanie called her son. She texted. Still no answer. When she checked her own PortSys account, she realized that Jeffrey had unfriended her that morning, leaving her unable to see his port history. By the time Monday morning arrived, she had turned frantic, porting to Jeffrey's chosen pin on the beach and wading through hordes of unimaginative tourists to look for her son, a human needle in the haystack. When she called PortSys to try to verify his current location, they refused to disclose it.

"Sometimes," Melanie says, "You trust your children too much, you know? Jeffrey was such a good kid, I'd have trusted him with any decision he made. But then I would forget he's still just a kid."

What Melanie didn't know was that Jeffrey's trip to Santa Monica was actually a premeditated ruse. He and Gallagher weren't going to California at all. Rather, they had spent the better part of a month sketching out a plan to port to the summit of Mount Everest. They studied storm patterns. They borrowed mountaineering gear from a friend (lightweight, to adhere to PortSys' YOU PLUS TWO guidelines, which allow for teleporting an extra two kilograms on your person in addition to the mass of your naked body) plus bottles of supplemental from a more experienced summiter. They went on long runs in high altitude cities: cities that Jeffrey had truthfully told his mother he was going to visit, while keeping hidden his ulterior motive for the jaunts.

The plan was port to increasingly high altitudes, get acclimated, and then hit the summit. Once on the roof of the world, Jeffrey and Paul would take in the view of the surrounding hemisphere, get a selfie, and then leave in an instant.

It is, of course, not legal to port to the summit of Everest. Since the advent of porting, only the South Slope of the mountain is open to climbing, with the North Slope formally closed by a Chinese government that outlawed porting from the start and has no plans to reverse that policy. Thus, oversight of Everest's unlicensed port tourism has fallen mostly to overwhelmed Nepalese officials.

The path to the summit was awash in litter and human excrement long before the advent of PortPhones, and porting has only exacerbated the problems at the top of the mountain. As with other national landmarks all over the world, port tourists have overwhelmed and desecrated what were once carefully preserved lands. In a bit of morbid irony, the deadly environs of Everest have help protect it from being *completely* overrun. Other parks and attractions lack such natural deterrents.

And standard tourist attractions are even more vulnerable, particularly spots highlighted by popular WorldGram travel accounts like @GoHere, which can create nightmare crowding situations the instant it recommends a porting destination. The Eiffel Tower in Paris is patrolled by armed forces at all times because port tourists stampede in at all hours, but the Tower is fortunate enough to be able to afford that security. Prominent amusement parks like Cedar Point in Ohio now must charge by the ride instead of charging gate admission because they can't build a portwall large enough to secure the grounds. Pebble Beach golf course in California now has PINE agents on carts patrolling the holes 24/7. Other hotspots, such as Monte Alban in Oaxaca and parts north of the aurora oval in Alaska, lack the funding to afford a portwall *or* beefed-up security, and have thus suffered environmental and ecological decay due to massive increases in foot traffic.

The summit of Everest, despite its hostile climate, has also suffered likewise. Perhaps it hasn't suffered the same amount of damage as Uluru in Australia, but *any* damage done to the roof of the world is substantial and permanent. New mountaineering laws have not helped. Anyone caught porting to the summit of Everest is subject to arrest and fines in excess of $500,000. But catching violators and enforcing fines is nearly impossible. While Nepalese officials were glad that porting eased some of traffic *to* the summit, they have had little control over the inevitable overcrowding that now routinely happens *on* it, especially when weather conditions prove favorable. How can you control the top of a mountain when anyone can get there by pushing a button and stepping into a wormhole? You can't keep a police force 33,000 feet up in the sky. You can't patrol it from the air. Proposals to create a portwall around the summit have proved unworkable.

To prevent being identified at the summit, Jeffrey Greenberg and Paul Gallagher left their passport lanyards behind in a still-unknown location. Jeffrey's callowness meant that he had vastly overestimated his ability to execute the Everest plan. As they ported from one acclimation point to the next, Jeffrey complained to Gallagher that he felt nauseous and dizzy: unmistakable signs of altitude sickness.

An encroaching storm system—not exactly a surprise development around Everest—forced Jeffrey and Gallagher to accelerate their plans and shorten their acclimation intervals so that they could port to the summit and get out before the squall bore down.

That would prove to be a fatal error, because Jeffrey's lungs were already starved for oxygen. At the peak of Everest, the air only has roughly a third of the oxygen contained in the air at sea level. That thin air, combined with the drop in air pressure, can tax the lungs of even a seasoned climber. And Jeffrey was far from that.

The instant the two boys ported to the South Summit, with an altitude of 28,704 feet, Jeffrey collapsed and began to convulse, the result of a cerebral edema. Gallagher, now terrified, tried to program Jeffrey's PortPhone to port his friend back to safer ground, but couldn't get his bandmate's finger to hold steady on the phone's scanner prompt. Even if Gallagher had succeeded in this, Jeffrey never would have been able to take the crucial step to complete the porting. He was stuck seizing at the summit, his body desperate to hyperventilate but too weak to do so. His diaphragm cramped into a hard knot. The oxygen supply to his brain got cut off entirely. When Gallagher called American medical startup 1RSPND and begged them to have first responders port to the summit, the company told him that they were over their monthly porting data limit, and that PortSys had throttled their service. Mountaineers that had secured official permits to summit the mountain began to openly grouse at the two boys clogging up the summit, which has a surface area roughly the size of an apartment closet. No one was going to help Jeffrey Greenberg.

It was all over in less than a minute. A nearby team of experienced climbers, who had made the summit the old-fashioned way, rushed to administer CPR to Jeffrey, but by then he had no pulse. With the storm closing in quickly, Paul Gallagher, who would only agree to speak on background for this story, had little choice but to abandon his friend right there, 100 meters below the highest point on Earth.

Jeffrey Greenberg's body remains on Everest to this day, scattered among the hundreds of other corpses resting on the mountain that cannot be removed, neither by porting nor by law. He is far from alone in being the only young person to meet a gruesome fate by porting somewhere he didn't belong. There was the case of Taylor Garrison, a college student who accidentally ported into the middle of the Pacific Ocean and drowned. There was the case of Megan Abay, who got stuck in a faulty wormhole that teleported her back and forth from her apartment in Chicago to her parents' home in Addis Ababa every microsecond, splitting her into two places simultaneously and destroying her mind. There was Leann Egan, who was ported 200 feet above her intended pin in Maui thanks to what PortSys described as a "glitch" in its famously guarded algorithm. She fell to her death.

And then there was the strange case of Anthony Drazic, a seven-year-old who, through yet another system "bug," ported directly into the body of a full-grown man named Joshua Klim, killing both instantly. Drazic's body had to be surgically removed from Klim's abdomen in a gruesome Caesarian section that would take a Serbian coroner thirteen hours to complete. To this day, it remains the only violation of PortSys's supposedly ironclad law that solid matter cannot port into other solid matter. And then there are, of course, the tens of thousands of runaways and refugees shot and killed by interior patrols lurking in the United States, the United Kingdom, Spain, Russia, and every other country looking to crack down on port migration.

These deaths, be they the result of direct failures in PortSys's algorithm, or the result of PortSys failing to curtail its users' more reckless impulses, have invariably resulted in solemn statements issued by the company, along with any number of discreetly agreed-upon cash settlements. Melanie Greenberg was offered $28,000 to settle her case against PortSys. When she refused and filed a formal lawsuit, the case was thrown out in Federal court after Congress passed a law that made it illegal to sue "any porting carrier" (curious wording, given that PortSys is the only porting carrier in existence) for accidents resulting from the use of their products.

Calls for PortSys to restrict how users port—into private homes, into war zones, and to dangerous terrain—have been rebuffed by the company in the name of port neutrality. The closest PortSys has come to fixing the problem is establishing two-factor confirmation for any user wishing to port into "conflict zones," areas marked as dangerous by the company (of course, those designations have often been met with vehement protest by residents of said zones). They promise that the bugs that killed Josh Klim and Leann Egan have been fixed in later software updates. The company's parental controls, ostensibly introduced to help parents monitor where kids port, remain cumbersome and lightly used.

When Jason Kirsch was confronted with these facts in an email exchange with me, he remained defiant.

"Our terms of service are clear," he told me. "Our port moderators do not advise people porting to certain areas they have declared as unsafe, but we are not going to close off those areas and restrict the God-given freedoms of those who are experienced and hardy enough to tackle that kind of terrain. I myself have ported to such locations. Have you been to the top of Devil's Tower? I have. It's breathtaking. It is incumbent upon users to follow both their better instincts and the laws of anywhere they choose to port."

"So you're absolved of all responsibility in these deaths?" I asked him.

"Let me make it clear, Katy: This company saved the world. You know that. I know I speak for my mother when I say it's a terrible thing any time someone experiences a porting malfunction."

You mean a porting death.

"No, these are unfortunate *malfunctions*. In the event of someone harming himself during the porting process, we mourn just as his family mourns."

I don't believe that.

"Believe what you want to believe," Jason Kirsch wrote back. "I have the facts on my side, and what the facts say is that porting solved this planet's energy crisis, along with its housing crisis and its traffic crisis. People can now evacuate from natural disasters in a snap, and rescue workers can port into those same areas with equal speed. Once we get China on board with porting, we'll have improved modern civilization by orders of magnitude. To me, it's insane that some people don't appreciate this. **WE INVENTED TELEPORTATION.** How can you not be astounded by that? I'm astounded by it every day! Do you understand how many lives this company has saved? Forty thousand automobile related deaths in the United States alone. Every year. All saved. Why is *that* not the focus of your story?"

(Jason Kirsch is not entirely correct here: While passenger automobile deaths are now nearly extinct, trucking fatalities have increased over 500% since the advent of porting, thanks to decaying highway infrastructure plus huge increases in demand for construction and shipped goods in formerly remote areas.)

Melanie Greenberg has never seen her son's body. To visit Jeffrey, she would either have to pay an outrageous amount to have it removed from Everest, or she herself would have to port to the summit, something she is terrified to do both from a physical and legal standpoint. For now, Jeffrey's body remains on display in a permanent, open wake she'll never be able to attend. She long ago forgave Paul Gallagher for his role in Jeffrey's death. Instead, she saves the bulk of her ire for PortSys and the Kirsch family. Sometimes, when she wakes up in the morning, she discovers that she's written hundreds of words in frantic night scribbling. She shows me the notes, which take up an entire filing box.

Are all those notes for the Kirsches?

"Not all of them. I spare more than a few for myself."

I don't think you're alone in having a hard time reckoning with how much freedom to give your children.

"Yeah but my son is dead, so I have hard proof I did a lousy job, don't I? I caved when I should've been stronger. And I let him have this power, because I wanted to have it too."

This is when I notice a rectangular bulge in Melanie's pocket. She takes out her old PortPhone6, the screen slightly cracked and the chrome edges nicked and scarred. She knows what I'm about to ask, so she goes ahead and answers in advance.

"It's for the Kirsches. It's my only way to get to Emilia and Jason. When they do one of their bullshit listening tours, or when

Jason stages one of his insufferable new product launches, that's when I'm gonna port in and tell them about my son."

And then?

"And then, I swear to you, I will throw this thing in the fucking ocean."

Mom

You didn't come to the gate last night

I know, mom. This week has been hell

Why? What happened

Well my roommate disappeared. My only friends are two weird boys. The dean of students is apsychopath. Everyone else hates me

Everything will be fine. I promise

I wanna die

Please don't joke about that

I said I WANTED to. I didn't say I was GONNA

Charming

I'll be at the Gate next week, all right? I'm just punch-drunk right now

DEAN'S RESIDENCE

Anna arrived at Vick's small white house at 7pm on Wednesday, as instructed. She dressed light, clad in only a white t-shirt and black leggings. It was a sad dumpy house located a block off the main campus. The exterior looked like it hadn't been painted in over a century. She stared at the front door, wanting to throw up. When she finally rang the bell, Vick answered immediately, clad in generic chinos and a black t-shirt. There was apparently no one else in the house. *Doesn't he have a family? A wife? Kids? Where are they right now, at dinnertime on a weeknight?*

"Come in," he said curtly. There was no difference between Vick at the office and Vick at home. One time, a seventh grade teacher of Anna's invited the whole class over for punch and cookies. When she ported to Ms. Navarro's house, it was like a completely different person was greeting the class at the door. Her hair was down. She was out of her work clothes. She flashed a smile at the kids that she *never* flashed in class. She was at ease and relaxed, almost uncomfortably so.

But Vick was consistent: face of stone, zero pleasantries. He didn't even bother to offer Anna water. When she walked in, he locked the door behind her. The whole house smelled like wallpaper glue. There were no toys lying around. No pictures on the walls. Nothing cooking on the stovetop. No life of any kind. She nervously tugged at her leggings and snapped them back against her hips. Vick passed her and then opened a creaky basement door underneath the main staircase. He flicked the light on and the basement glowed with a sickening fluorescent light.

"Follow me," he told her.

Don't do that. He'll fucking kill you, or worse. Shove his ass down those stairs instead.

He took one step down and then turned, scowling at Anna because she was still frozen in place.

"I said to follow me, right now."

She did as she was told. *You coward. You total fucking coward.* Why was she voluntarily following this man to her doom? She kept

84

her head down and thought hard about holding hands with Lara, so that she wouldn't feel quite so alone.

The basement was unfinished; just a dusty slab with a CFC bulb on a bare wire dangling from an exposed ceiling. Vick walked to the other side of the basement and opened up a thick iron door. Anna could tell she was about to enter a soundproof room. Isolation on top of isolation.

She followed Vick inside to a bare white lab. There was an X on the floor marked with black electrical tape. Vick put on a lab coat and cracked open a laptop resting on a table to the side. To Anna's shock, the peppy Brendan McClear was also in the lab, staring at a tablet and not looking up.

"Where's your name tag, Brendan McClear?" she asked him. He didn't respond.

"Stand on that X," Vick told her.

"What is this?" Anna asked him.

"Stand there." God, talking to him was so miserable. Every word swatted down. It was like talking to an anti-person.

She took her place on the X. Vick walked over to a rack on the left-hand side of the room and grabbed a kettle bell marked 2.5kg. He handed it to Anna.

"Take this."

"I wanna know what you're doing and why the hell sailor boy is here with you."

The corner of Vick's mouth spasmed upward ever so slightly. Seeing him smile was worse than seeing his eternal scowl. It was a gross smile. There was no happiness in it, only cruelty. Anna wanted to peel his face off of his skull.

"Take the weight," he told her.

She grabbed it and it tugged down on her shoulders. She felt so hollow and bare, the kettle bell could have pulled her arms right of their sockets.

Vick walked back over to laptop and opened up a video call. The screen was turned away from Anna. He aimed an external camera at her.

"You all set over there?" a voice from the computer asked Vick. The voice sounded oddly familiar.

"Ready."

"Okay. Send the pin."

Vick punched ENTER and suddenly a wormhole opened up in front of Anna.

"Where am I going?" she asked Vick.

"Nowhere. Now step forward."

Again, Anna did as she was told. In an instant, she was burning. This wasn't like regular porting. There was no shiver and snap. No, this was like five thousand needles were piercing the front of her body at once: stinging hot pain everywhere. Her back was still in the basement lab. But the front of her body was now elsewhere. *Everywhere*, like it had been transformed into an aerosol. Her eyes, if they still existed, were sealed tight but she could see a strobe of hot light rat-a-tat-tatting through her eyelids.

This was taking longer than normal porting. Much longer. There was no time inside this particular portal; only crude, brutish pain. She tried to scream but her mouth was absent. She had no face at all. She tried to let go of the kettle bell but now she had no hands. Someone had sawed off the front half of her and blown it into space. A great, horrible spreadening.

And then, with suitable disrespect, the wormhole spat her back out onto the lab floor. She dropped the weight, clutched at her face, and screamed. Technically she was still alive and intact, but inside she had disintegrated. The burning in the front of her body settled into hostile numbness. Her face had fallen asleep. She rubbed her eyes furiously to bring back the feeling. When she finally opened them, Vick was sitting at the table, typing away. Brendan McClear was eyes deep into his tablet.

"What's the status?" the voice on the laptop asked.

"Rejected," said Vick.

The voice from the laptop grew angry. "YOU PEOPLE ARE FUCKING USELESS. I WANT THREE, AND I WANT IT BY DECEMBER."

Vick clicked out of the video call, then swiveled in his chair toward Anna. "Do you remember your name?" he asked her.

"Anna Huff."

"Do you remember *my* name?"

"Yeah. Asshole. Your name is Asshole."

He gave her a menacing stare. Her own feline scowl was no match for it.

"Sorry," she said. "I must have forgotten."

"Say my name."

"It's Charles Vick, dean of students."

"Good."

"What did you do to me?" she asked him.

"Nothing," he said. "You failed."

"Failed what?"

"Come back next Wednesday. Same time. Dress light."

"I won't."

Vick stood up and looked down on her pitilessly. "Same time. You will not tell anyone. I'll know if you do." He gave her a sharp kick in the ribs, nearly parking his shoe inside her lung. "Now get up and leave."

Gasping in pain, Anna tried to scramble to her feet but her muscle memory wasn't quite back yet. Whatever was in that wormhole, it had put her in a space-time coma. She was suffering from a kind of physical amnesia, and the idea of it being permanent terrified her. Everything was off balance. The ground itself felt unsteady, constantly moving and shifting. She had been robbed of her vestibular functions.

Then, after a few seconds, it all came back. She stood up, wobbly but still erect. A touch nauseous. Neither Vick nor Brendan bothered to guide her back to the front door. She bolted up the basement steps and ran back to Sewell as fast as she could. When she got to her room, she pulled the blankets over her whole body and shook.

KIRKLAND HOUSE

Whatever grand plans Anna Huff had for wallowing in her trauma and lovesickness—spending her days curled into a ball and eschewing personal hygiene—were thwarted by the punishing regimen of fair Druskin Academy. Classes went till 6pm every night. Saturdays featured a cruel slate of additional *morning* classes. Every otherwise open crevice of time was stuffed full with work and sports and more work.

The schedule provided an occasionally effective diversion from her misery, but that didn't lessen how crushing the workload was in its own right. Even the kindly Mr. Nolan regularly assigned 200 pages a night, and they weren't easy pages. Her first diving meet wouldn't be for another four months but her coach, a white-haired bastard named Mister Willamy, had them in the well for seventy-five minutes a day right from the start. The satisfying bounce of the springboard under her feet was the only good part of those seventy-five minutes. For simulated meets, Willamy appointed himself judge and dished out merciless, unfair scores that had Anna and the rest of the team cursing his arbitrary judgment under their breath. He also had the team do interval sprints every day around the dirt track inside Druskin Cage, a decrepit brick fieldhouse choked with dust kicked up from athletes constantly running laps. Anna would end those laps caked in gray dirt, grit seeping into her mouth.

Oh, but that wasn't the end of practice. Hardly. After running came strengthening. After strengthening came calisthenics, including Dying Cockroaches: a ten-part leg lift sequence that Willamy had cribbed from an amateur militia training video he found online. After calisthenics came balance: Willamy would force them to stand on one leg for minutes at a time and stare at a small X he had marked on the wall of the cage. You couldn't look away from the X or else Willamy would force you to run suicides. Anna hated that X. She was getting really sick of Xs marked in places. If they ever tested her on what that X looked like, she would have grudgingly aced it.

When Willamy's back was turned, she would let her eyes wander around the cage, keeping her head perfectly still but focusing on anything else could find, even lines in the dirt. Sometimes she would steal a quick glance at cute girls who were still doing laps, but they weren't Lara. No one was Lara. Only Lara would do. This longing would always be with her. She could tell. She knew it would be her eternal companion if Lara couldn't be.

After balance came stretching. Endless stretching. Willamy would have all the divers hold a split for minutes at a time, until Anna could feel her groin muscles about to pull off the bone. If anyone broke into a giggle, more suicides. She *hated* suicides.

Piano lessons occupied just two hours a week, but they always seemed to come when Anna could least afford to sequester herself inside the Music Center. Even getting ready in the morning was a chore because of Druskin's antiquated dress code. Boys had to wear a coat and tie. Girls had to abide by a far more detailed section of the code that demanded "non-revealing, appropriate attire." Skirts had to run past your fingertips. Straps had to be more than two fingers wide. Tights were mandatory and *awful*. One girl had already violated the dress code by having the gall to try to pass off leggings under her skirt. She was immediately remanded to Vick's office. Anna shuddered to think about what awaited that poor girl in Vick's basement. Kids who were neither male nor female had to get special permission for their own set of dress guidelines and for residence in unisex housing. Druskin, being Druskin, made the application process for those privileges its own taxing courseload.

Anna was forced to return to Vick's awful house every Wednesday night. Same time. Same dress. Same wormhole. Same kettle bell. Same Brendan McClear acting as toady. Same horrible, burning result. There were new flavors of pain to the experience every time she stepped forward, but in the end the wormhole still spat her out right where she was. If this bothered Vick, he didn't show it. He would simply ask her once more to recite his poisonous name, and then he would send her back into the crush of Druskin as if nothing had happened.

There was barely time to eat. Anna would make sloppy PB&J sandwiches at Main Street Dining Hall and then smash them into her mouth on the go. This conveniently absolved her of finding people in the dining hall to sit with, but that bit of antisocial maneuvering came in handy given that Main Street sucked. A full quadrant of that dining hall was perpetually occupied by the football team loudly talking shit to one another and adhering to an all-steak diet. One afternoon, she was walking out of the hall when she spotted some other kid peeling an orange and tearing it carefully so that it was in the shape of a man, with the central column of its pith sticking out like a penis. She shuddered and doubled her walking speed out of there.

She finally found her precious energy drinks at the school Grill, refilling her dorm room fridge over and over with cans of the stuff and snacking on Grill owner Cecilia's black beans-and-rice every afternoon. She racked up a tab that had a piqued Sandy angrily texting her in all caps. Every day, Anna had enough sugar and caffeine coursing through her body to power a city block.

And then there was the walking. So much walking. Robbed of the ability to port, Anna felt every tedious step from the dorm to the academic buildings to the dining halls to the gym, the last of which was a mile away from everything. Before Druskin, Anna saved the bulk of her walking for new, exciting places. London! Paris! Phuket! *Miami*. She had forgotten how boring it was to tread the same ground over and over again. The soles of her mary janes were coming unglued and flapping around. Her cheap New Day tights kept slipping down and bunching all over, greasing her poor feet with sweat. She had never been forced to carry books so thick (and dull).

Everyone, save for Bamert and Burton, continued to ignore her. Everyone had to ignore everyone anyway because they were just as put-upon. Unlike the inside of a wormhole, there was no manipulating time and space at Druskin. Those were definite entities here, and they were *relentless*. She did her best to look glum, wanting everyone to *see* that she was lovesick without having to announce it, but all of the evil stares from classmates she had gotten along the quad paths for a few days had given way to general indifference. She was nobody.

Worst of all, she had virtually no time to break out of school. The coursework was making her smarter, and the walking and endless diving practices were making her fit. Yet it all felt like a grand distraction from the real work that she wanted to do. For the three weeks she was locked down by Vick's imposed restrictions, she was forced to check into Sewell at 8:30pm and remain there for the rest of the night in her half-deserted room, with cursory web access and a pile of work that only grew in size the more she hacked away at it.

Even when she procrastinated, she couldn't bring herself to do it productively. Instead, she would daydream about shoving Vick into a wood chipper, or she would run down to Mrs. Ludwig's apartment for a free macaroon, or she would check in on (stalk) Lara through Lara's WorldGram account.

She didn't formally follow Lara. She was content just to lurk, forced to accept that she had been demoted from Lara Kirsch's real life back to being just another weirdo ogling pictures of her online. There was Lara at the Arctic Riot festival. There was Lara partying on a very large boat with a gaggle of unimaginatively named DJs. There was Lara scoring a table at Arsen Lang's newest restaurant, accompanied by an unidentified guy. *Who's he? Why's she running with* that *dipshit?* She comforted herself by assuming Lara didn't really like the guy. She assumed it over and over until, in her mind, it was outright fact. After all, *he* didn't get a bracelet.

She also caught a photo of Lara in Sassari, Sardinia. Anna knew Sassari. Sarah took her to Sassari two years earlier because it had become a popular meeting ground for lesbian women, many of them ten to twenty years older than Anna at the time. With porting, like-minded people tended to cluster themselves in various locales, a trend that was bordering on self-segregation. It seemed like a good idea for Anna to give Sassari a shot. But with its gleaming piazzas packed with festive women and old Sardinian Catholics loudly protesting the now-consistent presence of those women in their town, the town proved more overwhelming than Anna could absorb at fifteen. She may have had something in common with those tourists, but they were tourists all the same. She quickly ported off of Sardinia with Sarah and didn't have the nerve to give it another chance.

Now here was Lara in the Piazza d'Italia, posing for a selfie with another woman, a few years older: pecking that woman on the lips and tagging her post with #NewWorldPrideDay and #LoveIsLove. Maybe she was kissing that woman out of support, maybe out of passion, maybe both. Either way, Anna wanted to clock that woman right in the jaw. First, she'd chase down Sarah's killer. *Then* this jackass. The woman only appeared in that one post on Lara's feed, but that was one too many. She probably had a dumb name, too: Cantaloupe or something.

Hands off, Cantaloupe.

Anna logged all of Lara's new locations in her Notes app while re-reading the Post-it Lara had left behind over and over. *Roomie.* Sometimes Lara would go for days without posting to WorldGram, hiding out in some undisclosed location. Anna wondered where she was. She pictured Lara all over: serenely wading through the Lily Beach shallows in a white one-piece, smoking dope with her legs dangling off the Cliffs of Moher, dancing with the street crowds in Rio. She pictured Lara visibly aching for the one person she wanted to dance with the most, and maybe marshaling a few rogue PortSys employees to gather up every last scrap of info about Sarah Huff. Anytime Anna tried to put Lara out of mind and focus on work, there she was again. She remained undaunted in seeing her once more. Impatient, too. In bed at night, she would whisper Lara's name to herself as an invocation. *Lara, Lara, Lara.*

But if Lara Kirsch was sad about being pulled out of Druskin, there was scant evidence of it on her WorldGram. She looked free. *Alive.* There was one photo of Lara in Barbados wearing a fedora with the caption, "These are waking dreams." Another post was actually branded content, complete with a #ShareSpace hashtag. Anna had "Really, Lara?" typed out in the windowpane of the comments for that one, but never hit PORT. If Lara wanted to be corny, that was her right. Anna wished she could be that corny herself, frankly. To be corny, you needed to be happy, or at least pleasantly deluded with false hopes.

Help me learn to be happy, Lara. Please cure me of this stupid brain.

Yes, Lara Kirsch felt betrayed by Anna the last time they spoke, but that only helped fuel any number of redemption fantasies in Anna's brain. Lara *wanted* to be wrong about Anna. Yes, that was it. *And if she really does think you betrayed her and can't get over it, then she really, really cares about you.*

Anna stared at the photos of Lara for minutes at a time before closing them. There was one photo of Lara at a cocktail party where she was wearing a short, fringed dress, like a flapper. Anna noted the black fringes gently brushing across Lara's smooth, unblemished thighs. Whenever she saw fringes dangling from anything else after that, she'd think of Lara in that dress—a faint crease of muscle running down the outside of her legs—and that made Anna want to bite through a knuckle. Random men and women would propose to Lara in comments of her WorldGram and Anna vowed to hunt them all down.

She had to ration the photos carefully, to keep from becoming obsessed and to wean herself from that seductive ache that came every time she glanced at her old roommate. It was addictive, that pain. The way it tortured Anna's mind and whispered to her that Lara hungered for her equally.

To distract herself, she'd go over to the GizPo comment section and do some shitposting: writing up opinions she *knew* would cause a fuss. "Actually, lemonade taste like shit," etc. Anna was only seventeen but she already knew that people online were just stock characters: influencers, wingnuts, lecturers, dorks, trolls, etc. It never got old setting off digital bombs that sent all those stock characters into endless beefs.

I trust my soul. Anna replayed the line over and over again in her head, then she'd look at Lara's picture and the phrase would vibrate. It would swell and take on bright neon colors. That's why she needed a hit of acid to balance the sweetness: either by lightly trolling the GizPo commenters or opening up a new tab and reading everything she possibly could about Emilia Kirsch and the corporate empire she lorded over alongside Jason Kirsch, Lara's considerably older half-brother. Best to temper her fixations just a bit. This was all very healthy. Definitely.

93

Finally, after nearly a month, Anna was freed from 'stricts and allowed to roam the campus at night again. Bamert could hardly contain his excitement at the news. Before Nolan's class, he jabbed an elbow into her side and declared, "We are celebrating tonight. At Kirkland! I'll provide libations."

"I don't drink," Anna reminded him.

"Again, that's of no concern to me. You will be there at 9pm. Burton will join us and show you what we've been working on."

"Hey! I have tambourine tonight!" Burton said.

"Not anymore," Bamert told him. "Shake your little idiot drum another time. This is a goddamn *rager*, son."

Kirkland was a house of fifteen rowdy boys located across from the gym down a relatively quiet stretch of Elliot Street. When Anna walked in after diving practice, there was a white greaseboard in the common room that had, "Tyler, your sister called. She's pregnant" scrawled across it in green dry erase marker.

The whole house smelled like feet. In the corner of the common room was a hamster cage with a single, malnourished rodent huddled in the corner, a big K shaved into its fur. Anna walked over to the cage and felt around for the little ball bearing inside the hamster's water bottle. The ball had gotten stuck, so she poked at it until it came dislodged and the little hamster could finally get fresh water to drink.

She went over to Coach Bergerini's door and gave a knock. He opened the door in nothing but tighty whities.

"Yeah?"

Anna held out her permission slip. "I'm here to visit Bamert."

"Yeah yeah, go ahead." He didn't even bother to look at the slip before shutting the door.

She climbed the stairs warily and passed a half-dozen doors blaring a half-dozen strains of obnoxious music. From behind Room 6, she heard a boy mashing buttons and screaming out "OH HO HO HO YOU JUST GOT FUCKING WRECKED!" Finally, she knocked on Room 12, even though the door was already cracked.

"Entrée!"

The foot smell was worse in Bamert's room, like he was pickling his own in white vinegar. She nearly choked.

"Bamert, this room smells awful."

"I can fix that."

He lit a cinnamon candle and now the room smelled like cinnamon *and* feet. He took out a tin of Kodiak and stuffed half of it into his cheek, then kicked back on a futon couch that sat half a foot above the floor. He was still in his suit: jet black with fire-breathing dragons all over. There was a giant wooden spool in the center of the room that served as a coffee table, with a bunch of cowboy boot-shaped shot glasses and a single Clemson football helmet resting on top. In Room 12, Bamert served Merle Haggard two ways: through his wireless speaker and on a poster that covered the entire back wall. He had also run a length of twine from one end of the ceiling to another and hung a full country ham from it: salted and preserved in a stockinette and already cultivating a sickly mold around its dark pink flesh. It was too much odor for too small of a space.

"Should I leave the door cracked?" Anna asked. Druskin policy stated that girls could have visitations with boys and vice versa after 7pm so long as the door stayed ajar and three feet were kept on the floor at all times. The rumor around Sewell, which Anna read about in the Shit Memoirs, was that Jubilee circumvented the latter rule by having sex with her boyfriend in the closet.

"You can close the door," Bamert told her. "Bergerini doesn't care. It's the only perk of sharing a house with a hockey coach and half his Neanderthal roster."

"What if I need actual air to breathe?"

"You can have air or you can have privacy, but you can't have both."

She shut the door and then pointed to the floor below, whispering, "Bergerini answered the door in his underwear!"

"Believe me, that's outright formalwear for him. His girlfriend is still in college, you know."

"What?! But he's, like, 40!"

"Judging by the sounds they make down there, I don't think the age discrepancy bothers them in the slightest."

"That's disgusting."

"It's legal, though. Funny what's legal and what isn't."

"There's a hamster dying in your common room."

"Yeah. Technically it's Moriarty's, because he bought it and named it Fucko. But I'm the only one who bothers to feed the poor creature."

He pulled out a handle of spiced rum.

"Where on earth did you get that?" she asked.

"The answer to that, dear Anna, is so obvious that you'll want to smash your face in with a textbook."

"That's how I feel all the time anyway."

"Want a drink?"

"I just got off of 'stricts, so no. Besides, I don't wanna throw up and then have to report to diving practice with a hangover tomorrow."

"I don't know how you do that diving business," Bamert told her. "Too high over water for my comfort, yessir."

They heard the doorknob rattle and Anna grew horrified Bergerini would be on the other side, fully naked and angry. Instead, it was Burton, carrying a small black instrument case. The second Burton saw the handle of spiced rum, his shoulders slumped.

"How are we gonna get anything done if you're drinking that?" he asked Bamert.

"We're not."

Burton snuffed out the noxiously sweet candle. Then he lit a bare match and the smell of the room grew nearly tolerable. He and Anna sat down on Bamert's cot, which was piled high with canvas army blankets. Bamert mixed himself a rum and Coke in a single, dirty Solo cup. He raised his cocktail to Anna and Burton.

"To Clemson. May they win the CFBCSA National Championship at the WallTech Seoul Bowl yet again."

"Why do you like Clemson so much?" Anna asked him.

"Well, my granddaddy went there, and my daddy did too. One day I'll go there."

"I thought you didn't like your dad."

"Can't stand the man."

"Then why do you like Clemson if he likes it?"

"Beats me. Anyway, *contraband,*" Bamert declared triumphantly. "Tonight we celebrate your ever so slight liberation, dear Anna. But also, we can finally show you what Burton has been working on." He nodded to Burton. "Show her."

"Show her what?" Burton asked.

"The things!"

"You didn't say to bring them."

"I said we'd show her what we'd been working on. You came all this way from Gould House and you didn't bring the damn things?"

"I have a picture on my pNote of them," Burton offered.

"Oh god dammit. Where's the *drama* in that, I ask you?"

"What the hell are you two talking about?" Anna asked.

Burton took out his Druskin-issued tablet and showed her a photo of half a dozen white transponder bracelets scattered on his desk.

Anna gasped. "How did you get those?"

This was Bamert's cue. He stood up from the futon, hopped onto the wooden spool, which openly groaned at having to support his considerable mass, and sang out:

"Dayyyyyyyyyyyyy stuuuuuuuudents!"

"BAMBAM!" came a voice from the room next door, "SHUT THE FUCK UP!"

Bamert ignored the order. "Day students, Anna Huff! *Day students.* Kids whose folks live within twenty miles of campus. They walk through Druskin Gate in the morning, and they walk right back out at night. They're not allowed to port directly onto campus every day, because security! Savor that irony, my dear. Baste it with its own juices. These day students, they're like mules: beautiful, workmanlike mules."

"You know a day student?" Anna asked him.

Bamert pointed at Burton. "Not me. Him."

"I may have met a girl," Burton confessed, playing with the sleeves of his tweed jacket to distract himself.

"You got a girlfriend?" Anna asked him.

"You know, I wouldn't consider her a 'girlfriend' necessarily."

"She's *smitten*," Bamert said. "She'll ford raging rivers for him. I have no idea why, but girls fawn over this man. They find him *mature*."

"I *am* mature."

"Well, most grown adults I know are annoying, so yes, I could see someone accidentally conflating those two qualities. These girls see our boy complaining for nut milk in the dining hall and they think he's cosmopolitan. It's astounding, Anna Huff. Our little mule ported to Vancouver for Burton, hit up a pop-up market, and found a bunch of those little Blackheel anklets on sale for nothing at all."

"What about the rum?" Anna asked Bamert.

"Oh, I just stole that out of Bergerini's closet while he was at practice. He has cases of the shit."

"Will you sit back down already?" Burton asked. "You're drunk."

"I don't get drunk. And why should I get down?" Bamert asked. "Technically, there are still at least three feet on my floor!"

"You're making me nervous. You're gonna fall and die, and then Anna will rat me out for it."

That was the wrong thing for Burton to say. Anna stood up in front of him and glowered, her skin knuckle-white all over.

"What'd you say about me?"

"I'm sorry," Burton said. "That was in poor taste."

"Hooooooooo, Burton. She's gonna fuck you up now, and with a *quickness*."

"Everyone thinks I'm a rat and I'm not," Anna said. "I've had to walk the quad every day with people looking at me like I'm the scum of the earth, and so I really don't appreciate it coming from either of you two."

"I said I'm sorry, all right? I get how much it sucks," Burton said.

"No, I don't think you do. Not even close."

"All right, maybe I don't," he admitted. "But what exactly happened in that office, anyway?"

Anna went from white to red. There was Vick's hateful face again, his snarl so permanent it may as well have been chiseled into rock. She hated that she knew that face so vividly. Sometimes she would see Vick's face right before taking off from the springboard in diving practice and she would skip a rotation just so she could get into the water faster, to clean the image away. Then Willamy would ream her out for poor execution. Everywhere she turned, there was an angry face awaiting her.

Tell them what happens in Vick's basement. Tell them what a sick asshole he is.

"I don't wanna talk about it," Anna finally told them. "I can't even think about Vick without going into panic attacks, so please don't ask."

Burton relented. "I didn't mean to."

"No one ever means to."

"Okay," Burton said, about to change the subject. "Why don't we talk about the anklets, then? The problem remains that you'd have to sort out how to clone these anklets and have them transmitting our biodata to the narcs in Student Services while you'd be busy porting somewhere else. And then you have to figure out how to port."

"Can your new girlfriend sneak in a phone?" Anna asked Burton.

"She's NOT my girlfriend, and the answer to that is no. They still make you drop your phone into the day student bin."

"Can we visit your girl... your *friend's*... house?"

"Vick turns down those requests all the time. He hates day students in general anyway, because they don't pay the full tuition. That's why only, like, a dozen of them get admitted every year. He thinks their folks are all faking New Hampshire residency to get the deal."

"God, he's such a bastard," Anna said.

"He's no gentleman," Bamert said. "He's a craven, vile coward. We should steal his phone."

"What are you, suicidal?" Anna asked.

"Occasionally."

"Actually," said Burton. "There's a germ of an idea there."

"It's a stupid idea," Anna said. "What, you steal his phone? Then he reports it stolen and it goes dead. What's the point of that?"

"Not the whole phone," Burton said, "But the battery. I've seen his phone. He walks around with it on a clip because he's such a big dork. He's one of the only faculty members on campus who can keep a phone on his person whenever he wants, and he doesn't have a PortPhone7 or an 8 like cool people do. He's a cheapskate. He has a Worm 4e. It's a piece of shit! You could crack it open and grab the battery out of it easily. That's the only part of a phone that would set off security at Druskin Gate."

Anna's eyes widened. "So you could actually do it."

"In theory, yeah," said Burton. "All you'd need is his battery. It's compressed antihydrogen. You can't trace it, and you sure as heck can't deactivate it. You bring the other parts of a phone through the gate, put it all together, and then you have a working PortPhone. You'd need a data plan, though."

"I think I could get one," Anna told him. "I would need a VPN to set up a dummy account for it, and I would need money."

"I HAVE MONEY!" Bamert screamed. "Old money is the *best* money. God, this plan is so perfect, and so *naughty*. Let's dance right into it." He took a big swig of his lukewarm mixed drink. "This could absolutely work, and even if it fails, it'll be a complete blast. Now, when do we steal his phone?"

"Oh I'm not gonna help steal it," Burton said.

The other two cried out WHAT?! loud enough to earn another "SHUT THE FUCK UP" from next door.

"Shut the fuck up *yourself*, Dippy Dog!" Bamert shouted back. Then he fumed at Burton, "What do you mean, you're not gonna help steal it? You had Cindy bring in the anklets!"

"Her name is Alyssa, and what she did for me was perfectly legal. You're suggesting that I help you steal Vick's PortPhone, which is not."

"You just sat here with us and figured out how we'd do it!"

"I never said anything about WE. I was explaining how *you* might do it. I have no interest in getting booted from here, Bamert."

Bamert held out his hands, each palm large enough to hold a watermelon. "You see these hands, do you not? You are enthusiastically pleading to catch these hands right now."

"Bamert, nothing you do to me could be worse than what my parents have already done." Burton tugged at his shirt collar and there was a small, button-shaped scar protruding out, precisely the diameter of a cigarette. "I'm on a full ride here. I get booted, and then I go back to them, which means I run away and end up like all the other port runaways. Not all of us can afford your level of disdain, do you understand?"

Anna had never seen Bamert chastened until that moment. He got off the stool and sank back into the dirty futon. Then he grabbed an empty Snapple bottle and drooled down a line of dip spit that seemed to have the tensile strength of a circus tightrope. The saliva broke, then made a little lasso and settled down on his lapel, where it sat upright for a few seconds before settling down into a permanent stain.

"You're right," Bamert finally said. "I shouldn't have assumed."

"Why do you even wanna break out of here?" Burton asked him.

"You know me, I get bored. And this place is too orderly. Everything is too clean. All the kids go to class on time. There's no mess. And New England *sucks*. It's a flavorless region. I need a taste of chaos or else I'll go mad here."

"I'll steal Vick's phone," Anna said. Both boys quickly forgot what they were fighting about. "I got no problem with that."

"Are you sure?" Bamert asked.

"I'm not gonna make Burton steal it, and there's nothing *you* can do quietly. That leaves me. Burton, can you show me how to take out the battery?"

"Yeah. In fact, I have an even shrewder idea for what to do once you get it."

"Our girl is so brave," Bamert said proudly. "Gets smacked down at the big boss level and wants to go right back at it! Unreal. You're the *real* dash of pepper, my dear."

He took another swig of his drink, only this time the spiced rum didn't sit right. Anna could see it: that moment when drunk people realize they've taken it one drink too far. Bamert's eyes seized up and his whiskers went limp. His face turned gray. He let out a small hiccup that acted as a warning sign to the other two. He held his breath, terrified of how the next taste of air might make him feel.

"If you'll excuse me."

He broke into a run out the door. They could hear him projectile vomiting into the sink even though the bathroom was at the opposite end of the hall.

Burton stood up and grabbed his tambourine case. "Check, please."

"Does he do this every night?" Anna asked.

"He wouldn't be Bamert if he didn't. I'll walk you back."

They paused in the Kirkland common room to feed poor Fucko the hamster, then made their way across South Campus, along the perfectly manicured trees with spotless dedication bricks, past the cube-shaped edifice of Helton Library, where half the student body willingly hotboxed themselves every night to cram for tests in monk-like silence for hours on end.

She paused outside Helton for a second and took in the air. The walking was still a drag, but Anna was already learning that the best parts of Druskin came in between being wherever you were supposed to be. All the stolen places and moments, those were the true gems. These were the dark parts of Druskin. September here was truly perfect. Even a cynic like Anna would have been a fool to deny it. It felt like living in a world that had been set designed. The air tasted better than anything on the menu at Main Street.

"I hate that library," Anna told Burton.

"You should. The architect who designed it had three families on three continents, and each family had no clue the other two families existed. I'd tell you to read all about it but the school strangely has no biographical volumes on him in the library that *he* designed."

"Funny, that."

"Yeah. Listen, Anna."

"Yes?"

"I'm sorry. What I said tonight, I was out of line."

"It's all right."

"You sure you wanna go through with this? I know what an awful start this has been for you, but you're full ride like I am."

"How do you know that?" she asked Burton.

"Because I can hear your shoes coming from two blocks away."

Oh God, another thing for people to gawk at. "I keep meaning to go to George & Phillips to replace them, but there just hasn't been time."

"It's very easy to get caught up in Bamert's Bamert-ness, you know? But as much as this place sucks, it's valuable to you and me, right? It means more to us than it ever could to Bamert, or even to Lara."

"I know."

"But you still wanna break out. Why? You worked hard to get in here. Why risk all that, and why risk it so soon?"

She clutched at the shoulder strap of her back pack. Pulled it close, nuzzling against it.

"Everyone else gets away with everything," she told him. "Why can't I?"

"You *know* why."

"Yeah well I'm not just gonna sit here and accept that."

"You're not gonna like me saying this," Burton told her, "but you should forget Lara. There's no shortage of rich girls here to chase after."

"That's not my angle," she insisted.

He took a step back. "I swear I wasn't implying that."

"She's not just a rich girl and I'm not just a sucker with a crush. Plus I have other people I'd like to find, and deans I'd like to ruin, and that's all gonna be a valuable learning experience on its own, Burton. I promise you that."

"Deans? You mean Vick."

"Of course I mean Vick."

"Why do you go to his house every Wednesday?"

"How do you know I go there?"

"I saw you walk in once."

"He makes me go."

"Why?"

"I can't tell you."

"Jesus."

103

"I don't even know if I can tell you that I can't tell you, do you understand? Keep your trap shut about it, especially to Bamert."

"I will."

She walked away, covering her paces all the way back to Sewell, past chatty seniors and quiet couples on their way to the chapel to hold hands for Evening Prayer. She reached the dorm and began the trudge up to Room 24. The stairwell existed inside its own cruel dimension, growing skyward and adding on extra floors in accordance with her level of exhaustion.

When she finally reached her room and cracked the door, she realized that she wasn't alone.

SEWELL HALL

Anna's bed had been stripped. Her clothes had been torn from the dresser and stuffed hastily into boxes. Someone had tried to move her mini fridge too, dragging it roughly six inches before giving up.

You've been expelled. Somehow they caught Bamert and Burton and you conspiring on video, and now you're all doomed. Except maybe Burton.

Maybe Emilia Kirsch had ordered her room trashed, which would have been strangely awesome. Then, in her quiet frenzy, she spotted a pink rollerboard suitcase and a stack of cardboard boxes next to the window. Also, the room smelled like butter now.

What the hell is going on? The bitch who moved your shit is a dead girl. Wait a second. Oh no.

She had been a fool to assume that her room would remain a single for the rest of the year. This was Druskin, after all. The Druskin admissions office could barely suppress its glee whenever they told new enrollees, Anna included, that they had been selected from an impossibly deep pool of applicants. It provided those kids with a cheap thrill that lasted far beyond what it merited. Now another new junior had scored a magic ticket. Still, Anna wasn't ready for Lara to be replaced. It hadn't even occurred to her. It also hadn't occurred to Anna that her new roommate would move all of her crap without asking.

A squeaky, British voice came from directly behind her. "Right, I can explain."

There, in the doorway, was a girl wearing a flower dress and sporting a mound of frizzy hair that could have filled a moving box of its own. She was barefoot, her legs and ankles painted in a black mendhi pattern: a perfectly symmetrical whorl of flowers and curls and ornate latticework. Anna was so mesmerized by the design that she could barely look up. The girl held out her hand.

"I'm Asmi," she said Anna. "I'm your new roommate." She had a fantastic accent. Anna wanted to grab it and try it on. But first, anger.

"You moved my shit," Anna said.

"About that, yes. It's horrible, I know. Awful. You probably think it's rude and just ugh! But actually it's ace. Once I explain it, you'll understand. I'm diabetic, you see."

"Okay."

Asmi grabbed a small black kit from the front of her suitcase, then removed a slim black pen.

"You have to vape when you're a diabetic?" Anna asked her.

"What? No. AHAHAHAHAHA bloody Christ no. I wish. I only like sniffing glue; none of that vaping nonsense."

"You what?"

"This is not a vape pen, dear. Like I told you, I'm a diabetic, which means that every two hours, day and night, I have take out this fucking pen and jab myself with it to get my blood sugar level. PRICK PRICK PRICK! all the time. If it's too low, I get to eat candy, which sounds brilliant but is not something I'm in the mood to do at 3am, and it *always* happens at 3am and never at a proper time, like after tennis. If it's too high, I take insulin. Another lousy prick. But I have to do it. My mam ports to Canada to get me that insulin for cheap."

"All right."

"And I have a weak bladder, which means I have to go pee whenever I wake up to do the whole blood-and-candy thing. So there you have it. Candy munching, needles pricking, doors flapping open and closed. It's a whole bleeding racket, and I don't wanna have to subject you to it at odd hours when you're down for a kip. Hence—"

"I take the small room," Anna said.

"Right. But I have a peace offering, because I figured you would be mad. Are you mad? You're probably mad even though I've explained it perfectly."

"I'm not." A lie.

"I'd be mad. I'd say to myself, 'Who does this Pakistani dickhead think she is barging in and moving crap around and munching on Cadbury Dairy Milk in the middle of the night?'"

"I swear I'm not mad," Anna said. Again, a lie. Anna was furious. The worst part of it was that all of Asmi's reasons for the switch were perfectly acceptable. Anna wanted to have the *right* to be mad, but all of that had been cut off in an instant: her rage tied into a knot and left with nowhere to go.

"I can make it up to you. In fact, this is well beyond what you probably deserve," Asmi said. She reached into a plastic bag resting next to her rollerboard and took out a container with a plastic top. When she popped off the lid, the entire room became perfumed with an even heavier scent of butter. After sitting in Bamert's room for so long, Anna had forgotten about all the good smelling things. She looked down and saw a bowl of perfectly fluffed rice, topped with a generous helping of chicken that had been carved off a spit: all dark meat, freckled with reddish sumac, glistening with fat and ready to break apart at the touch of a fork.

"It's the best you'll ever have," Asmi promised. Anna dropped her boulder of a backpack to the floor and took the kebab. She ate while standing in place. Asmi was right. It was heaven in styrofoam. For the moment, there was no homework, no lovesickness, no forced relocation to a new bedroom, no Vick, no Coach Willamy screaming at her to keep her legs straight. There was only buttery paradise.

"Do you want hot sauce?" Asmi asked. "I keep it on me at all times."

"I wuld but I don wanna thtop," Anna said, her mouth full.

"I made it."

"You make hot sauce?"

"The kebab, stupid."

"Oh, wow. *You* made this?"

"I could bring some back to you after any holiday break. But you better like it, you slag, or else I'll split your head open."

"I like it!"

Anna was finished within two minutes. She gamely scoured the bottom of the container with her fork to pick up every last grain of pillowy rice, every last drop of juice. She could have licked the thing clean, but wasn't about to do that in front of her new roommate.

"Thank you," Anna said quietly. She placed the garbage into the paper bag and cinched it up. "I can throw this out. Then I'll move my crap."

"I can help, although your fridge is stunningly heavy."

"We can get that in the morning. I'm tired."

"I understand." Asmi went over to the window and looked over at the Academy Building, lording over North Campus in all its brick majesty. Asmi took out a tube of Gorilla Glue and took a deep whiff. Anna was aghast.

"You really do that?" she asked Asmi.

"Why? Do you want some?" Asmi asked. She started giggling from the fumes. "You have to get your own at some point if you like it."

"Should you be doing that if you're a diabetic?"

"If you had to prick yourself with a needle a dozen times a day, love, you'd need to take the edge off occasionally as well. Give a shit. Now, you want a huff or not?"

"I'm good," Anna answered.

"What's your name, dear?"

"I'm Anna Huff."

"Fuck off. That's not your name. You're mental."

"That's my real name, swear to God."

"A huff for a Huff! Fucking hilarious."

"There's a Jubilee in this dorm, too."

"Well *that* name is just shit, innit?"

"Yeah, and a fitting one for that girl."

From the widow's walk on the roof of the Academy Building rose a clock tower with an oxidized copper dome. The dome was crowned with a weathervane hammered into the shape in of an old ship: anchored in place, prey to the fickle winds, lazily twisting in the growing chill, forever without a route or destination.

Asmi stopped giggling for a moment. "I can't believe I got into this place."

"Why not?"

"Why do you think, Anna Huff? Because I was waitlisted forever! Imagine spending three weeks in the dirtiest, poorest, most crowded comp in England, with bobbies outside the door constantly asking you for your papers because you're not some cream-white little English shit. Imagine all that, only to have a letter arrive one day telling you, 'Um actually, no. You, Asmi, get to go to fucking

Druskin!' I mean, Jesus! Top. Just a fucking top night. Tell me I should be excited."

You should not be excited. This place will suck you dry within days.

"You should be excited."

"Have you been alone in this room the whole time?"

Anna had no crisp block of prepared text at her disposal this time around. How could she have? She wasn't ready for ANY of this: the ransacked room, the sudden move, the considerable presence of a new human being in the room (one with significant medical needs), the incredible late night dinner. She needed life to slow down, yet all it seemed to do was accelerate.

"I had a roommate for a day," she told Asmi. "But then she left."

"After one day? What'd she do?"

"Nothing. I guess she just changed her mind about being here."

"Did you like her?"

"She was all right," Anna lied.

"I'm a fucking warrior, Anna. I can beat just all right."

Anna mustered the best possible smile she could. "I bet you can. That kebab…"

"You will dream about that kebab."

But Anna didn't. Instead, after dragging her relatively paltry assortment of belongings to the inner room, she lay down on her new bed, *Lara's* bed, and spent all night rustling. Three weeks had been enough to purge the room of Lara's presence. The air was stale. The sheets were laundered and smelled like industrial Uline detergent. The walls were barren. There was no Lara here, and frankly, there never really had been.

And yet, Anna's love only grew. That first night was all she needed. In her imagination she was always winning Lara over; much easier than trying to do it for real. She would listen to bad love songs on her school-issued phone all day long. This was shit she would never be caught dead listening to on a loudspeaker. She even played songs from the *90s*. Then she would concoct elaborate fantasies of her reunion with Lara and the relationship blossoming forth from it. Lily Beach. Vancouver. A stolen alcove somewhere on Sardinia, near the crowds but not of them. VIPs for life. Sometimes Anna imagined asking Lara to go steady, like 1950s teenagers, and Lara saying yes. Sometimes she fantasized about becoming a massive pop star and giving her body to the stage, whaling away at a grand piano and performing elaborate four-hour sets that would leave her physically and spiritually drained. She dreamed of retreating backstage, bypassing all the himbos and the PR stooges to find, in her dressing room, a waiting Lara: wearing that fringe dress and brandishing a wicked smile that told Anna everything she needed to know.

Sometimes she pictured the two of them making out in a London penthouse (replete with another grand piano for serenades, of course), or on the bearskin rug of a ski lodge in Park City, or in the sun-kissed surf of The Maldives. This was Lara Kirsch after all; you couldn't help but concoct moneyed daydreams about her. That was no sin. Every time she thought of Lara, new reasons to love her materialized. Their imaginary rapport only grew stronger. There were so many more things she would tell Lara, so many *real* things. Sometimes she pictured Sarah's killer abducting Lara, with Anna then mowing him down and rescuing Lara from harm. These were workhorse daydreams, as easy for Anna to return to as a movie that's been paused.

You could have kids together. You two could live on a farm if you wanted to. Don't push it. You're going overboard.

It would have been nice if Anna still had her sister to talk to about all of this. Sarah had a boyfriend one time, in between attending the occasional global HotPort "speed greet" party: parties that Sarah would inevitably beg Anna to rescue her from. Sarah had been in love before. Sarah was the only person Anna ever seriously entertained advice from. Everyone else, even Sandy, gave her advice as a poorly disguised order, tinged with the certainty that they knew everything and that she knew nothing. Sarah wasn't like that. Sarah was much older than Anna, but still young enough to be fucking up in real time and be continually learning from it. Her wisdom was fresh, always passed along to Anna with zero premeditation.

In return, Anna was herself a balm to Sarah, who suffered from insurmountable bouts of depression before and after their father abandoned them. Sarah knew the black curtain of depression as well as anyone: its texture, its heft, the way it would close around her. It would manifest itself as an influenza upon her psyche: deadening her muscles and numbing her senses. But Anna could occasionally liberate Sarah from its curse, dragging herself out bed and demanding they go where the curtain couldn't enshroud every last thing.

And the places they ported to together! They ported to the Boundary Waters and surveyed the mighty river bends from an A-dock, with Sarah saying to Anna, "There is a peace here I'll always wish for you to have." They ported to Plage de la Bocca in Cannes to gaze out at the Mediterranean while perched upon the riprap guarding the shoreline from erosion. Bronzed old French men in too tight Speedos, their skin sagging down from their spines, strutted past them with far more confidence than their fleshy bodies merited. Sarah swore to Anna that she would return to this coast one day as a director, premiering her own work at the Film Festival. They ported to the top of Table Mountain above Cape Town, standing upon the overlook atop the cliff face and running their hands along the stone wall as they marveled at the corduroy swells of the Indian Ocean and the sight of paragliders jumping off Signal Hill in the distance.

They ported to Centennial Park in Atlanta and stared at the public fountain that choreographed its sprays to Tchaikovsky. Then ported to Rehoboth Beach in Delaware, where they picked up dead horseshoe crabs by the tail and hammerthrew them back into the surf. They trampled abandoned sandcastles and played a game where they ran away from the waves, trying to not let the cold surf touch them. They ported to the Boneyard in Tucson and played hide-and-seek along rows of hundreds of grounded Boeing 737s.

They ate pizza on every continent. They scouted out new beaches for playing the wave game. They rode every roller coaster. They attended free poetry readings and lectures on second-wave feminism. They did "port-bys," where you ported to a random place for two minutes, snapped a WorldGram, and then ported right back out.

They played World Hunt, in which you were given a photo of an unknown location and then you won $1,000 if you could port to it and snap a photo of yourself there before anyone else could. They never won.

Everywhere they went, Anna wanted to pack the air into a tin and keep it, like a handful of dirt.

Now a soft breeze came through the dorm window, and now Anna was remembering back before porting, when Sarah had a car. It was a used, cherry red 1994 Civic they christened Rhonda. A truly lovable piece of shit. Anna thought it was the coolest car ever manufactured. Sarah would let Anna ride shotgun in Rhonda and take her to Rockville Town Center Cinemas to see any movie Anna wanted, even the PG-13 ones. She spoiled Anna like that, using her own allowance money to buy her little sister candy, terrible apps, plushies, and whatever else she wanted. Anna worshipped Sarah and treasured that drive to Rockville Town Center intensely: watching her big sis bounce along to the radio, rolling every window down on the brutally humid Maryland nights, and dancing in her seat amid the wind blasting through the car's interior.

One time, after pulling into a spot a block from the theater, Sarah turned to Anna and asked her, "What do you think of boys?"

"I don't like them," Anna said.

"Good. I know you already know this because you're seven, but stay away from boys. They're disgusting."

"Yeah! They're squicky!"

"Ha! That's a good word for it. *Squicky*. Stay away from the squicky boys."

When Anna was alone, as she was now, she could shut her eyes and take herself to a shadow dimension where Sarah was still alive, where what happened hadn't happened at all. She could build new, imagined memories of Sarah on top of the real ones. That shadow dimension was a better patch of spacetime than this one. When Anna put enough work into her illusions, they felt more real than reality.

She reached under her pillow, slipped on the rose pink bracelet Lara had given her, and kissed it for good luck. She finally fell asleep and the alarm pounded away an hour later. The whole suite still smelled like butter when she woke up.

From The Account Of @ErickMartin
Writer, Analyst, Assoc. Professor of Economics
Featured in @nytimes, @TNR, @washingtonpost, @NBCNews
Author of *The Architect Of Heaven: The Rise Of Emilia Kirsch*
and PortSys
Posted from 9:30am to 10:05am, 9/28/30

Okay, so my FOIA request for PortSys's internal emails re: personal privacy and antitrust practices was denied, which isn't exactly a huge surprise. 1/

PortSys is technically based in the "country" of Western Sahara, the bulk of which was uninhabitable pre-porting, but now hosts shell businesses for any global company that wants to plant an empty storefront in the middle of the free zones. 2/

The U.S.-based "arm" of the company, PortSys America, lobbied successfully to be exempt from FOIA laws when their lawyers argued that their algorithm and the ways the company use it are "trade secrets." 3/

Of course the judge that sided with PortSys was appointed by the President, whose re-election campaign received an $85,000,000 from a PAC with known ties to—who else?—Emilia and Jason Kirsch. 4/

So I came up empty on that request, BUT… 5/

Like every other corporate monolith, you can get a clear picture of what PortSys is doing by gathering info on the people they do business with. And hoo boy, do they do business with a lot of other companies! 6/

Here are four of them: Blackheel, WorldGram, WallTech, and ShareSpace. Take a wild guess where those companies are based. It rhymes with Mestern O'Hara. 7/

I got tax records from all of those companies. They're all insanely overleveraged. We're talking about billions of dollars. Just a staggering amount of debt. 8/

You might think that's because of labor, or overhead costs, or R&D, but it's not. It's because all four of these companies pay over half their operating budgets directly to PortSys. 9/

Take ShareSpace, for example. Here is how much they paid PortSys over the past three years:
2027: $42.6b
2028: $45.9b
2029: $50.4b
10/

Why the hell would an apartment-sharing app fork over that much money to PortSys? Well, the reason why is because ShareSpace is constantly borrowing money to pay PortSys for YOUR porting data, even though PortSys says they don't sell it to anyone. 11/

But that's crap. Ever try to adjust their privacy settings? I tried to navigate them just now on my phone. They're a labyrinth with no exit. 12/

PortSys, which is already a monopoly, is charging these companies billions to give them a working knowledge of where consumers port to the most, and when they do it. The rumor is they do this thru a private app called Network Z. No one is allowed to talk about Network Z unless they want to find themselves "accidentally" ported to the bottom of the Mariana Trench. 13/

Once those secondary monopolies take hold, you can expect PortSys to swoop in, assume majority ownership once the stock has tanked enough for their liking, and then offload the debt onto taxpayers. 14/

So not only is this blatant collusion, but PortSys is illegally giving over your location to complete strangers, even as they deny that same information to loved ones, personal attorneys, and even law enforcement in the event of an emergency. 15/

It's sickening, and it's only getting worse because as the company keeps getting richer, it can easily afford to buy the kind of policy that allows it to operate unfettered. 16/

We haven't even gotten into some of their other shady practices. I mean, Tennessee won the "sweepstakes" for a new PortPhone manufacturing facility by A) issuing an exemption to the state's minimum wage and mandatory time off laws and B) offering PortSys 15% of all state income taxes. 17/

Not just state income taxes paid by PortSys employees. ALL state income taxes. 18/

In the end, the facility PortSys built doesn't actually make PortPhones. All it does is produce a single Bluetooth terminal for PortPhones that are then fully assembled in Poland. 19/

A grand total of 38 people work at that plant. Thirty-eight. 20/

Good luck trying to investigate any of this. Our Secretary of Transportation is a former PortSys lawyer who says she cannot exercise any oversight of her former company not because of a conflict, but because she says it's a TELECOM company, not a transportation company. And the head of FCC is Emilia Kirsch's grandnephew! They've stonewalled anyone asking about PortSys, and worse. 21/

After I submitted my FOIA request and then ported to Punta Cana, I swear to you that I was approached by a man in a suit, who ported onto the beach and then walked up to me and told me, verbatim, to "knock it off," then ported right out. 22/

They know everything. EVERYTHING. 23/

BTW I'm tweeting all this from the Outer Banks, and when I ported into Corolla there was a timeshare sales rep right there, on the beach, asking me if I was looking for a place. He knew my goddamn name. END THREAD

GOREN HALL

Anna needed a microwave, a suction cup, a thin plastic spudger, a heat-able gel pack, a small flashlight, and a smaller-than-smaller set of pentalobe screwdrivers. These were screwdrivers designed for a forest nymph should she ever decide to become a handyman, but they were necessary for the heist all the same.

The microwave was the easy part of the plan, since Asmi had a cheap, light one from home that her mom hand-delivered directly to Druskin Gate. Asmi even brought her own spice blends to the dining hall to "remix" (her word) all of the bland cafeteria fare into passable versions of biryani and other more enticing dishes. Then she would box up the leftovers and nuke them during late-night cramming sessions. One time Asmi hacked her way into making a fish curry than stank up the stairwell for two days. The offense was noted at length in The Shit Memoirs. Asmi made up for it by stealing a few sundries from the kitchen while she was doing her work-study job and then making mug cakes for all the other girls in the stairwell.

Burton's courier, the mysterious Alyssa, smuggled in everything else Anna and Bamert needed. Anna stayed after in Nolan's class every Saturday morning to sign into a VPN account she had created that let her go online incognito. Then, she studied web tutorials of how to crack open tablets and PortPhones over and over, making sure she wouldn't miss a step when the time came to execute the plan for real. She must have watched hours of footage of dudes with pasty, greasy fingers handling and mishandling PortPhones. They were bad hands; incapable hands. Anna took pride in comparing that sorry parade of hands to her own nimble extremities. One time, she granted herself a break from heist study by checking in on Lara's WorldGram. The first post was a photo of Lara, sitting in the middle of what appeared to be an empty apartment in Manhattan, with the following caption:

Oktoberfest was fucking nuts, but sometimes I also love the day after the party, when you can just be you. I miss roomie spots like this one.

Anna was convinced that the way "roomie" was spelled was no accident. She went back to feverishly binging DIY vids.

It was, naturally, against the rules to tamper with school-issued electronic devices. After all, it wasn't as if Anna was alone in dying to engineer a way to port off campus and back. A lot of other great minds were behind a lot of dorm room doors, scheming to work similar magic.

Finally, everything was ready. With Asmi out at volleyball practice that Saturday afternoon, Anna wasted little time. She took out the dwarf screwdriver and unscrewed the bottom of her tablet. The second the screws came loose, they skittered off her desk and fell to the floor. Anna would have had better luck seeing microbes with the naked eye.

"Shit."

She felt around the hardwood, never realizing until now just how dirty the floor of her own dorm room was. Sticky *and* dusty. She felt crumbs of unidentifiable foodstuffs, hardened grains of stale rice, long hairs of unknown origin and color. Just when it seemed like the whole plan was dead before she had even taken one lousy step out of Sewell, she felt two pinpricks of cold metal and grabbed the screws, placing them in a small cup to make sure they would never go rogue again.

Next, she heated up the gel pack in the microwave. She only had to nuke it for twenty seconds to keep it warm for half an hour. That was enough time for the gel pack to absorb the oven's entire history of smells: dinners, popcorn, old tea, instant ramen, canned pasta, etc. She laid the gel pack over the glass touch screen to loosen the glue. Then, she attached a suction cup and jabbed the little spudger between the glass and the chrome casing. This was an oddly satisfying process. Her hands were busy and productive. They were happy.

It took a little English, and Anna began to freak out that the screen would suddenly come loose and go flying out the window, winding up in the beak of a pigeon that would then air mail it directly into Vick's office. Instead, the screen lifted off with gentle ease. *Phew.* Now she could see the guts of the tablet: all hard black chips and tiny circuit board terminals.

She kept the screen lifted at a 90-degree angle as she carefully unscrewed the battery cover. Druskin was a luxurious school in many ways, but cheap and shoddy in others. The dreaded lack of lack conditioning could make even fall oppressive. The food was one step up from a hospital cafeteria. And the tablets were mass-produced Monarchs with a battery that was the same shape and thickness as discount Worm PortPhones.

Anna disconnected the battery from its cable clip, pocketed it, and then reassembled the tablet. When she was finished, it looked the same as it had before she cracked it, and was still roughly as useful.

Now came the hard part.

Vick left his door open at all hours on school days, offering his availability to any student on campus. No one ever took him up on it. Even the brownnosers knew to stay away. Every day, Anna would go to her little snail mail cubby in Goren to check for school alerts and postcards that Sandy delivered by hand to the guards at Druskin Gate. On her way back to Sewell, she could glance into Vick's office and sometimes notice his PortPhone sitting out on the conference table, there for the taking.

The horrible indelibility of Anna's visit on Vick's office on her first night had a peculiar utility to it. She remembered, with high-definition clarity, a closet just off to the right of his office table, large enough to fit a person and also dark enough to hide them. She also remembered that Vick's office was manned by his assistant, Mrs. Kursten, who smoked five packs a day and had the bullfrog voice to prove it. Indeed, Anna Huff had remembered a great many details of the dean's office and was determined to take advantage of them.

On this Saturday morning, Kursten was out and Vick was working alone in the office, the door wide open. Goren Hall stood between a row of three boys' dorms off Water Street and the rest of North Campus, so it got a lot of foot traffic from the Walton Hall and Korenjack Hall boys passing through on their way to eating and studying elsewhere. Otherwise, no kid ever hung around Goren for any reason.

Bamert, who lived on the opposite campus, had no business being there that Saturday. But that didn't stop him from confidently striding up the stairs in a bright orange suit festooned with white Clemson tiger paws. He was whistling, a brilliant move to get attention that wouldn't raise suspicion because honestly, no one would ever find it unusual for Paul Bamert to make himself as conspicuous as possible.

When Bamert got to the final stair, he tripped and spilled a quart of ice cold Coke all over the floor.

"CHRIST AND EGGS!" he cried out. "THIS IS A FUCKING PECKERHEAD OF A DAY, YES IT IS!" Unsure he had laid it on thick enough, he added a few more: "SHIT! PISS! ASS!"

That did the trick. Vick stormed out of his office and over to the scene of Bamert's misdemeanor.

"What did you just say, young man?"

"Oh shit, Dean Vick! Oh, sweet ginger brown, I just said shit, did I not? FUCK!"

Vick swelled with rage. Bamert expected spikes to start sprouting out of the dean's face. Vick was so purely livid that he didn't notice Anna slip down the opposite staircase and into his office, snatching Vick's phone from the table and quickly ducking into the adjacent closet.

She turned on the pen flashlight. Cracking open a tablet in the comfort of her room was one thing, but now she was quivering a little. She could hear Bamert carrying on with Vick from afar.

"I am so, so sorry, sir."

"Do you think it's appropriate to use such foul language? If you're this casually profane outside of my office, I can't even begin to imagine what kind of sewer talk you use around your peers. I oughtta put you up for Un-Druskinlike Conduct right this instant."

Anna got the screws out and jammed them into her overalls pocket. She was getting more adept with the pentalobe screwdriver, handling it with the dexterity of a safecracker. She pressed the gel case, which she had microwaved just ten minutes earlier, against the screen and counted ten Mississippis to herself. Then she attached the

121

suction cup and worked the spudger under the glass and pulled. It wouldn't give.

Come on.

"You're right sir, and I beg your pardon. I beg it genuinely, as I am already down on my knees here. It's just…"

Do it, Bamert. Sell it.

"It's been a very difficult week for me, Dean Vick. A difficult month, really. I get terribly lonely. I have trouble making friends."

"Perhaps your comportment is the reason for your struggles," Vick told him.

"I have little doubt of that," Bamert said. "The worst part is that I have no one to talk to about it."

The screen came free. Anna lifted it ninety degrees and started in on the battery cover with a tiny Phillips-head screwdriver.

"Would you want to get a cup of coffee with me, sir?"

"I don't drink coffee," Vick told Bamert.

"Nor do I. It was just the first liquid that came to mind. I didn't wanna suggest Coke, lest I drudge up memories of my gauche outburst. Tea? Juice?"

"I could maybe get some tea. Let me just grab my phone."

Shit. Anna bit down hard on the flashlight.

"You know what?" Bamert told Vick. "Forget it. It was a silly idea anyway. I've wasted enough of your time, sir."

What the hell is he doing?!

The ensuing silence made Anna want to die. She finally got the cover off the phone and carefully unclipped the precious antihydrogen battery. Then, she swapped in the lithium tablet battery from her tablet and clipped it. According to Burton, she had to break one other component of the phone so that it would power on, but then get bricked shortly thereafter if it *stayed* on. The goal was to convince Vick his phone was broken, not that it had been tampered with.

"Actually," Vick told Bamert. "I don't need the phone. Let's go get your tea now."

Holy smokes, he did it.

Anna heard both of them clomp down the stairs to the Grill, the sounds of their footsteps blessedly fading away and leaving her with all the time she needed to finish the job. She screwed the battery cover back on, clipped off a single terminal off the memory card, and slowly lowered the touch screen down into the casing. She felt around her right-hand pocket for the tiny screws, but only found a hole instead.

Crap.

Suddenly, there were new footsteps growing louder and coming toward the office. A rhythm of mounting dread. Anna crouched down with the flashlight and searched frantically for the little bastard screws. The floorboards of the closet were so aged and warped that the screws could have easily fallen between the cracks and been lost forever, as surely as a climber disappearing down a crevasse.

The steps grew louder. Whoever was coming was coming nearer, and quickly.

Please God, let me find these screws.

"HEY!" she heard a voice cry out. That was it. She was dead.

But then, another voice. "What?"

"Hurry up, man! We gotta be there twenty minutes before practice!"

"Quit busting my balls. Bad enough when Willamy does it. Christ."

The footsteps faded away. Anna had little time to process her relief, because the screws were still nowhere to be found. Then she reached into her *left*-hand pocket, and there they were. She had forgotten which pocket she had put them in the entire time.

You. Moron.

Once the pentalobe screws were in place, she pressed down hard on the POWER button and said a little prayer. The screen glowed a bright enough to make her flinch. The phone worked, at least as much as it needed to. She turned it off before it could brick, and then the closet went dark again. She cleaned the phone down for prints with a soft eyeglass wipe. Now to just quietly slip out of the closet, put the phone back onto the table, and get the hell out of—

CLOMP CLOMP CLOMP

Anna couldn't leave the office, but she also couldn't stay. Back in the closet she went, leaving the door cracked the exact way it was when she broke in. Her breathing was heavy and labored. She tried desperately to corral it so that it wouldn't give her away. Stuck in that closet, she became all too aware of the wide variety of ambient sounds she could make: floppy shoes, heavy breathing, swallowing, sniffles, coughs, farts, sneezes. Her entire body was one big stupid booby trap.

She moved to the back of the closet and slid down into the corner behind a row of stiff blazers, then covered her mouth even though she had no intention of speaking. Vick walked into the office and grabbed his phone off the table. Minutes after he unlocked it, he was met with an endlessly spinning wheel.

"Ugh. Again?"

He cursed the phone, the lousy hypocrite, then sat down at his desk and picked up a landline.

"Mrs. Kursten? I'm aware it's a Saturday, yes. My phone has frozen up again and I need a new one delivered to Druskin Gate tonight. No, not Monday. Tonight. It's a ten-minute call and then you can have the rest of your day in Paris. Goodbye." He slammed the phone down and began running through a pile of manila folders on his desk.

Come on, you son of a bitch. Leave!

But Vick wouldn't. Maybe he knew Anna was in that closet. Maybe he knew she was there and was content to sit at his desk and leave her there with her fear for hours on end. That would've been a classic Vick move.

Instead, what happened next was even more torturous. Vick caught a whiff of something and took to it like a hound. Anna quickly took an inventory of her own musk: menthol dandruff shampoo, stinky old shoes, honeydew body wash, enough sweat to fill a fish tank, and more. But there was one more thing.

The gel packet.

Oh no, that gel packet smelled like a dorm room made from concentrate. That's what Vick had latched onto. Vick rose from of his chair to hunt the scent down. Anna was only feet away from expulsion, and that was the *nicest* possible outcome.

Then a hard port wind blew in, and there was Emilia Kirsch, dead in the center of the office. She looked irritated.

"Have you gone through those profiles yet?" she asked Vick.

"Most. Not all," he told her.

"I want them done tomorrow, no later."

"I understand."

"Any of the new ones stand out?"

"A couple."

"Such as?"

Vick walked back over to his desk and pulled an envelope from the stack.

"The boy, Jamie Burton," Vick said. "Polymath. Very talented. Also, he's a strangely mature kid for his age." Anna rolled her eyes at that.

"Any hang-ups about him?" Kirsch asked Vick.

"He spends too much time with Annie Huff and Paul Bamert."

The name is ANNA, you bastard.

"Ugh, Paul Bamert," Kirsch said. "Charles, why can't any of my friends have *normal* children?"

"The boy is a mess, and everyone knows his track record is abysmal. I doubt he graduates."

"And what about the Huff girl? Is she worth anything?"

"She's clever but otherwise unremarkable."

"She didn't rat out my daughter to you though, I'll give her that. How is she as an R&D subject?"

Vick's mouth drew up a single corner into that grotesque half-smirk. Anna looked away, clutching her knees and trying not to scream out in rage.

"She fails," Vick said. "And then she screams."

"I keep telling you to go to Southeast Asia for lab rats, for crying out loud."

"They're too easy to break."

"I'm a wealthy woman, Charles, but I am tired of doling out lunch money settlements on behalf of this school. That one Marshall girl, I had to shell out $500,000 after she walked out of your house lobotomized."

"The Huff girl won't give you any trouble."

"She better not. I bet she only got in here as a pity case anyway. What'd her sister do, kill herself a month before applications were due?"

"Actually her tests scores were remarkable. Shockingly so. And Coach Willamy says she's already one of the best—"

One of the best what? Divers? Why couldn't he compliment you to your face and not to that *pile of shit?*

"Oh, who cares what that lump of chewed gristle says about her?" Kirsch sneered. "Our admissions office needs to stop taking in every stray dog with a sob story hanging from its collar."

Anna turned lycanthropian, ready to break through her skin and burst out of the office closet door to devour everything in sight. Stealing Vick's phone battery was a sordid little thrill, but it wasn't enough. She could dash out into the center of that office, hold a samurai sword high in the air and let it catch a blinding glint of light before she brought the steel down on both of those fuckers.

"How's Lara?" Vick asked Kirsch. Anna leaned forward.

"You don't ever need to ask me about my daughter, thank you."

"How's business?"

"Charles, this company is solving far too many problems. Business cannot thrive if no one out there has any problems that require solving. Expanding access to Network Z and widening the porthole will disrupt things just enough to make consumers place even greater value in our security products." *Network Z!* "Sold effectively, they could soon be as profitable as our porting products. Do you see how that works?"

"I do."

"No, you don't. You're a common administrator with a head made of wet cement. That is why you help manage the players and why you are not a player yourself. Get through those reports and send me five names, including the Burton boy."

She exited with a portclap that shook the closet door. Vick stood there with his head bowed and for a moment, Anna pitied him. He was never going to grow into anything beyond what he was now. This was his permanent station in life. He was a pawn and a coward and a loser: a man surrounded by genius but possessing none of his own, and she knew with ironclad certainty that he would always be that way.

That sympathy had a quick half-life, though. Anna had granted Vick the courtesy of seeing him as a human being, while Vick had never granted her any such favor. He belonged in hell and she was ready to kick him down there. She wasn't afraid of him anymore. She didn't dread his sour mug the way she had for the past month, because now she knew the truth: *You're better than him. You got his porting battery to prove it.*

She could stay quiet in that closet for as long as she needed. She could have stopped breathing for hours and still outlasted him. It was actually quite cozy in there. Maybe she'd hide in there again sometime. Make it her home. Maybe she'd get that jackass to spill everything he knew about this poisonous school. The anger was cooling now, hardening into determination. You could have seen wisps of steam come off her body.

To pass the time as Vick continued poring over files, she practiced piano in her mind: *Sonatina No. 1 in G Major*, moving her fingers along an invisible piano in the dark, breaking into a private smile whenever the notes turned on the charm. She loved that piece right up to the day she sorted out how to play it. That's when the magic disappeared from the music and it just became a rote series of keys to press. She didn't want to become the kind of muso snob who was more impressed by a difficult piece of music than by a *good* one, and yet here she was, writing off *Beethoven* as kiddie stuff once she had mastered it.

Anna won second place in the junior division of Nationals playing that little scrap of his brilliance. The competition took place at Bingham High School, south of Salt Lake City. She sat on the floor of an angled hallway outside the school's assembly hall all that afternoon, waiting for two hours to take the stage. The hallway didn't even have a vending machine. While the other insufferable prodigies were getting in their respective turns, Anna went over the

127

sheet music in her head so many times that when she was finally called up to perform, she didn't hear the notes. It was an easy piece compared to what the other kids were playing, but that simplicity was what gave her the freedom to arrange it herself and to strike the keys with such careful timing and pressure that no one else could have played it similarly. Anyone else trying to replicate her performance of it would fail, and be left at a loss as to why they had. That was Anna's musical gift: the ability to play music precisely as she heard it in her own mind.

Sarah was so, so proud of Anna that day. It was the soon-to-prove bittersweet accolade that would start Anna on her path to Druskin. Now, once more, she could hear the notes from the piece—each one sharp as a diamond—in her mind, providing an appropriate soundtrack to the sight of Vick laboring away at his pathetic little existence.

Two hours later, Vick had finally plowed through all the reports. He turned the lights off and left the office door open behind him. Anna waited ten more minutes, poked her head out of the closet, and then ran back to Sewell. She ran so fast she could barely feel her feet.

SEWELL HALL

Bamert secured visitations for Anna's room the night of the theft. All the girls hanging in the common room stared as he politely greeted Mrs. Ludwig at her apartment door and then bounded up the west stairwell in a flowered suit featuring tailored shorts instead of pants. Halfway to Anna's room, he craned over the railing, stared up at the filthy plexiglass skylight at the top of Sewell, and sang out as loud as he could:

♫ *Here comes your man*
Here comes your man
HERE COMES YOUR MAAAAANNNNNN ♫

Anna burst out of Room 24 and loomed over him.

"Will you get up here, you jackass?"

"Coming!"

He walked straight through to the inner bedroom, kicked off his brown oxfords, and splayed out on her bed.

"When do we start rasslin'?" he asked her.

"Three feet on the floor," Anna reminded him.

Bamert dangled a hairy leg off her bed and let a single toe graze the hardwood.

"Did you get it?" he asked.

She pulled the slim battery out of her jeans pocket and brandished it in front of him.

"I got it."

"Anna Huff, you are incredible."

"How was your teatime with Vick?"

Bamert ran his hand over his greasy mop of hair and let out an exhausted groan. "That man is some bad weather."

"Yeah well, you weren't trapped in his office for three hours."

"And how *was* your quality time in the ninth circle of hell?"

"Awful and then quite soothing."

"Yeah, I bet you can't wait to darken that particular door again."

"Kirsch ported in," Anna told Bamert.

He sat up. "What?"

"This school isn't just a school, Bamert."

"I know that. The brochure wouldn't shut up about it."

"No. You don't understand. This place is a recruiting facility for PortSys, and more than that. They want Burton."

"For what?" he started laughing. "Are they putting together a folk band?"

"For I dunno, PortSys stuff! They think he's a genius."

"Well, he is. He's also an idiot. They say anything about me?"

"Uh, no."

Bamert grinned until the corners of his mouth were nearly hitting his earlobes. "You're lying."

"Dammit! They said you were a mess, and that I was a pity case."

"One of those two claims is accurate, at a minimum. Anything else you found out?"

There was also the matter of the hush money Kirsch doled out on behalf of Vick and his ghastly porting experiments, but Anna wasn't ready to talk about that just yet. Sitting in that closet, she agreed to place a gag order on herself for the time being. It was silence begetting more silence, and she hated that it was so necessary for her at the moment. Silence was an awful thing: the foremost tool of the corrupt. Every secret was an untreated wound. One day, Anna would see to it that everyone knew everything about everyone, and then the world would finally have to deal with itself. But for now, it was the most evil of necessities.

"You never told me your father knew Kirsch," Anna said to Bamert.

Bamert laid back down on the bed and rolled onto his side. He propped his head on his hand, like he was posing for an underwear ad. "How do you think I got in here? All the old weird rich people know each other. They really said I was a mess, huh?"

"I shouldn't have even told you. Ignore it."

"What else did they say? I won't tolerate odious slander."

"Nothing else, I swear. All they said was you're a mess."

"There's nothing worse than when people I hate are right, and they're right about me an awful lot." He stood up and gazed out the window. "Whatever. Soon enough we'll break out of here and I can be back with all the other messy people again."

"The Wall is still an issue."

"Heh. You mean Emilia didn't stand there and say, 'Now Charles, don't tell anyone my password is BananaButt69.'"

Anna started laughing. Whenever Bamert made her laugh—and it was often—she felt a little less lost. High school is when you laugh the hardest.

"Yeah no, she didn't do that," she said. "But she did mention something about a Network Z, which was something Lara also knew about."

"Aha! Maybe Z is how Emilia gets past the wall and all the nasty digital barracudas guarding it."

"Maybe. Or maybe they're selling the ability to track other people and..." *Sarah. You could get Sarah's porting history, even without Lara's help.* Now that was something the police couldn't do, even if they had bothered to try.

"And?" Bamert had been left hanging.

Anna snapped out of it. "I forgot what I was gonna say."

"You could track Lara with it."

"Yeah but that's not my priority. I mean, I know that's why you think I'm doing all this, but there's something else."

"Well, what is it?"

"Bamert, I can't." More of that poisonous silence.

"Well, here's an idea I've been kicking around: you told us about that one guy's feed, right? Erick Martin? The guy who said PortSys was selling porting data to any asshole with a checkbook?"

"Yeah, but Burton had a point about that guy. Who knows if his feed is worth anything. He's just some bored lawyer. He got his account banned."

"The point is, I know an asshole with a checkbook."

Just then, Asmi came flying into the room, her flowered dress matching the pattern of Bamert's suit. She had her hands held out in front of her in a full I-can't-even pose, ready to dump out the day's travails for Anna to take in.

"Anna, you would not *believe*—" She noticed Bamert, who put a touch of extra effort into his underwear pose the moment he spotted her. "Oh shit. I've come barging in like some complete ponce, haven't I? Are you two—"

"Hell no," Anna told her.

"Right. You're not even into lads."

"Nope."

"Is this the fabled Asmi?" Bamert stood up and did a little curtsy before extending a hand. "It can only be."

"You're Bamert," Asmi said. "I've seen you out in the quad, off your tits. Lucky bastard."

"I'll take that as a compliment before you elaborate further. Your dress is stunning, my dear."

"Oh you're double funny. Fuck off already." Asmi was giggling now. It was almost as if she found Bamert charming. Handsome, even?

"Are you flirting with her?" Anna asked Bamert. "Stop doing that."

"But I'm a free agent!" he cried. "You said so yourself! Jealousy is not a good look on you. That is *it* between us, my sweet little buttercup!"

"What were you lot doing in here?" Asmi asked them.

Anna and Bamert answered simultaneously and the combined reply sounded something like *hang-udying out.*

Asmi pointed to the battery in Anna's hand. "What's that then?"

"It's a PortPhone battery," Anna deadpanned. "We stole it from Vick and we're gonna build a PortPhone of our own."

Bamert played along. "It's true. Then we're all gonna whizz out to a Clemson tailgate for Bojangles and fruity drinks."

There was a breathless moment before Asmi burst into laughter. "AHAHAHAHAHA, aren't you the cheeky pair. Where did you *find* this boy, Anna?"

"In the toilet."

"Does he wanna sniff some glue?"

"Do I *what*?" Bamert asked.

"He doesn't want any," Anna said to Asmi.

"How do *you* know I don't?"

"You don't."

"Prude. Anyway, Miss Asmi, we're starting a business," said Bamert.

"What kind of business?" Asmi asked.

"We haven't actually gotten that far yet," he told her. "But we are extremely *into* business. Supplies, demands, shipping, things of that nature."

"Have either of you dickheads ever run a business?" Asmi asked them.

They answered simultaneously once more, but this time in cohesion: "No."

"Well, I have. I ran three of my dad's kebab vans in Oxford. You won't have time. Look at you, Anna: you're so knackered you can barely stand."

This was true. Anna was shot through with fatigue. Her face felt like was in her neck. Her bones were cheap bendy straws. Her feet were dead clumps. Every time she looked into a mirror, she expected it to crack.

"So your dad has a business," Bamert said to Asmi.

"A good one. His vans are the best in England. I used to work them every night work till 5am and serve a bunch of drunken wankers. They'd call me a Black Shard terrorist, Black Shard doesn't even exist! Then I'd hand them a tray of food, and then they'd call me a goddess. Did my fucking head in. British boys are the absolute strangest assholes. Learned all their racism from the Kirsches, I figure."

"Where's your dad's business based?" Bamert asked.

"I told you: Oxford."

Bamert shook his head. "No no no, I mean where's it *really* based? Where's the money get dumped? Come on now."

"Why should I tell you, you madhead?"

"Because life is better when the beautiful people tell each other their secrets. Tell me I'm wrong."

133

Asmi hesitated for a second. "You tell anyone and I'll have you, geezer. You're big but I'll use your face as my fucking welcome mat if you do me wrong."

"Please do that. *Fuck me up*, Asmi."

"Not a word, dickhead. I mean it."

Bamert ran a finger zipper across his lips.

"Pakistan. That's where my dad is from. That's where I was born before we fled the war. We round up the kitty from the night's business, we port to Kandahar, we leave the cash with my na, and then we port back to England. If the bobbies ever pop by a van, we have a stash of money on hand to make it look like we're on the up and up. They usually swipe half of it anyway: a tribute we gotta pay for them to leave us alone. Bastards. Again, tell anyone and it'll be *you* roasting on my dad's spit."

"You make that sound like a threat but I would be *delectable*," Bamert boasted. "I think it's a nifty bit of corruption your family has going and I salute you and your elders for it. If Emilia Kirsch doesn't have to pay taxes, why should you?"

"Bollocks to that thieving old hag," Asmi said.

"God, British profanity is so much better than our own."

"You two should get a room," Anna told them.

"We have one!" Bamert said. "We have a room and we're literally in it. And so, while we've got our little room together, let me ask you something, Asmi."

"What's that?"

Bamert stiffened his spine and tugged on his sport coat. Anna could tell his genius was booting up. You could see it in his eyes. His brain was a fickle, inconsistent organ. But when Bamert sensed a wave approaching, he knew when it was time to begin paddling furiously. The idea was coming to him now: every step of the plan emerging in full, from conception to execution. And it would all begin with a simple question to Anna's new, exquisite roommate:

"Is your father looking for investors?"

From The Account Of @KandyRichards
Thoroughly down this wormhole
Posted from 2:34am to 3:01am EST, 10/01/30

Okay this is my THIRD time setting up my account again because PortSys had me BANNED from this site the other two times. Because they own everything now, so why not?! But you cannot hold a good girl down! 1/

Now look at this: Here's a photo of Jason Kirsch, head of design for PortSys and Emilia's shit-for-brains son, leaving a hotel with Vietnamese premier Tuy Xuan Phan. Now what is the guy supposedly in charge of designing PortPhones doing meeting with HEADS OF STATE? 2/

Well, this isn't the first meeting he's had with foreign dignitaries! We know from @MeyerLemonParty's feed that he also met with officials from Thailand, Costa Rica, and Italy. Now what do those countries have in common? I'LL TELL YOU! 3/

They've ALL had violent crimes committed on their soil by American port tourists, and they've all had CIVIL demonstrations to keep Americans from porting in and out of their countries. 4/

Then Jason Kirsch visits and guess what happens? The government keeps the port border open to Americans. Even when we SHOOT their tourists dead for coming HERE! 5/

They also pay off opposition candidates to go away and/or rig elections against them to keep those port borders FREE and OPEN to Americans. And what do those Americans do? They build HOUSES, and RESORTS, and they put big portwalls around them so that they have control over the most desirable areas of those countries. They are gentrifying everything they can gentrify! 6/

This is Colonialism all over again. Go ahead and ask the North Sentinalese. Oh wait you can't because they GONE now. The haves get their oasises (that a word?) and the have-nots get to ROT in the free zones! 7/

If you think this is just about MONEY, yeah it's definitely that, but I wanna show you something ELSE! 8/

Here's a screenshot from the r/Conquistadors forum, where a dude named K15 goes on longwinded rants ALL THE TIME. And he believes some truly WILD SHIT! 9/

K15 believes women assaulted by port stalkers should accept it as the COST OF DOING BUSINESS and "move on" after being attacked instead of "branding themselves as martyrs". He also believes that porting is the "ideal Trojan Horse" to bring "White European cultures and values" to the rest of the world. 10/

He's glad public schools have basically died, and he's glad the health care system here fell apart because now it's a "truly global" marketplace. This is SICK! 11/

Now I have no definitive proof that K15 is Jason Kirsch, but you damn well better believe that @MeyerLemonParty and @RedSauce have been on his ass from DAY ONE. This is him. End of story. 12/

PortSys keeps talking about "port neutrality" and "true globalism." Meanwhile they give money to PINE to shoot people at will, then they turn around and lobby the government to conduct light infantry raids on ANY country that gives them trouble. 13/

The end goal isn't to create a global community. The goal is absolute DOMINION of the best parts of the world. 14/

That's why they've shut my accounts down TWICE. I have had people in my mentions tell me I'm "too close". It brings me no pleasure to endanger myself saying this, but the Kirsch family must be DESTROYED! 15/

Watch them deactivate this account in 3, 2, 1... <END THREAD>

GOULD HOUSE/CRATER

It took Burton's non-girlfriend girlfriend a week to smuggle all the parts. Somehow they ended up costing Bamert more than a fully assembled PortPhone out of the store—considerably more—but that was of no concern to Bamert and his daddy's credit card. Using Anna's VPN, he loaded up at PortDirect on chips, flex cables, taptic engine vibrators, an LCD screen, and more. Then he ordered a two-gallon drum of Cheez Balls delivered to the Goren Hall mailroom just because he could.

Again, Anna had to watch more tutorials featuring more nasty close-ups of pizza hands. The extra time was cutting into her already meager sleepload. She was running on less than three hours a night and it was deadening her body and mind. She had become a rock tied to a heavy rope, dragged around and across campus without end, leaving a trail of dull white chalk behind her.

They met in Burton's room in Gould House on a late Saturday afternoon to assemble the phone. The place was spotless. Burton made his bed with military precision every morning. He kept a small row of herb plants on the windowsill and fastidiously tended to them with a pair of shears and a spray bottle filled with distilled water from the cafeteria. Like a good nerd, he had all of his notebooks and papers color-coded and arranged in a perfect stack. He even vacuumed the floor twice a week. Bamert was openly disgusted with how immaculate the place was.

Anna laid out all the parts on Burton's bedspread and got to work, carefully tucking the circuit boards into the 3D-printed casing and packing the wires tight so that no interior space was wasted. Again, Anna was left to toil away with the pentalobe screwdriver. Her wrist ached as Bamert loomed over the assembly, contributing nothing while calmly perusing scores from the AP Top 25. He stroked one of Burton's chive plants.

"Don't do that," Burton told him.

"Why not?" asked Bamert. "Are you presenting these at some sort of garden show?"

"Yes."

"Wait, you are? I guess I should have expected that answer."

"I think I got it," Anna told them both. The boys huddled around the bed and gazed in wide wonder at the dull gray box before them.

"It's ugly as hell," Bamert said.

"Bamert," said Anna. "I will kill you with my bare hands."

"My apologies."

She slipped her bulldog cover over the phone.

"A bulldog?" Burton asked.

"I have my reasons," Anna said.

They sat in reverent silence around the homemade phone for a few minutes, praying it would come to life when they hit the Power button but dreading the potential letdown; that awful, distinctly 21st century sensation when a piece of technology fails and crushes your spirit for the day. Finally, Anna slipped her hand under the pebbly casing and pressed down firmly. A single agonizing second, and then the screen came alive.

"Oh my God, it works," Anna said.

"Well, it works, but does it *work* work?" Burton asked.

There was only one way to find out. Bamert had already done the legwork of hopping online and creating an entirely fictional businessman that he christened Chester Bumlee. From there, he took a demented glee in rounding out Chester Bumlee's resume. Bumlee was a 37-year-old barrister, single with one child, and living comfortably in an apartment complex in Oxford, England. His parents were deceased: killed, according to Bamert, in a tragic locomotive collision. Chester collected vintage mustard bottles and played in a bluegrass band called The Desired Effect. His profile photo was a Shutterstock image of a man in a seersucker suit holding a parrot.

PortSys demanded a social security number for any new American customer. UK residents, like Bumlee and his manufactured child, were under no such obligation. All he needed was a proof of address. The forwarding service Bamert set up for Bumlee sent all his snail mail, hand-delivered by PortSys-approved couriers, directly to Bamert's cubby in Goren Hall. Once he had opened up Bumlee's own personal credit card account (billed, again, to an address in New Hampshire), a PortSys account in his name and his daughter Sarah's name were both approved and active. Chester Bumlee matched Bamert's height and weight exactly. Ditto for Anna and Chester's daughter.

Leaving Burton behind in his room, Anna and Bamert ran out of Gould House with the phone and a weighted blanket that Bamert had ordered the week before, explicitly for their clandestine porting mission. When the blanket arrived at Goren Hall, Bamert ended up using it as his personal comforter because he liked sleeping with it so much.

It was getting dark enough now to provide Anna and Bamert with a bit of cover, but not so dark and late as to have security roaming around with Mag-Lites. Behind the Druskin infirmary there was a decent-sized patch of woods where kids would go to get high and drink hard soda. They called it The Crater.

"We shouldn't do it right in this spot," Anna said when they arrived. "It needs to be offset a little."

"I concur."

They walked another ten yards west and then turned south, following the towering Harkness Wall, stepping over and around felled trees that had been euthanized after emerald ash borers had snuck through the perimeter. Autumn was coming on strong now, every step they took causing the dead leaves to crackle and snap. The wind grew hostile. Anna got dizzy from looking around so much to make sure they were alone and unseen. She needed eight more sets of eyes to feel secure.

"Here," she said, stopping next to a thick oak tree. Bamert hung the blanket on one of the branches and she slipped underneath. The branch broke and the fifteen-pound blanket tackled her like an oncoming linebacker.

"Are you okay?" Bamert asked.

"I'm fine. This is fine."

They hung the blanket on a sturdier branch this time. She ducked underneath, opened up the map, zoomed in on her location, and chose a pin two feet away from where she was currently standing. A fly landed on her shoulder. She laughed out loud before shooing it away.

She hit PORT, took a step, and felt the shiver. Now this was proper porting. No burning. No needles. She had never been so happy to feel so cold. She took her step into the hole and, for a fraction of a fraction of a second, the cold encased her. You didn't pass through spacetime so much as spacetime passed through you. It was like a sneeze: a strange reflex that sealed your eyes shut and would probably kill you if lasted any longer than it did.

The great vacuum of air created by her exit from this plane sucked the blanket toward the void and left it stick–straight for a millisecond before it flared back out and plummeted to the ground. That heavy covering was enough to keep the port clap from echoing beyond the woods.

Anna appeared again right next to the blanket, the gust from her reappearance blowing Bamert's tie over his shoulder. He covered his face to keep from squealing with delight.

"It works!" he whispered.

"It works."

They looked up at the Harkness Wall, its battlements blocking out the coming moonlight.

"Think we'll get past it?" Anna asked him.

"As sure as sunlight, we will."

Body Identified At Bettendorff Beach As Local Woman
AP
10/1/2030

(COOS BAY, OR) — State Medical Examiner Dr. Carmen Headley confirmed today that the body of a previously unidentified woman that washed up along Bettendorff Beach on September 27th matched the fingerprints and dental records of anti-porting activist Melanie Greenberg. Official cause of death was listed as drowning. No foul play is suspected. Her body was found, unclothed, by a group of port surfers four days ago. No PortPhone was found on her person at the time. Toxicology reports showed massive amounts of alcohol and sleep medication in her blood at the time of death.

Greenberg, who gained some mild renown when her son died porting to the top of Mount Everest, leaves behind no surviving family or legal will. Her remains will be cremated and stored at the Coos County Sheriff's Office for a predetermined period of time before being remanded to Bay Area Public Cemetery for formal interment.

ROUTE 101

The next morning, Anna chugged three energy drinks in a row and knocked on Mrs. Ludwig's door. When no one answered, she knocked more forcefully. A cop knock. Mrs. Ludwig came to the door in hair curlers. Anna was admiring her fluffy white slippers before realizing that they weren't slippers; they were actually two cats sitting at her feet.

"Yes?"

"I'd like to take a ride, Mrs. Ludwig."

"Oh. Oh, *really*?" she said archly. Anna didn't know what she was in for.

"Hell yeah, I would. Let's go fast."

"I'll get my coat. This will be verrrrrrrrry interesting."

Within fifteen minutes, Anna was passing through Druskin Gate for the first time in over a month, her passport hanging dutifully around her neck. For so long, Anna had schemed to outwit that stupid wall. Now she could just prance right through it, if only for a moment. The five-week baptism into Druskin life had cleansed her mind fully of what the rest of the United States was currently like. Now it was all coming back. The small roads were bloodshot with dying vegetation. The sidewalks were crumbling. The crosswalks had faded away to stencils. Old, abandoned cars rotted in front of colonial houses. Spent shell casings were ready to ambush unsuspecting pedestrians anywhere they stepped.

Loud bangs went off all over town: a handful of remaining Druskin town residents taking their Sunday morning to venture places far more exotic. A few leafpeepers came popping in to gawk at the foliage and exited quickly after they had gotten their fill. A couple of PINE agents wandered around the sidewalk, bored but still fingering their trigger guards.

Anna heard the low roar of Route 101 in the distance, the only passable thoroughfare for trucks and tanks to get to I-95. Trucks and tanks were nearly all that were left of the automotive universe now: big lumbering beasts crisscrossing the country, frantic to either supply porters with goods or to wipe them out entirely.

Mrs. Ludwig led Anna over to the dilapidated remains of a nearby parking lot. There was only one car on the lot that hadn't been entombed in rust, and it was the low-slung, black 1965 Shelby Cobra that Mrs. Ludwig talked about more than she did about her own husband. Anna reached out and led her hand along the Cobra's voluptuous frame, feeling along the ragtop fastening studs and steel gas cap, grazing her fingers down the glossy white racing stripe down the center of the hood like she was a hot spokesmodel in an old car ad. In the sunlight, the frame shone like vinyl.

Mrs. Ludwig pointed to two black, bazooka-wide tailpipes running under the doors and alongside the chassis.

"These pipes, they get very hot," she warned Anna. "Don't touch them, yeah?" She unlatched the passenger side door. Attached to the seat was a body harness with a heavy iron buckle at the sternum, a thick leather guard flapping down from it. "What you do is you put your butt against the top of the seat and then slide down."

"Slide down?"

"Yep."

Anna stepped in, rested her butt against the top of the concave, leather-upholstered passenger seat, and then nestled down into the belly of the Cobra. The dashboard looked like it belonged inside a small airplane: nothing but black switches and tiny gauges, all with beveled corners and rimmed in chrome. The windshield was so tiny that the wipers each measured less than a foot long. The car was so low to the road that her ass was nearly touching the pavement. Between the driver's seat and passenger seat was a fire extinguisher. Anna had never seen one so prominently featured inside a car and worried that there was a good, proven reason that it needed to be kept so handy.

Mrs. Ludwig latched the passenger door shut and ran a hitch pin through it.

"Put the harness around your shoulders and buckle it tight," she told Anna.

Anna complied. She felt like she was about to go skydiving. Mrs. Ludwig came around, got in, took the Club lock off the steering wheel, and gunned the engine to life. Every other ambient sound was drowned out in an instant. Earplugs. Earplugs would have been a wise idea. Mrs. Ludwig shouted more instructions but all Anna could she see were moving lips. Then her dorm mom knocked open the glove compartment, revealing a pair of driving goggles that were better suited for World War II bombing sorties over London. Anna strapped the goggles to her face. Mrs. Ludwig put on a her own plus a pair of fingerless driving gloves, then she shouted more inaudible things before laughing and grabbing the stick shift.

The coupe reared back a couple inches and then exploded out of the lot and down the road.

Thirty miles an hour in the Cobra felt like 60. Sixty felt like 90. Every time Mrs. Ludwig hit the gas, the car seemed to lift off the ground and blast them into orbit. When Mrs. Ludwig got onto Route 101 and could really let it out, it was like passing through a wormhole with her eyes wide open. The wind and the engine ganged up on Anna's eardrums and pummeled them without remorse. Mrs. Ludwig hit 120 on the speedometer. The rearview mirror mounted on top of the dash started to rattle. Anna's passport card flapped up and smacked her in the face. When they zoomed past trucks and military supply vehicles it was like watching a time-lapse video. Anna was nauseous and thrilled all at once. The raucous wind blowing all around her reminded her of Sarah and those evening drives to Rockville Town Center.

"FASTER." Anna ordered. Mrs. Ludwig couldn't hear her. Anna pointed to her lips and shouted the word again.

"Yeah?" Mrs. Ludwig mouthed back. Anna nodded.

Mrs. Ludwig upped it to 140 and now Anna's insides were turning to paste. She discreetly put a finger to her throat and checked her pulse, which now roughly matched the speed of the car. She was dying to grab the stick shift and give it a little wiggle.

"Faster."

Mrs. Ludwig was incredulous but took it to 160 anyway. This was not a road built for such speeds. While Route 101, unlike residential thoroughfares, was blessed with semi-regular maintenance, that didn't stop it from accumulating potholes the width of a small dining table. Shredded tire bits dotted the road like black tumbleweeds. There was litter everywhere. Mrs. Ludwig swerved and careened around all the potholes and stale asphalt brownies littering the road at top speed. The hard molding of the door dug into Anna's upper arm. A tiny ball chain dangling from the cigarette lighter swung wildly with every nudge of the steering wheel. A horse—a fucking horse!—trotted across the highway and they had to swerve to miss it. Mrs. Ludwig laughed as they passed it. Anna did not. Alongside the road she saw makeshift crosses and piles of rocks left to honor Route 101's assorted victims. Beyond the crosses were neighborhoods with houses built directly on top of old, now-unused residential lanes.

"Faster."

The Cobra couldn't go any faster. Anna checked her pulse and it was similarly maxed out, frantically tapping out emergency cries for help in Morse Code. Here was the "shit white" moment Mrs. Ludwig had talked about. This was good enough. She turned to Mrs. Ludwig and stuck her thumb out.

"Go back."

Mrs. Ludwig nodded and pulled onto an exit ramp that was choked with quackgrass and spent dandelions. They buzzed over 101 and got right back on the highway, Ludwig ratcheting the speed back to 160 as the Cobra blitzed west, dodging fallen pines and deer carcasses. At cruising speed they sank so close to the road that Anna felt like it was poised to sand her ass into fine dust.

When they pulled back into the lot, Anna jumped out of the car, careful to avoid the broiling tailpipe lurking beneath, and frantically ran in place. They went through Druskin Gate and Anna kept high stepping furiously, pushing her heart rate until all the beats were poised to join together into a single, frozen contraction. Sweat came off of her in sheets and she almost slipped on the runoff. The armed guards openly laughed at her.

"What are you doing?" Mrs. Ludwig asked.

"I'm just fired up!" Anna said. "I forgot how much I enjoy going fast and now I'm just so goddamn fired up!"

"Would you like a pretzel?"

"Gimme ALL your pretzels, Mrs. Ludwig."

Mrs. Ludwig led her back to Sewell and opened her apartment door. Anna bounded in and kept running in place.

"May I use your bathroom?" she asked.

"Are you going to keep running while you do your business?"

"NO."

"All right."

Anna chopped her feet down the hall and grabbed one of Mrs. Ludwig's white cats along the way. She locked the bathroom door, whipping off her mary janes and her damp socks. Then, in one swift motion, she took the tracking anklet off of her leg and placed it around the cat's neck, discreetly tucking it under her collar. The cat didn't make a sound. Anna checked the collar for a name tag.

SHELBY.

"Heh."

She took out one of the Blackheel anklets that Alyssa had smuggled into past the Harkness Wall for Burton and slipped it onto her opposite ankle. Then she dried off her entire body with a hand towel, threw up into the toilet, walked out, and helped herself to a Bavarian pretzel the size of dinner plate. She'd earned it. She had passed a cat off as herself quite capably. Burton was wrong. Go fast enough and you *can* fake anatomy.

One hour later, Bamert knocked on Mrs. Ludwig's door, holding a bouquet of daisies and asking for his own joyride.

DEAN'S RESIDENCE

Wednesday struck again. Anna built up a healthy dread for every session in Vick's lab. The dread would ebb on Thursdays, and then slowly work back into a froth as the days ticked away. All over again, she would be back in his little dungeon clinic, staring daggers at a mute Brendan McClear and listening to the familiar voice on the laptop ticking off instructions to Vick as she held the kettle bell and stepped into the wormhole and her body exploded. Over the past few weeks, she could tell that the hole was sucking in *more* of her body on each attempt, grabbing what it could of her and pulling her apart like string cheese before rejecting her.

But on this night, something different happened down in that basement. Vick sat at his laptop and ordered Anna to step forward, and when she did this time around, she felt the crisp, refreshing snap of a successful port take hold. In an instant, she was ten feet from her original spot, the kettle bell still firmly in her grasp. No pain. No pins and needles.

Vick cocked his head and then went back to typing.

"Status?" the voice on the laptop asked.

"Passed," said Vick.

"I ported," Anna said, in disbelief. Brendan McClear looked up at her, and then stared right back down at his tablet when she caught him.

"You're done now," Vick told her. "You don't have to come back."

"I don't?" She hated feeling grateful to him for the news. She hated feeling like she had accomplished anything.

Vick didn't answer her.

"What is it you did to me?" she asked him.

Again, nothing. He kept on typing. She looked at the door and dashed away. On the way back to Sewell, she dropped to her knees on the asphalt path and burst into tears. *You shouldn't have to cry. They should.*

Other kids stared.

THE LATIN ROOM

Edgar Bamert awaited his son in The Latin Room: a small room next to the fetid Assembly Hall with its own distinct stench of wood polish and mildew. This was the room where Druskin students were put up for getting into trouble, subjected to a kangaroo court of deans and humorless seniors who already knew a troublemaker's fate well before the poor troublemaker did, but still allowed the offender a meek defense before casting him out. There was no shortage of trust fund kids and overachievers waiting for a spot at Druskin, so expelling a student was a relatively minor hassle for the powers that be. Vick happily condemned kids to the Latin Room any time they were caught drinking, vaping, fucking, cheating on an exam, cursing out loud for spilling a Coke, or doing one of the zillion other things that constituted "Un-Druskinlike Conduct," as outlined in the school's 300-page student manual.

On this day, Paul Bamert and Anna Huff were awaiting a wholly different form of judgment. Here now was Edgar Bamert: scion to a banking dynasty and a man as staid and conservative as his son was flamboyant. The elder Bamert sat opposite from Paul and Anna at a giant wooden table (by now, Anna had decided that the school's affinity for large tables was officially a fetish). He was clad in a crisp blue suit, a gold watch chain running from his lapel to his breast pocket. His fingernails were perfectly cut and buffed. His skin was smoother than fresh cream. The only telltale sign that he was J. Paul Bamert's father was a gold-plated tie bar adorned with a Clemson logo that kept his orange tie pinned to his dress shirt. He didn't get up to greet Paul or Anna when they entered the room. Edgar Bamert was a proudly severe man, rarely smiling because so few people were worthy of his approval, not even his own son. *Especially* not his own son.

"What is all this?" Edgar asked Bamert. He had a thick Virginia drawl that made Bamert's sound like a cheap knockoff by comparison.

"We have a business proposal, sir," Bamert told him.

"And what kind of business would that be?"

"Kebabs."

149

"Kebabs ain't a business, son."

"Actually, they're quite a lucrative one. I've run the numbers."

Bamert slid a small folder over to his father, but the old timer raised a palm.

"I don't need to see the damn numbers. Your idea for sellin' a bunch of Arab food is nonsense, boy. Besides, you already got your own line of credit, and you got the fundraising skills of a Bamert. There's nothin' else you require from me, boy. Sink or swim."

"Dad, that line of credit isn't enough."

"Is that right? Because it's downright ostentatious from my vantage point."

"It's not. And the Bamert fundraising prowess you canonize is hindered by the fact every rich kid here at Druskin cries broke if you so much as ask them to spot you a chicken finger sub from Romeo's on a weeknight."

"And what's with the young lady?" Edgar Bamert cast an eye on Anna. Anna was wearing a pair of eyeglasses with non-prescription lenses to the meeting, to pass herself off as an intellectual. "Who are you, sweetheart?"

"My name is Anna Huff, and I have offered Paul my services as CFO of the consortium."

"Don't you two lovebirds have classes to go to?"

"We're not that," Anna told Mr. Bamert. She offered little beyond that. She had a feeling Bamert's father would offer a strong opinion if she further elucidated her sexual preferences.

"Well, I shoulda known you two weren't a pair," said Edgar. "That would have been far too reassuring."

"Dad." Bamert began.

"Ahem."

Bamert rolled his eyes. "*Sir*. Sir, you sent me to this place because you wanted me to get my act together. Well here I am, doing just that. I've found a business partner, and we've showed initiative by outlining a solid, workable business plan on top of an already heavy course load. What more, sir, do I have to do to prove myself worthy of your largesse?"

"Well, you could shave. You could tame that wild mop on top of your head. You could wear respectable clothing instead of dressing like some sort of ghetto street pimp."

"Why?" Bamert asked him. "So I could look like you? And what have you done with that polite, respectable look of yours?"

Bamert, stop.

"Young man—"

"Who's the young man? You're the ne'er-do-well, *Dad*. You go to your golf club and you port to Bermuda and you throw very polite Derby parties that make you look like a captain of industry, but tell me a thing you've made that's been worth a damn. You sit there like you *earned* all this, like you didn't win at birth and coast along on the backs of industrial titans who were bones in the ground before you were even a thought in grandpappy's head. You could have spent all these years in glassblowing school and it wouldn't have mattered because our money makes money anyway. Rip me all you want with your antebellum disdain, *good sir*, but at least I *know* I'm a fraud. At least I know I am the absolute worst kind of freeloader, and I don't try to pretend I'm some kind of bullshit paragon of rectitude."

Anna didn't move. It was like she had a personal Harkness Wall around her entire body. She already knew the seed money was gone. She just hoped Mr. Bamert's reply wasn't as verbose as his son's, so that they could get out of that room before Vick stumbled in and decided to hold a spontaneous put-up.

Edgar Bamert gave his son a wide, condescending smile. He was like Vick; his smiles were rarer and angrier than his frowns.

"I'll give you your money, boy."

Juh?

"Know this, though," Edgar continued. "It's the last dime you'll ever get from me. You're gonna fail yet again, and you're gonna fail *hard*. And it'll be the best damn gift I ever gave you."

"I haven't told you how much I want," Bamert said.

"Send the number to Louise, and then never hassle me about money again. I have a golf date with Robb Caraway now. Go Tigers."

151

"Go Tigers, sir."

Mr. Bamert took out his phone and hit PORT, the portclap resonating out of the Latin Room and echoing through the innards of the barren Assembly Hall next door. Bamert the younger rocked back in the ancient wooden desk chair and tucked his hands behind his head.

"Well, that was highly on-brand for him," he told Anna. "I just love him so much. And he's golfing with the head of PINE! What a delightful pair."

"That was very dramatic just now!"

"We have that same fight twice a year." Bamert stood up and offered her his elbow. "He's so bored he'll fight with anyone. Let's get a sandwich."

The Man Behind PINE
Broadcast Date 10/8/30
Correspondent: Elena Roth
Segment Producer: Grant Holloway
Transcript posted: 10/9/30

ROTH: With nearly $200 billion in annual funding, the Port Immigration and Naturalization Enforcement Bureau, or PINE, now represents the largest independent branch of the U.S. Department of Defense. And with WallTech's Great Smartwall Project—the largest smartwall effort ever undertaken—experiencing massive delays and cost overruns, PINE's role in controlling port immigration into the United States has become even more vital.

But critics, including members of Congress, say that the bureau lacks oversight, operates in near total secrecy, and eschews due process in favor of brute force, a great deal of it targeted at port immigrants from non-Western countries.

The man in charge of the agency, Robb Caraway, has never given a public interview until now. Sitting with me tonight, he gives a robust defense of an agency one major news outlet has branded "a government-sanctioned hate group."

CARAWAY: This is not an easy job. That's the first thing you need to understand. We were given the thankless task of enforcing the laws of this nation and to secure its borders when its borders were, in an instant, destroyed. For centuries, we were one of the most secure and powerful nations in the world because we were surrounded by ocean on both sides.

ROTH: Those oceans have been rendered irrelevant.

CARAWAY: 100% irrelevant, okay? The two greatest natural military barriers in history: gone just like that. That means any Black Shard terrorist or drug smuggler who wants to port into this country can now do so. They are coordinated and extremely dangerous. This is a crisis. You saw what happened in Austin.

ROTH (narrating): Caraway, of course, is referring to the 2024 port attack on the Austin City Limits music festival that left nearly 500 people dead. According to a Congressional investigation, three members of the religious extremist group Black Shard allegedly ported in en masse, each one carrying a SIG516 carbon fiber assault rifle, preferred by port terrorists because its carbon fiber frame is light enough to fit within the YOU PLUS TWO rule of antihydrogen teleportation. It was that attack that prompted the formation of PINE and gave birth to the law that stated U.S. citizens have to wear passport or state ID lanyards at all times when out in public.

CARAWAY: Can I tell you something, Elena? I don't like these laws. I really don't. I hate that we had to make visible identification mandatory, but this is what is necessary to protect us from Black Shard and from the thousands, I mean literal *thousands*, of terrorist syndicates that are taking advantage of this technology, using it to arrange meetings and plot out sudden attacks.

ROTH: But Mr. Caraway, we spoke to multiple eyewitnesses who were in Austin that day and said that all three shooters spoke with American accents. Some people say that Congress names Black Shard in the report strictly for political purposes.

CARAWAY: And I'm supposed to believe "some people" over Congress? Why would I do that?

ROTH: Even if you find the Congressional investigation credible and the resulting laws justified, does that mean you're allowed to open fire on anyone not wearing a lanyard, or that you can stage raids anywhere you please?

CARAWAY: Who said we're doing that? "Some people" again?

ROTH: It happens every day.

CARAWAY: That's a gross exaggeration and I frankly resent it. Do your homework next time. You can grill me all you want, but at least do me the courtesy of using facts to do so.

ROTH: Is it true that you have a weekly security debrief with the Kirsch family?

CARAWAY: That's none of your business.

ROTH: You were a groomsman in Jason Kirsch's wedding party. Aren't you concerned that being close to him is a conflict of interest when it comes to overseeing this agency?

CARAWAY: You're reaching. The Kirsch family is the greatest success story in the history of this world and their generosity knows no bounds. I'm a free man and I can socialize with whomever I please. If you think that hinders me from acting like a professional, I again wish you had better facts on your side. You're coming to me with beliefs. Beliefs are a luxury for your kind that I cannot afford. People go into war with beliefs, but they come out with facts. *I* have facts.

ROTH (narrating): But facts are difficult to come by when you're investigating PINE. The Department of Defense does not publicly release the numbers of port immigrants killed by PINE agents annually, although the human rights group BlueWatch says it runs in the tens of thousands.

David Suchoff is a Professor of International Studies at Colby College in Maine, and he says PINE is little more than an enforcement arm of PortSys, the multinational conglomerate that controls all global porting bandwidth.

SUCHOFF: PortSys could end this crisis today simply by denying port access to anyone with a gun and anyone, non-citizens included, with a violent background.

ROTH: But they don't want to.

SUCHOFF: Of course they don't want to! We could even—gasp!— make laws demanding they do it. We could stop exporting mass shootings to other countries! But no one else in power wants to do that because too many people are making too much money from port tourism and from the expanding terrestrial commerce. Look at what Germany did.

ROTH: You mean when they passed a law banning all non-citizens from porting into the country.

SUCHOFF: Right. What happened? No one came, the economy cratered, and they opened up the port borders again five days later. China can outlaw porting and be fine, because China is China. Germany isn't. So why would America bother to replicate their failed experiment? You really think that smartwall is ever gonna work? Of course it won't. PortSys owns nearly half of WallTech. They don't *want* it to work. They want virtual construction fees for it to come rolling in forever while they keep the network subscription base maxed out.

Americans don't want the wall to work either, because they favor port neutrality and stricter regulation of PSP providers, i.e. PortSys. But they certainly don't want violent offenders or enemy combatants being able to port. God forbid Emilia Kirsch or her son lift a finger to prevent that. In fact, if you want to restrict porting for gun owners or for declared flight risks or for the mentally ill, they're ready to thwart you. The porting jailbreak two months ago at Stanworth Prison? They don't care.

This is a classic example of greed warping what ought to be a miracle of technology. Mankind has a tragic inclination to take any miracle and do the wrong thing with it, even when the right thing is plainly evident. That's what is so crushing about all this. We could have a vibrant, safe porting world. We don't. We're not even trying. We destroyed borders and yet we still harbor an irrational, homicidal obsession with protecting them. That's why PINE is gunning people down, or interning them, or confiscating their phones so that they have no way home.

ROTH: Robb Caraway says these measures are necessary to protect the country.

SUCHOFF: What country? There are no countries anymore! Anyone can go anywhere! We have a global currency! Languages are emulsifying together! And yet we want the freedom to move about as we please but we don't want everyone else to have it. We've upended the physical and spiritual notions of community but never bothered to reckon with how to redefine them. What *is* a community anymore? What's a neighborhood? Are there any? We've never answered those questions in a satisfactory manner, nor have we considered the monumental impact those answers might illuminate. Instead, we've opened up all the property of the world to one another, and then guarded our own more violently. It's folly. If you want porting in and out of your country to be legal, borderism is absolute folly.

And yet people fall for it anyway. So now you know why our government hands out "virtual addresses" to citizens at birth for tax collection—tagging babies like they're tracking sharks in the ocean—and why we're dumb enough to entrust a $700 billion public works project to a private company affiliated with the very company we're trying to corral. It's all a boondoggle that plays to our worst tendencies. PortSys and PINE want you to feel like a working wall is coming, but really they would rather let people come into the free zones and get shot than keep them out entirely. Never underestimate's man ability to take miracles for granted.

CARAWAY: The wall will be built, and it will work. But until that time comes, we have brave men and women out there in the field who have to make split decisions regarding people who may be porting into this country with bad intentions. And we haven't even gotten into port immigrants who mean well but haven't had their vaccinations.

ROTH: But what even *is* an immigrant now? We let people port anywhere they like, but if they want their kids to be citizens, they have to either port back here for delivery or pay a large fee to give birth at a designated "American soil" hospital abroad.

CARAWAY: That's not my problem. If you want your kids to be American citizens, you know the laws and you respect them. Furthermore, we lose 15,000 people to smuggled diseases every year. Prominent leaders are ambushed and assassinated with regularity now. Security is a constant, endless task. Every time you want to ease up, someone is trying to port into a bank vault, or a museum archive, or a law firm's confidential file room. You try doing this job, Elena. Everyone complains about the work we do, but I don't see them complaining when they're porting to the Swiss Alps in the morning to ski and then porting to a sandy beach for a nightcap. This is the price you pay for that kind of freedom of movement.

ROTH (narrating): But a disproportionate amount of that price is being paid by non-citizens who port in not to commit wanton acts of violence. Advocates say PINE has deliberately targeted workers in trendy, "insta-city" free zone porting spots in the Smoky Mountains, Western Montana, and off the Gulf Coast of Northern Florida, where seasonal clusters of both port tourists and the destitute can swell into the hundreds of thousands, causing dangerous overcrowding in an instant. Just last year, a bystander with a camera caught PINE agents gunning down a young laborer from Tuxtla, Mexico named Marco Ramirez. Ramirez was fully vaccinated and had secured a legal porting visa from PINE, and he wore it around his neck every day when he ported outside of Busch Gardens near Tampa, Florida to sell fresh mangoes on a stick to tourists. You can see the visa around Ramirez's neck in the video seen here. Please be warned that it is graphic in nature.

When Marco's mother, Yasmin, ported in to Busch Gardens to retrieve his body and arrange for transport back to the Mexican state of Chiapas, the lanyard was gone.

YASMIN RAMIREZ: They took it off his body.

ROTH: Did you see them do it?

RAMIREZ: No, but people there told me they saw the PINE agents do it.

ROTH: And you believe them.

RAMIREZ: Why wouldn't I believe them? PINE kills everyone. I had to get a special visa printed out just to go see my son dead on a sidewalk, and even then I was scared because they'd probably shoot me anyway.

CARAWAY: Our agents are incredibly well-trained and methodical. They don't make mistakes. When they act, it's because they perceive a real threat. Anyone disputing our methods is just part of the outrage machine, looking for attention.

RAMIREZ: Do I not get to be outraged over my son being shot to death? Who gets to be outraged in the world today? Who gets to be angry? Is it only Mr. Caraway? PINE? Emilia and Jason Kirsch? Because I am shaking with anger and I deserve to be. These monsters accuse people like me of being outraged about everything,

159

calling me crazy, because they don't want anyone to be outraged about anything that *they* do.

CARAWAY: I'm not here to indulge the hysterics of people who have no grasp of the situation. You can afford to be hysterical when you haven't been tasked with any leadership or responsibility in addressing what has become a very real national emergency for us Americans.

ROTH: Are you casually dismissing a grieving mother?

CARAWAY: I'm doing my job, is what I'm doing. Maybe she should stick to doing hers, if she even has one. The Americans I'm tasked with protecting cannot afford to have me emotionally compromised when I need to make hard decisions on their behalf.

ROTH: But since Austin, incidents of port terrorism have remained relatively flat, while violent crime among U.S. citizens has increased over four percent *every year*.

CARAWAY: I can't speak to that, since that isn't our purview.

ROTH: But local police departments sometimes work with you in human smuggling roundups. Don't you find that to be a misallocation of resources when incidents of *domestic* violence, suicide, and stalking are rapidly increasing?

CARAWAY: Again, that's not my purview. Even if I believed that incidents of port terrorism are flat, then that would tell me that we're doing our job effectively and keeping the threat contained. And truthfully, we could save these immigrants a whole lot of heartache if they simply wore their vaccination bands and followed our agents' instructions when they're being questioned.

ROTH: But, in the video of Marco Ramirez being shot, agents don't bother to question him before opening fire.

CARAWAY: I'm not going to speak to a lone video that could have been easily manipulated or filmed out of context.

ROTH (narrating): But that's not the only video that shows PINE agents using deadly force. In another video taken just three weeks ago, a group of agents is seen gunning down American sixteen-year-old James Hendry, who is walking around without proper identification. In the video, agents shoot Hendry a dozen times in the back before porting back to PINE headquarters in suburban Virginia.

SUCHOFF: They're accountable to no one, and they're gunning down legal porters and American citizens who are too poor to afford a passport or a state ID.

CARAWAY: Those are false allegations, and it makes our job infinitely more difficult when that kind of garbage gets circulated around and legitimized by the mainstream media. Here's what I know, Elena: We're the most open, welcoming nation on Earth. We have never passed a law that forbids legally porting here, because we believe in freedom. But we also know that PortSys can't control what you bring with you into a wormhole, and so we have to be fair but strong. It's not a perfect system we have right now.

ROTH: But you're counting on a wall to fix it.

CARAWAY: No, that's a mischaracterization. Everyone wants to be free and everyone wants to be safe, and those two desires aren't always compatible. So we're not sitting here on our duffs, praying some computer nerd at WallTech can solve that conundrum for us. We are doggedly looking for alternative solutions that keep our border legitimate while also reducing the need to employ deadly force.

ROTH: Can you tell me some of those possible solutions?

CARAWAY: Not right now, I can't.

SEWELL HALL

Bamert, aka Chester Bumlee, was now a very prolific businessman. He had a $200,000 stake in a growing fleet of Oxford-based kebab vendors, and he shrewdly decided to use 25% of that seed money for a targeted advertising campaign run by a company called Boola. The Boola rep was extremely enthusiastic about securing Mr. Bumlee's business, even going so far as to offer him exclusive access to something called Network Z.

"And what is Network Z, pray tell?" Bamert asked over the phone in his best British accent, which sounded very much like a Virginia teenager poorly imitating a British accent.

"It offers preferred vendors special porting capabilities and provides them with access to consumer demographics and porting trends that you cannot get anywhere else. This is a new offer!"

"Oh my! Jolly good! I would quite fancy that, I would! Oh, but I do want to take care that such things are within the bounds of ETHICS, my good lad."

"It's 100% ethical. We only collect data from porters who agree to share it. Would you like me to send you the materials?"

"With all due haste! Crumpets and brandy for all!"

The rep sent Bamert a PDF that included a nondisclosure agreement that ran over 30,000 words. Anna scanned the document and quickly noticed FAILURE TO COMPLY COULD RESULT IN JAIL AND A FINE OF $20 MILLION in bold. That was the nut of it. The rest of the fine print was window dressing. They signed Chester Bumlee's life away to this shady Boola outfit and received a confirmation email granting him one year of access to Network Z. Bamert hit DOWNLOAD on the DIY PortPhone and an ominous app icon loaded on screen: a sheet black tile with no name under it. When he opened the app, it looked just like PortMaps, only now the map of the world was black and had billions of small blue pins on it.

"Bamert," Anna asked, "what is this?"

She touched one of the pins and Network Z spat out the life story of a woman named Frances Gallery: her age, her date of birth, her current location (Atlantis Resort in the Bahamas), her top 10 favorite porting locations, her last 100 ports, everything. The screen blinked for a second and now the woman's dot was on another continent. This wasn't like the Friends section of the PortSys app, where only your circle of friends could see your location. This was the whole *world's* movement, a pulsing blanket of humanity bopping around in real time and in recognizable swells and patterns, swarming toward all the warm and bright places, leaving the nightlands lonely and barren.

"Well shit on a shingle," Bamert said, "We can see everyone!"

"This seems bad," Anna said.

"It *is* bad," said Burton. "Atlantis is a 50,000-room resort with no portwall. Why would anyone ever subject themselves to that kind of tourist trap?"

"Burton, please don't Burton all over this. Visitation time is almost over. This is a crisis. This is not something people should be able to have."

"But they already do," he said. "Brands and celebrities and anyone else with a million port friends, they can see this kind of movement and monetize it. This is the logical extreme of that."

Bamert leaned toward the screen. "What's that search bar do?"

Anna put her finger on the little bar at the top of the screen and a keyboard prompt popped up. She looked at Bamert, who gave her a nod.

"Come on," he told her, "You know you wanna."

Her fingers trembled as she typed in the name SARAH HUFF.

"Wait," asked Burton, "I thought you were gonna search for—"

When she hit the ENTER arrow, her sister's face and profile appeared. There was no pin to indicate her location.

"You're looking for your sister, Anna?" Bamert asked her.

"Not exactly." She brought up Sarah's porting data and it listed Rockville with a timestamp of August 9, 2029 as her final pin.

"Oh Anna," said Bamert. "I'm really sorry."

"What happened to her?" asked Burton.

"I'm trying to sort that out." She brought up Sarah's entire porting history. Before Sarah died, she had turned off location sharing and cleared all her porting data. But thanks to Network Z, all of that data had been resurrected for data miners and anyone else looking to scavenge her sister's digital remains. There, right below Sarah's home pin in Rockville and her work pin in San Francisco, was another pin: Houghton, Michigan. Underneath the pin was a tiny bit of text that read, "Shared with one other person." She pressed on the text with her finger and brought up the profile of a dirty looking guy named Bryce Holton.

"Who is that?" Burton asked.

"I don't know," said Anna. "But I'd like to talk to him."

"This was the person you were looking for?"

"Maybe." She opened up Bryce's porting data. He was currently milling around his grimy sales corner near the railroad crossing in Rockville. "I wanna go where he goes."

"Anna," Bamert warned her, "these are dangerous affairs."

Anna swiped over to her mom's old address in Rockville. No one had bought the old house from Sandy and no one ever would. No one wanted old houses out in the free zones anymore, much less one that had played host to a suicide. She queued up the porting history of that address and was greeted by a list of random names: likely squatters and bored real estate hoarders. She scrolled all the way back to August 9, 2029 and saw only three entries listed: Sandy Huff, Anna Huff, and Sarah Huff. No one else.

"That can't be right."

But it was. There was no record of anyone else being in the house the night Sarah died. No pin. No profile. Not even a default avatar. Whoever was in the house that night, whoever killed Sarah Huff, was nothing more than a ghost.

THE CRATER

Anna and Bamert trekked out to The Crater at 5am, the earliest time that students were technically allowed to leave their dorms. She draped the weighted blanket over a branch and ducked under it once more, like a fifth grader reading in the dark. She opened up Network Z and chose a pin on the opposite side of the Harkness Wall, then took a deep breath and steeled herself for the cold as she hit PORT.

But nothing happened. Instead, she was greeted with an error prompt: "Portwall ACTIVE. Please enter user ID and password."

"Shit."

"Anna? You've still got my blanket on you."

She pulled it off. "It doesn't work. Network Z doesn't get us past the wall."

"Ah," said Bamert. He thought about it for a moment and then slapped his hip. "Well then, that's it. We're just gonna have to climb it."

"What? Are you out of your mind? Do you remember what happened to that stupid boy who crashed assembly after climbing the wall?"

"Hell yes, I do. That owned."

"It doesn't own as much when it happens to you," Anna told him.

"Well, *yeah*."

"You're a physicist. You should physicist yourself past the wall some other way."

"Don't you think I've considered that? Physics grants you a miracle once a century, if that. And our century already got its miracle. Every time I try to engineer a way past that thing, I hit a," he looked up, "well, *you know*. Listen, I'd only have to climb it once."

"How do you figure that?"

"Don't you recall the wonderful visit Edgar paid us? He ported right out of that room."

Her eyes widened. "He's a trustee. He's got a password to get past the wall."

166

"And I have a password to get past *his* wall back home. Now tell me that isn't lovely. All I have to do is scale the Harkness Wall, port to the old man's house in Richmond, make sure he's asleep, swipe his phone, unmask his user ID and password, port back, leave his phone exactly as I found it, and port back here again."

"That plan seems completely workable and seamless," Anna told him.

"Stay right here."

"I was being sarcastic."

"Sarcasm is for the unwilling. Stay here."

He sprinted back to Kirkland while Anna stood out in the dark. The first traces of blue morning were creeping in from the East, and she was getting nervous. Overachieving losers would soon be streaming out of the dorms and heading to Main Street for breakfast and early cramming. She heard a rustle nearby and then saw a beam from a flashlight probing around.

The dreaded Wade. His bulky shadow preceded him.

Technically, Anna was allowed to be out here right now, but it didn't *feel* legal. Wade would have questions. Frantic, she flopped to the ground, covered herself with the blanket, then frantically hand-raked a pile of leaves and pinecone grubs on top of the blanket to camouflage herself.

Wade drew closer. She had no idea if she had hidden herself well. The small pocket of air under the weighted blanket took on her body heat, and now Anna Huff had the privilege of living inside her own little sweat lodge.

This is probably what being in a coffin is like. Oh god.

The footsteps came closer, gradually faded, and then gradually came closer once more, stopping right by Anna. Footsteps were the worst. It was nicer to live in a world where they remained an anachronism. Someone grabbed the blanket and whipped it off. Her chest cramped up as she stifled a scream.

It was Bamert. He was holding two Army blankets and a pair of box cutters.

"Let's get cutting."

"I'm not staying out here another minute."

167

"You mean I gotta bring all this back?"

She did. They punted on the morning's effort and schlepped to class. That night, Anna sat in her room with one of the army blankets and a box cutter, hacking away at the thick green canvas. Lots of sweating. Lots of hand cramps. Asmi caught her slaving away.

"Ooh, a box cutter! Can I play with it?"

"No."

"Do you need to glue any of those strips together? I have extra."

"No."

The next day was a Saturday. Bamert and Anna were back at the wall at 9pm that night, both of them carrying a knotted ribbon of shredded canvas. They joined the ribbons together and the makeshift rope stretched out to twenty-five feet. Bamert walked over to a sturdy pine tree that towered above the wall. He gave it a hearty shake and got showered in old brown needles. He wasn't in a suit this morning, opting instead to climb in school-issued grays from the gym equipment room. He was barely recognizable, right up to the moment he took out a tin of Kodiak and stuffed his beard with a fat dip. The smell of menthol and tree rot permeated the whole forest.

"And you ready for this?" Bamert asked Anna.

"I'm not the one who's gonna die."

"Remember me if I do."

"Are you in shape to do this?"

"How dare you. Never ask a Southern boy if he can climb a tree."

Bamert tied the rope around his waist, pocketed their phone, and started up the pine. For such a large boy, he was shockingly nimble, slithering his way through the gauntlet of sticky branches and live needles. When he reached the top, he grabbed onto the wall with both hands.

Now Bamert was hanging off the side of the wall. Anna backed away to make sure he didn't fall directly on her. No sense in *both* of them dying. He swung a gamey leg over the masonry and tied a highwayman's hitch around the posting. Anna watched as he performed a series of elaborate moves to safety re-wrap the rope around his own body.

With the rope secure, Bamert tucked his hand firmly against his butt and gave Anna a thumbs up before rappelling down the other side. She watched as the knotted canvas struggled against the posting, dying to be free of it. After a moment passed, the rope went slack and slipped off its mooring. Bamert was either past the wall or dead. The BANG she heard from the other side didn't do much to relieve her apprehension.

For five agonizing minutes, Bamert was MIA. Anna held her right hand up to the moon and cupped it in her palm. Suddenly, there was a fresh gust and there he was, bursting into laughter. There were still pine needles stuck in his beard.

"WOOO! That was *cold*! The user name is BigBam2020 and the password is *parfive*, with the number spelled out." He handed Anna their PortPhone. "Your turn."

"Just like that?"

"Just like that."

"But how'd you get the password?"

"Edgar was in the shower. A ghastly sight. Anyway, the nice thing about old people is they never remember their passwords, so they never use them. Where are you gonna go?"

"I dunno," Anna said. "I need a test pin. Somewhere quiet and deserted. Someplace where no one would ever bother to port, so that I can go in and out without anyone laying eyes on me."

"Aha!" Bamert cried. "I have just the place for that."

CLEVELAND

Anna reappeared in the middle of what remained of downtown Cleveland. Cars, a few of them occupied by the destitute, sat forever idle in the middle of Sixth Street. Skyscrapers lay empty and rotting in the dark. Half the streetlamps were toppled and not one of them was illuminated. The nearby Browns stadium was packed with bad memories and little else. This was a squatter's paradise now, with orphaned office buildings home to small hordes of porters from South Asia and Africa who were searching for temporary shelter from both the elements and from any PINE agents that might roll by.

She was out of Druskin. Free. She reached into her pocket and pulled out a small, lacquered bulldog made from crushed pecan shells. She had stolen it just the day before, sneaking into Vick's office and hiding in his closet just because she could, watching him come in and tend to his evildoing. In the dark, she practiced her piano tutorials for the week, tapping out each key in midair and hearing the notes peal out in her mind as clearly as if she heard a hammer striking a string. She made shadow puppets despite having scant light to cast them. She weaved her hands into a dragon and turned the dragon on herself, watching as it let out breaths of invisible flame. After Vick left for his house, she slipped out of the closet, swiped the little bulldog off his desk, and went on her merry way.

Anna's grandma Eileen always said she had "ten busy little fingers," because Anna would touch everything, examine everything, *break* everything with comical regularity. She could think with those fingers, see with them, remember with them. When Anna was much younger, Sarah taught her how to play blackjack, and what Anna loved far more than memorizing the basic strategy chart (which took her all of a minute) was shuffling the cards, growing addicted to the feel of the glossy card stock. No games. No magic tricks. The physical satisfaction of riffling those cards was all Anna needed. How could something so cheap be so perfect? Sandy had to confiscate her deck, she was so tired of hearing cards flapping at all hours.

Now Anna was in Cleveland for no good reason, but she took a moment to open the camera on Chester Bumlee's PortPhone. She ported over to the waterfront and put the bulldog on top of the script CLEVELAND sign overlooking Lake Erie. Against all reason, she liked it here. It was a peaceful little ghost city. Nothing but dark parts.

She opened up Network Z and typed LARA KIRSCH into the search bar, without any nosy boys looking over her shoulder.

You could port to her right now. She'd be fucking blown away by that.

The search results came up empty. As far as Network Z knew, Lara Kirsch didn't exist. *Huh.* But it only took Anna Huff a moment to shrug it off. Lara Kirsch was the daughter of a trillionaire. It stood to reason that PortSys protected her privacy in ways it would never do for common folk.

No matter. Anna would still find her. She needed a plan to find Lara as breathtakingly reckless and stupid as the plan she and Bamert devised to get out of Druskin. Oh, and she had to avenge her sister's death. It was a lot, as far as intramural activities went.

She ported to Vancouver and bought Bamert a PortPhone.

KEWARRA BEACH

Anna ported back to Druskin with an extra phone and Bamert set up a dummy Boola account for Chester Bumlee's daughter, Sarah. The company allowed for up to five of the elder Bumlee's contacts and/or employees to have access to their benefits. Thus, Sarah Bumlee was granted special privileges to Network Z.

They got under the weighted blanket together.

"Where to now?" Anna asked Bamert.

"You're letting me pick?"

"You climbed over the wall. It's only fair."

Bamert took out his phone and zeroed in on Cairns, Australia. Kewarra Beach was, for the moment, miraculously unmolested by the swarms of blue dots roaming across hemispheres. Here was the nefarious gift of Network Z to Anna, who hated crowds but always managed to port directly into places crammed with them marring the view, milling about, putting down lightweight sleeping bags anywhere they pleased, challenging strangers to pickup soccer games, and taking up precious space without cause. She could dodge all that now, even if empty spaces in 2030 never felt truly empty. Invisible hordes were always waiting on the periphery.

Bamert toggled to the CONFLICT layer of the map and it showed zero combat alerts. Another small miracle. The weather layer was clear, as was the ground hazards layer. He sent the pin to Anna. They locked eyes as they hit PORT, feeling the shiver as they stepped forward in unison.

The sunlight gave them a hard slap the second they appeared on the Aussie coast, but Bamert was unfazed. He shed his gray shirt to reveal a torso mossed in curly black hair, then took off his shoes and closed his eyes as he dug his toes into the sand. He groaned with pleasure, like someone had just fed him a hunk of steamed lobster.

"Oh, Anna Huff, this is what life should always feel like."

"We should go back to school soon. It's gonna be lights out."

"We just got here! Give me a moment, please. Let me have this."

A man walked by with an ice-cold rack of beer strapped to his shoulders and Bamert ran at the poor vendor like he was about to tackle him.

"YOU!"

He threw cash at the beer man and plunged a mighty hand down into the crushed ice for two cans of Tropics Lager, then he ran back and offered Anna one.

"I don't drink," she told him.

"More for me, then." He sat down on the beach and worked his toes down into the cooler layers of sand, kneading the grains and shaping them into tiny dunes. "Come on. Sit for a moment."

Anna slipped off her mary janes and plunked down next to Bamert. Small gusts of sand kicked up whenever other port tourists came popping in and out, but that did little to spoil the vista before them: the beach curling along Palm Cove, palm trees shooting clean out of the sand like tiki torches. The Aussie government enforced a No Posting law at this beach, which left it pristine compared to other global destinations that had become littered with obnoxious flyers and billboards. A nearby Malaysian tourist stood by the water, taking dozens of selfie-stick pictures and making a different facial expression in each one. A fat little 11-year-old waded out into the surf with a rented kayak, and then fell into the water every time he tried to get into it. It was hard to tell whether the boy was more unsteady than the kayak or vice versa. In the distance, they spotted a twentysomething parasailing high above the Coral Sea. Bamert stared at the woman in midair and shook his head.

"Now that I don't care for."

"Why?" asked Anna. "She's just parasailing."

"I don't care for it. Too high over water."

"What is it with you and heights over water?"

"Oh it's a long story. And I hate long stories."

"You must hate Nolan's assignments then."

"That I do." He chugged the first beer and let out a mighty AHHHH, like he was in a commercial. "This beer I hate far less."

The palms bent toward the sunlight radiating off the pink sea and Anna did as the treetops did, pulling her knees to her chest and leaning into the warm, happy light.

"We shouldn't abuse these phones," she told Bamert. "We need some kind of rule to make sure we don't do this too often."

"I agree. We'll only do it every day, all the time."

"I'm serious. I honestly don't wanna get kicked out."

"I suppose I don't either," Bamert said. "What are your parameters?"

"Well, we don't tell anyone except Burton."

"Duh."

"And we only port at night on weekends, or at 5am on weekdays."

"You're wounding me with these 5am wakeup times, Anna Huff. The other night I had to stay up late to study after our little sojourn and I hallucinated. A pig appeared in my room and asked me if I had a cigarette."

"I've been in your dorm. That probably actually happened. But look, the only way we can do this is by setting some limits on how much we do it."

Bamert let out a sigh and extended a giant hand. His palm was cold from fresh beer can sweat. "Deal."

Anna took out Vick's bulldog and snapped a candid of it resting on the beach. Their small moment of peace was interrupted when a man ported in directly in front of them, his arrival blowing sand into their faces. He wasted no time going into an elevator pitch.

"ARE YOU MR. CHESTER BUMLEE?" the man shouted. "IF SO I HAVE AN INCREDIBLE OFFER FOR YOU."

"Go away," Anna told him. "You see the No Posting sign, fucko?"

"I think you'll find that this offer is worth your time!"

"If you don't go away right now, I'll kick your ass."

The man didn't like that very much. He opened up his sport coat to reveal a loaded Glock tucked into his waistband. Anna's feelings about Druskin were conflicted at best, but at least there weren't any guns there. She did not miss all the big stupid guns, or all the pushy assholes porting from place to place and brandishing weaponry to make sure they got an audience.

"That was very rude, Ms. Bumlee."

For another five minutes this aggro port spammer held them hostage with vague offers of "market-based solutions" until someone nearby screamed out "CROC!" and the beach cleared to accommodate a 20-foot long saltwater beast that had arrived at Kewarra Beach the old-fashioned way. It moseyed along the sands with dead eyes and an open, neolithic jaw.

The port salesman had no choice but to cut his pitch short and bang out as crassly as he had arrived. Bamert and Anna ported back to Druskin. When Anna went to clean up in the Sewell bathroom, she still had grains of gleaming white sand pooled in her socks. She shook them out in the shower with a knowing smile before looking in the mirror and having her mood turn sour. Twenty minutes in Australia had been long enough to turn her face as red as a rum punch. As soon as she had discovered a way to port out of Druskin, she had managed to ruin it.

Anna Huff had herself a sunburn.

SHIT MEMOIRS ENTRY
Date unknown

Hey you people,

If you wanna know what happened the night Lara Kirsch left Druskin, you come talk to me about it. I'll tell you whatever you want to know, and I'll tell you what Dean Vick does with girls who displease him.

I didn't rat anyone out. And if you think I did, ask yourself why I got in trouble and Jubilee never did.

¯_(ツ)_/¯

SEWELL HALL

"Anna!"

It was Asmi running in from the larger bedroom. Anna was all the way under her comforter, but Asmi wasn't having it. She sat down next to the big lump on the mattress and began shaking it.

"UP UP UP. Anna, you have to wake up!"

"Says who?" she asked, still buried beneath her covers.

"Says *me*. When you guys told my dad to move his trucks from his usual corners, his sales doubled in ONE night! How in the great fuck did you know where he should put them?"

"I dunno. That rules, but I'm still sleeping in."

"Oh come on, let me take you to the Druskin Inn to celebrate! If we get there before the crew team does, they might even have some bacon left."

Asmi tried to pull Anna's comforter away. Anna gripped it like a mother hawk.

"I can't. I'm sick."

"You muppet. Quit playing around." Asmi grabbed the corner of the duvet and gave it a hard tug. Anna screamed loud enough for the whole dorm to hear as Asmi stared at her roommate's lobster-red face, now fully exposed.

"What the—"

"I told you I was sick!" Anna said.

"Fucking nonsense. You been on holiday?"

"Asmi, you're the greatest, but I can't talk about it."

Just then, an enraged Jubilee exploded into the room and pointed her finger at Anna. Something about those angry fingers always got to her, more than any verbal abuse ever could.

"YOU BITCH!" Jubilee screamed.

Asmi stood up and planted herself between Jubilee and Anna. She was a good four inches taller than her blonde dorm-mate.

"What do you want?" she asked Jubilee.

"Get out of my way."

"Pardon? This is our room and I don't recall inviting you in. Can't you see my roommate is gravely ill? Look at her! She's appallingly red! Her temperature is 103! This room has microbes in

177

it the size of gorillas! She needs rest, and certainly she doesn't need the stress of answering to some bouncy twat like you!"

Jubilee stepped back. Asmi put her hands on her waist and cocked a hip.

"Piss off." Asmi told her. "Piss off or I'll pitch you down the fucking stairwell." She held up her fist and pointed to an ornate spoon ring wrapped around her middle finger. The grooves in the ring were encrusted in black gunk. "You see this shit in my ring? That's old blood. From a boy. If I can make a geezer bleed, I can do much worse to a two-bit slag like you, *Judy*."

"It's Jubilee."

"I'll call you what I please and there's fuck all you can do about it."

"All right," Jubilee said, slowly backing into the big room but giving Anna one last jab. "But you, Anna Huff: you're a fucking rat dyke. And everyone knows it."

"Jubes," Anna told her, "You have no idea how big my mouth can get."

"BITCH."

Jubilee stormed out. Asmi locked the door and leapt back onto Anna's bed. Anna thought Asmi was about to strangle her. The way that girl told off Jubilee, it was clear that she wasn't shy when it came to kicking off violence.

But now, Asmi flashed a devilish grin. "You! What *have* you been up to?"

"I can tell you some of it but not all of it."

"Can you tell me why you're sunburned?"

"No."

"Whatever. Give a shit. So tell me then why Juniper—"

"It's Jubilee. Please don't get her idiotic name wrong."

"Jumper Cables. Whatever. Naff piece of shit that one is. Spill it. What's tickling her ass about you?"

So Anna told her about Lara, and their night out on the bridge, and the dastardly security guard, and the visits to Vick's basement. She left out the small detail of how she truly felt about Asmi's predecessor. Maybe everyone already knew, but she didn't wanna know if they did.

"Oh my god, Vick! The fucking gall of that man. Shouldn't you go to the trustees? The police?"

"I don't think so," said Anna.

"Well, I promise I won't tell a soul."

"Actually, tell everyone. Paint it on the Academy Building for all I care."

"You don't mean that."

"Yes, I do. If people are gonna talk shit about me, I'd at least like them to get the facts straight. And no one's gonna believe it if it's coming from me. Better they hear it secondhand. Just don't tell anyone I managed to get sunburned in October."

"Fair enough. I can tell Mrs. Ludwig you're ill, but I can keep it vague, so she doesn't send you to the infirmary. You really could pass off as feverish if you tried, love." She put the back of her hand to Anna's forehead and Anna flinched in pain.

"GAHHHHHHH!"

"Oh. Right. Sorry about that."

"I think I need aloe. And maybe that bacon you mentioned."

"I can get you both of those things, but first…"

Asmi walked back into her bedroom and grabbed a small gold pocketbook. She took out a crisp hundred and laid it on top of the comforter.

"What is that?" asked Anna.

"That's your cut from last night. I figured you could use it in advance. My dad left it at the Gate. Says there's gonna be a lot more where that came from."

Mom

You didn't come to the gate again

I know. I'm sick

Are you in the infirmary

No just in bed

I should call the nurse

Do NOT do that. If you do that I swear I will murder you

Anna.

Mom.

Why didn't you just tell me you were sick

I'm sorry

I know said you didn't have to come to the gate if you didn't want to but I miss you

I'll come to the gate next time, I swear. Actually, maybe I'll just come visit you in dc

Very funny

How are you

I'm so tired. Working in dc all night, then porting over to Hong Kong for more work all thru another night. I haven't been outside in a week

Take a break

They don't give me more work if I do that

Ugh

Ugh. Anything else you wanna talk about?

I think I can find Sarah's killer

Mom?

I don't wanna talk about this over text

Armenian Separatist Leader Denies Group's Role In Austin Massacre
AP
10/10/2030

(YEREVAN, ARMENIA) — Serj Magulian, publicly identified by PINE officials as the leader of terrorist group Black Shard, has again equivocally denied playing any role in a 2024 mass shooting in Austin, Texas, that left over 500 people killed.

"We do not claim responsibility for that attack," Magulian said in a video released on his official WorldGram this morning. "U.S. officials have not produced one shred of evidence that our people were involved in this unholy massacre. If you watch the video of the events on October 5th of that year, you will see that the gunmen's faces are completely covered by masks. We do not do this. We are proud to show our faces because we are proud to be Armenian."

Magulian has long been the leader of the "Guardians of Ararat," an Armenian nationalist group dedicated to maintaining the Armenian border in the wake of, in his words, "port colonization," and to lobbying the government of Turkey to recognize the Armenian Genocide of 1915, something that Turkish President Kemal Uskudar has steadfastly refused to do. U.S. officials claim that the Guardians of Ararat are a political front and that Magulian's real intention is to coordinate terrorist attacks under the banner of Black Shard.

"I have a problem with America, it is true," says Magulian in the video. "They won't recognize the horrors inflicted upon our people. They invented porting, which kills the soul. We are flesh and bone. We are not data. And yet Americans want us all to reduce ourselves to mere files, to be sent around here and there and everywhere. They think everyone should be able to port where they please. This is *our* land. Barbarians have attempted to wrest it from us and kill us all, and yet here we remain. No matter what new technologies they invent to try to steal our land away from us, and no matter how docile our current government remains in the face of these threats, we remain.

"No place can be special without its people, and we're not going anywhere. Like the Chinese and the Israelis, we are borderists. The Guardians of Ararat will defend Armenia's proper boundaries at all costs, but we are NOT murderers. Robb Caraway calls us Black Shard? There is no Black Shard. What does this name even mean? They say we are Muslims. Our group is not affiliated with any religion. I myself am a Christian man. This is all made up to scare dumb Americans. It is fantasy. There are only the Guardians of Ararat, and we were born to defend ourselves, not to attack."

Magulian says that his group could not have ported to Texas because he and his members have taken a consecrated oath to never port, nor to ever venture outside their defined border of Armenia, which occupies a greater landmass than the officially recognized borders and includes the officially Turkish area around Mount Ararat, the fabled resting place of Noah's Ark.

Regardless, U.S. officials immediately condemned the video, dismissing it as extremist propaganda and reasserting that Black Shard does, in fact, exist.

"If you watch the whole video of Magulian's tirade," says State Department spokeswoman Sarah Strong, "you will see that he contradicts himself by promising to hunt down executives of PortSys, including the entire Kirsch family, and 'drowning them in their own blood.' And if Black Shard doesn't exist, then why are militiamen wearing Black Shard emblems porting around the globe and opening fire on people at random? There's ample evidence of that." Indeed, one such gunman named Aren Vulcanyan was detained by PINE agents after gunning down three tourists in Palm Beach, Florida, and proudly swore loyalty to "General Magulian and the holy struggle of Black Shard" in his written confession.

Magulian denies having any association with Vulcanyan, and remains adamant that the existence Black Shard is a fabrication. In the full video, Magulian propagates a theory some have dismissed as "truthering" that U.S. Officials conspired with PortSys to stage the Austin attack as a way of frightening the masses into submission.

"If you want to find the true murderers, look to the vipers in your own midst," he warns in the video. "For if you do not cut out their hearts, we are surely prepared to."

HOUGHTON, MI

Anna didn't want to port to Michigan alone and unarmed. She enlisted Bamert to be her muscle. In true Bamert fashion, he embraced the job with gusto, borrowing a varsity Druskin Football jacket from Matt Raidl down the hall in exchange for a six-pack of smuggled Molson Ice. For security, he ported back to Virginia and grabbed a light handgun from his old man's arsenal. Edgar Bamert owned so many guns that he had an entire subsection of the basement remodeled to house them. Bamert offered to grab a gun for Anna too, but she politely declined.

She missed nearly a full week of classes. Her skin was peeling off in wide flakes. She snuck into to the bathroom twice a day, making sure it was deserted before entering, and then sloughed her face raw with a sweet-smelling apricot scrub, destroying as much physical evidence of her time on that pristine Aussie beach as she possibly could. Asmi covered for her by taking notes in the chemistry and ethics classes they shared, and bringing her paper trays from the dining hall piled high with cold, chopped fruit.

Anna followed along with the class syllabi online, sequestering herself in bed and plowing through one unreadable book after another. For Nolan, she typed out rote papers in the largest font and spacing she thought she could get away with, following the time-honored format of quoting the book, writing a little about that quote, quoting the book again when she couldn't think of anything else to say, and repeating the cycle until finally nailing the page requirement.

By Saturday, her sunburn had cooled off for good. At 5am that morning, Bryce Holton's blue dot showed him loitering around the Lake Superior canal. Anna and Bamert assumed their usual positions near The Crater and got under the weighted blanket. By now, Bamert had slept with the cover so much that it had taken on all of his personal attributes: the feet, the meat, the sweat, even a trace of stale urine.

"You know," Anna told him. "There is a laundry service at this school."

"They lost one of my suits last week," he complained.

"You have a hundred suits."

"Only one that's teal with bananas on it, though. The cleaners are dead to me. I won't let them touch Moby Dick."

"You named the blanket Moby Dick?"

"Yes, and do you know why?"

"Why?"

"Because it's *heavy*, man."

Bamert laughed at his joke so loudly that Anna hit PORT before he did to leave him behind. When she emerged in Houghton, it was colder than the wormhole. She was on a bike path right beside the Michigan Tech campus, along the canal. In the distance, a massive vertical-lift bridge opened up to let an icebreaker pass through. In the predawn darkness, the rising lights of the bridge made it look like a flying saucer was lifting away from the Earth before jumping to light speed and zooming back home. Jupiter, that great ball of violent sky, hovered far above the canal.

You know it rains neon on Jupiter, don't you? Wouldn't that be gorgeous to see?

Oh, to leave this planet and leave it fast. Anna was certain there was intelligent life out there, and that it was better than life here. PortSys claimed they hadn't yet engineered a way to safely send yourself away from the Earth's surface, but maybe that was a lie. Maybe they already knew how to pull it off, but wanted the Earth spent before introducing that particular option exclusively to their most elite customers. Lara would be one of those customers. Lara would need a trusted shipmate to keep her company on that long, quiet voyage across the cosmos.

Bryce was standing on the canal and spotted Anna right away. He pulled out a gun. Bamert popped in right beside Anna, his timing once again faulty.

"Okay that's very funny," Bamert said to Anna. "But don't—"

"Paul."

Anna nodded toward Bryce.

Bamert cocked his eyebrows. "Ah."

"Who the hell are you two?" Bryce asked. He was drunk.

"Are you Bryce Holton?" Anna asked.

"None of your business." He took out his PortPhone.

"There's no point," Anna told him. "We know where you go."

"My ass, you do."

He hit PORT.

ROCKVILLE, MD

They tracked Bryce to the corner of Nebel Street and Randolph Road, porting onto a strip of unkempt grass tucked between a row of shabby auto mechanic shops and the train tracks. Bamert had his own gun drawn this time. He tucked his chin into his neck to finish off the intimidating football player look. Bryce reached out with his own gun like he wanted to slap them with it.

"I don't want any of the crap you're selling," he shouted at them.

"Sarah Huff," Anna said. "Do you remember a girl named Sarah Huff?"

"No."

Anna showed him Sarah's photo. "She looks like me, but older. And prettier."

Bryce cautiously walked forward to get a better look at the screen. "Ehhhhh, could be a lot of customers I've met."

"She was with you in Houghton on the day she died. August of last year. Did she buy something from you?"

"Are you guys cops?"

"We're high school students, sir," Bamert told him.

Bryce lowered his gun and Bamert did likewise. He squinted at the photo of Sarah and nodded reluctantly. "Yeah, all right. I remember her."

"What did she buy from you?" Anna asked him.

"I don't remember."

"Don't lie. I fucking hate liars."

Bryce took hit off a vape pen. "She bought a .22."

"Why?"

"I dunno, some asshole was stalking her."

"Do you know who?"

"What am I, her goddamn bestie? Look man, I'm just a dude out in the free zones selling shit to people who need it. Your girl bought a gun, a couple bullets, and that was that. It was a zit on my day."

"Did you know someone killed her with that gun?" Anna told him.

"So what? People get got all the time. Doesn't make a difference to me."

"Watch it."

"*You* watch it. Watch me port to the desert and open fire the second I feel a stiff wind. No one's gonna give a shit about another pair of deadass teenagers."

Bamert put his hands up as a gesture of peace. "We've stumbled out of the gate, it seems. We're not here to harass you."

"Speak for yourself," Anna said. "I'm gonna follow this guy around and throw a dildo at him everywhere he goes."

"Hush up, you," Bamert told her. The only thing Bamert had ever learned from his years observing his old man, apart from how to mix a Cuba Libre, was how to charm people using fluent business-ese. "In fact, Mister Holton, I would love to make a purchase of your fine, sticky wares if I might." He pulled out a fifty-dollar bill. "Personally, I don't smoke weed. It makes me believe I'm fireproof, which I am not. But I might know a fertile market for your product, one to which you would have *exclusive* access as long as we do business together."

"Bamert."

"Anna, he has already given us information out of the goodness of his heart. It's only fair we offer something in return. Isn't that right, Bryce?"

"You're full of shit," Bryce said.

"I'm not. You see this jacket?"

"I'm not impressed."

"Nor should you be. It's not even mine." He pointed to the great *D* on his breast. "But this school, Druskin, is protected by a portwall that you would shit hot knives to get past. Because there are many angsty teens past that wall in need of your contraband services."

"Weed?" Bryce asked him.

"Weed, vape carts, booze, molly, Adderall, *especially* Adderall. Tell me that's not worth something. Tell me that isn't worth regaling us with every last possible detail you know about Sarah Huff."

"I told you, man. I only sold to her once. She said a guy was harassing her, and she said that no matter where she ported, he could find her. He could get past even good portwalls, like whatever your dipshit prep school's got."

Bamert held out the fifty and Bryce stared it down. He took out a prescription bottle with a small nugget of weed resting inside.

"This is sativa," Bryce told them. "The pure stuff. They don't even spray it for bugs. Pass that around and see what the little rich kids think. And I got carts of the same shit that can last kids months. But if you come to my pin again, you better text me beforehand, or I'll put you the fuck down."

Bryce ported out and left them standing among a tangle of uprooted cement parking stoppers, the rebar sticking out of them like broken bones. A mighty CSX train came roaring down the track: a set of four linked locomotives pulling over 100 hydrogen tanks behind them. When the train cleared and continued on its way to Illinois, Bamert exulted in his purchase, taking a heavy whiff of the weed nugget.

"That's good and stanky. We can sell this for triple on campus, darling."

"You just made a deal with the guy who helped kill my sister."

"You're right. We should have chased him around the world and then gotten shot. That would have been highly productive."

"Screw you, Bamert."

She walked closer to the tracks and sat down in the dying zoysia. *She said that no matter where she ported, he could find her.*

The sun was knocking but that didn't make this part of Rockville any warmer, nor any prettier. People had left this stretch for dead long before porting came along. A couple of stray dogs ran by, their tags jingling frenetically as they searched for owners who had abandoned them in favor of roaming the world as yuppie Newmads. Across the tracks there was a rusted, empty playground, the ambient winds nudging the swings back and forth. Anna wanted to swing on those swings with Lara, and she didn't know why. Just two girls in love, swinging merrily in the predawn moonlight.

Bamert walked over and sat down next to Anna, patting her on the shoulder with his big wet paw.

"You all right?" he asked her.

"We used to live near here. Over in Garrett Park. We had a real house. It wasn't very big, and I remember hating it. My parents never talked to each other. I guess they stayed together for our sake, but it didn't help much. Anyway, that's where Sarah died."

"I'm sorry, Anna."

"Yeah, I know you are. Everyone is when I tell them."

"Did you and your mom get counseling or anything?"

"We couldn't afford it. We couldn't afford a burial either. We donated her body to a Bethesda hospital and they forgot to return the ashes to us."

"Judas Priest."

"We had a memorial and no one came, not even my old man. I try to remember my favorite times with Sarah and sometimes I feel like I mix the places up. My life has no chapters to it, Bamert."

"Druskin is a chapter of your life."

"Yeah well, it's a lousy one," she told him. "Maybe that's why I look back on that lousy house so fondly. I don't even like it, but at least I know that part of my life was *real*, you know? I had a home once. A real home. Sometimes I worry maybe that was the best I'll do."

"I don't believe that."

"The worst part is that my mom couldn't sell our house. She had to default on the loan. So now, she's slaving away in these kitchens, chasing working hours, and all the money goes to some asshole bank, or to ShareSpace so she can bunk up with a bunch of randos."

"We can give her the money from the kebab trucks, plus maybe whatever we sell off of Bryce."

"I'm not giving Bryce Holton another dime of my money, and I'm not gonna become some bootlegger for the rest of Druskin. Vick would snuff us out within a week."

"The truck money, then," Bamert suggested.

"We might need that for something else, seeing as how Edgar says you're cut off again."

"What did you have in mind?"

"You Bamerts wouldn't happen to be members of MyClub, would you?"

"Goodness yes, we are. You should see me at the omelet station on Sunday mornings. I am a tank."

"How much is a guest fee?" Anna asked.

"$500 for the day."

"A little bit more kebab van money, and we should have enough for that."

Anna's PortPhone buzzed. She touched the screen and there was a News Alert for Lara that read: "PortSys Heiress Wilding Out In Fiji!" Bamert laughed and Anna got angry at him all over again. She wished he had a suit on so she that could strangle him with his own tie.

"Oh come on," he said. "I'm not laughing at you. I think it's adorable."

"That's just what people who are heartsick wanna hear. That they're *adorable*. Pretty much the ideal reaction."

"And where is our girl right now?" Bamert asked.

"The South Pacific."

"I bet she'll wrangle an especially lame WorldGram out of that trip."

"Stop it," Anna said.

"Oh come on, you have to confess: it's kinda lame. I clicked on her feed and it was nothing but hats and ads."

"Let her live."

"Why? She bailed on school and left you to twist."

"I don't wanna hear it. The best thing that's happened to me since that day is falling in love with her. I think about Lara and I'm happy, Bamert. I can feel joy right there beside me."

He rubbed her back in penitence. "You're right. You're right. Love's a marvel, isn't it?"

It was. God, it was. It was a stubborn thing, this love. Needy. But the moment Anna felt it, she knew she wanted be in love for the rest of her life. Life before love was just a dress rehearsal. "I love her, Bamert. I have to find her."

"Maybe she's with Emilia Dearest. You could search for her mammy."

"I don't want to do that. Emilia'll know someone is looking for her."

"Yes, and what a profound shock that would be to her system. I can't think of anyone else looking for Emilia Kirsch, except for Presidents, and dictators, and angry customers, and exploited laborers, and the family of that kid who died on Everest, and the Guardians of Ararat, and the Israeli Defense Forces."

"Ugh, fine. You're deeply annoying this morning."

"Look how early I had to get up! You are not getting optimal Bamert here, and that's a detriment to us *all*."

She put her finger on the search bar and typed in EMILIA KIRSCH. Nothing came up. Kirsch was porting around wherever she pleased. But, as with Lara, PortSys had rendered her invisible.

FORMAL LAUNCH OF THE PORTPHONE 9P
Partial Transcript
Presentation date: 11/01/30
Keynote Speaker: Jason Kirsch

[applause]

JASON KIRSCH: Thank you! What a day. What an audience. Are you guys ready for a great day?

[applause]

JASON KIRSCH: That's a shame, because I have nothing for you.

[laughter]

JASON KIRSCH: Okay, I might be kidding. My name is Jason Kirsch, and I am the Chief Creative Officer here at PortSys.

[applause]

JASON KIRSCH: My mother, Emilia—who I think is not only the most important innovator of this century but also the most important *person* of this century, full stop—once said to me, "Jason, it's not about what our products do, it's about how they make people *feel*." And that's been our North Star since our inception. *We* reintroduced the world to itself. *We* rendered horizons obsolete. *We* pulled the world out of the New Depression. *We* made it possible for Ian Berenson to rebuild the original World Trade Center twin towers in Dubai, to give new life and hope to those who lost their loved ones on that terrible day.

[applause]

JASON KIRSCH: But while we take pride in our genealogy of PortPhones, from the One to the Eight, we know that they are the

193

means and not the end. A PortPhone doesn't leave you breathless, the way the majesty of the Grand Tetons will. It's not your mother smiling as she welcomes you into her dining room at Thanksgiving. It's not the incredible rush you feel gazing out from the Kirsch viewing platforms installed off the Antarctic Peninsula, where, I would just like to note, global sea ice thickness this year increased for the first time since *1979*.

[applause]

JASON KIRSCH: Thank you, thank you. Is that awesome or what? So while I personally find our phones beautiful, elegant—even a touch mischievous—I know they are merely a conduit to the things and places and people that make us feel joy, or wonder, or perhaps a touch of danger. It's not just porting that saved us from climate change by ending our addiction to fossil fuels and allowing us to resurrect the oceans with iron fertilization. No no. It's that porting allowed us all to gain a greater appreciation for this massive, strange, wonderful planet we call home. It made everyone on every continent *want* to save the world. Why? Because we could finally *see* all of it with our own eyes. We saw what was ours, and felt an instinctive need to protect it.

[applause]

JASON KIRSCH: That's why I'm so excited to be here today. Because you see, when my amazing team and I set out to design a new product, we're not just satisfied to add on bells and whistles. We don't update the blueprint. *We throw it out*.

[applause]

JASON KIRSCH: Earlier this year, I ported with my team to a retreat outside of Kathmandu where we studied the practice of Nyungne: a fasting ritual that fortifies the immune system and brings forth *total mental clarity*. We learned so much about our

194

intentionality in those thirty-six hours, and our time fasting also gave us a renewed focus: the kind of determined visioning the world expects from PortSys. At the end of our fast, we, as a team, personally butchered a long-haired yak and prepared a banquet from its carcass, nose to tail, for our hosts at the Kopan Monastery. Best meal I have ever eaten. I did not port out *once* during that retreat, I'll have you know.

[applause]

JASON KIRSCH: Thank you, thank you. After that incredible feast, we went back to the PortSys lab—and I know a lot of you reporters here today would like a peek inside there—and said to one another, "Starting from scratch, how do we build the perfect product for *today*?" And we did. If our products are truly less about what they do than how they make people feel, I think that you are about to feel a great many things when I show you what I'm about to show you. Because THIS is the PortPhone 9p.

[applause]

JASON KIRSCH: Ooooh, it's blue! Excuse the pun, but that is *cool*. What you're looking at is a galvanized steel casing with a ceramic finish, guaranteed to withstand fluctuations of over 200 degrees without cracking. And thanks to our beautiful, expanding global ice sheets, I doubt you'll have to worry much about such insane temperature changes these days, no matter how far your travels take you. Also, we've reduced porting time by 1/32nd of an angstrom, which doesn't sound like a lot, but I assume we'd all like to spend even less time freezing our butts off in wormholes.

[laughter]

JASON KIRSCH: The camera is entirely new. It can shoot video at a rate of forty-eight frames per second and get this: I'm gonna shoot a movie right now. Are you guys ready for your close-up?

CROWD: YES!

JASON KIRSCH: Good, because I've hit Record. There you all are up on the screen. Looking good, you guys. Now watch this.

[ports a foot away]

[crowd gasps]

JASON KIRSCH: Hey look at that. That movie is *still* recording. Yes, we've engineered continuous video *through* wormholes.

[applause]

JASON KIRSCH: I know a lot of you would still like to see what the inside of a wormhole looks like, as do I. But that we haven't quite cracked that yet. You're just gonna have settle for live, continuous video of your globetrotting efforts. Are you ready for chained port-bys?

CROWD: YES!

JASON KIRSCH: There's more. Now, you might have heard rumors about this, and while I am not usually a big fan of gossip, this time I'm happy to confirm it's true: YOU PLUS TWO is now YOU PLUS THREE.

[gasps]

JASON KIRSCH: Yes. We have engineered a way to increase the spatial orientation of our wormholes across our 9P network, so that porters can accommodate up to *three* extra kilograms of mass. This is one kilogram that is going to change *everything*. Think about what it means to volunteers delivering food to those in need, or to construction workers who won't have to make multiple port trips to bring all his accessories to a work site. Think about what it means to new mothers whose infants may fit in under that threshold. Think about how it will further reduce the traffic burden we place on trucks, ships, and railroads. Think about what it means to a young man who wants to bring extra Valentine's Day gifts to his girlfriend, especially now that there's no such thing as long-distance relationships anymore. That's for better or for worse depending on the couple, I suppose.

[laughter]

JASON KIRSCH: Think about what it means to Doctors Without Borders, who are now *truly* without borders.

AUDIENCE MEMBER: What about guns?

JASON KIRSCH: We at PortSys have always made your security our top priority.

AUDIENCE MEMBER: More people are gonna die because of you! Only people who can afford a decent portwall are gonna be safe! You are inviting more death into our lives!

[boos]

JASON KIRSCH: No no no, let him say what he has to say. I value transparency.

AUDIENCE MEMBER: If you did, you wouldn't sell porting data to hate groups and terrorist organizations!

JASON KIRSCH: Okay, this is not the forum for this. We're gonna have a question-and-answer session on this a week from now during my Jase Dismissed portcast, and that's going to be a better venue for that particular line of inquiry, rather than you causing a disruption here.

AUDIENCE MEMBER: HE'S A FUCKING LIAR! THEY'RE GONNA SELL US ALL! THEY'RE GONNA SELL US ALL TO HELL!!!!

OTHER AUDIENCE MEMBER: You promised all of us a PortWatch last year and never delivered, asshole!

JASON KIRSCH: Security?

ASSEMBLY HALL/DRUSKIN GATE

When Anna emerged from hiding with a properly ashen November complexion, she was amazed to find that other girls in Sewell acknowledged her presence. Some of them even talked to her. Stares that had been rude on her second day of school were now curious, some even a touch sympathetic. When she nailed a back tuck in diving practice, Katie Gray gave her a high five. The dreaded Jubilee still hated Anna with a blazing fury, and the rest of Jubilee's crew gawked at her like she was a lying nutjob, but otherwise she was a now viable human being on the Druskin campus. She wasn't quite sure if she liked it or not.

Halloween came and went with little fanfare, save for another torpid Dunbar Hall mixer. Some of the more enterprising kids walked around dressed up as WorldGram posts, and as PortPhones with screens that actually lit up, and as daredevils like Steve Fryman, who once jumped off the Petronas Towers in Kuala Lumpur and ported, in midair, safely over to the top of the Empire State Building. There were more than a few kids dressed as Lara Kirsch—or "Lara Kush"—complete with pot leaf hairstyles. Every time the fake Laras walked by Anna, she got equal doses of joy and longing.

Out in the free zones, Halloween was always a roiling cauldron of crime and debauchery. Little kids skipped through time zones, chasing dusk to amass candy from every continent (in Antarctica, they doled out Zero bars as a gag), while the adults ported from one shrouded time zone to the next, looking to either terrorize people or fuck them. Sometimes both. The Huffs traditionally made a point of staying in for the night. But this Halloween, Anna could walk campus freely. She dressed as Brendan McClear. Bamert dressed as Burton. Burton dressed as Bamert.

The next morning, during a leisurely roll across the quad, Nolan told Anna that she was getting a C+.

"When you write for this class," he said, "Take it seriously. Tell me how the material makes you feel, and then tell me why I should care."

No more quote-mashup English papers for her. No more big fonts. Nolan began assigning her short stories. Within the work, she discovered writing stories had the power to take her away from Druskin and from herself, mentally porting away to Cinque Terra, to Hans Island above the Arctic Circle, back to Kewarra Beach, and to anywhere else far away. She poured hours into each assignment because they didn't feel like work at all. One of them was a love story between two young women, set in Lily Beach. Her grade in the class skyrocketed.

She didn't port for another two weeks, keeping her secret phone stashed on the top shelf of her closet underneath a buffalo plaid blanket that her mother insisted she take for extra warmth. The blanket looked, smelled, and felt like 1982. She would have rather frozen to death than sleep under that thing.

One Wednesday morning, they streamed into Assembly Hall and were greeted not with the usual guest speaker, but by a very angry Dean Vick, who ordered them to sit down even before it was technically time to sit down.

"Two weeks ago there was pecan bulldog on my desk in my office. That bulldog was purchased for me by my late mother when I was growing up in Georgia, and I have kept it with me in the five decades since. One of *you* took it."

He jabbed his finger out at the crowd. Anna grinned and quaked at the same time.

"Not only did one of you take it, but apparently you thought it would be fun to do this with it."

He queued up the big screen and there was Vick's little bulldog hanging out by an unidentifiable railroad crossing, and out on a tropical Australian beach, and also in the middle of Cleveland for some reason. The kids cheered and Vick shushed them sharply, like he was blowing a poison dart at them. Anna, Burton and Bamert—all self-exiled to the balcony—kept mum.

"I'm sure whoever did this also finds it funny, but they won't be as amused when we track them down. The photos have been scrubbed of metadata but I can assure you that we will find this person, and we will step up night patrols until we do."

When Anna left Assembly that day and trudged over to Goren to get her weekly postcard from Sandy, she saw a small camera mounted right above Vick's door. A roving eye. Its motion detector blinked red as she scooted past.

On a deadly cold Wednesday Night, Anna met Sandy at Druskin Gate. Her mom's fingernails were caked in black grease. Her hair was stringy and thinned out. The guard refused to open the gate despite Anna giving him her best puppy dog eyes (admittedly, she wasn't that great at playing cute), so she and Sandy had to settle for reaching through the wrought iron bars to embrace one another, like a monitored prison visit.

"Mom," Anna said. "Are you all right?"

"I'm fine."

"You don't look like you've slept."

"Ugh." Sandy looked around. She used to hate early winter nights, when it would go dark at 4:30 and you'd be seemingly trapped in night forever and ever. But now she missed this anodyne darkness. The day brought work, the late night brought fear, and there was little rest to be found anywhere in between.

"I'm a mess," she told Anna. "But look at you! My god, you look so *healthy*! It's like you went on vacation!"

"Nope, nope. No vacation," Anna insisted. "I've been here the whole time."

"Well, you wear Druskin well." Sandy was nodding in strained enthusiasm, trying to be peppy but visibly failing.

"Mom, what's wrong?"

"I'm just so happy to see you flourishing. This place is a miracle. You're so safe here."

"Mom," Anna pleaded.

"I can't."

Sandy was gripping the bars to keep from collapsing. Anna wrapped Sandy's hands in her own.

"There was a man who came into our ShareSpace," Sandy confessed.

"Oh no."

"It wasn't me. He didn't get me. There was a woman staying there, and they had broken up, but he still had the password, so he came in with a gun and…" She slid down to the ground, keeping her hands locked around the bars, a silver charm bracelet on her wrist delicately clanging against the iron. Anna slid down with her. Sandy's jaw hung open, but she couldn't summon the energy to scream.

"I used to dream about places," Sandy went on. "But you stop dreaming about them when they're right at your fingertips. When you've seen what I've seen in those places."

"Mom, I love you so much."

"Promise me you won't leave here."

"I won't."

"*Promise* me," Sandy begged her. "And be sincere about it."

"I promise."

"I know you're a clever girl and I know you wanna find whoever made Sarah do what she did. But Anna? I cannot lose you."

"You won't."

"They can heap all the work on me. All the debt. They can force me to port from one crap dishwashing job to the next and I will hold on. I know it doesn't look it, but I swear to you I am as light and strong as bamboo."

"I know you are."

"But if you go looking for Sarah, you'll only be wading back out into this awful *shit*. And you're still my little girl."

"I know, Mom."

Anna slipped the hundred Asmi gave her from her pocket and closed Sandy's fist tight around it.

"What is this?" she asked Anna.

"It's from a friend."

"You don't have to do this."

"Take it and get a single ShareSpace room for the night. Hell, get a SharePod and make it two nights. Get some sleep for once. You're rotting and I can't stick around here playing Happy Schoolgirl if I know you're in this kind of shape."

"You're right."

"I'm gonna take a work-study job at the dining hall."

"*No.* You focus on your classes."

"I can do that and still give you some relief."

"No. No job."

"What if *you* worked here then, Mom?"

"Is that something you *really* want, Anna?"

No. "No."

"I bet you don't."

Sandy stood back up and wiped the tears away from her face. There were light portclaps ringing out from the countryside, but otherwise the night was calm and peaceful. No choppers. No PINE men. Only a few private armed guards on patrol. From nearby came the crisp smell of fireplace smoke piping out of a chimney.

Sandy closed her eyes and took a big whiff. "It's pleasant here," she said. "Almost too pleasant."

"There's a ShareSpace complex in Portsmouth with singles. Treat yourself."

Sandy nodded. "I know. It all sounds so nice, doesn't it? I just wish someone had told me that when people can go anywhere, they ruin everywhere. I wish it was easier to stick to your own business, but no one ever can. At least you can here."

"It's not as easy as it looks."

"No, but you're anchored here. You'll appreciate it more and more as you go along. Druskin will give you what you need. No one wants a small life anymore, but they ought to."

Sandy zapped away, leaving her only remaining daughter with her hands wrapped around the frozen bars of Druskin Gate. One of the guards politely tapped Anna on the shoulder, and she trudged back to Sewell as the first flurries of wintertime came swirling down on her.

THE ACADEMY BUILDING

She wasn't prepared for Ethics class the next day. She hadn't done the reading. Burton was on the other side of the table and gave her a furious topline before Father McDuff came rolling into the room, but she didn't absorb a word of it. Meanwhile, Bamert was fondling his Druskin-issued smartphone under the table, gawking at a recent direct deposit sent to Chester Bumlee's checking account from Asmi's grandfather.

"We have the scratch for the thing," Bamert whispered to Anna.

"I can't go."

"Why not?"

"I can't go anywhere. We can talk about it after class."

"Well, this is heartrending."

"After. Class."

McDuff moseyed in, all seven feet of him. Two kids scooted over to make room for his towering frame at the round table. He smiled wide, straightened his Roman collar, and stretched out his slender arms, long enough for him to shake hands with people from across the room.

"Good morning!" he said. The class dutifully repeated it back to him. "Now, who has thoughts on last night's reading? Anna Huff?"

Oh, come on.

"Anna, what did *you* think of what Marcus Aurelius has to tell us?"

"Um…" She was dead already. "Um" was big red flashing signal to the world that you hadn't done the reading, and that your brain was devoid of working thought. Anything coming after that "um" was destined to be a grand waste of everyone's time.

"Father, I tried to do the reading last night but I was too upset about something."

Father McDuff tented his hands and gave Anna a searching gaze. "Mind if I ask what it was?"

"All right," Anna said. "I met my mom at Druskin Gate last night and she had just watched a man kill his wife in a ShareSpace. I couldn't get that out of my head. It's so messed up and awful out there, and it just makes me feel like nothing matters."

A bare chuckle came from the other side of the table. It was David Farris, a sophomore. He was giggling into his fist and not making much of an effort to hide it.

"What's so funny?" Anna asked him.

"Nothing," David said. "It's just that y'all are spoiled."

"Excuse me? My family has no money."

"I ain't talkin' about money. I'm talkin' about peace. Y'all are spoiled by peace."

"What the hell does that mean?" Anna was gonna lunge across the table and bash his head into the mahogany.

Farris took a deep breath and rolled his shoulders. "It's like this: you act like this kinda stuff is shocking when it's been around you this whole time. It was just hidden from you, that's all. Where were all the wars before porting, huh? They were in the Middle East. They were in Africa. They were in Asia. They were nice and far away, but it ain't like that anymore. War is free now. Violence can go anywhere it likes, and that scares Americans, especially whiteass Americans, to the bone. And war is gonna *stay* free because ain't no profit in peace. Y'all were fine with violence when it was in Syria or somewhere else. Now you see a person get killed next door and you go OH NO THE WORLD IS ENDING! when it's the same shit— sorry, Father—that's been going on everywhere else forever and ever. Y'all didn't have to *see* the ugliness before, so you could just chill out and watch some prestige TV while our boys were over in some country you didn't care about, killing folks you *definitely* didn't care about. So when a bunch of those Black Shard boys—"

"Well actually, Black Shard is a fabrication," Burton cut in.

"When a bunch of those Black Shard boys *or whoever else* come over here and tear it up, everyone freaks out and calls PINE. Then we send a bunch of Army commandos on port raids where they shoot up entire houses safely out of your line of vision. But you oughtta see 'em do it! You oughtta see the body count PINE racks up, and you oughtta see it up close."

"I hate PINE," Anna insisted.

"That ain't the point. The point ain't you. The point is America. Americans don't say shit—sorry, Father."

"Thin ice, son."

"Sorry. Americans don't say nothin' when we got hate groups porting over to Afghanistan and going on shooting sprees. They only kick up a fuss when they gotta port off of South Beach because they heard a gun go off and got freaked out."

"Should you be able to port with a gun, though?" Anna asked him.

"I don't fuck with guns—double triple super sorry, Father. They gotta sort out the gun stuff. All I'm saying is that white folks were a whole lot cooler with violence when they knew where it was gonna be at."

Asmi, who had come in late and grabbed a seat next to Farris, began to subtly nod. There was a weight in her eyes that Anna had never seen before, and she knew in an instant that Asmi's usual feistiness existed to beat back a very old, earned sadness.

"He's right," she told Anna.

He may be right but he still sucks. This is what you get for not doing the reading.

"I guess you're both right," Anna admitted. "But David doesn't have to be so smug about it. I was just sad a woman was murdered."

"Well yeah!" said Farris. "It's sad as hell! I ain't tryin' to downplay that. I'm just sayin' that I see folks out in the free zones all the time with sadass faces, actin' like the world is ending because they saw something awful that they used to be protected from. They're like 'oh, nothing matters,' and 'oh, this world sucks,' and blah blah blah. Sister, you can port to Tahiti! I say that's worth making people a little more fearful and uncomfortable than they used to be. And these rich scumbags who use portwalls to keep people off of beaches and clubs and bigass country properties? I say *screw* those people. They deserve more danger, too. They deserve to have the world see *them* doing their horrible shit. I say we break in and swipe some of the Dom Perignon bottles out of their fridge."

"They deserve to have the world see them *doing their horrible shit." Okay David doesn't suck anymore. He's fucking nailed it.* Anna said nothing as she filed his feedback away in a mental safe deposit box. She knew exactly who would break the silence anyway.

Bamert pointed at Farris. "Can you teach this class?"

Matt Raidl wasn't having it. He waved his hand at Farris' speech. "I think that's all nonsense."

"Young man," said McDuff, "What is that you're wearing?" He was pointing to a cap resting in front of Raidl on the table that had a crude symbol stitched above the bill:

"It's just a hat," said Raidl. "And I'm not technically wearing it right now."

"That's a Conquistadors logo," McDuff said. He wasn't looking so jovial anymore.

"Yeah, and?"

"You know a fan of that site violently assaulted a girl on this campus last year, do you not?"

"The club had nothing to do with that! Vick said we could still wear their swag!"

"I did not agree with him on that point, nor do I now. I would ask that you leave that hat back in your dorm when you attend this class."

Anna did a fist pump under the table. Father McDuff knew the right side to butter his bread on.

"It's satire, Father," explained Raidl. "The forums are satire. People are getting all worked up over jokes, man."

"That site is garbage," said Farris.

"Maybe you should try reading it."

"I have. It's fucked up."

"David!"

"Sorry, Father."

"I'm going to make you a shirt that says that, David. That's one garment that won't be banned from this class."

Raidl tried to change the subject. "All I know is that what David said about war was a big load."

"Why is that?" asked McDuff.

"There's gotta be order, man."

"Whose order?" asked Farris.

"I dunno, just order."

"Why?" Farris asked him. "Why has there gotta be order? The whole of mankind's evildoin' comes from people trying to instill order on other people. That's how you got slavery."

"Whoa whoa whoa," Raidl said. "I wasn't saying slavery is good. Don't put that in my piehole. I just want people protected."

"Which people?"

"Everyone!"

"Don't work that way, quarterback. And I don't think you or your *hilarious* Conquistador buddies want everyone protected. But guess what? Y'all ain't protected, either. Emilia Kirsch is one greedy bitch—sorry again, Father. She *totally* killed that Oregon lady. But at least she went over the top of all those old guys' heads and let loose the whole damn world."

Okay he gave Emilia half a compliment. He half sucks again.

"Is that worth people getting killed?" Anna asked him.

Farris stood up. "Was it worth people getting killed before?! Look at the stats, girl. Same amount of people got killed before porting. But now it's spread out. Beat that! They democratized war and violence. They spread out the danger that used to be just for poor folks and refugees, and now we all gotta share it. We all gotta *see* it. So I ain't feeling sympathy for *any* Americans who act all horrified when they see an immigrant get gunned down, or when a woman gets murdered, or when a big pack of port refugees comes in from Syria hoping for food and water. That all sucks, but y'all should have had to look at this stuff your whole lives! We each get a little a taste of the suffering now, and that's the way it should be. So, Anna Huff…"

Anna was afraid. It was way too early in the morning to be this thoroughly owned by a smarmy bastard.

"Anna Huff, I get why you're sad. Now, you can let that sadness get you down. You can curl up into a teeny tinyass ball and act like everything is the worst. Or you can accept the real costs of this world, and then be free. So what you gonna do? What's it gonna be?"

SAN FRANCISCO

MyClub International was the biggest of the private porting club conglomerates. The company had 50 locations worldwide, including flagships in London, Tokyo, New York, Marrakesh, and Paris, along with scouted-out locations in Patagonia, the Canadian Rockies, and French Polynesia. But the original San Francisco branch, in a building formerly occupied by another private club called The Battery, was still the largest and the swankiest one in the MyClub portfolio.

When Anna and Bamert ported into the top floor of the club, a hostess wearing a black earpiece greeted them at a reclaimed wood desk that had been stained a deep walnut for maximum neo-rustic appeal. Anna felt terribly underdressed. Bamert, in a purple pinstripe suit and mosquito tie, had no such concerns.

"Hello again, Mister Bamert!" the hostess said. "Would you care for a seat at the bar?"

"Would I! Do you still have the happy hour buffet?"

"Oh, yes! All complimentary."

"Splendid. Do you still have those little duck rolls, with the bacon and the jalapeno and the farmer's cheese?"

"We do, yes."

"Hot damn! That's all I needed to hear."

Anna held up a picture of Sarah on her phone. "Do you remember this girl ever working here?"

The hostess barely blinked. The staffers at MyClub were a remarkably well programmed species: superficially pleasant but impervious to actual human feeling. If they did have empathy, they would have had to scroll down a VIP list to find it.

Brendan McClear would have made for an excellent host at this dump.

Past the hosting station, a bartender noticed Sarah's picture. When Anna locked in on him, he quickly looked down and went back to drying off coupe glasses.

"I'm sorry," said the hostess. "I don't recognize her. Even if I did, club policy is to not discuss employees or disseminate employee information."

"I bet it isn't," Anna snapped.

"You'll have to pardon my friend," Bamert told the hostess. "She takes lithium." He grabbed Anna by the arm and escorted her to the bar.

"Anna, there is a delicate waltz to this sort of thing," he told her. It was as quiet a voice as he could muster, still loud enough to be heard from Marin County. "You can't walk in here cold and brandish images of dead women at these people."

"Screw that lady," Anna said.

"Calm down. Let's have an amuse-bouche and then reassess our strategy, shall we?" He leered at the buffet. "I am having so many inappropriate thoughts right now."

It was clear that Bamert had been savoring this jaunt for weeks, but for altogether different reasons. A waiter walked by with a tray of free champagne flutes and Bamert snatched two of them off the side of it, leaving the tray unbalanced and nearly causing the server to drop it. Then he grabbed a scalloped edge plate from the end of the Happy Hour spread and loaded up on crispy pig ears, duck rolls, miniature banh mi sandwiches, lobster tempura, and fatty slabs of raw toro arranged in a flower pattern. An older couple took too long at a hotel pan filled with gummy pasta and Bamert cruised around them, loading up on pickled red onions and potatoes fried in goose fat.

The bartender discreetly wandered toward to Anna. He couldn't have been more than twenty: an Indian-American man in buttoned crew neck shirt with the top button open. A small flap of the collar hung down with fashionable precision. Two other bartenders had the exact same flap. There must have been a MyClub company style guide mandating the exact angle and cut of the flap.

"Would you like a cocktail?" the bartender asked her.

"I'll just have a Red Bull," Anna said.

"On the rocks?"

"Uh, sure?"

"One Red Bull on the rocks, coming up."

"Wait."

The bartender gave Anna a swift and somber shake of his head. This wasn't the place. When he came back with her Red Bull, she shifted into loose code.

"We were thinking about going to dinner after this," Anna told him.

The bartender looked over at Bamert, who was still loading up on food like he was at a mafia wedding. "Really?"

"Yeah. My friend will still be hungry. He's insane. You have any places you like?"

"Around here?"

"Anywhere."

"Well, I work here all night so I usually save my big meal for afterward. It's kinda like my breakfast, actually."

"Breakfast works for us," Anna told him. "I mean, which meal is which anymore?"

"Yeah, it's all mixed up now, isn't it? Anyway, my spot is a joint called Pho Hoa in Ho Chi Minh City. It's incredible. I usually pop over there around 4pm Vietnam time."

"4pm?"

"Yeah."

"Thanks for the rec."

"No problem. You better get yourself an appetizer at the buffet before your friend houses them all."

Bamert came back as the bartender walked away. Another tray of champagne flutes glided by and Bamert grabbed two more.

"We should endeavor to do this every Saturday," he told her.

"You told me this was a delicate waltz. You just attacked that buffet like you were a sperm whale."

"*You* are the guest, Anna Huff. You must be delicate. I, on the other hand, am here to serve as the artful diversion that I was born to be." He stuffed two spring rolls into his mouth at once. "Now whatffs the planth?"

"It's already taken care of."

"Whuh?"

"Just finish eating so we can get back to campus."

"We juffth got here!" Bamert double-fisted the new champagnes with urgency. "Relaxth! Take a load off!"

Anna got up and walked over to the buffet. She took a tasteful portion of Korean fried chicken wings and fresh salmon belly rolls, then sat back down at the bar. The food was better than anything at Main Street, and yet she didn't enjoy it all that much. She hated the club with a spiritual fervor. A set of double doors led out to an open roof deck, where a group of perfectly dressed twentysomethings gathered around at outdoor fireplace, sipping Moscow mules from copper mugs and laughing like they were in an ad for tooth-whitening strips.

This place deserves a war. Burn it. Burn them all down. That hostess up front had Sarah's old job, and yet couldn't even summon the modicum of solidarity required to ask around about her. What a pile of shit that lady was.

Anna drifted out to the patio and looked down at Broadway below. Two city buses were frozen in place on the sidewalk and had been converted, long ago, into ad hoc homeless shelters. To the East, tourists were porting in by the waterfront and then porting out again the instant they saw how many port scavengers and refugees had set up camp along The Embarcadero. Before MyClub took it over, the Battery Club got rid of all its formal entrance doors and swathed the first level of the building in a layer of reinforced steel, with a single loading dock the only way for people and goods to get inside from the ground. You could do that sort of thing when fire codes were no longer so burdensome.

PortSys was also headquartered in San Francisco, over in a massive compound that occupied the entirety of what used to be The Presidio. The second PortSys employees clocked out of work on any given weekday, they would port far away from the compound and bunker down behind another portwall somewhere else. Every major business in this city, every fancy apartment building, every private club: all of them were cordoned off so thoroughly from the free zones, they may as well have been on another planet. *David Farris was right: nobody acts on anything until it happens right in front of their faces, and they'll go to great lengths to preserve that blindness.*

That was San Francisco now: a workday haven for the wealthy and the strategically indifferent. There was a lot of hate in the world, but it was the indifference that did the most damage.

Anna looked over to the Bay Bridge. She and Bamert had come at just the right time to see its deck lights kick up and twinkle in the burgeoning dusk. Sunset chasers popped up along the Embarcadero below to catch a glimpse and shoot a port-by. A steady convoy of trucks were roaring back and forth along the bottom level of the bridge. The top level was now reserved exclusively for the United States Army and for PINE. It was very important that U.S. troops were visible to everyone: stationed in the most prominent spots, holding the nastiest possible weapons, constantly reminding you what they could do if you didn't have an ID hanging from your neck.

Anna fiddled with her passport card, which she dutifully hid under her sweater anytime she ported away from Druskin. It had a special watermark on both sides that glowed in the dark, so that PINE agents could see it on people. Of course, PINE agents saw only what they wanted to see.

She gathered up a big loogie and hocked it over the railing. Then she slipped Vick's pecan bulldog out of her pocket and took a photo of it in front of the Bay Bridge. Bamert stumbled out to the roof deck with another mountainous plate of food. He was drunk and bubbly.

"Look at that view! A view like this, Anna Huff, is soaring. My heart feels brand new."

"I promised my mom I wouldn't leave Druskin."

"I dare say that you haven't held up your end of the bargain."

"I know. I suck. Duty called. I'm gonna go to Vietnam tomorrow morning, and I'm gonna talk to that bartender about Sarah, and then that'll be it. I'm not gonna port out of school again."

"Why not? We've only just begun!"

"Bamert, there's a lot I want to do out there, and there's a lot of people I wanna make uncomfortable. But I'm not ready. I'm gonna make this and Vietnam an exception, but after that, I have to concentrate on being an actual student."

"Okay. All right. It's the wise thing to do." He held up his PortPhone. "But I say we hold onto these jusssssssst in case duty pays another call, hmmm?"

HO CHI MINH CITY

There was already a line at Pho Hoa when Anna and Bamert ported in the next day. The serpentine procession of foodie tourists heading out the door represented the only people standing in place around Phuong 8. The rest of the neighborhood was mass chaos, with locals porting in and out at will, sometimes just two blocks away from where they had originally stood. All the port winds blew harsh over Anna, knocking her into other pedestrians who appeared less than thrilled by the contact. She saw one customer port away from Pho Hoa while holding a hot bowl of soup in his hand, which was incredibly bold. The bowl didn't even have a lid.

The roads were alive: choked with vendors on motorbikes carrying crates filled with jackfruit and whole chickens and tiny fish to the thriving restaurants and markets. And of course, there were soldiers. You could port into Vietnam without a visa and without checking in at port customs. But the VPA was rightfully skeptical of Americans all the same. One of their men kept his rifle trained on Anna and Bamert as he roared by on a motorbike of his own. All around them was a hot funk of broth and gasoline and sweet milk flowers and rotting garbage.

Through the front window of the noodle shop, a crowd of early diners sat on metal stools inside, hunched reverently over huge bowls of cinnamon- and anise-spiked beef broth. Anyone without a seat lapped at their bowls while staring angrily at the stool havers.

Bamert was sweating through his suit. He took a hearty whiff of the air, like he wanted to inhale the whole sky.

"You know that Druskin does a senior semester abroad in this country?" he told her. "I'm applying *tomorrow*."

Anna ignored him. She had spotted the MyClub bartender standing in the line, with a hat pulled down over his face. The bartender was sweating, although maybe that was just the heat.

"Hey," said Anna.

"Listen," the man said, keeping his voice low. "You cannot tell anyone you heard this from me."

"I won't. I don't even know your name."

"And you won't. You wanna know about that girl, right?"

"It's my sister."

"Yeah well, I have to be far, far away from it," he told her. "That fair?"

"More than fair."

"And I would prefer you not go back to that MyClub branch ever again."

"What about me?" asked Bamert. "Can I go back?"

"Who is that?" the bartender asked Anna.

"He's Bamert. Ignoring him is hard, but I promise that you can get the hang of it."

"Hey!"

"We'll never go back to that club," Anna told the man. "You have my word."

"Double hey!"

She hit Bamert with the laser eyes. "Bamert, not now."

He took a step back. "As you wish."

She turned back to her source. "I just wanna know what happened to my sister. That's it."

The bartender swallowed hard and looked around. The three of them didn't necessarily blend into the surrounding crowd, but the neighborhood was such a churning blender of humanity that it hardly mattered. To talk at a normal register was to whisper. Besides, the line for Pho Hoa on its own was as gentrified as downtown Oakland. They blended enough. As the bartender told his story, the din of the tourists and workers snuffed out his words before they had the chance to echo another foot beyond.

There was a member of the club, he told her. A man. Mid-40s. Wealthy beyond imagination. While Sarah was hosting one night, he hit on her and she politely rebuffed him. But that was far from the end of it. The man later held court out on the roof deck, quaffing cocktail after cocktail. He demanded Sarah wait on him, even though that wasn't her job. It didn't matter. The manager told her to serve the man as best she could. At least she would get a decent tip out of it. Sarah's hands were visibly shaking when she delivered cocktails and small plates to the man and his cohorts. When she put a wedge of lime in his old fashioned by accident, he grabbed her by the wrist so she couldn't walk away.

"Is this what you think goes in an old fashioned?" he asked her.

"No, sir."

"It's all right, cutie pie. At least you're something to look at."

Sarah ended her shift that night shaken, but still standing. The man came back the next week. And the next. Whenever she turned down his advances, he would berate her while keeping a smile on his face. Initially, this all came across as light teasing. Only he would keep at it. He openly blamed her if something else in the club wasn't to his satisfaction, like when the lighting was a shade too bright, or when the music was too docile. Whenever he was displeased, and it was often, we would call on Sarah and ask his "little piggy" to address the issue. Sarah begged the manager to let her port home whenever the man came in, but the boss refused because it would have been his ass if he did. This man was far too important to displease.

Eventually, the obnoxious patron learned Sarah's name and took to stalking her outside of the club.

"What'd he look like?" Anna asked the bartender. A pedestrian walking by gave her a crude elbow to make room for himself, but she didn't feel it.

"Tall guy. Thin, black hair parted down the middle. Fake tan. Big gums and tiny little teeth."

"Why didn't you do anything to stop him?"

"No one could. You don't understand."

"No, you're right. I don't. Was it someone who owned the place?"

"It's someone who owns *every* place," he told her. "Do you see what I'm getting at?"

"Wait."

"You understand now why I can't have you ever going back there? You don't need a police sketch for this guy. It's someone everyone knows."

The loose details the bartender gave of the man now fused into a single image. She felt so much worse than she had minutes ago.

"Is it—"

"I'm not gonna tell you his name," the bartender told her. "All I can tell you is that I don't get as hyped up for the unveiling of a new PortPhone as I used to."

SEWELL HALL

Anna sealed herself off in Room 24. Bamert had stuck around Ho Chi Minh City to brave the line and get a bowl of pho (two bowls, actually), but Anna was in no such mood. She found herself frenzied and nauseous, the way she felt that first night coming out of Vick's office. Her mind was a pressurized tube with no release valve.

Simple vomiting wouldn't do the trick. There was no way to purge the dread. It was a permanent installation, as nagging and permanent as a chronic pain. Nothing soothed it. The black curtain was coming over her, heavy and thick. She opened the window of her bedroom to get a shock of cold air, but it tasted acidic. She got into bed, but every position felt more uncomfortable than the last. She wanted to sleep in all morning like a normal teenager on a Sunday, but it was impossible.

Does this happen to other people? Do their bodies and minds turn on themselves so viciously? And why is this room so dusty? Someone is trying to poison you. Asbestos. Asbestos everywhere. You're breathing it in. It's burning.

She had a face to her nightmares. Jason Kirsch. Jason Kirsch was the Chief Creative Officer at PortSys and Lara's half-brother. He was forty-five years old and married with four children. He was the presumptive heir to Emilia and the entire PortSys dynasty. He was also a stalker and a murderer. What did he do that night to Sarah, anyway? Did he shoot her and plant the gun? Why? Anna took out her smartphone and looked at all the photos of Jason Kirsch online: standing on a stage in a pristine black t-shirt, wireless mic tucked discreetly by his cheek, a fancy PortPhone prototype looming on a big screen behind him. She watched a product launch video and listened to Jason regale a bunch of fawning tech reporters with his standard, airy-fairy horseshit about changing the world.

That voice. You know that voice.

That was the same voice that emanated out of the tinny speakers of Vick's laptop. Jason Kirsch was there when Vick used her as a guinea pig. That's why she was holding a 2.5kg weight every time

220

she stepped into the wormhole. Anna Huff was a test subject for an expanded port network.

She went over to the r/Conquistadors forum and read some of K15's assorted works. The group met in person every week to hoist pints of beer and stoke their collective grudge against the rest of humanity: a toxic pocket of humanity spreading itself across terra firma. Every post of K15's ran over 5,000 words long, written in a brutalist intellectual-ese that had her pining for the relative lucidity of her homework assignments. He wrote of a "true globalism," in which "great men" could exercise dominion over any land they wished. One passage slapped her hard across the cheek:

"It is not a concern of the Great Man to heed rejection: be it from an institution, or from an agent of commerce, or from a member of the female persuasion. That last group is perhaps most pertinent of all, such is their need to *reject*. This appeals to their virtue and, at the same time, allows them to use that false virtue as a cudgel against those who might want to level the playing field of the battle of the sexes. I see no reason to indulge these strumpets and their lamentations over what is chivalrous and what are the actions of a cad. I do not believe in rejection. I only believe there are those who recognize my greatness and submit accordingly, and those who are pathetically, willfully blind. I find the latter, frankly, a more satisfying nut to crack."

God, he's as much of a pig as your old man was.

She created her own anonymous account and sent K15 a private message.

"Hi yeah you say you don't believe in rejection. Is it because rejection is probably all you've ever known?" she asked him.

Surprisingly, he was swift to react. "And you are?"

"I'm nobody, which is weird because a nobody like me should be in *awe* of a supposedly Great Man like you."

"Indeed, you should be. That I've deigned to reply to you means you're touching greatness you would otherwise never be able to approach."

"Some people may be 'great' but that doesn't mean everyone else is worthless."

"Well, you are. Why don't you kill yourself?"

"Why don't I report you to the moderators for that?"

"LOL go right ahead. I own this site, you stupid cow."

That was enough DMing for her. She thought about the night at Druskin Gate with her poor mother. Now, the truth tightly wrapped around her heart.

You can't love Lara now. You know that. It's an impossibility. You were a dumbfuck for ever thinking it wasn't. It was a mistake to keep porting. It was a mistake to break your promise to Mom. It was a mistake to find out the truth because now it's going to ruin you. You'll never escape it because you don't have the smarts or the courage to beat it. You should have stayed dumb and selfish, like every other teen out there. This was all a mistake. You're a mistake. You suck. The world would be better off if Sarah had lived and you had fallen into a sewer. You should—

"You know," Asmi said from the doorway, "I felt bad when I nicked the big room for you, but it turns out you like to sneak out of here more often than a bloody diabetic does."

See now, Asmi was the clever one. Asmi knew when to take shelter from the world when it was offered.

"I'm sorry I woke you up," Anna said.

Asmi sat beside her. "You stink."

"I know. I'm a terrible roommate."

"No, I mean you literally stink. You get sunburned in October. You stay up all night cutting up blankets like a freakshow. You duck out of here at 5am in the morning and you come back here with the smell of lotus blossoms and warm piss in your hair."

"Um…" There was that "um" again. Dead. "The diving well. So much chlorine. I have to use a strong shampoo."

"Come off it. You're porting. You really *did* steal a battery from Vick!"

Anna groaned. "I'm not gonna port off campus again, I swear to God."

"Is that why you needed a business alias? Is this how you knew where to put the vans? Has my dad been paying you to go on holiday in Vietnam all this time? Did you also lie to me about what happened with Dean Vick, you shitstain?"

"No. Look, all the shady things we did to help with your dad's business were *legitimate* shady things. Boy, that sounds awful the way I phrased it."

"Why are you porting?"

"There was something I had to find out and I didn't want you to get in trouble. I didn't want them to send you to Vick."

"You don't think *I'll* get in trouble if you get caught? Whose number is in your PortPhone contacts? What's the address on his PortSys bill? It doesn't take a fucking genius to get it sorted, Anna Huff."

"I promise I'm not going to do it again."

The school-issued smartphone blew up on Anna's nightstand. She grabbed it and there was a push alert that read NEW MESSAGE FROM: LARA KIRSCH.

"What the fuck?"

"That's your old roommate, right?" Asmi asked.

"Yeah, it is," Anna said.

"Well, what's it say?"

"I, uh, boy now there's a whole bunch of stuff I gotta decide if I should tell you or not."

"You tit!"

"Bear with me! It's 6am!"

"I know that because you just woke me up, dickhead!"

Her phone blew up again. This time, it was actively ringing. *Who makes an actual voice call in 2030?* It was Burton.

"What could *he* want?" Anna asked. "God dammit, there is too much stuff happening right now."

"Go on and answer it!"

"Okay, okay." She picked up. "Burton?"

"You need to get rid of your phone, *that* phone, and you need to get your transponder anklet back on," he told her. He wasn't fucking around.

"Why?"

223

"It's Bamert. They got him by The Crater. He's getting put up tomorrow night."

MRS. LUDWIG'S APARTMENT

Mrs. Ludwig offered fresh pastries and tea to the Sewell girls every Sunday morning. She baked all her goodies from scratch, the heavenly scent of jumbo Bavarian pretzels slathered in *Allgäu* butter and airy *Franzbrötchen* floating up to the top of each stairwell, gently rousing the girls and welcoming them to their day off.

On this particular Sunday morning, after stashing her PortPhone above a gypsum ceiling tile in the Sewell bathroom, Anna Huff was ready to partake. She was so excited for fresh pretzels, in fact, that she knocked on Mrs. Ludwig's door a full half an hour before they were ready to come out of the oven.

Mrs. Ludwig cracked open the door. "Yessss?"

"Is it too early for teatime?" Anna asked.

"No. But look at you. You look like you haven't slept at all!"

"I haven't."

"You should sleep, then. Sleep sleep sleep."

"I can't."

"Ugh. Well, come in then, I guess."

She opened the door all the way and Anna surveyed the living room. Mrs. Ludwig had "Mustang Sally" playing on a loop on a wireless speaker. It was the only song she liked.

Anna really should have studied Shelby's features more when she first met that stupid cat. All she remembered was that Shelby was white, fluffy, and surly. As it stood at the moment, there were a dozen such cats lounging around the apartment: on the sofa, under the sofa, behind the drapes, on top of the china cabinet, etc. A dozen more were secreted God knows elsewhere in the place.

Shit.

"Sit down, Anna Hoof."

Anna sat down on the hard loveseat and stroked the cat sitting at her feet. She reached down and gave its collar a little tug, revealing the name HENNY etched in the tin name plate. No beginner's luck for her this time. She grabbed a madeleine and munched on it to compensate.

"*Schmecks?*" Mrs. Ludwig asked.

"Mmm-hmm."

"Why haven't you slept?"

"Can I invoke confidentiality with you?" Anna asked.

"That is not a thing."

"Can it be?"

"Eh, I suppose. Although if you tell me you have killed a man, I break this promise. Yeah?"

"No, I haven't killed anyone just yet."

"Good. I have."

"What?!"

Mrs. Ludwig let Anna twist for a moment before breaking into a giggle. She had a flawless deadpan. No one could ever tell when she was fucking with them.

"A friend of mine is about to get put up," Anna confessed.

"Oh. Is it the Virginia boy? The one who wears all those hideous suits?"

"Mrs. Ludwig, only *I* get to make fun of Bamert."

"Awful suits. So loud. I'm sure he's a fine boy otherwise. What did he get caught doing?"

"He ported."

"Ohhhhhhhhh! Now that's something! How'd he do *that*?"

"I don't know," Anna lied.

"I mean, how would you even trick the little anklet?" Mrs. Ludwig asked her. "Kids have been trying to do that for ages!"

"Not the faintest idea. Could I have an energy drink?"

"At seven in the morning?"

"If I'm gonna be awake, I may as well be awake."

"Let me put on some tea. They'll fire me if I give you kidney stones."

She walked to the kitchen and Anna examined seven more cats: Buddy, Max, Moritz, Wilson, Pickett, Liam, and Georgina. All duds. *Shit shit shit shit shit shit shit.*

Mrs. Ludwig came back with a tray carrying a teapot, a creamer, cups, saucers, and sugar packets.

"Lemon?" Anna asked.

Mrs. Ludwig sighed. "Right. The lemon. One moment."

She fled and Anna groped four more cats: Bilbo, Kaiser, Bacon, and Shelby. *SHELBY*. She wanted to shave a giant X into Shelby's fur to keep track of him, Kirkland-style. Alas, Mrs. Ludwig was already back with the lemon.

"There we go. Everything you need. Now, we have Darjeeling, Earl Grey, chai, green tea, and something called Morning Zinger, which sounds very American and bad."

"Got chamomile?"

Mrs. Ludwig hung her head. "Oh, what the shit."

"Earl Grey is fine."

"No no no! You want chamomile, I get you the chamomile."

She got up again. Anna grabbed Shelby and ducked into the toilet. When Anna tried to pull the anklet off her, she screeched, bared her thin fangs and raked a claw across Anna's forearm. Anna dropped the cat and bit down on a hand towel to keep from crying out in pain.

"You all right in there, *schatz*?" Mrs. Ludwig asked from the kitchen.

"I'm all right! I just went to pee and a cat joined me. No worries!"

"Is that Shelby in there? Let me know if you want me to come in and smack her on the head."

"Nope! Everything is way cool!"

Anna wrapped a wad of toilet paper around the scratch to stanch the bleeding. There was a bacon-scented candle resting by the faucet. Anna sniffed it. Smelled like bacon, all right. Now Anna wanted bacon.

She held the candle down for a coiled Shelby.

"Please don't die from this," she whispered to the cat.

The cat took a tentative step over and licked the cold wax. Anna gently slipped the anklet off Shelby's neck and then onto her own foot. By now, the laceration on her arm had bled through the toilet paper. Droplets of blood dotted Mrs. Ludwig's shag bath mat.

Anna pulled the bacon candle away from Shelby and the cat screeched once again. So she let Shelby have at it while slipping out the door.

Mrs. Ludwig saw the blood. "What the—"

"Just a flesh wound, Mrs. Ludwig."

"Did the cat do this? I should throw her out the window, the little shit."

"It's fine, really. I should go."

"You didn't have the tea! Or the *Brötchen*!"

"I know, I know. Listen, Mrs. Ludwig: confidentially, I feel like I'm losing my mind."

"You're losing blood, is what you're losing."

"I don't know what to do."

Mrs. Ludwig wrapped Anna in a hug: firm and tight. Mrs. Ludwig was a skilled hugger, almost as good at it as Sandy.

"In the end, it'll be okay," she told Anna. "If it's not okay, it's not the end."

"Thank you so much, Mrs. L. Hey wait a second, that's what your couch cushion says!" Anna pointed to a small crocheted pillow in the living room that, indeed, expressed that exact sentiment.

Mrs. Ludwig winked at her. "That's my favorite pillow for a reason, Anna Hoof. You're going to be fine."

Anna was crying, her blood dripping down onto the rug and a parade of cats coming to lap it all up. Mrs. Ludwig let go of Anna and fetched a First Aid kit from the kitchen, cleaning off Anna's arm and smearing it with unguent.

"No matter what you do and no matter what happens, everything passes," Mrs. Ludwig said. "Life moves forward, yeah?"

"When?" Anna asked her.

Mrs. Ludwig laughed. "You want me to set the oven timer for it? Whatever you do in life, do it with a good heart. That's all you can control. And get some sleep."

"Okay."

Anna went to leave, but Mrs. Ludwig stopped her.

"No tea?"

"You told me to sleep."

"I guess I did! Huh."

Anna walked out, then doubled back and peeked through the door one last time. "Oh hey, the cat started eating the bacon candle. You might wanna check on that."

Lara

Hey

Hey

How u holding up?

Everything's a disaster, so I'm having a super normal one

Lol

Lol

I heard about the stuff Vick made u do

Yeah

Is it true? Did that really happen?

It did yeah. Fun times!

I'm so sorry. I never should have doubted u

Vick is a bastard and I'm gonna take his soul

He deserves that

Yup

Is there a chance we can meet?

Yeah of course. Altho I don't quite know how to pull that off

I'll be at the rowing dock at 8pm tonight

Uh, okay

I miss you, roomie

Same

GOULD HOUSE

The "I miss you" text was ruining her. She needed to talk herself out of love and all it took was one text for the job to become Atlas-esque. Was it a cursory "I miss you"? Was Lara just being nice? Or had Lara Kirsch—freed from Druskin to roam the world and party with literal rock stars—really missed her short time confined to a tiny, smelly dorm room with her weirdo roommate? It was a maddeningly vague thing to say. A thoughtless pleasantry but also a gateway phrase to "I love you." To be missed and to be needed was just a tease compared to being loved, but it was also a start.

Lara wanted to meet. And talk. Alone. Anna remembered when she sprang a "can we talk" on Emma Chance at homecoming freshman year. Face-to-face. Not over DM. They walked out to the school parking lot together, the October night air so brisk you could crack it. At the time, Anna thought that Emma agreeing to have a talk meant she *wanted* Anna to ask her out. That's what "the talk" is for in high school. Emma Chance wanted no such thing. She thought Anna had a beer connection.

Now Lara wanted a talk of her own. The texts burrowed into Anna, making her hot and flush, her mind taking them and running with them through the hills and fields. She could hear Lara saying "I've missed you" to her face, in low and breathy tones. *I've missed you, baby doll.*

Stop it. Sarah wouldn't want you doing this. This is just puppy love. You're a dumb dog.

She treasured the text chain from Lara like it was a handwritten postcard, reading it over and over and picturing what Lara's face might have looked like as she was typing each missive. But now she had firsthand evidence that this love was virulent. This love had no ethics. It was compromising her soul's immune system. Every second she held onto it was a betrayal of her own sister. Sarah wanted Anna to find a girlfriend, nagging Anna for love life updates the way Sandy might have if Sandy'd had any free time to ask. Now Anna finally had an update for her sister, and it was a fucking disaster of one. *Okay Sarah, so the deal is… oh God you're gonna hate my guts.*

231

She needed a plan for their meeting at the dock. But there went Druskin again, digging into her schedule and stealing every last scrap of time yet again. She was in Burton's room, commiserating over the situation with her guy friends. Even there, she encountered a critical distraction. Bamert only had a day to prepare his defense before the disciplinary committee. He sat on Burton's bed in a pink flamingo suit, legs spread wide.

"How'd you get caught?" she asked Bamert. "What happened?"

"What happened is that Wade happened. I reckon they upped his donut allowance to go after Vick's precious bulldog with more gusto. I never saw him coming: a truly incredulous development given that boy's girth."

"This is all my fault," Anna told him.

"Pfft, don't be an idiot," Bamert said. "As far as I'm concerned, that soup was worth it. Now gimme the bulldog."

"No, come on. I'd be framing you."

"Just give it to me. Let the unholy Vick have his lame tchotchke back. I bet it wasn't even *made* in Georgia."

She slipped the bulldog out of her pocket and felt its smooth, polished body. She understood why Vick liked it, though the idea that they might share a common interest was yet another unwelcome revelation. She wanted to drive a steamroller over the figurine and mail Vick the pieces. Instead, Bamert grabbed it out of her hand, dropped it into his shirt pocket, and gave it a little pat.

"There we are. Safe and sound, little fella. And your phone?"

"Hidden."

"Well, that'll do. Legally, they weren't allowed to break into my PortPhone, although I'm surprised your nemesis didn't put a gun to my head and demand I do the retinal scan."

"What about your anklet?" Anna asked. "Do they know it's fake?"

"Nope. They were so mad at me they forgot to ask how I got past the wall."

"And Vick didn't take you to his basement?"

"No. Bless his microscopic heart, I guess he's choosy about who gets to be a lab rat."

"Don't call me a rat."

"You know what I mean, Anna."

"I can speak for you in front of the disciplinary committee," Burton offered to Bamert.

"You're a true gentleman and I accept your offer, so long as you *stay on topic*. If you start actively bitching about the upholstery in The Latin Room, they're gonna put me up for porting *and* for murder."

"I would talk for you, too," Anna said. "But I'd be worthless."

"I don't want you anywhere near that room," Bamert told her. "Vick put me under the lights for three hours to get me to sing about the both of you. I don't know what it is about this school. All this horseshit about honor, yet you so much as fart in another person's face they're dying to have you blame a friend for it."

"It's to scare everyone else into falling in line," said Burton.

"Yeah well, fuck 'em." He took a swig from a bottle of clear fluid and grimaced. "Blech. Burton, what the devil is this swill you've given me?"

"That's called 'water,' Bamert."

"Well, it's disgusting."

"I'm gonna confess to Vick," Anna told them. "They'll kick you out if I don't."

Bamert smacked his own thigh. The ensuing clap rang out as loud and true as anyone porting out. "Anna Huff, I will be damned to hell if I let that man near you ever again, or if I let you be a part of this wicked process."

"But—"

"No buts. I can survive this ordeal and you can't. Edgar'll make a call and this'll all go away. Even if they boot me, there's another dipshit prep school out there more than willing to dip into the family coffers."

Bamert wrapped his hulking arms around his knees and squeezed like he was trying to pop them. Anna could see his beard twitch. He stared up at the bare ceiling, like he was in a chapel to make a plea to God.

"Bamert," Anna asked him, "Are you okay?"

He whipped out a tin of Kodiak and tucked a fat, moist dip under his lip.

"I'm fine. Just gonna be another pleasant exchange between Edgar and me. Same as it ever was. You know, when I was old enough to walk and talk, my folks didn't bother with nannies or any of those child care accoutrements. When they left the house they'd leave me behind all by myself, with some food and water on the counter. They may as well have put a doggie dish on the floor for me. They'd tell me not to answer the door. I spent whole days alone in that fucking house, talking to the walls and conjuring up invisible friends and painting my face with magic markers. Then they'd come home drunk and yell at me because I'd made a mess. I was *six*, mind you. So, you know, trouble's no trouble for me. Trouble is the primary form of communication for the Bamert family."

They sat quietly before Burton asked, "Oh hey, I never asked you: Why'd you draw on your face?"

"Aw hell Burton, does it even matter? That's enough stewing about me. Now, Anna Huff."

Anna looked up at him. "Yeah?"

"Don't you worry about me. I'm nothing. You, my dear, have far more pressing matters to tend to. Do you know what you're going to say to Lara Kirsch?"

"No."

"Well, you've got a few hours," he told her. "Should I prepare a sonnet?"

"I don't know what I even *can* say."

"Then let her talk first. Everyone wants to say the right thing, but sometimes that's the other person's job."

SALTON BOATHOUSE

Lara was late. Anna was standing behind Salton Boathouse, situated just north of the Druskin bookstore and overlooking an enclosed 2km stretch of the Hobscott River that stretched all the way to the gym and the playing fields. Follow the river and it ducked under the stone bridge where Anna had spent that first, magical-yet-horrible night with Lara. Now her only company was a flock of double-crested cormorants perched at the edge of the dock, their long necks curved like question marks.

She felt stupid waiting. Entrances mattered and here was Anna, dressed plainly and standing alone in the cold with her teeth chattering, like a dope. She had the rose pink bracelet on but why? *Why'd you wear that?* She alternated between hiding the bracelet in the sleeve of her letter jacket and leaving it out and proud.

Across the placid river, past the crew launches moored to the dock, she could see a large faculty apartment complex that housed the teachers fortunate enough to not have to live with their students. With its cylindrical chimneys piping away in the grim artificial light, the residence glowed like a working factory. Along the opposite riverbank was a scrupulously landscaped esplanade where families of staffers could stroll and where couples could hold hands inside a gazebo built atop the inside edge of a sharp meander. Anna let out a bracing exhale that made her breath look like a plume of cigarette smoke. During the day, the crew team set sculls and shells down in the still water and sliced through it like it was soft cheese. Their rowing was always perfectly smooth and even. The sight of those dagger-like boats always stopped Anna when she was on the paths. This really was a beautiful school. Druskin could grind you down and abuse you and yet it still had the gall—the naked gall—to enchant you in quiet, hidden moments.

She felt a light wind. Lara was there on the dock. Leather jacket. Tight jeans with no back pockets. She was shivering in the raw autumn wind, grabbing at her lapels and wrapping them around herself like a swaddling blanket. The cormorants flew away to give the two girls time to themselves.

"I really need to check the weather before I go porting places," Lara said. Then she ran over and hugged Anna tight, as tight as when she hugged Anna that first night. In Anna's brain, there was a very small and angry man sitting in a director's chair with a bullhorn shouting reminders to her:

Her mother is a monster! Her brother killed your sister! She called you a liar and left you to twist! You two can't happen!

It didn't matter. Anna held onto Lara and felt the cold, worn-in leather of her jacket. She took in Lara's sweet scent and heard gentle keyboards and 12-string guitars providing background music in her mind. Their hips were touching and Anna fought like hell to keep hers perfectly still.

"You found me," Lara told her.

"Well, I mean, you kinda came back and found *me*."

"Doesn't matter. We're real again. You're still wearing the bracelet."

"I am."

"Looks good on you. Anyway, I'm sorry," Lara said. "I'm sorry for everything." She meant it. Green eyes can't lie.

Bamert was right. She said the right thing.

"I *was* wrong about you, Anna. I was wrong to say what I said to you that night. I should have believed you. I was right to need you."

"Why did you leave school?" Anna asked her.

"Emilia freaked out. Emilia didn't even want me to *go* here. That was all my idea. She said I wasn't serious enough for it, but I enrolled anyway. Then that first night happened and that was just the excuse she needed to pull me out. Meanwhile, you got fucked over. They don't have actual justice here. They just judge people however they please and they think that's fine because they're the grownups and every kid should fall in line. But it was me who left you in that office with that asshole. I left you to take the heat when *I* was the one who could afford to take it. That's something Emilia would do and I'm not her. I'd drain every last ounce of blood out of my body to not be her, I swear to you. I feel like shit about what happened. I don't expect you to have much sympathy."

"I don't, but I still like you."

Lara smiled. "I'll take that. I knew there was something true about you. I don't deserve you."

"It's okay. We're cool."

"How are things otherwise, Roomie?"

"Not good."

"I heard about your friend getting put up."

"I was porting with him."

"Get out. That's wild. You broke out without me! I'm a little jealous."

"Jealous? You broke out after less than twenty-four hours at this dump."

"It's not the same."

"Well, you told me to find you," Anna said, "I figured I would have to crack the Wall to do it."

"How'd you pull it off?" Lara asked. "How'd you get past the wall?"

"If I told you, it would ruin the magic."

Lara laughed. Oh, how Anna had missed the burst of unadulterated joy that came from cracking Lara up. Still never got old.

"I guess that's fair," Lara said. "Did you find out about your sister?"

Tell her.

"I found out some things. It's not good, Lara." She burst into tears. "It's so bad I can't stand it. It's not right, what they can do to people now."

Lara grabbed her tight. Her touch remained a universal cure-all. No one outside of Anna's family had ever held her. It was such a simple, perfect thing to feel. *If you two hold each other forever nothing can touch you.*

"Do you wanna tell me?" Lara asked.

"I wanna tell everyone I see," Anna said, "But saying it out loud makes me feel insane."

"I know how that feels."

"Do you?"

"I do. I can prove it," Lara whispered. "You're the only person I can prove it to."

"Why me?"

"Because I trust your soul. You've got no right to trust mine, but I'll earn it. I have a plan."

"What is it?"

"Now it's my turn not to spoil the magic."

Anna busted out laughing and relented from their embrace to dry her eyes. "You fucker!"

"I have my reasons. So your friend got caught porting and you didn't."

"Yeah," Anna said. "Survivor's guilt."

"I know about that. I feel guilty all the time because I know everyone else has it worse."

"How exactly did you port here?" Anna asked.

"Ah," Lara said. She took out her phone and opened up a golden app icon. "That's a bit of magic I *can* show you: VIP status. Gets you past any portwall undetected. Gotta be a Kirsch to have it though."

A Kirsch with VIP status could go anywhere they pleased. Like into Sarah's bedroom.

"How does it work?" she asked Lara.

"It just does. You feel like a spy when you use it."

"Or like something else."

Lara traded out her phone for her vape pen. "I know you don't, but I gotta offer. You'll feel like an astronaut."

"Sure, what the hell." *Can't be worse than that joint that made you barf.* "How long does the high last?"

"Until you want more." Lara took a hit and handed the pen over. "Breathe smooth."

The pen was long and surprisingly weighty, capped with a stainless steel mouthpiece that had Lara's lip gloss still imprinted around it. Anna liked holding the pen. She brought it to her mouth and inhaled too fast. Just like her to somehow breathe wrong. The vapor hacked away at her throat and sent her on a coughing jag that echoed across the river and back. Lara giggled, a step away from laughing at Anna outright.

"I should have warned you," Lara told Anna, taking the pen back and tucking it into her inside pocket. "That's a strong cart I use."

"It's okay," she wheezed. The smoke left her throat stripped and burning, but then the weed took hold in a way that the first joint she smoked never had. Anna felt light, like she was on a porch swing and someone was gently rocking her back and forth. She looked over to the twinkling apartment lights and they went soft in the growing cold, tiny stars of light that she wanted to reach out and hold in her hand. She wiggled her happy fingers. This wasn't Lily Beach. This was still Druskin, but this quiet, dark part of campus was good enough for her high. Her joints felt motorized. She stretched her hand out in front of the river and stared at it. Her bones felt ready to shine out of her skin. She could feel all the levers and pulleys inside her body doing their precision busywork with good cheer. Her heart felt like it was going to float out of her chest. Her muscles relaxed and stretched like taffy. Self-traction. When she looked at Lara, she saw an aura of pure neon.

"Where'd you port?" Lara asked her. The question dulled Anna's newfound high, her neuroses giving the porch swing a rude jostle.

"I dunno," she told Lara. "Nowhere as cool as where you've been."

"I doubt that," Lara said.

"I dunno, I've seen your WorldGram."

"You have? You stalking me?" laughed Lara.

"Only a small amount."

"You follow me on it?"

Anna thought about all the times she lingered over that stupid FOLLOW button, hemming and hawing over whether or not to click it. "Follow you? I, uh, I don't."

"You didn't give me a follow?" It was impossible to tell if Lara was seriously aggrieved or if she was just playing around.

"Okay, here's the truth. I have a hard time looking at everyone else freely porting around when I'm stuck at Druskin." *And who was that piece of shit she was kissing in Sassari?*

"But you ported out!"

"It's not the same," said Anna. "And I didn't want you to think I was some psycho following you after you left."

"So you just lurked instead."

"Like a totally normal person, yeah."

"I don't blame you for not following me. That account is all horseshit," Lara told Anna. "It's not like *your* page. Your WorldGram rules."

She saw your WorldGram. On her dormant WorldGram account, Anna posted only the most unremarkable photos of places: weeds, shoes, old wads of gum on the sidewalk. She never included herself in her own WorldGram photos but always added a sarcastically cheery caption like, "Seeing all the BEST sights in Vienna!" under a picture of an Austrian trash can. Sometimes she'd get a like from a stranger and Anna enjoyed that feeling more than she ever cared to admit.

"You really liked it?" she asked Lara. The porch swing began rocking smoothly once more. "You never followed me, though."

"Well I didn't want you to think *I* was stalking *you* now, did I?" Lara joked. "But I *am* gonna steal your bit and post photos of dry cleaning bags from hotels."

"I'll sue," Anna joked.

"You won't win."

"You should keep posting photos of yourself, or Emilia's marketing team should. I like seeing you there." *Whoa hey. Easy, Cheesy.*

"Emilia claims I'm not a thinker, so she decided to use me in other ways. I don't even write the captions on those posts. They had a rum company sponsor one of them. Meanwhile, I just turned 17."

"But you went to all those places, right?"

"Everywhere gets old if you're alone. It's like you're on tour. But you're not on tour for, like, a *reason*. You're just a package being shipped around. It's beautiful world, but I know it too well now. I'd rather stay home, if only I had someone worth staying home for. You know where my favorite place to port is?"

"The place you wouldn't tell me?"

"That one, yeah. The place I go more than Lily Beach."

Paris? Lucerne? Kyoto? Sassari? The top of the Burj Khalifa?

"It's fucking Cleveland," Lara confessed.

"You're shitting me."

"No one's there. No one expects me to go there. Finding a place to be alone is easy when you port somewhere shitty, you know. And I *love* how shitty Cleveland is. It's gorgeous to me. I can port to Cleveland, by myself, and not have to pretend I'm having a wild time in Mallorca or wherever."

"That's out in the free zones though," said Anna.

"I don't care. It's deserted anyway. And it's dark. I like to move in the dark, Anna Huff. The world zigs, I zag. Emilia got me a place there and it's mine. I can treat the joint like shit if I want to. I can leave empty beer cans around and not do my laundry and just be however the fuck I wanna be. You feel me? You ever been to Cleveland?"

"Maybe once." Anna felt all that hot blood rush to her cheeks and hoped that the chilly darkness was enough to mask it.

"I'll take you," Lara promised. "I'll show you my place. We can eat top ramen there together."

"I do love top ramen."

"I wanna be part of the world. I don't wanna act like I'm too good for it, because I'm not. If it rains when I go to Ohio, then all the better because it'll be even more deserted. No one uses the Burke Lakefront Airport anymore, so I can port alone, stand on a big fat tarmac in front of the lake, get high, feel the rain, and be still. One night I was standing out there and I saw a star and got to have a moment with it. Just me and that star. That's what's beautiful to me."

"I saw a bunch of friends with you in all those other places you went though."

"Fuck my friends. They mean nothing. Get high and everyone is your friend. They'll get you a beer. They'll give you a kiss. They'll treat you like Queen Shit for a night. Then it wears off and you're right back where you were."

"What about me?" Anna asked Lara. "Does the high of my friendship wear off, too?"

Lara dismissed her with a fierceness. "Never. You're different. You're not them."

"Then come back," Anna said to her. *Oh my God, shut up already. Keep your mind to yourself.*

"I've thought about it. I miss being surrounded by smart people. *Actual* smart people, not people acting like they are. You save my room for me?"

"I took it over. I started cooking meth in it."

Lara squealed with laughter. "How dare you."

Anna smiled hard. Could feel the smile forming: her eyes crinkling and the corners of her mouth drawing upward and her cheeks dimpling and her face going red in the whipsaw November air. She felt, for the first time in her small existence, *adorable.* Flirtatious, even.

"Actually, another girl took your place."

"Is she cool?" Lara asked.

"Yeah. She's cool."

"How cool? You guys an item?"

"No! No no no. She's into guys. I mean, she *hates* guys, but she's into them. I don't quite get how all that works."

"Ha! Neither do I. Guys all want things, but they don't wanna *understand* them. That's their whole deal. I go to these MyClubs and walled-off resorts and it's usually a bunch of gross older guys, or it's some dumbass hanging with me to angle for a job with my half-brother."

"Your brother seems like a dick." That came out of her mouth quicker than she anticipated. That was the weed's fault. She didn't want to kill the moment. Sometimes the moment grows so profound that nothing else before or beyond it matters. Anna was in the moment now. Her grief was on the mat. Lara sat at the foot of the dock and let her legs dangle over the peaceful waters. Anna sat down next to her but kept a respectful distance.

"I'm sorry," she told Lara. "I shouldn't have—"

"Jason is a demon," Lara said, not looking up. "Your thing with Vick isn't the first time I've heard about our company torturing people. That you agreed to let Vick experiment on you for my sake makes me wanna throw up. Jason is in charge of all that testing. He's a horrible person."

"He's there in the lab when they torture me."

"You know he likes to hunt, right?"

"Seems the type."

"He poaches, like the rest of them. He doesn't care. He's why there are no more rhinos. He ports over to Africa to hunt all the time. There are a lot of posers out there who port to Africa and take their selfies and act like they just cured racism, but he goes there to *kill*."

She told Anna about an elephant hunt Jason forced her to go on once in Tanzania. He hired a full team: guides, five-star chefs, porters. He brought crates of guns from a gun locker he kept in Cape Town, and he dragged Lara along even though she despised hunting and despised him in even greater measure.

"Why'd you go?"

"You have to understand: Jason has this way of making you do things you don't wanna do. He's very scary when he bosses people around, like if you don't do what he says, then something awful will happen. I know I warned you about Emilia, but her I can deal with. Jason scares me to death."

"Jesus."

"Yeah, so he takes us out into the bush with enough guns to start World War III. We see this elephant mom and her baby and I'm sitting in the jeep, about to burst into tears. You should have seen these animals, Anna. I mean, it's a pair of fucking elephants! They're these big beautiful, unspoiled creatures. It's like *seeing* love. That sounds so…"

"Trite?" Anna asked.

"Yeah. Trite. God, you know just how to put things the way they are." Another line from Lara that went directly into Anna's memory bank.

"It's not trite, though. You saw love." *You said* love *to her. You still love her. Tell her you're into her. She's so close to you. It would be perfect if you two kissed, wouldn't it? Okay, maybe now is not the time. But God, she looks shit hot right now.*

"Yeah. I was so happy to be looking at these animals. I wanted to be them. Just love, without any of the bullshit."

"You wanted to protect them," Anna said.

"I did." Lara started to cry. "But I couldn't. All of sudden the gun goes off and the mom and the baby, they go to the dirt. I couldn't save them. I couldn't save you. I'm so sorry."

They scooted closer to one another. Anna put her arm around Lara and Lara leaned her head on Anna's shoulder to sob. She was dying to tell Lara *I love you*. The mere idea of saying it felt wondrous on its own. The weed wasn't helping beat back her temptations. Lara's touches were lingering. Faint portclaps coming from Druskin proper went off like fireworks in the distance.

"That wasn't even the worst part," Lara whispered to Anna, wiping tears away from her pink eyelids. The worst part was afterward, she said. Jason had brought local tribesmen with him, and his accompanying film crew shot a video about how the elephant meat would feed the tribe for a month. Jason shook hands with the chief at the end. It was all bullshit. Those locals were paid to be on camera. The chief wasn't a chief at all, just a member of the tribe named Ed. Lara told Anna that the natives sat in the truck and waited while Jason took out this machete and hacked away at the elephants' bodies, alone. Their hides bled out and deflated in the baking sun.

"All this blood and it's making him hack away even harder. He called to me and held up the machete, like I was supposed to join in. I said no and I swear, when I did, he looked at me like he was gonna hack me up next. It's not the first time he's looked at me like that either."

Anna's high turned to vinegar. She felt extraordinary and awful all at once. This was a very Druskin feeling, every day. But with the weed, the dichotomy was pulling her brain apart.

"I'm gonna go back to Tanzania and seeing those elephants again," Lara said. "I'll protect them this time around. All their lives they'll be free to be. And I won't go with Jason. I'll go with you. Port out of here again and we can do it."

"Lara," Anna told her, "there are things I *have* to tell you."

"What are they?"

Lara took Anna's hand. *Gentle.* Feeling a touch bold, she fiddled with the signet ring on Lara's freckly white finger, then she squeezed her hand and felt a tender squeeze back. Lara playfully returned the favor and fiddled with the rose pink bracelet hanging off Anna's wrist. Anna's hand, normally so hyperactive, was happy now. It was home.

She slipped Lara a printout:

8/9/29
Rockville, MD

"What is this?" Lara asked.

"Can you see where other VIPs port?"

"Only if I'm friends with them, and I keep all that on lockdown."

"Are you friends with Jason on WorldGram?"

"*No.*"

"I need to know if he was in Rockville on that date, and I need to know what time he was there if he was."

"Why?"

Don't lie. "I just need to know. It's important."

Lara prodded. "What happened on this date? You can't just *almost* tell me things."

"Oh God."

"Your sister," Lara guessed.

Anna burst out weeping. Lara followed suit. Between them, they could have flooded the Hobscott with tears.

"My sister," Anna confirmed. She braced herself for Lara to become defensive, to show her family blood. But instead, Lara straightened her spine and tucked the Post-it into her inside pocket.

"All right," Lara said. "I'll find out for you. I can friend Jason and then unfriend him again quickly. He won't think anything of it. He hates me."

"I can't believe anyone hates you."

"Oh, Roomie." Lara scooted closer and leaned into Anna to feel warm and safe. There they were: two girls huddled together, rootless and cold and bone tired from being so frightened. How Anna wished they could run away together. Oh, and the places they could run. *Run away with me, Lara. Let's run away together. To Cleveland.*

A hard wind blew in behind them. In the lights of the boathouse, all that Anna and Lara could make out was a tall figure with tight coiled hair and long bony fingers.

"Oh, am I interrupting?" Emilia Kirsch asked them. The two girls sprang up from the edge of the dock, keeping their hands locked tight.

"What are you doing here?" Anna asked her.

"Well, I *do* own the place," Kirsch said. "The question is: what are *you* doing here, Anna Huff?"

"I'm not doing anything illegal, *Emilia*." Something about Kirsch made Anna Huff bolder and ruder, which was gratifying for a solid half a second before the inevitable return volley came roaring back at her.

"Oh but you *were*," Kirsch told Anna. "Lara, what did she tell you? Did she tell you she was porting?"

Lara took a step back. "I don't remember."

"I'll take that as a yes. Not your best work, Lara, although I don't know why I would expect good work from you regardless."

"What are you talking about?" Anna asked. "Did you put Lara up to seeing me tonight?"

"What, did you think she just *wanted to hang*?"

Anna spun to face Lara. Spun so fast that her hair got caught in her mouth. "Lara?"

"You don't understand," Lara told Anna. "She made me. I swear I wasn't trying—"

"Here's a story for you, Anna Huff," the elder Kirsch began, her bloodhound eyes tearing away at every stitch of Anna's clothing. "Two sloppy and rude teenagers walk into a MyClub in San Francisco, flashing photos of a dead girl to the hostess, who, being a professional, alerts a manager, who then sees one of those teens play ace detective and make jayvee small talk with a soon-to-be-extremely-fired bartender. Then they port to Ho Chi Minh City, where the bartender tells them a completely farcical story about the

Chief Creative Officer of PortSys being a bad little boy. Feel free to fill in any holes in my narrative."

"You pile of shit," Anna said.

"Save your anger and put it to a more constructive use."

"How could you do this to me?" Anna asked Lara. "*You* ratted *me* out?"

"I swear I didn't mean to hurt you," Lara told her. "Mom just told me to come talk to you, that's it. I don't know anything about a dead girl. I don't know anything about San Francisco. I don't know anything about Jason."

"She's mostly right about all that," Kirsch said. "Little Lara, always carefree, always blissfully above it all. But you, Anna Huff: you're more clever than I gave you credit for. How did you get past my wall?"

"I attained the privilege, *dear*," Anna cracked.

"Again, clever. You're not quite smart yet, though. Once you're both things, you'll be quite the prospect."

"Screw you."

"Oh please, I'm too old and tired for that sort of business. Now, your friend Bamert is in dire straits, but I think we can see to it that *you* are not put up alongside him, so long as you know your place and get back to your studies."

"I'm gonna burn this place to the ground and make sure you're in the center of it."

"No, you won't. Think about dear Sandy, Anna. Think about how disappointed she'd be to find out her little girl blew her best chance at becoming somebody. It would crush her to see you not only expelled, but potentially *prosecuted*. Oh my! That would be dreadful, wouldn't it? And what if your mother's work dried up? All her income? What if she couldn't even afford to stay in a ShareSpace, behind a decent portwall, hmm? What if it were just the two of you, alone in the free zones, where anyone could come get you?"

Anna was never gonna get high again. That was the first thing. She was never gonna be this messed up when messed up things happened. Nope. She would remain stone sober for eternity if it meant avoiding this sort of bad trip. She was violent inside now, ready to spew out thick, venomous blood at Lara's mother.

"I'm doing you a favor tonight," Emilia Kirsch told her. "I'm wiping your slate clean. You'll never have to see the inside of Vick's office again. You'll never have to worry about any of the things that worried you before. Now you can get down to the business of being a happy and productive student. You could even meet a cute boy!"

"I'll kill you." *Dude, don't say that in front of Lara.*

"Get in line, dear. Okay, this is as much time with children as I can usually handle in a day. Lara, please be on your way."

"No."

Emilia tapped her foot impatiently. "Lara."

Lara burst into tears and screamed at her mother, "I hate you!"

"Leave."

Lara stepped back and took out here PortPhone. "Anna, I'm so sorry. Anna, I—"

"GO," her mother ordered.

Lara hit PORT and a deathly chill swept over the dock. Anna was alone with Kirsch. With Lara gone now, she had no interest in being patient. She charged. Emilia sidestepped her and ported to the edge of the dock, leaving Anna to sprint directly into her shrill portclap.

There was a stray oarlock resting among the frosted weeds. Anna grabbed it and hucked it at Kirsch, but missed her wide right by two feet. It went splashing harmlessly into the Hobscott, breaking the pristine reflection and settling on the bottom, never to resurface.

"How'd you do it?" Kirsch asked Anna. "How'd you port out of here?"

"By putting my foot in your ass and seeing where it took me."

"Curious, I don't remember that. But you know what? I'll let you keep your methods to yourself. Only fair that we agree to keep each other's secrets."

"I agree to nothing."

"You already have. You made a fine test subject for our R&D lab, but your dealings with the Kirsch family are now over. And never call me Emilia, not if you ever want see what's left of your worthless family again." She took out her PortPhone. "Oh, and if you should ever decide to port away from Druskin in the future, just remember what's out there waiting for you. Your sister found that out the hard way. We always know where you are, Anna Huff."

Emilia pushed a button and was gone, leaving Anna alone on the dock, stung red and raw by the whole Kirsch family, who were now little more than traces of bare wind.

ASSEMBLY HALL

Bamert's parents hired a white shoe lawyer to present his case to the disciplinary committee and defend him on accusations of porting, stealing, drinking, having a loaded handgun in his room, and six additional official charges of Un-Druskinlike Conduct. For the hearing, Bamert wore a charcoal gray suit. No loud colors. No patterns. No funny little animals. All the color had been bled out of him. He may as well have been wearing a prison jumpsuit. Anna wilted at the sight of him as he and the lawyer walked up the endless Academy Building stairs and ducked into The Latin Room.

She waited in Assembly Hall while Burton testified on Bamert's behalf as a character witness. Anna tried to hear what was going on behind the Latin Room doors but the proctor shooed her away, leaving her to spread out on the front row of the orchestra section and stare at the bare stage. Everything in the Assembly Hall was old and dry as tinder. *This could all burn so fast and hot. And so easily.*

Burton shambled out of the Latin Room and took a seat next to her. His testimony lasted thirty-five minutes and included a brief history of the Arthur Ashe monument in Richmond for some reason. Purest Burton. But he was flustered from his session and could only initially recap it in a stream of *harrumphs* and *pffts* so authentic that he deserved to be made an honorary father-in-law.

"How'd it go?" Anna asked.

"Hmph! Well, the format was ridiculous. I laid out an ironclad case. Afterward, they just asked me a bunch of questions off a form, like I was giving out information to a dentist. An entire Keynote presentation, completely wasted. Do you know how long it took me to convert the video files for it?"

"Burton, is he gonna stay?"

"You're not hearing me, Anna. I'm already telling you: I made my case for him, and they didn't care."

"Oh."

"He'll be lucky if they don't actively *prosecute* him for anything."

"Yeah well, this school has a nasty track record for keeping things in house."

"How are you holding up?" Burton asked her.

"I'm not."

"You should go sleep."

"Everyone keeps telling me to sleep. Maybe I'm not sleeping for a reason."

"How'd your meeting with Lara go? Are you friends again?"

"I don't wanna talk about it."

"All right." He looked away from Anna and quietly clicked his tongue, rapid-fire. He pointed to the stage and asked her, "Did you know the man who designed this hall also designed a series of Polish concentration camps?"

"I did not," Anna said.

"Ah, but the story gets even better," Burton promised.

"How could it not?"

"The architect, a nasty little bastard named Klaus Horst, demanded to design and build a Roman Catholic Cathedral on Druskin school grounds. The administration said yes, even though they had NO intention of making it a chapel. What they needed was this hall. So when the contractors finished construction of Horst's blueprint and he came to visit, they brought in a pulpit and had one of the drama teachers dress as an ordained priest, like McDuff, to trick the man into thinking this assembly hall really was a church. Then Horst went back to Europe and made war prisons, never realizing he'd been duped."

"Was every building at this school designed by a complete asshole?"

"Pretty much." Anna laughed and Burton gently patted her hand. "It'll be okay."

"Will you promise me something?" Anna asked him.

"I can try."

"Promise me you'll never work for PortSys."

"Why would I ever do that?"

"Because money."

"I've come this far without money, so I think I can deal. I came here to be a professor of wildlife ecology, not some drone with a black card."

"Christ, what if Bamert gets kicked out? I can't stay here if Bamert gets the boot. What will we do?"

"We could start a band."

"What?"

"You play piano. I play the tambourine. We could start a band!"

"No. No, we couldn't."

The two of them played intense rounds of gin rummy against one another on the stage as they waited an hour for the kangaroo court next door to recess. Burton was one of the few people Anna couldn't beat routinely. She would occasionally shuffle the cards for too long, rapping the split deck against the desiccated hardwood until Burton shouted at her to just deal. Finally, the door to The Latin Room cracked open and they stopped playing to hear the verdict.

Bamert came out and hugged his lawyer. He walked into the Assembly Hall with a broad smile on his face. For a moment, Anna thought he had gotten off, but then Bamert drew his finger across his throat and her heart dropped.

"Oh no," she said.

"It appears," Bamert told them, "That Edgar really did want me to enjoy the gift of failure."

The three of them hugged as the committee of high-achieving suckups and taciturn school officials paraded out of the room and down the stairs. Vick caught Anna's eye and gave her one of his repulsive, crooked half grins. She nearly pushed him down the stairs, but then again she nearly did a lot of things. Nearly ready to kill someone. Nearly ready to tell people she loved them right before they betrayed her. Nearly ready to take down PortSys. Now her best friend was cast out and she was there in Assembly Hall, fully aware that she was just another helpless teenager, nearly doing vital things but never doing enough.

"What are you gonna do?" she asked Bamert.

"I don't know," said Bamert. "Probably get more of that pho."

"I can't be here without you. *We* can't be here without you."

"Actually, I'll be just fine," Burton told them. They both glared. Burton got defensive. "Well, I didn't want him to worry!"

"I know you two'll do fine," Bamert told them. "You both have strong ethics. And Anna Huff, you have the heart of an ox."

She wrapped her arms around Bamert, her hands barely meeting behind his hulking back. He gave her a loving slap on the shoulder.

"I should go," he told Anna and Burton. "They want me gone tonight."

He broke away and strolled toward the exit. Then, Bamert paused and looked up at the balcony. He pointed at their spot in the first row overlooking the orchestra section.

"Don't let anyone take my seat, all right?"

"I won't," Anna said.

"Y'all take care of yourselves. I'll be around."

Then J. Paul Bamert walked down the stairs, out the Academy Building door, and away from his Druskin career forever.

Lara

Anna?

Anna, I'm so sorry. I HAVE to see u. I have something that u need to see. It's important. If we can get it to Dr. Ciaran Stokes, we can beat them

r u there

Please, Anna

Roomie...

Anna, I'm sorry. Please don't hate me

The Man Who Invented Porting Has Nowhere to Go
By Sean Grann
Q Daily
Published: 11/27/2030

(UNDISCLOSED) — Dr. Ciaran Stokes won't be able to port when this article publishes, and he has taken all the precautions necessary for his future once it does. He purchased a quarter-acre of land in a remote area, if any area can be labeled as such anymore, that he has asked me to not disclose. He also asked me not to divulge any qualities of the terrain, lest it give him away. He deliberately kept his new parcel of land small, despite the fact that he could afford something much bigger. The house he plans to live in is also relatively miniscule—just a single room—but uncommonly bright, with plate-glass windows taking up a majority of the exterior.

"I need to be able to see people coming," he tells me.

He has guns. Several guns. To cover his tracks, he set up a shell company in Western Sahara to buy the guns and then set up a second shell company to buy the guns *from* the first shell company. Then he had the second shell company send the guns to a set location pinned within thirty miles of here so that Stokes could pick the guns up himself and drive them to his new abode.

Because even though he has done everything in his power to keep this location a secret—including never actually porting to this exact pin and leaving his PortPhone in a locker any time he visits—he suspects it's only a matter of time before he is found. When I speak to him, he sounds as if he wants it to happen.

"They know everything," he says.

The "they" in question is PortSys: the trillion-dollar megalith that, until seven years ago, was Stokes' employer. It was a good job. PortSys is famous for its employee benefits (at least, at the executive level), and Stokes was afforded every luxury that came from working in the company's R&D lab: a free private health system, a hospital devoted solely to PortSys employees, free food made by chefs imported from all over the world, and a salary well into seven figures.

"You also got a free company car to use any time you wanted one," says Stokes, "Which Jason (Kirsch) offered to everyone as a joke."

Ciaran Stokes, on the other hand, is not a joking man. He is an extremely grave and, frankly, humorless fellow. If you're wondering what he's been up to since he left PortSys, it's been this: securing his new home, outfitting it, carefully wiping away the few remaining traces of his existence, and preparing to be under siege.

"It hasn't been easy," he tells me, "All the houses I found were flawed. One house I looked at, the lighting setup was horrible. You couldn't intuit which light switch turned on which light."

My parents say the same thing about hotels.

"I know you think I'm being funny but it's a serious issue. Whoever conceived the house put no care into how it would be used. I couldn't function in that sort of place."

Even if you remodeled it the way you wanted it?

"No. I would not want the lingering atmospherics of whatever that person did to that house. It would bother me."

A lot of things bother Dr. Ciaran Stokes. He dropped out of MIT after two years to work at a Silicon Valley incubator because he thought the professors at the college were too deferential to classmates whom he felt were of inferior intellect. He divorced his first wife because, as he tells me matter-of-factly, "I realized that she wasn't my equal, in terms of intellect. Our conversations always devolved into meaningless pleasantries. It was like being married to a neighbor." He doesn't have kids because he finds children to be "embarrassingly incomplete." He eats all of his food with chop sticks, even breakfast cereal, because he believes that Western flatware promotes binge-eating and sloth. If people are even a minute late to meet with him (as I was for our second appointment, due to a family matter), he will refuse the meeting even if he has nothing else to do.

It was this kind of preening exactitude that made him a perfect fit at Kirsch Laboratories: an early incarnation of PortSys where Stokes worked in the R&D lab and was given broad latitude to follow his own ideas and turn them into tangible products.

"It was heaven," he tells me. "Anything I wanted, they gave it to me. If I needed a team of a dozen people to work on something, they had a list of candidates ready for me the next day. *Good* candidates. No retreads. I never had to sit in a status meeting. I was never given any metrics to hit. I could create my own rules and work fully within them. It was as pure a working environment as I ever labored in, as I will ever work in. But, of course, that was the great lie of it all."

How do you mean?

"Because I didn't know that I would invent what I invented."

Stokes is talking about the antihydrogen porting method that became the foundation of all modern teleportation: a formula that PortSys owns outright and has endeavored, with shocking success, to keep from being made public. When the PortPhone was first introduced in 2021, it was touted exclusively as the triumph of Emilia Kirsch and her son, Jason. Even Frank Lender's biography of Kirsch—believed to be the best in its category—fails to mention individual scientists at PortSys, instead referring to them as "the team" or "the lab" and framing the invention of porting as the product of Emilia Kirsch's iron will and her son's fantastical creativity.

"They got all the credit," Stokes says, "which is hilarious because I know the Kirsch family's dirty little secret."

What's that?

"I want you to turn your chair directly toward me before I tell you. The way you're offset right now makes me crane my neck a little bit, and I find that uncomfortable."

I scoot my chair so that we're now directly facing each other, like we're in a psychiatrist's office. Stokes snickers a little bit—the first time I've seen him even come close to laughing—and then leans in and whispers, "Emilia is dumb."

Dumb?

"The whole family. Rock stupid. She's a pitbull and so is her son. They can always get one person to agree in any meeting. When that first person agrees with them, the rest fall in line quickly thereafter. But that's the extent of their talents. They're incurious at best and gleefully ignorant at worst. Whenever I tried to explain porting to Emilia, she got bored within five minutes and asked someone to bring her a ginger ale."

Why don't you try explaining it to me, then?

Stokes stands up from his chair and looks out the tinted plate glass windows wrapping around his micro-home. There are guns leaning against each wall, and he keeps a 9mm strapped to his body at all times, even when sleeping. Prior to this meeting, he asked me to leave all of my electronics at home so that I couldn't be traced. He could shoot me dead in this house and no one would know about it for a long time, if ever.

"I'll explain *part* of it, and even that I'm going to keep relatively vague."

But how can I know you invented porting if you can't explain it to me in full?

"They'll kill me, you understand. And you! I don't think you understand the danger you've put yourself in by agreeing to meet with me."

As you might have guessed, there is a price for all of the creative freedom and neat perks that PortSys affords its employees. PortSys owns any IP formulated by an employee like Stokes. In addition, the company's nondisclosure forms are considered some of the most ruthless ever devised, with employees who sign on not only exposing themselves to potential liabilities if they disclose what they know, but in some cases facing criminal prosecution as well. Stokes says one prospective whistleblower, whom he won't name, was forcibly ported to Turkey, a PortSys-friendly nation, where he was sentenced to life imprisonment for embezzlement. Stokes claims the charge was fabricated. Immediately after sentencing, the whistleblower was killed by a gang of six inmates.

How do they forcibly port people? I thought only you can port yourself.

"It's very easy for them. They control the entire map, right? They know where you are on the switchboard. Then they can open up a hole and throw you in. You land where they decide, and if they decide that means a leftover landmine sitting in a Cambodian rice patty, they can do that."

You're suggesting they kill people.

"Oh, they do more than kill people."

Stokes says that Chief Creative Officer Jason Kirsch has used living humans—particularly port runaways—to find and correct bugs in the porting system, including "buffering" issues where porters step into a wormhole and don't reappear again for stretches that can go on for months, even while the porter himself cannot perceive the time lag.

"Every automatic software update you get for your PortPhone was the direct result of many human beings suffering. Sometimes Jason had us do tests on people just to see what would happen, like a teenager sticking a bug in a microwave."

Did you ever object to him doing it? Did you ever refuse to conduct any tests for him?

"No, because they owned me, and because I was making too much money to object. That's absurd in retrospect, knowing how much that company stole from my mind. But I wasn't wise enough to see that yet. I was so happy to be *in* the work that outside factors were negligible to me."

Okay, but why human subjects? Why not test the bugs out on lab rats?

"Because you can't! The rule is that only living humans can port, and that rule isn't there out of the goodness of Emilia's heart. If they could port objects, they would. If they could port a mountain and catastrophically alter the geology and gravitational field of this planet in the process, they would. But they can't. You need people. This was why all the old quantum physics experiments in teleportation were middling affairs where one proton appeared somewhere else for a trillionth of a microsecond. No one thought to start with humans until I came around."

So what makes humans the difference?

"You port through space-time, which means you must be able to perceive it. That is the key. A block of wood cannot port on its own. Something gets lost in the transaction. When a human teleports, there is an exchange they have with spacetime, although it's not an exchange that you or I are conscious of when we port. The wormhole *learns* you and what you're holding, and then accommodates you."

It sounds like you're saying you need to have a soul to teleport.

"I'll let theologians decide that. Besides, Jason Kirsch can still port, can't he?"

So why meet with me then? What's your grand plan here?

"There is no grand plan. I granted you time because my compensation for inventing porting technology has been repugnant. I'm not talking about mere money, either. I am talking about a compensation of *history*. This meeting here, between you and me, is at least an attempt at starting a legacy. That's what I deserve. History rewards the liars and the cheats and I won't have it anymore. *I* am the architect of heaven, Sean. The Kirsch family fired me and cast me out the second I suggested that I get the proper amount of credit due."

So this is an ego trip for you?

Stokes pivots his chair away from me, so that we are not longer facing one another. "If you're trying to paint me as arrogant or greedy here, you've got the wrong target. *They* are the thugs who wrested this technology away from responsible scientists. They are the ones who have made this world what it is now. Whatever hubris I'm showing you is nothing compared to the hubris they've demonstrated."

So why not bring them down? Why not leak the formula?

"To you?"

To anyone!

"Because it's already in the wrong hands, and I know which way information flows once it gets out. With the Kirsches, the people in control are evil but at least they're breathtakingly uncreative. Maybe that is the best we can hope for."

It's worth noting that when *Q Daily* contacted PortSys for a response to Stokes' accusations, they responded quickly without any threats, be they legal or physical. Instead, we received a statement that read, "Over the years, the PortSys lab has employed some of the greatest scientific minds in human history, and the Kirsch family has always been forthright about crediting this amazing team for their work and compensating them far above industry standards. We categorically deny Dr. Stokes' claims, and wish him nothing but the best of luck in his future endeavors."

As I wrap up with Stokes, he walks over to his living room window. There's a loaded AR-15 leaning against the window. He gently fondles the barrel, as if grasping the top of an umbrella. A few portclaps echo in the distance, each one making Stokes tickle the barrel, as if he's considering just how many people are nearby, and what their intentions are. It's a reflex to him at this point.

Then he turns to me, the same clinical expression he always seems to have, and says, "Maybe when they kill me, I'll finally get the recognition I deserve."

Is that really all you want? To be famous for creating this brave new world?

"Everyone expects a brave new world, but that isn't how it works. You only get the new part."

SEWELL HALL

A month passed after Bamert's expulsion and Anna Huff had settled back in as an anonymous Druskin student, shuttling from Sewell to class to the pool to the cage and back to Sewell again with all the enthusiasm of a factory worker screwing caps onto toothpaste tubes. She had become an automaton: a bag of meat that ate and read and cranked out (better) English papers. She coasted through diving practice and barely heard Willamy, even when he was yelling right in her face. She quit piano lessons because, as accomplished as she was, every new piece they taught her sounded like a love song designed specifically to smash her heart to pieces. Love was nothing more than a gift best left unopened.

Don't answer her texts. She doesn't care about you. She never cared about you. They killed Sarah and now they're just fucking with you because that's how they get off. You fucking loser.

She dutifully met with Sandy every Wednesday night at Druskin Gate, even as the nights got colder and darker. This part of the Northeast was incredible in the depth and texture of its darkness. No wonder Bamert had despised it so. Every time Anna thought it was already pitch black outside, an hour would pass and a new, more intense shade of blackness would shroud the campus. Everywhere Anna stepped, she felt enveloped by thick night as worn-out students kicked through the slush in black boots and drab winter coats. Even when she was hanging out at the gym, all the kids were dressed in gray. The administration should have shaved everyone's head.

Losing Bamert made it all worse. Everything on campus was lifeless without his presence: the Assembly Hall balcony, the Latin Room, any novelty tie she spotted on another student, etc. When she needed a laugh, she would bring up his WorldGram feed and gawk at him, still clad in suits despite not being obligated to wear them. He'd be sitting atop Teotihuacan, drinking water-clear beer in Uruguay, sucking on shrimp heads in New Orleans, and sneaking into Clemson tailgate parties. There was no sign that Bamert was intent on furthering his formal education, but there was every sign that he despised his freedom. It was a curious effect of Druskin: all the kids hated it and loved it in equal measure, she and Bamert included.

She followed him. No shame in that click.

One night, Asmi bounded into the small bedroom and sat on Anna's desk. The bags under Anna's eyes would have gotten her a senior discount at the movies.

"Guess what?" Asmi said.

"What."

"My dad wants you to come for Christmas. Says it would give him someone to talk to besides my 8,000 relatives who are *extremely* fucking annoying."

"And you want me to, like, meet them all?"

"I don't think you understand what a remarkable breakthrough this is. My dad doesn't *like* people, not even when they're handing him cash."

"Well then, why does he want me to stay with you guys?"

"Because I told him he'd like you."

"That's a pretty big conclusion to jump to."

"Oh, come *on*," Asmi said. "I've seen you moping about all month. You suck now, you pillock."

"Hey!"

"Come with me. Aren't you excited to get out of this loony bin for two weeks? And now you get to spend it with the most fabulous girl in all of Oxford. The batty old King would be beside himself with jealousy if he knew."

"I'm sure that's true. But—"

"But what?"

"There's my mom."

Asmi started to laugh. "D'you really think we wouldn't invite your mam? Bring her! We can cash in some of the kebab money and buy her a proper Christmas gift!"

The sales job was taking hold. Every Christmas, Sandy insisted on going to New York and strolling along Fifth Avenue, even though Fifth Avenue was choked to death with tourists and stillborn cars that time of year, and patrolled by roughly 68 million PINE agents. No matter. Sandy Huff loved the city at Christmas, scraping together money to stay in an actual hotel with her daughters. Not a ShareSpace, but a real hotel, with a room of their own and a door that locked and a small, functional portwall. They'd order cheeseburgers from room service and eat them on the bed.

But the Huffs couldn't afford a hotel this year. They would just be porting to Fifth Avenue for a lonesome afternoon among the throngs before heading back to a ShareSpace, somewhere. Oxford seemed a bit less frantic by comparison.

"You sure we wouldn't be intruding?" Anna asked Asmi.

There was that laugh again. The sound of Asmi's laughter painted every corner of a room. If anyone had an issue with her laughing—and more than a few kids would give her the side-eye in Main Street when she cracked up—that was *their* problem.

"Oh Anna, what does 'intruding' even mean anymore?"

OXFORD

The security guards by Druskin Gate handed Anna her PortPhone. Not the crude one still squirreled away in the crawlspace of the Sewell crapper, but her actual PortPhone. When she turned it on, there were a half-dozen more synced Push Alerts from Lara Kirsch.

All the other kids ported out immediately, the resulting series of portclaps blending together in a single, thunderous boom. Anna stayed rooted in place until she was nearly the only one left. The guards stared at her, wondering why she was so reluctant to go. She looked at the pin Asmi had given her for St. Michael's street. Not but five blocks away from that pin was the Oxford branch of MyClub International.

Every time you port, a Kirsch makes money.

"Ugh."

Asmi's family had room for the Huffs to stay over for the entire break. Sandy, locked into two dishwashing jobs, would still have to commute from DC and Hong Kong daily, but she could swing it. She and Anna would also have to share a bed, but Anna didn't mind that. Sandy was a heavy sleeper. She barely moved.

One of the guards tapped Anna on the shoulder. "You all right?"

She turned and held up the phone. "Yeah. So long, guard man." She walked through the gate, hit PORT, and felt as cold as she'd ever been.

Now she was standing on St. Michael's outside a blue apartment building: a complex two stories taller than the ancient brick rowhouses lined up alongside it. The English weather was on her right away, the cold, wet cobblestones reaching into her bones and leaving her as damp and dead as the ground she stood upon. Directly across the street was the Three Goats Heads pub. There was a ruckus coming from inside but Anna couldn't tell if it was happy screaming or angry screaming. Gangly college kids marched along the street in their scarves and peacoats while she stood out in the clammy air, waiting for Sandy so that they could ring the button for the Naru family's apartment together. Asmi had given the Huffs the password for the Naru family's portwall, but Anna hated porting directly into homes. She insisted on always ringing first.

There were soldiers around these free zones, but the Brits at least had the common courtesy to keep their rifle barrels pointed downward. Port marketers blasted in and hassled potential customers along the cobblestones. Two Americans ported onto a nearby corner and screamed, "You're an idiot" at one another before clapping back out. An unarmed cop stopped a woman on the sidewalk and demanded to frisk her for weaponry. She groaned before putting her hands up and letting him aggressively pat her down. No one paid the Huffs any mind.

Sandy ported onto the street and wrapped Anna in a bear hug before Anna even realized it was her own mother hugging her.

"Oh, Anna. Anna! This place is wonderful!"

"Mom, I can't breathe."

"Let me have a look at you again." She held Anna by the shoulders, like she was holding up a doll for inspection. "You looked healthier last month."

"I *was* healthier last month."

"How were your final exams?" her mom asked.

"They're *why* I was healthier last month."

"Well, let's get you warm and fed! I'm excited to meet this roommate of yours. I feel awful that I don't have the Prosecco on me. I couldn't port with it because my coat is so heavy."

"It's fine, mom. We can port back for the gifts."

"Oh, I have a zillion things we have to port back to the locker for. I'm glad it's the same temperature here as it is in Maryland right now. Maybe this Christmas we can finally avoid getting sick."

They rang the bell and Asmi greeted them in a jade green dress. "About time. Get in here, the both of you!"

She pulled them inside, locked them in a three-way hug, and then led them through a grimy hallway to her family's apartment on the first floor. Inside was mass chaos, with tiny children scurrying about, old ladies huddled around platters of steaming roti and jars of stewed lamb, and a Christmas tree so thoroughly weighed down by ornaments that half its branches were sweeping the floor. Sufi music flowed out from a wireless speaker. An old upright piano sat unused in the corner. *A piano.*

Asmi introduced the Huffs to the room. Everyone nodded and then went back to doing exactly what they had been doing before. Anna was taken aback by all of it. Not the noise, nor the sheer number of people, nor even the sensory overload of all the food and music. It was the joy. She had barely remembered what joy looked like. The Kirsches had absconded with all of hers, it was so light and pilferable.

"Is that all the lot of you have to say to me roommate and her mam?" Asmi asked her relatives. They all gave Sandy and Anna pleasant smiles, and then went back to their business once more. Asmi shook her head. "And where are the chips? Did any of you heat up the chips? You're all hopeless. Hopeless!"

"You coulda done it yourself," her eight-year-old sister told her.

"Why would I do that when I can make *you* do it, you little creep?"

"Eat shit!" the little girl snapped.

"Well I would, if one of you dickheads had bothered to heat it up!"

"Stop stealing my glue!"

"You're lucky I don't throw you off the roof!" Asmi turned back to Anna and Sandy. "Fair warning: it's like this all the time."

"I think that's okay," said Anna.

"My dad is out with the vans," Asmi told them. "Let me show you to your room." She led them down the hall and opened the door to a room that was smaller than Anna's room back at Druskin. There was a full-size mattress on the floor blocking the entrance to a lone closet.

"I know it's small," Asmi told them. "But it's safe."

"It's perfect," Anna told her.

"You're just saying that."

"No. It's perfect. We owe you."

"Actually, that would be wrong, *Miz Bumlee.*"

"Who's Ms. Bumlee?" Sandy asked.

"It's just an inside joke, mom."

267

"I have to go help my na with something," said Asmi. "All right if I let you two get settled in?"

"Of course," Anna said.

She and Sandy took out their phones and ported to the Rockville locker five times, groaning as they locked and unlocked it on every trip. When they were done, they had filled the small bureau against the window with enough clothes to last them the holiday, along with three bottles of Prosecco and an economy-sized tin of Old Bay-dusted blister peanuts as gifts for the Narus.

Anna sat down on the mattress to check its firmness, and then she lay down on her side and tucked her hands under the pillow. Sandy kicked off her shoes and slid between Anna and the wall, spooning her daughter and stroking her hair. When Anna was five, she snuck into Sandy's bed one night because Sarah showed her a video of a girl dressed in witch makeup, green skin and bulbous moles included. The video was supposed to be funny, but it scared Anna to death. She huddled by Sandy that night for comfort, and the two of them shared a bed for years after that. Sometimes, Anna's dad would port in after midnight, stand over the bed, mutter that he was sick to death of "all these girls in *my* house," and then either port elsewhere or pass out drunk on the sofa bed.

Now lying together just above the floor, Sandy picked at Anna's ear and Anna slapped her away.

"Mom."

"Sorry, there was a bit of dried skin there," Sandy said.

"Ask before you go poking at me."

"I know, I know. I'm sorry. How was your week?"

"Honestly, I don't even remember."

"I'm worried about you. You seem sparkless. Maybe you should meet a boy."

"I don't like boys, Mom. I like girls."

Sandy stopped stroking Anna's hair for a minute. "Oh. Oh, I didn't know that."

"*I* knew," Anna said.

"I always figured you might. But I didn't wanna be rude about it."

"You could have asked. I would have told you."

She went right back to stroking Anna's hair. "Well, I think it's great that you like girls."

"It's biology, mom. It's not some prize I won at the econ fair."

"Will you just let me mother you? Let me say my mom things."

Anna sighed. "All right. But no Twenty Questions. Sarah already asked me all of them."

"Sarah knew?"

"Possibly."

"Well, I wasn't gonna ask any questions." She held onto Anna tight. "But maybe you should meet a girl."

"Yeah." Anna stared at the barred window and heard the cacophony of port claps and jolly students right outside. "Maybe I should." She turned around and the two of them were nose to nose. "I'm tired, mom."

"Then rest now. I love you so much."

"I love you, too."

"I'm so proud of you."

"Thanks, mom."

Anna turned back onto her other side. Sandy held her tight and they drifted off into an afternoon nap. Druskin was always pushing you to be self-reliant and independent. For four months, Anna had bopped around the campus as a small adult with pronounced and pressing responsibilities, along with very real adult traumas to navigate with no help whatsoever. But now Sandy was here and Anna could be a girl again. She didn't dare upset her mom with the news about Jason Kirsch. Instead, she fell asleep in Sandy's arms. She could have slept clear through the rest of 2030, even with no earplugs in. Wasn't it so wonderful to sleep, and to forget.

But Asmi had other plans.

OXFORD/LONDON/STONEHENGE

An hour into naptime, Asmi gave a hard knock. Anna woke up in her mother's arms, her ear hemorrhaging sweat all over Sandy's cardigan sleeve. The Huffs shook off the cobwebs and opened their bedroom door. Asmi already had her phone out.

"Shall I show you around?" she asked them.

They ported to the Bodlean Library.

"That's the Bodlean Library," Asmi said.

"Can we go in?" they asked.

"Not really."

They ported to Christchurch College.

"That's Christchurch," she told them.

"Can we go in?" they asked.

"Not really."

They ported to Buckingham Palace.

"That's Buckingham Palace," she told them.

"Can we go in?" they asked.

"Not really. Big line."

They ported in front of a sandwich shop.

"That's Morton's. My favorite sarnie shop."

"Can we go in?" they asked.

"Yeah. We can go in that."

They each ate a chicken curry salad sandwich on fresh baguette before porting to Stonehenge.

"That's Stonehenge. Bunch of rocks," Asmi told them.

"It's kinda boring," Anna said.

"God, yes. It's shit."

"Has it always been by the side of a highway like this?" Sandy asked. Anna and Asmi stared at her. "Why are you two looking at me like that?"

They ported to the Turf Tavern, which had a patch of grass growing over the sign above the entrance. They pushed open its weathered, dark green plank door and passed through the stick-style cottage, ducking under low wooden rafters and emerging outside on the tavern patio. There was an open fire cage with free benches around it. Sandy grabbed a pint of Caffrey's for herself, plus two Cokes and a basket of thick, salty fries for the girls.

"It's nice here," Anna told Asmi.

"Innit? UK has their act together a bit more than the U.S., but that's not saying much. At least they do gun checks here in the free zones."

"It's more than that, though," Anna said. "It has your, I dunno, vibe. It's clearly *your* hometown."

"It is! I mean, Manchester was home first, but now this is. UK's not the same as it was, though. It's an angrier place now. Maybe it was always shite, and I was just too young and stupid to notice. I mean, look at me. I don't really remember a time when people didn't call me a bloody terrorist. It's like people want a home, but they don't want anyone else to have one." She leaned in and whispered to Anna. "I need to talk to you one-on-one."

Sandy overheard that and took her cue. "You know what, gals? I'm gonna walk around a bit." She got up and left them to their devices.

"You never told me how you ported out of school," Asmi told Anna. "You really stole the battery out of Vick's phone?"

"Yeah."

"Oh, that's brilliant. The bellend. What'd you do with it?"

"It's in the Sewell bathroom."

"Ew."

"Yeah see, that's why I hid it there."

Asmi sat back and put her arm around Anna's shoulder. The fire in the cage sent daredevil sparks whirling up into the coming twilight. Anna stared at the flames dancing around in the air like quick fingers.

"There are a lot of things you haven't told me," Asmi said. "I didn't want to pry, but—"

"No, I should have told you more, I just got overwhelmed and scared by everything. Druskin makes everyone keep their mouth shut and that's what I hate the most about it."

"Well, that and the food is shite."

"Heh." She focused more intently on the fire twisting and mutating. The Student Center at Druskin had a fireplace that kids liked to read around, but it was a gas fireplace. You flicked on a switch and the flames went up in a consistent row, fed by a burner hidden under a mass of fake logs. The fire looked the same every time. The logs didn't collapse. The coals didn't grow white hot. It was a bore. Thus, Anna was enjoying the chance to see a *real* fire burn and collapse. She got excited when barkeeps came around to dump fresh logs into the cage and kick the flames up again.

"Bamert and I ported because we were looking for the man who killed my sister," Anna told Asmi matter-of-factly.

"Oh my God."

"Yeah. Anyway we found out who it was and somehow that just made the whole thing a hundred times worse."

"Who was it?"

"You don't wanna know."

"The hell I don't. It's bloody fascinating."

Anna noticed a lone man sitting near another lit fire cage. He was wearing a brown canvas jacket and had a tweed golf cap pulled down over his eyebrows. He was looking at them, and not being all that subtle about it, almost like he wanted Anna to see that he was looking at her. Then he got up and left.

If you should ever decide to port out of Druskin again, just remember what's out there waiting for you.

She scooted close to Asmi and whispered, "Not here."

"Oooooh!" said Asmi. "Could this go all the way to the top?"

Anna didn't answer. Instead, she gave Asmi the look. Rather than press the issue, Asmi pulled out her PortPhone.

"I want to show you something, but your mam is still in there."

"Can you show me quick?"

"Yeah! Reckon it'd only take a minute or two." She gestured to the back door of the tavern, where servers ducked in and out with fresh, frothy pints. Sandy was talking to a man at the bar. "Although we could piss off longer if your mam is trying to get laid."

"Stop it."

"What? It's allowed! She can bring him back home but they have to keep three feet on the floor, love."

Anna started to crack up. "Oh God."

"We have a closet that you can duck into while they're shagging," Asmi suggested. "You won't have to watch."

"Fuck you!"

"AHAHAHAHAHA."

"I'm gonna port to the North Pole and get the hell away from you," Anna said.

"I tease, I tease."

Anna settled down and took a sip of her Coke, now all lukewarm and syrupy after being too close to the firelight. "I guess we could ALL stand to get laid, so more power to my mom."

"You ever done it?" Asmi asked.

"No. You?"

"I have. It was such a fucking mess I won't try it again for a while. You kiss a boy and he's always thinking three steps ahead. He just wants to get there, and then he doesn't know what to do when he does! You'd think a boy who's keen would know how to work his own knob. I reckon you'll have better handle on what to do when *you're* with a girl."

"Lord willing."

"Now, do you wanna see the main attraction or not?"

Asmi grabbed Anna by the elbow and stood her up. Now they were in London, right off of Piccadilly Circus. Asmi spun Anna around and there, in front of them, was a store front painted wedding cake white, with varnished beechwood benches and a kitchen awash in gleaming steel. A clay oven the size of a car sat in the back corner of it.

The sign above the restaurant wasn't finished yet but Anna could already see the outline of NARU AUTHENTIC stenciled in.

"Is this—"

"Brick and mortar!" Asmi said. "The foot traffic details you gave us were fucking spot on. You can make consistent revenue here, all year round. Come on in!" She unlocked the door and led Anna into the restaurant. It was so clean that Anna abhorred the idea of future customers making even the slightest mess.

"This is gonna be a hub kitchen for us, too," Asmi went on, "Working portwall. No more mobile kitchens. We can just run the food out to the trucks from here, the way the big franchises do now. And we can open new kiosks anywhere we want!"

A short old man was hunched over the counter, furiously jotting down notes on a legal pad. He didn't bother to look up when they came in.

"Dad!" Asmi shouted. "Dad, we're here!"

The man looked up. He was bald on top, save for a few stray hairs, and he had on a striped polo shirt than hung well past his waist. He came out from behind the counter and gave Asmi a peck on the cheek.

"Asmi."

"Dad, this is my roommate, Anna Huff. She's friends with the Bumlee family."

Mr. Naru's eyes lit up. "Ah, Chester Bumlee!" He shook Anna's hand vigorously. "*Very* good businessman."

"Thank you for having us in your home," Anna said.

"No no no, I insist. If Asmi says you're good, I believe you are good. Come."

He led Anna and Asmi behind the counter and into the back kitchen. There were porcelain bowls and plates piled high on the racks, along with stacks of flatware caddies and a power dishwasher large enough to clean off a baby whale. Mr. Naru gestured to it all with pride.

"Our first store. Thirty percent gross revenue to your friend," he told Anna.

"Holy shit."

"Come."

He led them into a small back office and opened up a buxom safe under the desk. He grabbed a weathered yellow envelope that was stuffed thick with cash, then handed it to Anna.

"For Mr. Bumlee."

"Jesus," Anna said. "What do I do with all this?"

"Shoes," Asmi said. "This Christmas, you're getting some shoes. Maybe even more than one pair."

Anna stole rubber cement from Mr. Dawson's art class to weld the soles of her mary janes back on, but the grip didn't last. They were already back to flapping and gathering up snow and mud.

"Okay, I could use some shoes. Mr. Bumlee thanks you for this, Mr. Naru."

"Thank *you*," he said. "Very good businessman."

There was a tap on the storefront glass. A group of pasty boys were waiting outside the restaurant. Asmi waved them off.

"We're not open yet."

"We're hungry!" one of them yelled. He was a scrawny boy in khakis and a black t-shirt with the Conquistadors emblem silk-screened over the left breast. More of his buddies ported in around him, and they weren't all British. There were some Americans. There were some Aussies. They all wore the matching khakis-and-shirt combination.

Asmi pointed East. "We have a van open on Broad Street in Oxford. You can port there."

"Aww, but we're hungry now, and your food looks sooooo good," the boy said with naked sarcasm. The others laughed.

"Are you thick in the head? We're not fucking open yet!"

"Excuse us, are YOU the one acting like you belong here? I don't think so."

The skinny boy, apparently the chief hooligan, kicked at the door. They weren't hungry at all. The glass pane on the door cracked.

"DAD!"

Mr. Naru came out from the back and put his hands up. "No no no no!"

The mob didn't care. The boy kicked until his boot finally broke through. The other boys hucked rocks at the windows as indifferent port tourists passed by.

"Can you call the police?" Anna asked.

"It wouldn't matter," Asmi said. She ran over to her dad. "We have to port out."

275

"No, I'm staying."

"Dad, please!"

"FOOKIN' LET US IN."

Asmi fished Mr. Naru's PortPhone from his khakis pocket and queued up a pin. "Dad, NOW."

The mob crashed through the plate glass window with the skinny boy leading the charge. They came rampaging inside like a virus replicating itself, uprooting tables and lobbing chairs over the counter. One of the Conquistadors took out a pocket knife and threw it end-over-end at Mr. Naru, nailing him in the shoulder. Asmi's dad slumped down against the counter as the mob ran into the back kitchen, emptying out the flatware bins and smashing fresh plates on the ground. They chanted "SHOW US YOUR PAPERS" over and over as one particularly nasty kid stood atop the counter like he owned the joint and lobbed a rock at Asmi's head.

Asmi grabbed a carving knife from a block and was about to start slashing through the boys when Anna held her back and gestured to Mr. Naru, bleeding all over the floor.

Asmi set the knife down and screamed "Hit PORT" at her old man.

"No," he said.

"I'll bloody do it for you." She pulled him up as a ceramic bowl whizzed past their heads. He hit the prompt while she pushed him forward and he was gone. She and Anna quickly followed suit.

By the time the police arrived, the mob of Conquistadors had already burned down the dining area, along with everything else inside Naru Authentic, and ported out before anyone could lay a hand on them.

JOHN RADCLIFFE HOSPITAL

The line for outpatient treatment at Radcliffe wrapped around the entire building and grew at a frightening pace: patients from America and continental Europe and even Africa all porting in and vying to get decent treatment. A cluster of armed guards scouted the line, demanding papers from people bleeding out from gunshot wounds, writhing in pain from broken bones, even giving birth right on the sidewalk.

Anna ported onto a patty of fresh dogshit. It found its way between her sole and her insole, and now she could feel it warming her toes.

They knelt by Mr. Naru, who fell out of his wormhole but was savvy enough to brace himself before landing on the sidewalk outside. He was bleeding profusely as Asmi tore away a part of his shirt to make a loose tourniquet to wrap around the meaty part of his wounded shoulder.

"I'll see how long the line goes," Anna told Asmi. She walked gingerly along the row of ailing men, women, and children, careful not to smear the poop inside her shoe further, though she knew that effort would be in vain. The smell battered her with every step as she tried to gauge the wait time.

"How long have you been here?" she asked one woman.

"Lo siento, no hablo ingles."

"Cuanto es la espera?"

"No se."

She asked another patient, who only spoke Hindi. Another only spoke Arabic. A nurse emerged from the admitting area and surveyed the line. She was besieged instantly by a frenzied crowd, begging for their loved ones to be let in.

"HELLO!" she cried out to them. "I have told you this already but we are at full capacity! If you have a life-threatening situation, please consider other alternatives!"

"We don't have any!" one patient shouted.

"We are doing our very best to treat as many people as we can, but I cannot guarantee your loved ones will get the care they need in time."

A handful of disgruntled patients and their families ported out, allowing the line to condense a hair. Everyone else stayed, either because they kept their faith in the shrinking line or because they couldn't port anyway. Anna saw at least three unconscious bodies on the sidewalk. Or, at least, she *hoped* they were only unconscious.

She ran back to Asmi, who was sitting cross-legged on the concrete and holding her dad upright in her lap. Mr. Naru was awake and alert, but still grimacing from the stab wound.

"We can't stay here," she told Asmi. "Maybe we try Denmark?"

"We don't have health privileges in Denmark," she told her.

"Back in Pakistan?"

"You're not a Pakistani citizen, Anna. You have to check in when you port there."

"I can do that while you go right to a hospital."

"Any hospital in the free zones there will be overrun anyway," Asmi said.

"America?"

"You're kidding, right?"

"That's it, then," said Anna. "We gotta get a port doctor."

"We don't have the money for that!"

Anna pulled out the envelope of cash Mr. Naru had given her back in the restaurant. "That's where you're wrong."

"No no. Wouldn't feel proper using that."

"Are we really gonna have this talk right now? I'm not trying to stick you with leftover birthday cake. He's gonna die."

"I'm not gonna die," Mr. Naru said.

"Well, he's not gonna feel *good* if we don't get him treated soon," Anna said. "You've got the energy to port, what, one more time?"

Mr. Naru nodded. Anna looked at Asmi and could tell she was relenting.

"Let's get your dad home."

ST. MICHAEL'S

Mr. Naru ported into his apartment and slumped to the ground, soiling the rug with his own blood. His family screamed out in horror and swarmed him. They propped him up, got him water, and demanded, in Urdu, to know what happened. But he was drifting in and out of consciousness due to blood loss. When Anna and Asmi ported in, the rest of the family stared back at them, expecting answers. Asmi said a single word to them that they all immediately understood: "*Conquistadors.*"

Asmi searched for an available port doctor as her little sister brought Mr. Naru a succession of items to make him feel better: water, tea, chapati, even a stuffed bear.

"Quit giving him all that!" Asmi yelled at her. "What's a bear good for besides mopping up blood?"

"I'm trying to help!"

"You can help him by pissing off!"

Every five-star doctor listed on MedPort app had a wait. Same for the nurse practitioners. Asmi had to scroll down into the three- and two-star listings to find anyone who was available right away. When she picked one, a short man with black hair ported in with his hand already outstretched.

"The money?" asked Dr. Fisher.

Asmi handed him the envelope. The doctor knelt down and looked over Mr. Naru's shoulder.

"Looks clean. I should be able to stitch him up here. He might need an x-ray later on. That isn't included, by the way."

"I bet it isn't," said Asmi.

"I have to get a few extra supplies and I'll be right back." He disappeared for twenty minutes. When he reappeared with an extra kit of medical supplies, Asmi glared at him.

"If you take that long again, mate, there'll be two stab wounds to treat here."

"Calm down," said Dr. Fisher. "You actually did a great job stanching the blood. He's already stable. You keep taking care of him like this and he should be fine in no time." That was enough hope and flattery to keep Asmi from cutting him. Dr. Fisher numbed up Mr. Naru and threaded eight dissolvable stitches through his shoulder.

The whole house smelled like dogshit now. Anna walked outside and tossed her soiled mary jane into a rubbish bin. Now she had just one sad shoe. Her mom ported in by the door.

"There you are! Where on earth did you go? Literally where?"

"Mom, I'm sorry."

Sandy shook Anna. "You can't do that to me!"

"Mom, stop."

"You don't know what it's like for me when you disappear, okay? You don't know the thoughts that come to my mind *immediately* when I don't know where you are, Anna. I know you're young and you want to be independent, but every second you're gone, it crushes me."

"I said I'm sorry, all right?"

"No, you're not. Make me your friend on that fucking phone." Sandy never swore. She saved up her cursing for times when it could mean something. "And don't unfriend me. I wanna know where you are at all times."

Anna sighed and accepted her mom's friend request.

"Why are you only wearing one shoe?" Sandy asked.

"The other one broke."

"Where did you go with Asmi?"

"We went to London but then something bad happened."

"What?"

Anna led her mom into the Narus' apartment. Dr. Fisher was already gone. The family had moved Asmi's dad to his bedroom, but the blood-stained outline of his upper body remained permanently dyed into the rug. Asmi leaned on the kitchen counter and took out a cigarette. No one in her family objected to her smoking right there.

"Is he all right?" Anna asked her.

"Yeah," Asmi said. "I told him weeks ago to get a shotgun for that new storefront and he wouldn't do it because he didn't want the police catching him with one. Now look what happened. Friend of mine says they burned the place down."

"Oh god."

"They're bastards. Utter fucking bastards. Why can't they leave people alone, Anna? I mean, I get hate. Believe me. I get hating someone like Vick, you know? That's proper hate. But this isn't. I've lived here my whole life and had to deal with it. Not once has anyone ever had the courtesy to tell me *why* they hate me."

"I don't hate you," Anna said.

"Oh, darling. I know that. Come here." She wrapped Anna in a hug and then beckoned Sandy into joining them. "You're both lovely."

"We're so sorry," Sandy said.

"There's nothing for you to be sorry for. There are people who want to share the world with others, and people who don't want to share anything. I try to ignore it but nights like this are when I know which side is winning."

"I won't let them win," said Anna.

"There's nothing to be done," said Asmi. "You can only be you."

"Yeah well, I'm gonna be more than me. I'm gonna crush them all."

"Well if you do," said Asmi, "Start with that fucking doctor."

OXFORD/COSTA RICA/RICHMOND

They stayed in Oxford another week, gorging on Grandma
Naru's home cooking until Anna felt like a giant rice ball rolling in
and out of bed. In the mornings, she stood sentry in the family room
as Asmi and her father filed police reports and insurance claims that,
combined, held about as much promise as a lottery scratch ticket. On
Christmas Eve, they wolfed down endless courses of nihari, korma,
chapshurro, and chapli kebab at the Naru apartment. After gorging,
Anna played Christmas carols on the piano, and then lay down on
the family room floor. She looked at the soft glow of the family
Christmas tree and allowed herself, against all better judgment, to
sneak in a dream about having Lara wrapped in her arms. She tried
to sub other girls into the dream, but her mind refused to budge. It
wanted a treat. It concocted an elaborate back story in which Lara
magically redeemed herself so that Anna could love her without
reservation.

*"If we can get it to Dr. Ciaran Stokes, we can beat them."
Maybe that text is just another trap. But what if it's not? A girl can
dream, can't she? Is that so wrong?*

On Christmas Day, the Huffs and Narus ported to the Mongolian
Wok for dinner and then five miles over to the Hollywood Bowling
Alley in Oxford, hewing to a Naru family tradition. Even with a bum
left shoulder, Mr. Naru rolled a 200. No one else was at the alley that
day, but that didn't stop Anna from constantly looking around to
make sure there weren't any pasty boys in Conquistador logo shirts
at the doors, frothing at the mouth. When they ported back to St.
Michael's, Sandy took Anna into their little bedroom.

"Look by the mattress," her mom said with a twinkle. Anna
checked and found a fresh pair of duck boots and a pair of red Pumas
with white soles hiding on the floor. "Do you like the sneakers?"

"They're very, uh, red."

"You needed something sturdier than those mary janes."

"I did."

"Do you want me to return them?" Anna could tell that Sandy
was hoping for a "no." The holiday had revitalized Mrs. Huff but she
still didn't look well. Her face was sunken. Whenever she brightened

up, Anna knew it was a temporary state: a bittersweet respite in the middle of an otherwise trying day, week, month, year, decade.

"I'll keep 'em," said Anna.

"But do you like them?"

"I'll keep 'em."

On the 26th, Sandy went back to her dishwashing job, hairnet and all. She gave Anna her blessing to port around that day with Asmi, so the two girls sent themselves over to the Papagayo Peninsula in Costa Rica, staring at the lackadaisical komodo dragons lining the beach paths and listening to the throaty calls of howler monkeys emanating out of the jungle. The monkey's hollow, guttural cry sounded as if it had swallowed another animal and *that* animal was screaming to get out. Their racket snuffed out all the port claps and lent the beach an otherworldly, almost industrial ambiance, like the whole peninsula was enclosed inside a jet hangar.

In the center of Culebra Bay, the two girls spotted a 300-foot yacht with a helicopter landing pad that had been repurposed into a spikeball court. No one was aboard. They sat back and lounged amid the turquoise bay and sculpted rock outcroppings. The sun coddled them in its supple heat. They snagged a couple of tamales from the constant stream of vendors bouncing in and out. Anna unwrapped a corn husk and rushed the tamale into her mouth to keep from burning her fingers.

"How's your mate?" Asmi asked.

"Burton? Burton went on a garden club tour."

"A garden club tour?"

"Everything about Burton makes sense if you just pretend he's an 85-year-old woman."

"I didn't mean Burton. I meant your other friend."

"Oh. Bamert."

"Yeah."

"Well, let's see."

Anna couldn't sign into Network Z on her actual phone, so she opened up WorldGram and scrolled through pictures of Bamert to zero in on his location. He was wearing a Santa hat throughout his feed, giving the camera a thumbs up and a deranged grin from

Bangkok, Rio, Vancouver, and other destinations chosen seemingly by hitting SHUFFLE. In one photo, taken from the north summit of Twin Peaks overlooking San Francisco, he held up a fifth of Jack and gave the camera another manufactured smile. Anna knew that smile. It was the same look Bamert gave her after he came out of The Latin Room that night. She looked at the timestamp on the post. It was 9:07am.

Everywhere gets old if you're alone.

"D'you wanna visit him?" Asmi asked.

"I probably should, but I don't know if that would be something he wanted."

"Oh please. He adores you. You're his best friend."

You have a best friend?

"Let's go see the boy," Asmi insisted. "Text him right now."

Ten minutes later, she and Asmi stood at the foot of a gated, winding driveway outside Richmond, Virginia. The surrounding lands were quieter than death. When commutes became blessedly extinct and the well-to-do porters could build houses anywhere they liked, all of the McMansions went underwater. Some of the suburbanites stayed, but plenty of them walked away from their mortgages and left soured dream homes orphaned across thousands of cul-de-sacs. They were off to live as Newmads, or to settle down in any one of the new, far-flung exurbs to pop up around a world that had been re-fashioned into a mad sprawl.

From a distance, many of the houses in this neighborhood still looked new, with their toothy HardiePlank shingles and ugly craftsman columns weathering the elements season after season. It was only once you stepped inside that you noticed the decay. Families emigrating from outside the country took advantage and squatted in the bedrooms, taking a calculated risk on free luxury accommodations in the hope that PINE wouldn't come snooping around for them.

Asmi nervously fiddled with her British passport, rubbing it between her fingers like a talisman. She had a temporary student visa to port, but being out in the American wild terrified her all the same. The Bamert estate had a portwall but the greater development did not. This was a genteel part of the free zones, but a part of them all the same.

"I don't like it here," Asmi told Anna.

"Not many people do, it looks like."

"Let's go in before some tank rolls by."

They rang the buzzer and the gate swung open without any response from the intercom. Lining the driveway were parallel rows of meticulously sculpted holly hedges. The residential road outside was thoroughly choked with weeds, but the Bamert estate remained conspicuously free of any encroaching overgrowth. The Bamerts must have had a landscaper sit sentry all day long, even in wintertime, trimming bushes and vaporizing any fallen leaf that had clung to life past autumn.

Anna and Asmi knocked on the mahogany double doors. Bamert greeted them in a red bathrobe festooned with small reindeer, holding a Solo cup filled with God knows what. Too drunk and filthy for them to hug.

"Ho ho ho," he slurred. He stumbled into the foyer without saying anything more.

Anna and Asmi followed Bamert into a marble hallway larger than any room they'd ever been in. In the center of the foyer was a pedestal featuring a bronze bust of Hoover Bamert, Paul's great-grandfather. Lining the surrounding walls were solemn oil portraits of other Bamert family luminaries. It reminded Anna of Assembly Hall at Druskin, only colder. So cold. She grabbed her elbows and shivered as she and her roommate trailed Bamert through his family's frozen domain.

They followed him into a kitchen that was outfitted with restaurant-grade appliances and lined in Andromeda granite, the countertops a celestial swirl of grays and purples. From the ceiling hung the same country ham that Bamert had been aging in his Kirkland single. He vomited into the sink. Anna rushed over.

"It's morning here!" she scolded him.

"Allow me to port to Istanbul and remedy that."

"You're not in a suit!"

"I'm a robe guy now, my dear. It suits me."

"Is there anyone else in this house?" she asked.

"AHAHAHAHHA no," said Bamert. "I wouldn't dare subject you to a second round of Edgar. He's in Telluride. Come with me."

"Why is it so cold in here?" asked Asmi.

"It won't be in just a moment."

He led them through another long hallway, past an open bedroom strewn with old toys and picture books that had been left there for years. Anna noticed a small set of wooden train cars in the shape of P-A-U-L lined up on a dresser. Through another set of museum-like hallways they reached a fabulous parlor, with a globe the size of a yoga ball spinning around on a maple stand. Bamert picked up a fire poker and jabbed at the ashen logs in the parlor's elephantine fireplace. Over the flames, there was a cast iron cauldron bubbling and spitting hot chili onto the coals below, making them hiss. He grabbed a pile of paper bowls and held them out for the girls.

"Chili?"

"No thanks," they both said.

"Suit yourself." He ladled himself a bowl and sat down on the leather banquette, letting stray bits of meat and onions languish in his tangled beard. "So, how was everyone's Christmas?"

"Bamert," Anna asked, "are you alone?"

"Well, not anymore!"

"Aren't you gonna go back to school? Any school?"

"Ohhhh, maybe. I dunno. There's a certain freedom in having everyone give up on you. I feel more productive than I've ever been. Plus I have to mind our burgeoning kebab empire." Asmi shook her head in sorrow. "What? What's wrong?"

"My dad put most of the money into a loan for storefront, and then a bunch of dickheads came and burned it down."

"Ruffians!" Bamert cried, stomping his foot on the floor. "Who were these men?"

"They all had the Conquistador logo on their shirts," Anna told him.

"Ahhhh," said Bamert. He took a large handful of tortilla chips, pulverized them over his bowl of chili, and engulfed a heaping spoonful of the mashup. "Conquistadors. Such proud boys. Real group of winners there. What was that principle they believed in? Accelerated Darwinism?"

Anna had done her homework on Conquistadors, scrolling through their endless subdomain in the few quiet moments when Druskin wasn't smacking her upside the head. Indeed, they believed teleportation was a gift from God and a ticket back to the age of colonial rule. K15 himself had written a very long, boring post about Accelerated Darwinism, which theorized that porting made conflict easier than ever before. This was posited as a welcome development because whoever asserted their "rightful dominion" in this Great Port War would become the prevailing species indefinitely thereafter. It was not hard to sort out which group of people K15 preferred assert themselves.

Bamert took a cigar from his robe pocket and jammed it in his greasy mouth.

"Don't do that," Anna told him.

"What?"

"Smoke that. It's disgusting."

"Excuse me, you are in my home. Furthermore, you are in the great Commonwealth of Virginuhhh, which has no regulations against smoking tobacco indoors, nor any other regulations of any kind!"

"Will you stop being *on* for five goddamn seconds?"

He slumped in his chair and put the cigar back in his pocket, the drooly end of it seeping through the fine satin. A delivery boy ported into the hall, carrying a sack of groceries.

"Did someone order a grocery delivery?"

"I did," said Bamert. "Just put it in the kitchen."

The boy did as instructed and walked with his paper bag down the hall. Bamert raised his Solo cup to the girls before knocking back a huge swig.

"Bamert," said Anna. "You have to stop drinking."

"I can't, Anna Huff. It's such a fantastic sickness. It's everything to me, always. People call addiction a battle but I don't recall this ever being much of a battle. When I chase this particular dragon, I always catch it. Now what other friend is as reliable?"

"I am."

"You shouldn't be. You're free from my bullshit now, don't you know that? Tell me you didn't enjoy a nice quiet month at Druskin without me. I would have." He stood up and tended to the fire, mindlessly stirring the big hefty cauldron. Then he turned around and looked at Asmi. His eyes held nothing but dark thoughts.

"Your friend really is beautiful," he said to Anna.

"Thank you," said Asmi. She was being polite. The whole room had grown uncomfortable.

"I couldn't say such things to you on campus, Asmi. But seeing you now ignites something within me." He stirred the pot more vigorously, gripping the handle until his hand could nearly bend the wood. "I feel *besotted*. Is that the British term for it?"

"Stop that," Anna said. "This isn't you."

"I told you I would disappoint you," said Bamert. "I told you that the first night we met. The night *you* fell in love with Lara Kirsch."

"What?" Asmi said.

"Bamert."

"What? You said yourself that you hate secrets. Allow these truths to be my Christmas gift to you. You had the hots for your old roommate. I have the hots for your *new* roommate. There. *Liberation*. Tell me you don't feel better about everything."

"This was a mistake," Anna told him. "You're drunk and you need help."

"I don't need help I need LOVE, god dammit!"

He threw the wooden spoon into the fireplace. It banged against the grate and sent embers flying onto the floor, coming into dangerous contact with the booze stains in the carpet fibers. Anna and Asmi took a step back as Bamert sank to his knees and fell to the carpet. He was crying: a sick, wet, drunken lump convulsing on the rug.

"No one in this house understands me," he said softly. "Love comes from people *wanting* to understand you, and no one in my family has ever bothered to try. I wish I was anyone but who I am."

Anna approached him cautiously and put her hand on his back. He reached around and gripped her gently with own soot-covered

288

paw. Then he looked up, nascent tears bulging from the bottom of his eyelids.

"I'm so sorry. To you both. It seems the only comfort I'm capable of offering comes from Edgar's liquor cabinet."

"It's all right," Anna said. "I mean, it's not all right. You're always so damn dramatic."

"That I am."

"Well it's no way to run a kebab business, you shit," Asmi said.

He snorted out a laugh. That was how a good breakdown always went for Bamert: a long wash of despair and sobbing until one sharp puncture of a laugh reset everything. Those were always the best laughs. Earned laughs.

"Oh, so that's it?" Bamert asked them, sitting up on his heels. "We're right back to shit-giving mode?"

"You're lucky we are," said Asmi. "You boys. All you have to do is be sweet once and people will forgive you for anything."

"I fear I've ruined what little rapport I had managed to establish between us, fair Asmi."

"You haven't. But you're not lean. And I fancy my boys lean. Not skinny, but lean."

"I shall endeavor to fit that description one day."

"You wanted love, right Bamert?" Anna asked him.

"I do," he said.

"Then here it is: Get it together. Stop drinking. Go back to school."

"Which one?" he asked Anna.

"What am I, your guidance counselor?"

"I know that's a rhetorical question, but the answer is yes, at least in an unofficial capacity." He crawled over to the banquette and dragged himself onto its cold, studded leather. "Look man, you guys are gonna head back to Druskin and then I'll be alone again. Edgar, bless his heart, never really taught me how to cope with that. He just left me here. May as well have chucked me in a river and told me to swim."

"Don't go on with the self-pity again," Asmi said. "You made yourself a good friend at Druskin, right?"

"The best." Bamert said, holding his cup up to toast Anna.

"Well then, I doubt you're as hopeless as you prattle on about."

"Maybe not."

"I'll be your friend too, you know, if you tell me more about Anna fancying Lara Kirsch."

"No no, I think maybe I've embarrassed her enough today."

They both looked at Anna and expected her to spit out a morbid laugh, but she didn't. She was staring at the cauldron in the fireplace, watching it bubble and hiss. It was exhausting, carrying all this. Even in the most relaxing times—joyously tossing gutter balls in an empty bowling alley, sleeping close with her mom on a wonderfully chilly Christmas Eve, eating tamales on a pristine, radiant coast—she felt weighted down by all the dark things. Soon she would have to go back to Druskin and pretend to be a normal student, all while watching Dean Vick saunter around the quad a free man and knowing that the two most powerful people on the planet could snuff her out any time they felt like it. This was what Emilia Kirsch demanded she do, and now she was falling in line. The fucking worst. *Does everyone else carry this much shit with them everywhere they go? How do they exist? Is everyone who walks around looking normal all day really just a flaming wreck like you?*

"Are you okay?" Asmi asked.

"Bamert's right," Anna told her. "I'll feel better if I tell you everything." So she did. She told them about Vick's basement, the night Sarah died, the bartender in Vietnam, Jason Kirsch, K15, and the night out on the dock with Lara and Emilia. She emptied out her mind in full.

"This is villainy," Bamert said of Vick. "Pure villainy."

"You're putting me on about Jason Kirsch, right?" asked Asmi. Anna shook her head.

"You got any proof of this?"

"Um…" That *um* again.

"Well, you need bloody proof!" Asmi shouted.

"For what?" Anna asked her.

"To bring him down! To bring them all down!"

"Someone might have proof."

"Who?"

"It's a long story."

Asmi put her hands on her hips. "Who? Spill it, dickhead."

"Lara might have it," Anna confessed.

"LARA?" the other two cried.

"She was gonna go through the confidential records and find Jason's porting history."

"What the devil makes you think she'll do fuck all for you after the way she fucked you over on that dock?" Asmi asked.

"Nothing," Anna said. "She keeps texting me but I haven't answered back. Something about Ciaran Stokes."

"*Fuck* Ciaran Stokes. He's a raw cunt, that one!"

Bamert stood up. He was about to ride a new wave. "If I may, I think you're being too harsh on Anna here, Asmi."

"I'm telling her what she needs to hear."

"People always use that excuse to justify being uncouth. And you're not the uncouth sort. You're too lovely for such things, are you not?"

"Careful, boy," Asmi warned him.

"Do I look reckless right now?"

"Quite."

"I promise you that my focus is on Anna here, who has all the bravery of a great mother elephant."

Wrong metaphor to use there, Bamert.

"Lara claims she has proof," Bamert continued. "And Anna still loves her."

"No I don't," Anna protested.

"Oh, please. Here is something you don't need to hear but will want to: the Kirsches have forced you into timidity. They want you to be common and polite and incurious. But that's not you, Anna Huff. Anna Huff, you are a *rude* woman, are you not?"

"I mean, I dunno if I can beat Asmi in that department," said Anna.

"I'm not talking about huffing glue and saying *dickhead* this and *dickhead* that, although I find all of that impossibly charming. I'm talking about a rudeness of the *soul*. I'm talking about a soul that

291

demands truth, no matter whom it may discomfit. That's you. And you won't find that truth if you capitulate and become yet another Druskin goody-goody. There is the unfortunate possibility that Lara Kirsch is more Big Bad Wolf than Red Riding Hood, but she's offered you the only decent lead you've got, yeah?"

"Yeah."

"If she's baiting you, what's the worst thing that happens? She breaks a heart that's already been broken, and she leaves you to mope around Druskin for another year and a half. How far away is that from your present condition?"

"Not very."

"Not very. But if she's pure and true, then you'll get your proof and you'll have crossed love's finish line all in one shot! Hope is *in* love, don't you see? They can't be separated. Why not take a chance?"

"Sarah. That's why. This isn't what she wanted."

"She wanted peace for you. Did you not just tell us that? Where is your peace now? Is *this* the life Sarah Huff would want for her sister?"

Anna wasn't convinced. At least, not outwardly. "Look, even if I had proof, I wouldn't know what to do with it. What is proof anymore? They could just deny it and everyone would believe them anyway. All I want is to not know the things I know anymore."

Asmi turned to Bamert and held her hand out. "Give me that cigar."

"May I ask what you intend to do with it?" Bamert asked.

"Smoke it, you stupid git."

He fished the cigar out of his pocket and tossed it over. Asmi rolled the stogie between her fingers before walking over to the fireplace and re-lighting it in the flame, then oh-so-casually took a big puff. A steak dinner puff. It was as natural to her as it would be to an oil baron. She grabbed a bottle of brandy off a nearby coffee table. Bamert's heart grew at the sight of it.

"This is a nice bottle," Asmi told them.

"I need everyone sober, please," said Anna. "For *once* in this goddamn life."

"I can't drink," Asmi told Anna. "Diabetic, remember?"

"Oh, right. You just huff glue solvents."

"Exactly. But if I could drink, I'd fancy this brandy. They stabbed my dad, Anna. Six inches to left and he'd be as good as dead. I don't like these Conquistadors. I don't like the Kirsches. Maybe they invented porting but they can piss off. I don't like any fucking bullies. And I don't accept that we're too young and inconsequential to do anything about it. D'you understand?"

"Yeah," said Anna.

"Good. Then there's work to do. I'll drink to that in spirit."

"Hell fucking yeah!" Bamert screamed. "Steal their secrets and then steal the girl, Anna. A stolen girl is sweeter than any other."

Just then, they heard a loud portclap from down the hall.

"Say," Bamert asked the girls, "was that the delivery boy? Why'd he take so long?"

They walked out of the parlor. There was black smoke rolling toward them from the kitchen, as methodical and deliberate as the living dead. They could hear the flames rumbling behind the great black veil: growing hungrier as they munched the drywall and cabinets. Then they heard a horrifying squeal as the ceiling of the kitchen caved in and drove the smoke into a frenzied rush.

"We gotta go," Anna said. She and Asmi ran, praying they knew the way to the front doors. But Bamert quickly ducked back into the parlor to retrieve his PortPhone as the smoke surged past the opening. The two girls had their phones out ready to port, but they already had put some distance between themselves and the smoke that had overcome Bamert and smothered him in choking black ash.

They busted open the double doors and ran out into the frosted gardens. The spreading fire lit up every window, making the house look like some horrible, thirty-eyed demon beast arising from its slumber. The flames gushed out of the roof. Every second waiting for Bamert felt like its own wormhole: a manipulation of spacetime that froze the body whole and kept it suspended in a nether-dimension.

Finally, Bamert threw open the doors and waltzed down the stone steps, his phone in one hand and his precious drink in the other. He was coughing and hacking, black spittle hanging from his nose and beard. He walked right past a shell-shocked Asmi and Anna, then sat down in the snow, breathing heavily and watching the estate burn. He took out his phone, casual as could be.

"Wait," said Asmi. "I can't be seen by the police. I'm not legal right now"

"I wouldn't worry about that," said Bamert. He made a voice call. "This is J. Paul Bamert. I'm at 2200 Old Georgetown Pike and the house is on fire. Yeah, I bet you can't." He hung up and slowly sipped from the Solo cup as his tar-soaked coughs died down.

"Ladies," he told them. "Edgar is not going to be happy with me."

DRUSKIN/DC/NEW YORK

The first thing Anna did when she got back to school was knock vigorously on Mrs. Ludwig's door. Mrs. Ludwig peeked out. "Mustang Sally" was playing on a loop again. Her Christmas tree was still up. There was a cat sitting, comfortably, in the center of it. It didn't even seem to notice the ornaments and tinsel hanging alongside it.

"Yes?" she asked Anna. She was peering over her glasses at her. Mrs. Ludwig always wore those owl-frame glasses but never seemed to look *through* them.

"I'd love another ride in the Cobra," Anna said.

"Now? In January? It's freezing out there, *schatz*."

"All the more invigorating."

Mrs. Ludwig sighed. "Let me get my coat."

One hour later, Anna sauntered out of Ludwig's apartment with a fake anklet and a rapid-fire heartbeat. The cat whose identity she stole this time was ELMER. She committed the black spot just under the left side of his whiskers to memory. Then, stomach still rumbling, she sprinted up the stairwell to barf into the toilet.

Asmi saw Anna rush into the bathroom and held Anna's hair for her as she emptied out her insides, using the SHIT MEMOIRS as a kneepad. When Anna was finished and wiped away the last traces of bile from her mouth, Asmi grabbed the notebook and flipped through the freshest pages.

"It says I'm a bitch in here!" Asmi cried.

"It says everyone is a bitch in there," Anna said.

"Well who's the bitch who wrote it? If it's that Junebug, I'll show her how bad a bitch I am."

"Jubilee."

"Who cares. Dreadful name. Did you enjoy the ride, dearie?"

"In parts."

"I'd nick a car like that. It's fantastic."

Early in the week, Anna dutifully tended to her usual campus routine. Classes. Diving. Cramming sessions all night. When she was able to steal a bit of sleep at night, she curled into a ball and imagined Sandy behind her, gently holding her and picking at her ears. Anna had grown fond of sleeping against the dorm room wall. There were so many goddamn walls in the world now—walls around houses and clubs and businesses and crummy ShareSpaces—but Anna's wall was one of the few good ones. It never judged her. It kept her safe and secure. Sandy was a superior bedmate, but this wall made for a fine substitute cuddle buddy.

On her Druskin-issued electronics, Anna unfollowed everyone she knew, communicating with the outside world solely through a dummy, old school email account she had created with her VPN. When she saw Vick walking around the quad, she stared straight ahead, neither seeking eye contact nor avoiding it. If he looked, he looked. Whatever.

At Gould House, she begged Burton for a new weighted blanket.

"I don't see Alyssa anymore!" he protested.

"Aren't you lonely, Burton?" Anna asked him. "Couldn't you use the company of a lady for the night?"

"Okay, A) You're not Bamert, so stop talking like him, and B) I have done just fine for myself since then."

"You have?" she asked, stunned at Burton's cocksmanship.

"Everyone loves a tambourine man."

"I don't."

"You don't like *any* men. The point is: I can't get you a blanket. I've been paranoid ever since they booted Bamert and you should be, too."

"Burton, if you only knew how deep my paranoia goes."

As a substitute, she grabbed the scratchy blanket her mom gave her out of her closet. It wouldn't be nearly as effective at muting portclaps as the weighted beast Bamert once had, but it would have to do. She couldn't use the spot by The Crater anymore, because Wade had that area locked down. Even the old school potheads were too scared to venture behind the infirmary anymore. Instead, Anna would have to port from the playing fields.

Druskin Stadium was built in 1948. Ever since its construction, trustees and alumni had steadfastly refused to renovate its aggregate concrete stands because they wanted it to look the exact same every time they came back to school to get loaded for Homecoming.

Underneath its washed-out bleachers was a grubby home team locker room that was left open at all times. In the dead of night on Friday, Anna slipped through South Campus with the blanket stuffed into her backpack, still wearing the bracelet Lara gave her around her arm for optimism's sake. It was not an optimism she trusted.

She crossed the practice fields in the cold and mud, and then walked along the old bridge overlooking the creek. No stars out tonight. The clouds had rudely shrouded them all. She stopped for a moment and looked over the parapet and down at the water below: now frozen and unforgiving. Nothing moved. She looked over to the banks of the river and felt a pull inside her, followed by a pang of guilt.

But Anna couldn't waste any more time. She scampered across the jayvee football field and rushed into the dark, exposed locker room. Once inside, she shut the door and turned on her counterfeit PortPhone, snatched from the ceiling tiles of Sewell Hall and still in working condition. Then she hit PORT and got an error message.

MASS LIMIT EXCEEDED.

"Dammit." She shed her scarf.

MASS LIMIT EXCEEDED.

She shed her knit Druskin hat, then hit PORT and felt the shiver.

There was a PortHut on Connecticut Avenue in the DC free zones that sold pre-paid phones with a set number of trips on them. She grabbed a 50-trip model off the rack inside and registered that phone to a *new* Bumlee daughter, who was born in 2005 but didn't exist until Bamert had drawn up her official proof of address a day earlier. After Anna got the phone registered, she calmly walked past the dead Cleveland Park Metro stop and paused at the casual steakhouse at the corner of Connecticut and Ordway. Armed PINE guards roving up and down the avenue took no notice of her, but she heard one of them bark at a port tourist for papers. Soon, shots rang out from that same spot.

No one else on the street paid the commotion any mind. It was a busy night, with customers porting to the door of the steakhouse to get a look at the room, give their reservation name to the maître d', roll their eyes at their table not being ready yet, and then vanish so they could spend that wait anywhere else. Vendors appeared at the back door to deliver fresh meat and julienned russet potatoes, two kilos at a time. A decent portwall and a $30 cover charge helped keep most of the street riffraff away, not to mention the innumerable PINE agents patrolling Connecticut Avenue all the way down into the heart of Washington. The area was smothered in choppers buzzing low overheard, scouring the ground for things to be angry about.

Through the steakhouse window, Anna watched the diners partake of high roller Cabernets served in bulbous wine glasses and slice into their grass-fed beef, hand-delivered directly from Estancia Ranch in Argentina. She saw a waiter come bounding through the double doors to the kitchen, hoping she might catch a glimpse through the doors of her mother scrubbing away at the plates and cutlery in back, but no such luck. Christmas break had only ended a few days prior, but already she missed Sandy terribly. There was an adjustment period in going back to being alone, and that adjustment remained its own form of hard labor.

She stepped aside from the window, hit PORT, and now she was in Manhattan at the corner of 57th Street and 6th Avenue. This part of town was hollow at night. The office buildings were mostly dead dark. The cross streets had long been cleared of taxis and cars to make the whole city a pedestrian zone. The only commotion nearby came from the line outside a Japanese mega-restaurant and a handful of tourists and drunks ducking away from the retail stretches of Fifth Avenue and Times Square to smoke weed and have sex down in the darkened hull of the F train station. On that station's platform was a series of open cars waiting for anyone looking to camp out or indulge in less restful activities.

A score of PINE agents were sweeping the area. They, along with the port immigrants they hunted, usually preferred scouting around warmer areas in the middle of January. But they never neglected Manhattan entirely. They could always find someone there who wasn't supposed to be there.

Anna was cold. Bereft of a hat or scarf, she covered her ears with her hands as the wind came hurtling through the skyscraper canyons.

It rattled the bare flagpoles: stiffened iron arms that stretched out above the shuttered revolving doors of virtually every office building. There were a handful of office lights still on, but people working in those offices rarely bothered to set foot on a New York sidewalk after filling out their timesheets for the day. She took out both her PortPhones and left them behind the bench of an abandoned bus stop. She had eight blocks to walk, and they were not short ones.

She crossed Fifth Avenue. During the day, it remained a tacky street fair of tourists and scammers desperate to hustle them with port tours and lightweight merchandise. The hordes of tourists had mostly dissipated now, but Anna still had to muscle her way through a small and raucous throng at the intersection before emerging on the East Side and finding herself back in the dark, menacing cold. Half the apartment buildings she walked by had a SHARESPACE banner draped across the front. The others were either filled with port squatters or about to be.

When she got to Sutton Place, she walked up the decaying access ramp and onto the promenade along the East River.

No one was there. Lara Kirsch was late yet again. From a nearby building, Anna could hear a couple of squatters screaming at each other from the inside of an abandoned one-bedroom apartment. It made her brace for gunfire that, blessedly, never came. Regardless, she felt naked out on the promenade, as if every window above was home to a sniper with a rifle scope trained on her.

You pushover. Lara's not coming. Emilia is coming to toss you in the East River, you absolute sucker.

She pocketed the rose pink bracelet in solidarity with her conscience.

There. Now you can't fool yourself anymore.

To stay distracted, she stared across the East River at the resurrected Domino Sugar factory. She would be stronger this time. She would obey the directorman in her head. Lara Kirsch owed her. Lara should have been on time, and she should have ported in on her knees, begging for forgiveness and dying to get back in Anna's good graces and not the other way around. *Furthermore—*

"Anna?"

She turned around and there was Lara at the top of the ramp, wearing sunglasses, ruby red lip gloss and a long blue wig. She was holding a plain manila envelope and looked scared to death. Like Anna, Lara felt eyes all over her. Both of them knew Emilia well enough to know what her evil eyes were capable of. She ran over to Anna and tucked the envelope into her hand.

"Take this." Lara told Anna.

"What is it? Why are you dressed like that?"

"Photographers can sometimes spot me by my hair."

"Oh."

"I did a bad thing, Anna. You're the only person I trust with this, even though you have no reason to trust me."

"What is it?"

"I'm sick of Emilia. I'm sick of my brother. They think they saved mankind but all they really did was port the can down the road. I may be seventeen, but I'm old enough to be ashamed of my family, Anna. Of who they are. Of what they did to you and so many others. No amount of weed makes that shame go away. I can try to run away from home all I like but that doesn't mean I can *get* away. And being a brat to Emilia about it isn't enough. So take this and maybe it'll do some good. Jason and Emilia saved these notes for posterity, but I took them. Valeria knew where they were hidden. I had her port into the family vault to grab them while Emilia was paying us a visit at—"

"Salton Boathouse."

"Salton fucking Boathouse," Lara said triumphantly. "I had to keep you in the dark about the real plan, otherwise it might have gotten all fucked up somehow. But it worked. Valeria wasn't too happy that Emilia had her deported after firing her, so she got the notes for us. She rules."

"But what are the notes?"

"They're the end of Jason and Emilia. I told you I knew things. Dr. Stokes will know what this is when he opens the envelope. Take it to him. If I try to deliver this to him myself, I'll be spotted. And if anyone tries to send a digital file of this, PortSys will know. Ask the reporter Sean Grann to help you find him. And warn Grann. Emilia knows where Grann lives. She has eyes on him. PortSys is her magic mirror. I'm scared of everywhere because of her."

"Lara, I'm tired. I can't hold in one more thing." Anna got zero warning about the tears. They erupted out of her, her belated attempt to contain them producing a HONK so loud, it was as if motor vehicle traffic had returned to New York City once more. Her lips crumpled. Her hands fell to her sides. Part of her didn't want Lara to see her like this, but another, stranger part was very much into the idea. Every moment with Lara was so primal and raw that it could only result in something this emotionally monumental. Lara was an event. Lara was the only event in Anna's life. She wanted every second with her to be real and indelible and *big*. Also, the wig on Lara looked terrific. No hope with love. No love without hope. *God dammit*.

"Anna, I have to go soon."

"You can't just summon me here, in this cold, then hand me this envelope and leave me again. You said it yourself: we can't almost tell each other things."

"I can't tell you right now. Ask Grann."

"August 9th, 2029," said Anna. "What about that?"

Lara put her hand to her mouth in grief. First she was nodding, then shaking her head, then nodding once more.

"He was there," Lara said. "Jason was there."

"What time?"

"11:56pm."

"Sarah's time of death was midnight."

"Oh, God." Lara leaned against an iron railing for support. "I should've known. I should've done something. I *could* have done something."

Anna, trying to keep her composure, didn't offer a hand. Hearing Lara confirm the news—consecrate it—brought Anna equal parts pain and vindication. "I need the proof that you have that he was there."

"I can take a screenshot. I'll have someone send it to your dummy number when I get back to my phone."

"Promise me," said Anna. Her jaw was stone when she said it. There was nothing flirtatious about the order.

"I promise." Lara limped away from the railing and offered a hand. Anna took it and her resolve ended its second brief cameo. Lara pulled Anna close and wrapped her in her neon-bangled arms.

"Roomie."

"Roomie."

"I'm so sorry," said Lara.

"I know," said Anna.

"We really need to stop making each other cry."

"I know."

They squeezed each other tight and the polyester fibers from Lara's wig got caught in Anna's mouth. It didn't matter. She kept her hands perfectly still but they were screaming to do more. They wanted to touch every inch of Lara Kirsch. Cold? What cold? There was no cold anymore. The air felt as hot as blood now.

It was this close to coming out of Anna's mouth. *I love you.* She had edited this moment into so many different scenes in her mind. Each time she imagined saying it to Lara, it felt realer than the previous fantasy. There was an *I love you* on the bridge by Druskin Stadium. There was an *I love you* on the white sands of Anguilla. There was an *I love you* at the top of Uluru in Australia. There was an *I love you* for everywhere. Now it was gonna pop out at the exact time she did NOT want it to.

But before she could say it, she had to acknowledge the harsher truth whipping around them.

"Lara," she whispered, "Your brother is a murderer."

"I know he is," Lara said. "Not just elephants, huh?"

"Not just elephants."

Lara stepped away. "They're both murderers, Jason and Emilia. Take the envelope. Stop them. You're braver than I am."

Before Anna could say one word more, Lara Kirsch kissed her on the cheek. She felt Lara's hot lip gloss press against her dried, ashy winter skin. It tickled her face and felt so wonderful that she couldn't bear it. Lara's lips lifted away and Anna could feel the gloss still on her, like someone had lovingly branded her. That part of

Anna's face belonged to Lara now. It belonged to Lara forever. She wanted Lara's lips. She wanted to press hard against them and have Lara kiss her back and know, in that moment, that Lara belonged to her as much as she belonged to Lara.

But it was too late. Of course it was. By the time Anna had stored all of that in her hard drive, Lara Kirsch was sprinting back down the ramp and disappearing into the sinister caverns of midtown Manhattan.

SHIT MEMOIRS ENTRY
Date unknown

Yesterday I saw Jubilee eating breakfast at Wetherell and she put mayonnaise on a blueberry muffin and ate it. That's a true story. And if she writes that I'm lying about this (I know what her handwriting looks like), I'll print out the photo I took of her doing it and paste it here. ☺

GOULD HOUSE

Anna held Lara's envelope in her hands and felt along its smoothed, unlabeled front. This little packet of secrets pleased her hands to no end, and they were fickle little monsters about what they encountered. If they couldn't touch Lara all over, this would have to do.

She sat on Burton's bed, legs spread the way Bamert used to do when he was holding court to an audience of two. She was wearing the bracelet again. Burton tuned his tambourine (which, he insisted, was a thing that tambourines required) while Asmi banged away at a history paper on her laptop. Earlier that morning, Asmi had taken her own ride with Mrs. Ludwig that, as with Anna, resulted in an emergency appointment with the porcelain of the Sewell bathroom. She herself had managed to pull off a round of feline identity theft: slipping her anklet around the neck of a cat named Noel, who was easily distinguishable from the others because he only had three legs. Asmi Naru now had the port identity of Esther Bumlee, along with the hardware to go along with it.

"Are you gonna open that envelope?" Burton asked Anna.

"I don't know," she said. "Lara didn't tell me if I could or couldn't."

"That means you can." Burton put down his tambourine and rubbed his face. He looked pained, like he was about to confess his sins.

"What?" Anna asked him.

"I'm going to say it, and you're not gonna like it."

"You could put that disclaimer in front of anything you say, Burton."

"Lara's not trustworthy," Burton said. "She hosed you once, and she'll hose you again."

"No," said Anna. "It wasn't like that." Hours after Lara had fled Sutton Place, Anna got a picture message from an unknown number. There it was: Jason Kirsch's porting history from the night of Sarah's death. That it was digital piece of evidence felt flimsy and wrong given what it inferred, but Lara Kirsch had kept her promise.

"Well, of course you don't feel that way," said Burton. "You might be biased!"

"Trust me: Lara is one of us, not one of them."

"I don't believe that for a red second."

"A 'red second'? Is that a real expression? Shut up already. Lara's solid."

"Open the envelope," Asmi told her. "Might give you a clue either way."

Anna ran her hand down the back seam before pinching the clasp and taking out a small sheaf of yellow legal notes. It was written in laser-precise longhand, good enough to be its own font. Yet it was incomprehensible: formulas and italicized variables and superscript numerals and Greek letters and random polygons and every other inscrutable mathematics symbol that Anna dreaded seeing whenever she cracked open an exam booklet. She was straight A's in trig, but these formulas were far beyond her high school-level grasp. Attached to the pages was a small yellow Post-it note that read, in glittery purple ink: FOR DOCTOR STOKES. Another Post-it note included the address of journalist Sean Grann.

"I know what this is," said Burton. He pointed to a symbol at the top of the first page.

$$\bar{H}$$

"That's antihydrogen," he said. "Your old roomie handed you the formula for porting."

"Sounds like Lara didn't screw Anna over at all," Asmi said.

"Oh, she hosed her, all right," said Burton. "Just not the way I thought she would. Anna, you're a dead girl if anyone catches you with that."

SEWELL HALL

Anna was in bed, the envelope tucked inside her desk drawer but still gnawing at her. Under the top sheet, she rubbed her fingers together like it was still between them. She stared up at the small neon stars she had stuck to the ceiling, the same kind of decorative stars Sandy got from the Dollar Tree and put on their bedroom ceiling back in Rockville. Those prefab constellations still couldn't push the envelope from her thoughts, so she turned to the wall and shut her eyes tight to make all the nagging questions go away. *How am you gonna find Sean Grann? And what was with that kiss?*

Okay, so the kiss thing took up the bulk of her mental gymnastics. A kiss should bring more certainty, not less. Anna kept reliving it on a loop: a mental TikTok for her to add to her Lara compilation. When she had gotten back from Manhattan that night and looked in the mirror, she could see the imprint of Lara's lip gloss on her cheek. She didn't wash it off until the next morning. She hated—*hated*—that this was the thing she focused on the most, given the crisis at hand. It was the shallowest, most 17-year-old thing possible.

But you are *a 17-year-old.*

She felt a breeze come over the room, maybe off of Sewell Beach, and checked the open window. It wasn't open at all. Looming over the bed, she saw the figure of a man—a squicky man—with his hair parted down the center of his scalp, clad in khakis and a black shirt with the Conquistadors logo adorning the breast. He was holding his extremely large butcher's knife. She could hear him breathing heavily: long, slow, deliberate exhalations, like he wanted to colonize the air of her bedroom. She felt a shiver of a whole different kind.

"If you move," the man whispered, twirling the knife, "this isn't the only thing that goes in you."

"Go ahead and kill me," she whispered back. "It would get me out of a physics test next week."

"Funny girl."

"Hello, Jason," she said. *The envelope. He's here for that envelope. He knows about the screengrab, too.*

309

"Hello, little piggy."

Jason Kirsch placed the knife on Anna's desk and spun it. Then he picked it back up and knelt down three feet from the bed, holding the knife out to the side like he was preparing to gut a newborn elephant. Anna wanted to turn on the lights and scream FIRE as loud as she could, fists clenched and mouth open wider than her own head. *FIRE. FIRE. FIRE. FIRE EVERYWHERE.* But Jason had the knife, and so again Anna Huff was forced to choke on her own words. They burned in her esophagus.

"I'm gonna kill you," she told him.

"That's exactly what your loser of a sister said. But she killed herself. So quickly, too. Didn't take much encouragement. It's a pity, you know. She was a good looking woman. Would have passed my naked test. Do you know what that is?"

"Go fuck yourself."

"There's no need for that when so many women are lined up to give me the pleasure. Now, about the test. I believe certain women look their absolute sexiest without a stitch of clothing on them. No heels or lingerie necessary. Those accessories only get in the way. Your sister had the kind of body to pass my test. You, less so. If your rotten mother hadn't stirred the night your sister ate a bullet, I think I would have had time to indulge myself."

Is this sack of shit giving a launch presentation on rape?

Anna was going to kill Jason Kirsch. There would be no *nearly* this time. She would kill him as surely as he killed Sarah. And he did kill Sarah, no matter who pulled the trigger that night. He was a murderer and he deserved murder. That would only be the crowning blow. First, Anna would rip his scalp off, cut off of his arms and legs, kill his children in front of him, and then burn him alive. She would visit every last bit of karmic pain upon this man, if only to get him to shut the fuck up.

"I bet you looked up to her," he went on. "I bet you wish she was still here, to be a big sis and give you all kinds of little piggy advice."

"Is this what you do?" she asked him. "Just hound people until they do whatever you tell them to do?"

"It's worked for me so far. Also, if they don't do what I say, I just slit their throats. Wasn't necessary for your Sarah though."

"Keep her name out of your mouth."

"*Sarah, Sarah, Sarah,*" he sang.

Wait. Timeout. He's not asking about the envelope. He doesn't know you have it. Maybe he doesn't know about the screengrab, either? He does seem stupid.

"It's not gonna work this time," she told him. "You can't make me do anything I don't want to do."

"That knife and I say otherwise. I'll be paying you more visits, so that you can understand the truth. That is my gift to you. There are things inside my head that are more coherent and visionary than the things inside anyone else's head. You should be grateful I'm sharing that vision with you."

"I'm not."

"Here's something I realized. When you have a mind like mine, life is enhanced in every facet. Isn't that amazing? All the places I can go, yet there's nowhere I can go on earth better than inside my own mind. When I'm in love, I feel that love stronger than normal people do. When I'm high, I have a better high than your average gutter junkie. If my sister ever bothered to think for herself, all that weed she smokes might be put to better use."

"You have no right to dump on Lara like that."

"I have every right to. Who are you to say otherwise? She's as much of a waste as you Huffs are. You didn't even know your own sister was in pain. You couldn't stop her from killing herself when she needed you the most. These are true statements."

They were. Love and Druskin had managed to distract Anna from survivor's guilt somewhat, but now Jason Kirsch was hauling it out of storage, porting her back to that night in Rockville, as she slept tenderly in her mother's bed without any inkling of what was going on in the room next door until the gun went off. *How could you not know, Anna? How could you not have been on guard, in this world? You're an idiot for letting that happen. A nothing.* She could feel the seed being sowed into her brain, along with the sickening realization that Jason Kirsch was good at this. He was good at making people suspicious of themselves.

But perhaps Anna Huff was good at it, too.

"When this is over," she told Jason Kirsch, "it's gonna be *you* dying by suicide. And that's the polite way of phrasing it, you fucking eel."

He suppressed a giggle. "You think I secretly hate myself," he said.

"No one's ever loved you. And it shows."

"The weak always soothe themselves by thinking the strong are miserable. Little piggy, my life is amazing, and I wouldn't trade it for anything."

"I'll have you trading it for the keys to hell."

"I'd keep those plans to yourself, if I were you. I think you've already seen what happens when you venture too far out of your comfort zone. How was Oxford?" he asked her. *Son of a bitch.* Jason knew it all. Orchestrated it. The Turf Tavern. The angry Conquistadors burning and looting the Naru storefront right after Anna ported in. Bamert's house burning to the ground. His people were there. His people were *everywhere*. He would never, ever leave her alone.

Jason Kirsch stood up, again asserting dominion over the room. He was bigger than he looked on video, with shoulder and thigh muscles so thick it was like he wore armor under his skin.

"I'll be back," he told her. "Be a good little piggy in the meantime for me. We've only just started."

He took out his PortPhone and tipped her desk chair. Just as the chair toppled over, he ported out, the clap in exact sync with it smacking the ground. She ran to the desk and yanked out the envelope from behind it, jamming it under her pillow.

Asmi swung open the door. "What was that?"

"Nothing," said Anna. "Go back to bed."

BANTAM, CT

Anna ported from the stadium locker room the following night. When she reappeared in the Northwest corner of Connecticut, the wind slapped at her, demanding she go away. But she held firm, standing at the bottom of a sloped gravel driveway frozen solid with slick black ice. There was a yellow clapboard house thirty yards up the driveway, but the portwall kept her from zapping in any closer to it. The surrounding countryside was dead. No other houses or people in sight. Nothing except cold and darkness.

Anna tried circumventing the icy gravel, walking along the withered patches of grass alongside the driveway. The skeletal fir trees poked and jabbed at her until she had no choice but to test the gravel once more. One step and she knew she'd made a terrible mistake.

Oh shit.

She slipped, landed hard on her poor tailbone, and then slid like a hockey puck right back down the driveway, settling at the bottom and leaving her with an incongruous, gorgeous view of the stars above.

Hey, is that Jupiter?

The front door of the house opened. Anna heard someone cock a shotgun.

"Who's out there?" a voice shouted.

She stuck her hands up, still flat on the ground. From a distance, she looked like a snowman that had melted.

"Hello!" she shouted. "I come in peace!" *Why did you say that? You're not a fucking alien.*

"I don't want any!" the voice cried.

"I'm not a port marketer! I am a very nice person!"

That didn't satisfy the voice. The man at the front door fired at one of the trees and a large branch came falling down on the ice, all damp on the inside and slimy bark on the outside. *God, everyone and their stupid guns.* Anna rolled out of the way and stuck her hands up again.

"Please don't shoot! I'm a girl! You wouldn't shoot a girl, right?! That would be a dick move!"

"That's why they always send girls."

"My name is Anna Huff and I'm a teenager!"

"I don't like teenagers."

"I don't either!"

"If you're looking for writing advice, I've got an email address."

"I'm not here for that! I'm gonna walk to you, okay? I'm not armed! I'm just gonna walk, one foot in front of the other, super slow."

The man at the door held still but kept his gun on Anna. Laboring to breathe in the icy gale, she grabbed a brittle tree and propped herself up. Then, she walked up the side of the driveway again, never daring to put her feet on that cursed ice. She reached out for another tree, then another, then another. She looked like she was traversing a ropes course from one inch up in the air. When she finally reached the door, the man holding the gun looked more befuddled than angry.

"Will you put that thing down?" she pleaded.

"What do you want?"

"You're Sean Grann, the reporter?"

"I don't have to answer that."

"Oh come on man, I just had to climb up your stupid driveway. Why don't you salt the thing? Okay, I know why you don't have to salt the thing. Whatever."

"I'm Sean Grann."

"I need to talk to you."

"About what?"

"About Dr. Ciaran Stokes."

CUBA

After visiting Sean Grann and warning him, Anna had to wait a full week to port to Cuba, hiding Lara's envelope behind a loud, farting radiator in her room. She went through the motions on campus: walking and eating and studying until her vision began to double. She could have fallen asleep in any place, in any position. As always, she frantically tried to keep up with her assignments but still felt as if she was doing the absolute bare minimum. Other kids, Burton included, had a limitless capacity for work and for extracurriculars, as if they had cloned themselves. Teachers and coaches always demanded focus, and the other Druskin kids seemed so much better than her at finding it. They compared their prospective GPAs with one another constantly. She hated all of them, Burton included. Him she hated a wee bit less than the others.

Cuba promised to be an all-day affair, which meant that Anna had to trudge out to the stadium at 5am on a Saturday morning, port out, and then return only after it was dark again back on campus. On her way to the stadium that morning, she looked back and saw a trail of perfect footprints in the snow behind her. That wouldn't do. She doubled back and, with her new duck boots, swept the prints away and made mad dashes in the snow to throw off anyone who might stumble on her path and grow curious.

Once more, she cracked open the fetid locker room door and grabbed the wool blanket she had stashed over in the corner. Then she hit PORT and found herself in a darkened alley in the town of Trinidad, with nothing but the sound of crowing roosters to accompany her. She sat down with the envelope and snuck a bit of extra rest, waiting for dawn.

When the sun finally rose, Anna slipped her little bulldog phone behind a crate of rotted oranges and walked out of the alley. The world turned pastel. Yellow sunshine. Living, light green vegetation. Rows of houses with clay tile roofs painted in light blues and pinks and oranges. The streets came to life as tourists began porting in, live spammers right alongside them. Unlike so many other cities, the streets in Cuba were still used, with refurbished American lemons lumbering down the streets as the music kicked up. That music wouldn't stop until well after midnight.

Anna flagged down a souped-up 1954 Hudson Hornet, a Hunter green step-down model that was the size of a barge.

"Cuanto cuesta un paseo al Parque Natural Topes de Collantes?"

"Un paseo?" asked the driver. He looked confused, then held up his hand and mimicked using a PortPhone.

"No tengo un PortFono," Anna said.

"No?" asked the driver. "Entonces, como llegaste a Cuba?" *Then how'd you get to Cuba?*

When Anna held up an American twenty, the driver ceased asking questions. He swung the door open and she sat down on a spotless tan bench seat. This was more comfortable than the Cobra. The Hornet was as wide as a house. Its dashboard was 100% steel, featuring all kinds of latches and doodads you could play with. Anna laid her hand on the glove box, looking at the driver to make sure it was okay for her to touch the interior. He nodded. He was proud of his big beauty.

They were off. The road was rocky and uneven and the floor of the Hornet was low to the ground, but the beast cut across the terrain with ease. Smooth and silent, like a shark on the hunt. The car took care of Anna's stomach in ways that Mrs. Ludwig's Cobra could not. Soon they reached the entrance of the park. She got out of the Hornet and gazed at a pristine lagoon down below, a crashing waterfall feeding it. She had forgotten, entirely, the feeling of old-fashioned travel: taking the long road toward a destination and then experiencing the supreme majesty of watching that destination come into view. It was a sensation of earned awe that shouldn't have ever gone extinct.

The sun above blazed so hot and bright that Anna couldn't even make out its sphere. A dip would have been nice. She held up another twenty for the driver.

"Me puedes buscar en cuatro horas?"

He nodded. She pocketed the twenty and walked toward the lagoon overlook. There were Americans lounging on a rocky beach alongside the lagoon, lollygagging in the coarse sand and porting back and forth to grab camping supplies before frolicking in the clean water. Anna made a beeline for the trailhead above and started the three-mile walk toward Dr. Stokes' house. She pulled out a rough map that Grann had grudgingly given her and followed it down to the paces through the lush parkland, ignoring the hideous Western advertisements that polluted the trail: stacked ads for phones, wart creams, escorts willing to port directly to your bedroom, and mediocre streaming movies. Once she veered off the path, the branded garbage disappeared and the jungle closed in behind her, reaching around and over her until she was walking in near darkness. She could hear wildlife but couldn't see it.

After an hour of slogging through the muck, she came to a river fifty yards wide. There, in the center of the river, perched upon two wet logs stretching out from either end of the banks, was a single-room house with big, tinted windows on every side.

"Oh, for crying out loud."

She edged closer to the banks and looked downstream, where the river picked up speed and became a white, foaming churn. Close to the horizon, the river disappeared, as if it had been lopped off with a giant cleaver. Falling into the river would be decidedly bad, but Anna hadn't come this far not to deliver the goods. She tested the log with her boot. It was so slick as to be untouchable. No friction of any kind. When she pulled her boot away and looked at the bottom, it was greased black with pure petroleum.

This is so typical. You finally want to walk places and this is what awaits you. Bullshit.

A voice rang out from the forest. "INTRUSO!"

Anna looked for the voice but only saw an endless tangle of greenery. Dr. Ciaran Stokes opened his side window open pointed a gun at her. Grann had warned Anna, "You're gonna kill yourself doing this." Here was proof.

"Good morning," Stokes said to Anna. "Feel free to test the log, but it's a long way down the waterfall when the river carries you there."

Anna held up the envelope. "I have something for you."

"Is that supposed to entice me?"

"My name is Anna."

"So?"

"This is an envelope taken from Emilia Kirsch's vault by her daughter, Lara. She wanted you to have it."

"What's in it?"

"The formula for porting."

"And how would you know that's what it is?"

"Because I get straight A's, motherfucker."

"A teenager who thinks she's smart. That's reassuring. Do you have a PortPhone on you?"

"I left it in Trinidad," she told him.

"Tell you what: you can talk to me if you cross that log."

"Can I have a rope?"

"You cannot."

Why is everyone such a gleaming penis?

Anna stuffed the envelope into her bra and grabbed two sharp sticks. Then she straddled the log and began the long, extremely painful scoot across to the center of the river, digging the impromptu spears into the log to keep her balance. She envisioned Willamy's dreaded X on the side of Stokes' house, focusing on it as best she could. The oil was seeping through her pants, her underwear, her everything. After three feet, she felt choleric. Her hands did not like this big gross log, not one bit. Midway through, she lost equilibrium and had to grab onto a tiny branch to right herself. The branch dug into her saddle as she wriggled past it. She was beginning to hate the outdoors now, almost as much as she hated people with guns.

When she reached the end of the log, Stokes didn't bother to offer her a hand. He kept his gun on her as she pulled herself through his door and lay gasping on the ground, sore and greasy. She wiped her hands on herself, then gave him the envelope. When the doctor pulled out the notes, his eyes went buggy and he dropped the gun so fast it nearly went off on its own. Anna got up and jumped away from it.

"Lara Kirsch gave you this?" he asked Anna.

"Yes," she said.

"Why?"

"None of your business."

"I've been looking for this for a very long time. You're an A student, indeed."

Stokes handed Anna a roll of paper towels and a spray bottle of disinfectant cleaner.

"Clean up the oil, please. I hate messes."

"Clean it up yourself," Anna told him. "I'm not your maid. I wanna know what those notes mean. I wanna know how porting works."

"It's beyond your feeble grasp."

"What's in there that you didn't already know, Doctor? Or are you the fraud everyone thinks you are?"

Stokes knelt down to spray away the oil stain.

"Look," he told her, "there is a portionality to this. It was my team that cracked the process. Without my innovation and leadership, PortSys would be nothing. We were already close, testing the formula on whatever losers and urchins Jason brought us. Some of them disintegrated in the process. Some of them are stuck in the wormholes for infinity."

"So it wasn't just Jason who experimented on people."

"Who cares?" Stokes asked. "Do you care about the poor Taiwanese laborer who made your little PortPhone when you go zooming around with it? People never say it, but in their every waking action, they endorse the human cost of *things*. So yes, we accepted that as the cost of changing the world for the better. And I'd wager you've accepted it, too."

"You don't know me."

"You're a teenager. You don't even know yourself."

"PortSys experimented on me, too."

"So?"

"So I deserve to know how PostSys works from the inside."

"No you don't. You're unnecessary. Besides, how should I know how they operate now? They fired me, remember? And do you know why?"

"Because you're an asshole."

319

"Funny girl. We hit a wall in development, until a colleague of mine, an *underling*, had a breakthrough and helped complete the formula."

"So you didn't invent porting," Anna said.

"If anyone invented it, it was I."

"But someone else finished the job."

"And then I was cast out before I could see it made whole! Don't you understand? It was *my* idea."

"Ideas are overrated."

"Says a girl who's probably never had a good one. The Kirsches fired me the second they knew they had a working product, so that only *they* would be privy to the final working process. The underling? Dead. Murdered in Turkey. The only reason PortSys kept me on call before the Grann article posted was to ring me up anytime they had bugs that the Kirsches were too stupid to sort out on their own."

Anna looked at the sheaf of legal notes in Stokes' hand.

"So those complete the formula?"

"Together with my files, this is everything," Stokes said, smiling. "The full picture."

"So what will you do with it?"

"Compete! Everyone thinks I'm a fraud because the Kirsches spew lie after lie after lie. But now, with this, we can take PortSys down. You see? We can make a better porting world. A *responsible* one."

"I don't believe you," Anna said.

"No?"

"You wanna bring them down, but you'll be just as bad. You'll be poisoned, like them."

"You make the worst assumptions about people because that's your generation's hobby and you have nothing better to do. Maybe you should try seeing both sides of this," Stokes suggested.

Anna picked up Stokes' handgun. She had never fired a gun before. It was a lot heavier than she thought it would be. She hated guns but her hands clearly did not.

"You're getting oil on that," Stokes pouted.

"That's your fault, isn't it? Give me the notes," she said. If she was nervous, her words didn't betray her. She was low and calm. She didn't care enough about Stokes to worry about his opinion of her.

The doctor gestured all around the river house. True to Grann's reporting, there was an assault rifle resting against every window. "You're new with that gun," he told her ominously. "I am not new with those."

Anna shot Stokes. She shot him before she could even consider the consequences, or the fact that the gun had a wicked kickback that sent her reeling into the glass wall behind her. Into that bullet went all of the hatred and fear and guilt and anger that she had dealt with for over a year. It felt *great* to shoot someone.

Stokes' right leg exploded: a great blood bomb sending out shards of hair and bone, soiling his precious floor and leaving him howling to the ground. He dropped the notes. Anna snatched them up and grabbed every other gun in the cabin. Through the window, Anna saw one of his assistants on the riverbank, his own gun drawn.

"You can't leave," Stokes said. "The windows may be bulletproof, but he'll shoot you dead the second you walk out. And the underbelly of this house is lined with explosives. I can blow it at any time."

"How?"

"With the push of a button, you brat." People in 2031 could do too many bad things too easily.

"Good luck reaching it now, pegleg." Anna stood next to the doorway and slipped the rifles into the river, one by one. Then she closed the door, walked over to the kitchen, pulled two Ziploc bags out of a drawer, and pointed at a sleek laptop resting atop a rattan desk.

"What are you doing?" Stokes asked her.

"How much does your laptop weigh?"

"What?"

"HOW MUCH DOES IT WEIGH?" she demanded.

"Three pounds, but don't—"

She did. She grabbed the laptop and ejected the hard drive. Then she dropped the hard drive, her phone, and the notes into one of the Ziploc bags. She sealed the bag up, sealed that bag in another bag, and then stuffed it all down her blackened pants. She opened the window facing downriver and looked out at the Stygian waters below. The river was a great serpent tongue, the waterfall at its end the back of a hungry mouth.

"Where do they experiment on people?" she asked Stokes.

"They move the lab and the servers around. You'll never find any of it."

"Then tell me where *you* did the experiments."

He sighed. "Outside of Bozeman, Montana. It's a compound. Unmarked. The smartwall is the best of its kind. Don't bother."

"That's not for you to decide, Doc. I'm leaving." But before she did, she peeled off her shirt, kicked off her boots, then walked over to Stokes and stared at him.

"What are you doing?" Stokes asked.

"Watching you bleed." She kicked him in the ribs. His cries of agony bounced crisply off the bulletproof glass.

She leapt into the river. Stokes' lackey opened fire from the side, but by then Anna was already so far down the river that it was an impossible shot.

The river manhandled Anna, overwhelming her anytime she thought she was about to gain control. This is why she wanted to be on a diving team and not a swim team. She reached her toes downward hoping to strike the riverbed, but only found colder waters and tiny biting fish. The river carried her past a rock and it scythed into her arm. The rapids were engulfing her now. Whenever she came up for air, the water nailed her and snatched away the end of every breath. Soon, there wouldn't be any more breaths to cut off. Soon, the water would flow into Anna's sinuses and down her throat and flood her system like amniotic fluid. The river would take her.

So this is what drowning is like. Feels very stupid.

The dropoff was coming at lightspeed. Back on the Druskin campus, Coach Willamy would have all the girls on the diving team tread water for long stretches, sometimes an entire practice. If a girl tired out and sunk, he would yell at her instead of rescuing her. Anna could hear Willamy now: *You're not even trying to stay alive, Huff. You're just giving up because you don't think you can give more than what you've already given, and that's why you suck.* If that was the last voice she ever heard before dying, she would be very angry about it.

And then, a branch. Sweet glory of life, the river offered Anna a reprieve and she clung to it with a superhuman fury. All she could think about at the moment was everyone she hated: Willamy, Vick, Stokes, two of the three Kirsches. No way Anna could die with all of them still alive and prospering. She wasn't gonna leave this world without owning all of them first.

On either side of the anchored branch, the river was waiting to throttle her. Only a few feet in front of the branch were the falls, kicking up a spray that decorated the plunge into oblivion with fleeting rainbows. The branch itself was part of a fallen tree that had gotten lodged behind a rock outcropping in the center of the river. Anna pulled and pulled until, at long last, her feet finally touched something solid. She scrambled up the rocky outcropping and looked down below. A group of tourists had ported into the lagoon to skinny dip. They were having a great time. Anna hated them now, too.

"MOVE." she shouted at them. The roar of the falls drowned her out. No matter. She stepped back on the slick black rock to get a running start and then jumped.

The diving technique came to her automatically, No overthinking it. Core muscles engaged. Legs tight together, as if bound with twine. Neck stiff. Toes pointed straight enough to make a ballerina wince. Anna swept her arms forward as the emerald glories of the Cuban jungle panned up into her line of vision. She joined her brilliant hands above her head and became a human arrow, taking aim as she rocketed toward the lagoon below.

When she hit the water, there was no pain. No rocks hidden under the surface to sabotage her entry. The dive was so effortless, she started laughing before she had even broken the surface. Flawless technique. It was a 10.0 dive and she knew it. She felt down into her pants. There was still a Ziploc bag full of Big Teleportation's deepest secrets comfortably lodged in her undies.

The nudists in the lagoon gasped before breaking out in raucous applause. Anna ignored them and swam for the banks. When she got to the parking lot, she slipped into the Hudson Hornet, in her bare feet and a sports bra, and held out a wet twenty for the driver.

"Rapido. Por favor."

Anna had been in such a rush that she didn't realize the driver's seat was unoccupied. She looked back at the beach and saw only naked white people. The paths and surrounding jungle were similarly barren, but the thrill of her dive was wearing off and paranoia was settling back in. Ciaran Stokes and his Cuban Wade would be coming down that path shortly.

Anna scooted over to the driver's seat. The key was still in the ignition. *Is that what it's called? The ignition? How does this work?* Everything she knew about driving she learned from old Dwayne Johnson movies and from Sarah driving her to the movies in Rhonda. Sometimes Sarah would let Anna sit on her lap and turn the steering wheel.

Now she remembered. *The pedal on the right. That's the one you mash with your foot.*

She turned the key and the big green boat shuddered and harrumphed its way to life. She grabbed the gear shift and looked at the letters on the dash: P, D, N, R. Rhonda and the Cobra both had manual transmissions. This refurbished Hornet had been blessedly restored with an automatic.

D stands for Drive, shithead.

She yanked the gearshift but it wouldn't move. Twisting it did nothing, either. She yanked again until the stick was nearly ready to break off. Only after nearly destroying the transmission of this fine antique did Anna Huff finally have a breakthrough.

Push the top of it down first, then *shift.*

She stomped on the gas so hard, the car went crashing into a NO CLAVADOS sign that stood between the Hornet and the steep hill down to the beach below. She shifted into Reverse and mashed the accelerator again. Now she was flying backwards and failing to remember the existence of the wide pedal on the left that did the stopping. This looked so much easier when Mrs. Ludwig was doing it.

"AYYYYY!" That was the driver. He was running out from the jungle, frantically zipping up his fly. Anna found the brake and shifted into Drive. The Hornet made a horrible noise, like she had broken something vital inside of it. She gave the gas a gentle tap and edged the wheel just enough this time to get back on the road to Trinidad. The poor driver's phone was still sitting on the passenger seat.

The thing Anna noticed the most about driving was that it was awesome. Here she was, a 17-year-old girl, just a few inches north of five feet, and now she was encased in a steel exoskeleton that could hit 80mph and cut through her enemies like they were weeds. Driving was freedom. Anna owned the road. The bump and potholes and looping curves were hers to conquer. Her stomach felt better than it had in months. And so many fun things to grab with her hands! Her busy little fingers could fiddle all they pleased with the radio and blinker and the headlights. She turned on the wipers and seeing them stand at attention thrilled her like she was a child at a carnival.

When Anna got back to Trinidad, she eased the Hornet next to a free stretch of curb, stopping in place for five minutes before finally realizing that P stood for park. She tucked the keys above the visor, grabbed the driver's phone, and tossed it in the glove box. She swore she'd come back to Cuba one day to beg his forgiveness. Then she ran out onto the street—men and women alike gawking at the sight of a wet teenager running around barefoot and shirtless—headed down the alley, found her phone behind the orange crate, and hit PORT.

The second Anna was back in the Druskin locker room, she saw another person's shadow. A man grabbed her from behind and wrapped his hand tight around her mouth. Dean Vick had been waiting for her.

"Where have you *been*, Annie Huff?"

DRUSKIN STADIUM

Vick's hands were disgusting. Terrible hands. Minor hands. Anna wanted to vomit through the five angry fingers he had firmly clenched around her jaw. He was clamping down hard on her face with his right hand and her bare stomach with his left, the latter mere inches above her precious Ziploc bag. The door to the locker room was slammed shut and all Anna could see were exposed wooden 4x4's extending up to the bleachers, nails crudely sticking out of them. This room, like Vick's basement, was a prison. She was gonna die here if she didn't think quickly.

He's hurting you. That means you get to hurt him back.

"Give me that phone," Vick hissed, reaching for Anna's hand. She thrashed around to break free, but it was no use. Vick was too strong, squeezing her belly so hard that her ribs were about to collapse. There was only one way to gain leverage over him. Anna dug her heels in, leaning back and taking him back with her, farther and farther back until she drove him into one of the wooden 4x4's. A single nail sticking out from the timber sunk into Vick's back and he squealed in pain as Anna wrested herself away from him at long last.

Vick was a great bulging vein of a man now. Taut as piano wire. How could anyone be so hateful? What was the point? He charged at Anna and she deftly sidestepped him. *Toro!* He took another charge and caught her with a shoulder to the hip. A lump as hard as bone formed on contact.

"You never belonged at this school," Vick told her.

"Yeah but you do," Anna said, giving him her own crooked, evil grin. "You're a common administrator, Charles. *With a head made of wet cement.*"

Vick charged once more and missed, with Anna slugging him in the puncture wound as he passed. He grabbed at his back and fell to his knees, weakened in strength but not in rage. He raised a final angry finger at her.

"You'll never get away with this."

Before Anna ported out, she made sure to get the final word in.

"Say hi to my bulldog figurine for me, you psychotic dick."

Then she stepped out of the locker room and away from Dean Vick's poisonous hands.

CAIRO

Anna was in the center of downtown Cairo in her bare feet. Men noticed her immediately. She took off running so that no one could grab her. It wasn't quite yet dawn in Egypt but the capital was still swathed in its signature bustling din, which was there before porting and would remain long after. Vendors lined the street with open carts to sell tea, appliances, cigarettes, vapes, and hair dryers. The asphalt was still clogged with moving trucks swerving around abandoned motorbikes, horses, and drunken port tourists. A guy who ported in near Anna and who had no sense of the city's rhythm immediately got clipped by a semi when he obliviously stepped into the street.

The sour tang of burning smoke was everywhere. It clung to Anna as tightly as Vick did back in the Druskin stadium locker room. A flare went off in the distance, followed by a volley of machine guns rat-a-tat-tatting. Cairo went in and out of Red Zone status every hour. While PortSys didn't ask Anna for two-step verification to go there this time around, that still didn't make it the safest destination.

It was strange, how tinny the gunshots sounded to her. Even the gunshot that killed Anna's sister, and in turn woke Anna up, sounded weak, like a dime store firecracker. She didn't even realize it was a gun until Sandy started screaming. The sound of gunfire still didn't frighten her the way it should have. It was everywhere in the free zones. When you live with war, she reckoned, you accept the ambience of war right up until the moment it blows you to pieces.

Anna ducked into a side alley, dutifully dodging all the stray dogs and cats wandering around. The alley was clotted with old bicycles and garbage left by thoughtless tourists. She slumped down against a cool stone wall and a light rain flicked off the tin roofs, drizzling fresh water onto her grimy feet and legs. She took a photo of a spat-out wad of chewing gum sitting in the dirt, knowing she couldn't post it ironically to WorldGram but still snapping ironic photos out of habit.

She had no money. She had an American passport that protected her back on U.S. soil but would do the precise opposite here. A man in camo fatigues with a red armband came walking down the alley carrying a gun. Anna hid her face and pretended to be crying so that the soldier would leave her be. Under present circumstances, feigning distress wasn't a problem for her. She had been attacked by Dean Vick a second time and had only barely come out unscathed. She had also shot a man, although that should have bothered her more than it did. She wanted a normal brain and she wanted to have normal feelings about the situation, but no. No, normal was an ongoing delusion. The whole goddamn world was psycho, and its psychosis was clearly rubbing off on Anna Huff.

Or maybe you were just always *a psycho.*

She was happy to be out of the New Hampshire cold. But she was still wet, the dusty Cairo air pulling sweat out of her skin.

The soldier passed Anna without breaking stride. When he got farther down the alleyway, she opened up Network Z and checked on her mom. There Sandy was, back in DC, a little blue dot on Connecticut Avenue in Cleveland Park. Anna could see other dots popping up outside the restaurant at a rapid pace. When she checked some of their profiles, all she got were blanks: the outline of a person's head and nothing else.

PINE.

Someone shouted at her from the alley entrance. It was another man in fatigues with a gun. Anna got ready to port but, before she could, the man was gunned down from behind by six *other* men in fatigues, their uniforms adorned with a single patch that displayed a long, black shard of obsidian. The slugs exploded out of the soldier's back and skipped along the concrete toward Anna, now split open like tiny flowers. The half dozen militia guards advanced on Anna. She could have sworn she heard their guns go off just before she felt the shiver.

WASHINGTON, DC

Anna ported onto Ordway Street, which ran perpendicular to Connecticut Avenue, and crouched in front of one of the opulent townhouses along it. The houses that were still occupied in this hood were tucked behind walls nearly as high as the Harkness and capped with barbed wire just to be extra nasty. The abandoned houses had no walls at all, left free for squatters and/or Mother Nature to occupy them.

A woman walking her Shih Tzu spotted Anna, all disheveled and barefoot, and crossed Ordway to get away from her. Anna looked down toward Connecticut Avenue and could see trucks blitzing by at 100 mph, not bothering to stop for pedestrians. Chinook helicopters above were crisscrossing so low to the ground it sounded like they were about to land on her head.

She ran to the back entrance of her mom's steakhouse, through the winter muck and past grease dumpsters that were already near full capacity. She slipped through the rear door and into a narrow hallway packed with full beer cases piled on top of one another. Two workers awkwardly slid by Anna and were too stunned by the sight of a shirtless stranger in the hallway to say anything. She ducked into the kitchen and saw Sandy, in her hairnet and kitchen clogs, spraying béarnaise sauce off plates and eating any big scrap of ribeye she spotted on its way to the trash. They only paid Sandy $12 an hour, so she viewed the leftovers as a deserved perk.

Anna tapped her mom on the shoulder. Sandy turned around and nearly dropped a serving platter.

"Anna! What on earth?"

"We have to go."

"Where?"

"We have to GO."

She gripped Sandy tightly and led her out the back.

"I need to grab my phone!" Sandy protested.

"You can never use it again," Anna said.

"What?!"

There was a commotion coming from the dining room. Sandy tried to pause to hear what was going on, but Anna wouldn't let her stop.

"Get out of here, you PINE terrorists!" shouted a man in the dining room. He was alternately cheered and castigated by other diners. A PINE agent came moseying through the swinging kitchen doors like he was entering a saloon.

"Let's go," Anna said.

Sandy didn't question her daughter this time. They sprinted out the back and headed west on Ordway. Anna gave Sandy her phone but kept the bulldog cover for herself.

"Take this. Passcode is 5272."

"Anna, why aren't you in school? And where are your shoes? Is that bracelet you're wearing new? Where'd you get that? What is happening, for God's sake?"

"Listen, there were problems," Anna told her mom. "People may be coming after you."

"Is this some kind of joke?"

"No. Also, I'm probably expelled. Actually, I'm *definitely* expelled."

"What?!"

"Mom, it's very important that you get mad at me later, not right now. Other, much more dangerous people are also very mad at me right now. Take the phone."

"Anna."

"TAKE IT."

Sandy took the phone. "What am I gonna do with this?" she asked Anna.

"Port anywhere but here. Wait for my text. Contact no one else."

"But our locker!"

"Mom, we can never go back."

"Anna, you promised me."

"Mom, *later*."

Just then, a skateboarder riding down the sidewalk smashed into Anna and knocked her over. Her skull hit the pavement with a sickening thud and her scalp tore open. When she sat up, she saw

331

PINE agents to the east rampaging down Connecticut Avenue, grabbing at lanyards and kicking people over.

The boy on the skateboard knelt down beside Anna and her mom.

"Is she all right?" he asked.

"No!" Sandy screamed. "She's hurt, you moron!"

"Mom, stop screaming." Anna stood up, blood trickling down the side of her head. "Gimme your phone," she told the skateboarder.

"What? No."

"I shot a man today. If you don't give me your phone, I'll shoot another." She patted the bulge in the front of her pants. It looked gun-like enough.

"I'm not giving you my phone."

Anna grabbed the boy's skateboard. Before he could protest, she brought it down on his head. When the boy dropped to the ground, she wrenched his phone out of his jeans pocket and slipped Dougie over it. Her phone now.

"What's your passcode?" she asked the boy.

"I won't tell you, you crazy bitch."

"You guys always accuse us girls of being the crazy ones. Well guess how we got this way, fella?" Anna raised the skateboard over him again. "I'm only gonna ask you one more time."

"3400."

"Anna!" cried her mom. "What are you doing?"

"I'll text you, mom. Go now."

They ported out just before PINE came marauding up the street.

PortSys CCO To Repurpose Private Resort As Experimental Sovereign Nation

MALDIVES (AP) — Jason Kirsch, Chief Creative Officer of PortSys, unveiled plans today to convert his family's private Lily Beach resort on Huvahendhoo island in the Maldives into a "sovereign incubator" for entrepreneurs and other captains of industry.

"The Kirsch family's mission is to open the world up to everyone, and our own properties are not exempt from that mission," the would-be heir to the PortSys empire told reporters at a press conference he convened out in the shallow waters surrounding the Lily Beach villas. Reporters covering the event were urged to take off their shoes and socks and join Kirsch in the surf as he outlined his vision for the property in a presentation that, surroundings aside, was not unlike the unveiling of a new PortPhone.

"We're gonna expand to more villas," Kirsch promised. "*Bigger* villas. Plus we'll build a major conference center. Lily Beach will become ground zero for future technologies, port-forward governing ideas, and creative storytelling."

But the World Wildlife Fund is concerned that Kirsch's expansion plans will endanger shivers of whitetip reef sharks who call the surrounding Addu Atoll home. Other groups decried the resort's handshake deal with web titan Darren Jackson to host an offsite for his company, Univeil, once the new facilities have been built.

"They say they're gonna be sovereign," says Rosa Wills, GizPo columnist. "That just means it's gonna be a playground for rich libertarian a**holes like Kirsch and Jackson."

Jackson's Rosetta network has been lambasted as a breeding site for hate groups and other divisive factions, including the "men's renaissance" forum Conquistadors. Questions about these concerns, and about concerns of Maldivian citizens over their government's $100 million subsidy of the project, were left unanswered by Kirsch.

The resort's expanded villas, each complete with a full kitchen and private spa and around-the-clock staff, are already available to purchase and will start at $76 million each.

"This is about freedom," Kirsch told reporters, before putting on a snorkeling mask to observe nearby whitetips, "And, as with the technological gift that PortSys has granted the world, this is a freedom that will prove contagious. Sovereignty here will soon mean sovereignty *everywhere*."

CAIRNS

Anna Huff had a great many things to do and not a tremendous amount of time to do them. First of all, she needed a shirt and shoes. Those were crucial. She ported back to Kewarra Beach north of Cairns, where she and Bamert had stolen those first few blissful moments in the sun outside the Druskin walls before everything went to shit. Groups of port tourists were frolicking gaily in the water, all rocking waterproof fanny packs to safeguard their phones and passports. Discreetly as she could, Anna strolled behind one of the palm trees and nicked a tie-dyed shirt and a pair of flip flops that had been left there. Then she ported to Holloways Beach, five miles to the south. When she put the shirt on, it was two sizes too big. Like wearing a mural.

Disappointed, she rested against another palm tree and woke up the skateboarder's phone. His name was Brayden Bundy.

That's a stupid name.

Before Brayden could report his phone stolen, Anna opened his PortWallet account and wired the remaining $200 in it to a Monarch vendor who was more than happy to port directly to her pin.

"Are you Candace Bumlee?" the vendor asked.

"I am. Do you have my phone?"

"Here you go." The salesman handed her a brand new Worm9 and a two-year contract to sign. "You sure you don't want a PortSys-brand PortPhone?"

"Fuck PortSys."

"All right then!" He cast an eager eye on the phone she was already holding. "Did you want to trade in your old PortPhone?"

"Oh this?" Anna asked. "Nah. I better keep it for backup."

"Well, if you want any upgrades I have some amazing covers."

"Go away."

"Right." The salesman clapped out. Anna put Dougie on the Worm9 and logged onto Network Z using her brand new identity. She called Bamert immediately.

"Hey."

"Your mom texted," he said. "I had her port to one of our estates in North Carolina. This is one that hasn't burned to the ground, which is nice!"

"Will she be safe?" she asked Bamert.

"Worried sick, but safe."

"Where are you now?"

"ROCK AND ROLL, BABY."

"What?"

He texted her a link. She recognized the logo for Desert Burn '31 immediately. *Oh god.* She hit PORT, closing her eyes before the wormhole could do the job for her.

PHOENIX

Now she was on a scrubby hill overlooking Phoenix Motor Speedway. At the far end of the track's infield was a massive stage rising up from the ground: great iron trusses stacked to the moon, speakers the size of city buses joined together and snaking down from the rigging above, spotlights brighter than the sun itself. The crowd filled the grandstands and spilled out of the speedway into the surrounding lots, a human swarm that easily numbered in the six figures. The whole desert smelled like weed and beer piss.

A halogen floodlight at the top of the hill cast an eerie silver glow down on the stoners and bros in flannel shirts riding around on souped-up bicycles. Port marketers zapped in to offer festivalgoers e-cigs and airplane liquor bottles and potato chips and other lightweight non-perishables. Everyone except for Anna was dressed in formalwear: suits, tuxedoes, frilly taffeta gowns, garish dresses with slits that ran all the way to the hip, and more. Meanwhile, she was wearing a tent and cheap thongs.

She was dead sober but felt drunk all the same. Just another day that had thrown too much at her too quickly. She walked down the hill, bobbing and weaving between couples aggressively making out on picnic blankets. Farther down the hill, she saw a dozen boys in black t-shirts and tux jackets and khaki pants huddled around a quarter barrel, chortling with one another. She kept that wolfpack at a distance and bumped into a girl in a tight white dress who was drunk into next week.

"I like your shirt!" the girl said.

"Thanks," Anna said.

That was enough small talk. The girl in the white dress wrapped her arms around Anna and kissed her full on the mouth. She slipped her tongue past Anna's lips and Anna was so shocked at what was happening that it didn't even register that she was slipping her own tongue back.

Are you really doing this? Are you kissing someone? Holy shit, you are *kissing someone.*

It was like she had just chugged twelve energy drinks in a row. This girl tasted like Mad Dog, but her mouth was still wet and soft.

337

Magnetically so. She pressed against Anna and Anna could feel the Ziploc bag digging into her belly.

"Ooh, what's in your pants?" the girl asked.

"Nothing. That's nothing."

She nipped at Anna's earlobe and whispered to her, "Why don't we port someplace quiet?"

"Now?" Anna asked her. "I… I can't." She had to turn the girl down for a million different reasons, and yet she still felt like a fool for doing it.

"Come on," the girl said, "Let's get out of here." She pulled away from Anna with a naughty look, then promptly dropped to the ground in a drunken coma. Her white dress was muddied in an instant.

Suddenly, there was a meaty paw on Anna's shoulder. She whipped around and punched the offending man in the stomach.

"OH, SWEET VIRGINA!" he cried out. "That was most uncivilized, Anna Huff."

"Bamert! Oh my god, I'm so sorry."

She rubbed his back and used her other hand to keep him from falling over. Bamert had already managed to sweat clean through the silken fabric of his chosen fashion statement for the evening: a beige suit decorated with little cacti. The sun may have gone down in Arizona, but the parched ground had taken in all its heat like cast iron. That trapped heat rose back through the crowd and permeated the living desert air, stewing everyone in a rich funk.

"That's quite all right," Bamert said. "That's what I get for interrupting your little rendezvous."

"I didn't know that girl at all!"

"That's the fun of it."

"Why is everyone dressed like it's prom?" Anna asked.

"Because that's the theme of this year's festival, my wild buttercup: PROM. Sorry I didn't remind you of that tidbit. You seemed to be in great haste."

Anna grew solemn for a second. "That was my first kiss."

"Helluva way to kick off your love life. Now, why are you bleeding?"

She touched her forehead. When she pulled her finger away, an infant scab came with it.

"Oh Jesus."

"What's going on?" Bamert asked her.

She pulled the Ziploc bag out of her waistband. "Can you take this?" she asked.

"And what might that be?"

"It's the recipe for teleportation."

He threw his head back laughing. "AHAHAHAHA. Does it require kosher salt?" Anna gave Bamert The Look. "Wait. You're serious."

"Half the recipe was stolen from Emilia. The other half I stole from Ciaran Stokes."

"Why'd you do that?"

"Uhhhhhhhhhh."

Bamert pulled a can of seltzer out of his trousers pocket. Two naked boys on dirt bikes came whizzing down the hill past them. "Anna Huff, are you telling me that you stole all of Big Teleportation's trade secrets and then stuffed them into your unmentionables, even though you have NO idea what to do with them?"

"That's all accurate, yes."

"Why, that is *marvelous*." He tucked the Ziploc bag inside his sport coat. "I have some thoughts on what to do with your goods, but first: how did you steal this from Ciaran Stokes?"

"I shot him," Anna said.

"Oh! You just up and shot him."

"I did."

He bit his lip and nodded. "Okay. Did you kill him?"

"If I'd been thinking clearly. I also might have punctured Dean Vick's lung."

"Busy day for you!" There was a buzz in Bamert's pocket. He took out his PortPhone and his eyes went open wide. "Oh wow, it really *was* a busy day for you."

"What do you mean?"

Bamert showed Anna a Push Alert from FreedomNews USA:

CRAZED DRUSKIN STUDENT GOES ON PORTING RAMPAGE; ASSAULTS DEAN, SPRAY PAINTS LOCKER ROOM WITH SWASTIKAS AND HATE SPEECH, FLEES

"I have an alert set for Druskin stuff," he told her. "Didn't expect FreedomNews to pop up there, though. They have the *best* headlines, I must admit."

Anna swiped opened the full report and stared in disbelief. It included doctored surveillance footage of her scrawling hate symbols all over Druskin Stadium.

"I didn't do any of that stuff!" she cried. "Well, except for the assault."

"I believe you, but I don't think PortSys has much interest in doing likewise. No wonder that girl wanted to make out with you. You're a sexy fugitive now."

Anna scrolled down and there, staring back at her, was a picture of herself in an argyle sweater, with a wan smile and her eyes halfway shut.

"Christ," she said. "They used my school photo."

"I think it looks quite fetching," Bamert said. "Also in your favor: David Farris said you were innocent."

"The guy from ethics class did?!" She skimmed the copy and found his quote:

Anna Huff is wild but the idea that she's a Nazi is some supreme bullshit. Don't tell Father McDuff I said "bullshit."

"I guess that was nice of him," Anna said, "but Christ, I'm screwed."

"You would have been if that girl over there hadn't passed out. Now, who stole half of that recipe from Emilia?"

Anna was so preoccupied with the news blast that she barely heard the question. She looked around and no one at the festival seemed to notice her or care who she was. But it was still clear that her life, as she knew it, was over. She had the cover of darkness on her side at the speedway, and she'd have to stay under it for a very long time, perhaps forever. Daylight would kill her, and it would kill her mom too. There would be no more Druskin. No college. No future. Just an endless slog through the free zones: a life in hiding from Jason Kirsch and all the other demons roaming the landscape.

"Anna," Bamert said.

"What."

"Who stole the other half?"

"Lara did."

"Oh, really?" He pointed to the speedway. "Well, speak of the devil."

"What?"

Bamert wrested his phone back from Anna and opened up the camera. He zoomed in on the festival's VIP area, situated atop a cantilevered platform behind the soundboard in the center of the infield. Anna saw a sharp black bob of hair bouncing up and down to the beat. Neon bangle bracelets. Hoop earrings. Neon blue eyeshadow. Her heart blitzed ahead of her aching body.

"She's here," Anna said, dumbstruck.

"Just your luck."

"I stink, though." It was true. She smelled like a rancid oyster.

"Everyone stinks here," Bamert told her. "That's why it's so wonderful. People scoff at body odor, then they go out dancing and suddenly they *want* that funk in the air. They need it. The funk is love, Anna Huff."

"I look like shit. I'm bleeding."

"Everyone's bleeding here! You fit right in. Go to her."

"It's too dangerous."

"You shot a guy and stabbed another guy today, right?"

"*I* didn't necessarily stab Vick. He kinda stabbed himself. But I did assault a skateboarder."

"Did you ever consider then, Anna, that *you* might be the dangerous one?"

All her life—which admittedly, had been quite brief—Anna Huff had never thought of herself as dangerous. Didn't *want* to be dangerous. Dangerous boys were cool and dangerous girls were psycho. Besides, it was always the shitty people who were dangerous: corporate tyrants, terrorists, armed PINE agents horny for

341

gunfire, people porting into strange houses in the dead of night to indulge their sickest impulses, etc. Anna Huff's life was built around either avoiding that danger or coping with it. But now that all felt like an enormous waste. Why did *she* have to be on the run? Why did *she* have to always live in fear? Fear was something the dangerous people counted on to keep everyone else in line. But they were all like Vick: sad, pathetic, and scared to death of having their illusions of power disappear. Those vacant illusions were everything to them.

"I guess I never thought of myself that way," she said to Bamert.

"You're a lion," he told her.

"I thought you said I was an ox. And an elephant."

"I'm upgrading you, darling. To lionhood."

"Are you gonna be all right?" she asked Bamert. "You're drinking water?"

"Do I look all right or do I look all right? Sobriety is a horrible thing, Anna Huff. But this is what I need to do to learn how to be a person again, isn't it?"

"Oh, Bamert. Bamert, I'm so proud of you. And I'm glad you're wearing a suit. You're you again."

"That I am."

"But you're in danger right now."

"Am I? Whoever nuked our Virginia house seems content to leave it at that. I owe them a favor, frankly. Edgar is pissed at Emilia now. The only thing weird old rich people hate more than the poor are *other* weird old rich people. The old man gave me my credit card back outta this."

"They might come for you."

"I told you trouble is no trouble for a Bamert." He gestured over to the VIP area. "Now go hunting, you deadly lioness you. Go on and *feel the noize*."

Anna marked a pin right by the stage that quivered in place as human bodies pinballed around the infield. The VIP section itself was off limits, but the rest of the festival itself was free; organizers didn't bother with the hassle of trying to charge admission. Instead, they took a cut of the merch and draped every square inch of the desert in ads for hard seltzer and shoddy WallTech hardware for personal residences. PINE agents were snaking their way through the mass, covering all possible ground. Maybe they didn't know Anna's port ID, but they knew her face. She grabbed a ponytail holder out of the hot dirt and tied her hair behind her head. It was the only disguise she could hope for at the moment. Then she hit PORT and felt the shiver.

Inside the speedway, the crowd noise coalesced into an ongoing, multi-octave WOOOOO that reminded Anna of the first time Sarah ever took her to a concert like this. It was at the Superdome in New Orleans, and the old school weed smoke was so heavy in the air that you could smell it in the plastic seats. The crowd that night also WOOOOOed like a flock of a million joyful birds. Two burly dudes bought Sarah beers before that show and she wisely moved with Anna to another row of seats so that she wouldn't be asked to repay the favor somehow.

Now Anna was in the middle of the same kind of hyped-up crowd, but as an only child. Lara Kirsch, in a bubble-gum pink dress with little satin roses adorning the shoulder, was leaning over the guard rail of the VIP section and screaming out for the band. The music was so cacophonous that Anna could only make out the bass distinctly. The ground under her quaked to the beat. Everyone else inside the speedway appeared to have someone else with them. But Anna was all alone, staring up at Lara and praying for her to stare back. There she went again: trying to feel important by looking around for someone important.

Lara caught a glance of Anna in her frumpy tie-dyed shirt, and her eyes went wide in happy surprise. She raced to the back of the platform, past the security guards and down to the barricade. The music—so brutal and relentless just a moment earlier—cut out as a new act got ready to take the stage.

"What are you doing here?" Lara asked Anna. "Oh my god, you're bleeding!" She took out a small tissue and spat on it to moisten it. Then she gently wiped the dried blood from the side of Anna's face.

"I can get you up with the VIPs," Lara said, taking Anna's hand. "The area has its own portwall. Come with me."

Lara ushered Anna up the stairs, where there was actual room to move. Freedom. Waiters in branded apparel walked around handing out vials of kamikaze shots. Obnoxiously wealthy scions and heiresses strutted around the platform in dresses that looked like they came fresh off a Milan runway. One girl was bathed in sapphires that shone brighter than the stage show. Lara took Anna over to a promotional kiosk for a designer named Baptiste.

"What are we doing?" Anna asked.

"It's prom," Lara said. "You need a dress. And better shoes."

"Your mom said I needed better shoes once."

"Fuck her."

Lara asked the woman behind the counter for a sample dress for her friend to wear. Asked it in perfect French. The woman ported out with a crisp snap and reappeared within seconds, her perfumed port breeze wafting past Lara and Anna. She was holding a sequined handbag, black flats, and a mini dress: black on the sides with a wide white panel running down the front and back. A racing stripe.

Holy shit, that looks like Mrs. Ludwig's car.

"This work?" Lara asked her.

"Yeah."

"Come on."

She took Anna to a trailer bathroom behind the kiosk. It was basic, but it was still a huge leap up from a port-a-potty.

"Let's get this on you," Lara said. "Take off your shirt."

"Okay." Anna pulled off the frumpy t-shirt.

Of all the times you gotta show off your beach body.

Lara put the new dress over Anna's head and pulled it down to her hips. Anna, so flushed with love-spiked adrenaline that she could barely speak, put her passport lanyard back on, then bent down and peeled off her yoga pants. With her legs freed, she was beginning to feel more human and less like a fleshy, beached walrus.

"I stink," she told Lara matter-of-factly. One day, by God, she would not have crippling body odor around this girl.

344

"Ha! I do too." Lara held up her arm and playfully waved the odor toward Anna's face. Anna didn't tell Lara she thought it smelled good. *The funk is love.*

Before she got the dress all the way down, Lara saw the bruise on Anna's hip and touched it. Each touch from Lara was like a kiss. Anna tightened her core muscles like she was about to leap off another cliff, then pulled the dress all the way down.

"You got into a fight," Lara said.

"With Vick, yeah."

"I heard about that. You're a hero, Roomie." She took out her PortPhone and brought up Anna's dormant WorldGram profile. She had 200,000 new followers.

"They said I painted swastikas on the walls but it's all a lie," Anna said.

"I bet. I know Emilia's playbook. It's a literal playbook. I can get that for you, too. Now turn around."

Anna turned and Lara zipped the dress up. The sound the zipper made was sweeter than any music coming from onstage. The fabric, so smooth and silken, caressed Anna like a lover. The rose pink bracelet made for a perfect accent to the ensemble. Anna stared at herself on the mirror. At long last, she looked exactly the way Lara Kirsch made her feel. She ran her fingers through her hair, feeling sleek and fast. Like she was heading out for a date. Was *this* a date? It took everything in Anna's power not to barricade the door and keep them in that bathroom all night.

"That dress," said Lara, "is flawless on you."

"Yours looks good too."

"I promise you that yours looks better. The concert bill said to wear a dress you don't care about. This was a bridesmaid's dress from Jason's wedding. I hate it." Anna believed her. Normally, Lara was impeccably dressed but simultaneously gave off the vibe that she didn't need to put any thought into it. The dress she had on now killed that vibe. This was a needy dress. She still looked dazzling in it, but it wasn't her.

"Why'd you wear that tonight if you hate it?" Anna asked her.

"So I could ruin it. But look at us now," she exulted. "We're not crying for once."

"Night's young."

"Do you want makeup?"

"Do I need it?" Anna asked.

"Maybe a little." Lara dug into her bag to grab an eyeliner pen and some lip gloss. "Hold still."

Anna leaned in and Lara gently brushed her lips with the sweet peach gloss. Then she took an ice pick-sharp eyeliner pencil and traced, ever so carefully, along Anna's eyelid. Anna drummed her fingers against her sides with near-concussive force. When Lara was finished, they turned toward the mirror and stared at one another.

"There," Lara said. "Flawless. I mean, you were already flawless without makeup."

"Don't give me that bullshit."

Lara laughed and handed Anna the pencil. "Keep it. You wear it better than I do."

"I don't wear anything better than you."

"Your turn not to give me that bullshit."

"Okay," Anna admitted. "I'm hotter than you right now."

"You really are. Roomie, do you remember what you asked my mother when you met her the first time?"

Oh, she remembered, all right. "'How do you know I'm not a superstar?'"

"And look at you now," Lara said, putting her hands on each side of Anna's dress. "You ARE a superstar."

"Hell yeah I am."

Lara giggled before turning serious for a moment. "Did you get the screengrab?" Lara asked Anna.

"I did. You kept your promise to me."

"I told you I would. Did you give the notes to Stokes?"

"I did," Anna said. "But then I had to shoot him."

"You are such a wiseass! Wait, you're not joking." Lara stepped back. "What did you do?"

"I kept the notes you gave me and stole all of his," Anna said. "I'm in very big trouble, Lara."

"Where is everything?"

"You said you trusted me, right?"

"Yeah."

"Trust me again. *Trust my soul*, Lara Kirsch. You owe me that."

"Okay."

"Stokes was a bastard. He can't have the notes."

"Then who are you gonna give them too?"

Anna looked away from the mirror. She couldn't take the sight of them together in the reflection, looking like a real couple, another second longer. If she kept staring, she would jump on Lara and feed her hot kisses. *You know how to kiss now, girl. You're not a rookie.*

"I gave them to someone already," she finally told Lara. "Someone on our side."

"You don't mean, like, the FBI. Do you?"

"Uh, no. Someone better."

"Emilia and Jason aren't gonna like it."

"They aren't gonna like anything I do to them," Anna said. "I know that puts us in an awkward spot, like it always does. But I'm ready to be dangerous. I'm ready to hurt Jason and Emilia. But I don't wanna do it without your permission."

Lara gnawed on her fingers. Someone outside knocked on the bathroom door and Lara yelled at them to fuck off. She took out her PortPhone and showed Anna her photo archive. There was Lara at Shutters in Santa Monica. There was Lara on the roof deck of the MyClub in San Francisco. There was Lara at the upscale Acacia Mall in Kampala, Uganda.

"You see any photos of my family here?" she asked Anna.

"No."

"All they care about is loyalty for loyalty's sake. They don't care about me. Plus Jason sold Lily Beach."

"No."

"He did. My beach. *Our* beach. I wouldn't have given you those notes if I didn't want Jason and Emilia to hurt."

"What about you? Will you be all right?"

"Will anyone?"

Anna looked down at her new shoes and stammered, "Jason. He came to my room. *Our* room. He said he'd be back. He wants me to kill myself, and that he'll slit my throat if I don't. I don't wanna drag down this night, but I had to tell you. He wants to do the same shit to me he did to Sarah."

"I know," said Lara. "He visits my room sometimes, too. No matter where I port, he can find me."

"Oh my God."

The visits began when Lara was nine years old. The first time Jason came into her bedroom, she thought he was looking for a phone charger. But that's not what he wanted at all. He loomed over his half-sister's bed, holding a knife and whispering horrible nothings to her. She was an untalented, revolting little shit. A responsible person should slit her throat, but why saddle them with that job when Lara could exercise a bit of wisdom and just do it herself?

There was no discernible pattern to Jason's visits. Sometimes a week would go by without him coming. Sometimes a single night. But the visits grew so vast in number that the pattern was beside the point. Every night, whether or not Lara was left undisturbed, she felt him. After three years of this sickening dance, with Lara steadfastly refusing to break, he moved onto what he considered easier prey. But he didn't stop visiting Lara entirely. She remained his most prized target. His big buck.

"Sometimes he spins his knife on the dresser," Lara told Anna. "Looks at me with black eyes and I can feel his evil all over me. Only reason I haven't hurt myself is because staying alive is the best way I can make him miserable. But god, it's hard to resist it. Sometimes I wanna use the gun just so that I never have to see him or hear him again, you know? And then I hate myself for the urge. Why do I end up with all of the shame and he ends up with none? That's not how it should be."

"Does he—"

"No, he never touches me. He doesn't have to touch people to violate them. It's why I stay out all night a lot. But eventually sleep catches up with me, and when it does, so does he." Lara shuddered at her own words. Her green eyes dimmed. "One time I paid a guy on the street to watch over me but when Jason showed up that night, he smooth-talked the guy right out the door. Other times I've tried to engineer ways to port without him noticing, but he always knows. And I've never spent the night with another guy or girl. Because if they ever had to deal with Jason…" She couldn't speak the consequences out loud.

"What if you just ditched your phone?"

"He can find me. I have to time it so that I sneak away when I know he's busy somewhere else. Only reason I made it to Sutton Place and back that night was because he was eating dinner with fucking Robb Caraway."

"Who else knows about this?" Anna asked.

"One person, and you probably guess who."

Maybe I should have Jason pay you a visit. That's what Emilia told Lara that first night at school.

"That piece of shit."

"I've never told anyone else this," Lara said. "Jason said no one would believe me, and I believed *him*. Sometimes you take the worst people at their word because you've already seen what they're capable of. And Jason is capable of anything. He ruined your family and he doesn't even care about his own. I hate him. You ever feel a hate that you know is so deep and so right?"

"I have." Anna had a list of such hates: Vick, Jason, PINE, Emilia, and on and on they went. But those grudges felt petty by comparison at the moment. Lara Kirsch was possessed by a hate that had profound roots within her. Evil was her family's blood heritage.

"No matter where I port to, he knows I'm there. And he can get past any portwall. There's nowhere to hide. That's why I wanted to go to Druskin, Anna. It's why I asked them to give me a roommate even though Emilia wanted me to be in a single." Lara confessed. *We'll bust out of here and then we'll go everywhere the shitty people aren't, and they won't ever be able to find us.* "It's why I wanted the inner room. I thought that extra buffer might help keep Jason away, especially because *you* were my roommate. The second you talked shit to Emilia, I knew you were the right girl. You're not someone to be fucked with, Anna Huff."

"Not anymore, I'm not."

"I hate that I have to tell you this. But I feel better now that I have. I feel safer."

"I'm gonna make him pay for what he did to Sarah and to you. You cool with that?"

"I am extremely cool with that. But how are you gonna do it?"

Before Anna could answer, the next act was on stage and the music shook the platform again, drowning out anything else they could have said to each other. Their quiet time was over. But that didn't stop Anna from trying to steal more time.

"Do you want to dance?" she asked Lara meekly.

"What?"

Anna leaned in and put her lips to Lara's ear. "Do you wanna dance?"

Lara nodded. "Let's dance all night. No one can catch us when we're dancing."

Anna's heart thundered. They ran out of the bathroom and to the front of the VIP area to shake their traumas off. The funk was building. Anna closed her eyes and let the music take over her body. She didn't care how she looked. When she opened them, Lara was closing in and wrapping her arms around Anna's waist. She stepped between Anna's legs and they flowed as one, swapping sweat as they pulsed with the night.

A pack of boys butted in to dance around them, one of them putting his arms around Lara from behind. Lara squirted out of his grasp and got even closer to Anna for protection. Anna could see photographers snapping photos of Lara and her from the infield.

The song ended to more WOOOOs and the lead singer grabbed the mic to banter.

"EVERYONE HAVING A GOOD TIME?!"

WOOOOOOOOOOOOOOOOOOOO

"We gotta lot of dancing to do, Phoenix! But since it's Prom Night…"

The entire crowd went "awwwww" in unison.

"We're gonna slow it down for all you lovers out there."

The snare kicked in and each of the couples below locked together as the slow jam washed gently over the crowd, making the drunks horny and the stoners romantic. The horde of boys encircled them again. Lara gave Anna a "save me" face" and they joined hands, dancing closely on their little parcel of the VIP area as other rich kids and yuppies filled up the platform. Lara and Anna got back in sync as the stage went dark and the ethereal silhouette of the two girls dancing in the glow of the halogen floodlights shone up on the hill, their shadows more graceful than they themselves could ever be. The boys backed off. Anna put her hands on Lara's hips and Lara wrapped her arms around Anna's neck. Her hands were at home on Lara's body. The two of them were so close now. It was them, and only them.

"You smell like wine," Lara whispered in her ear, her lips nearly touching it.

Oh shit, that girl you kissed. You cheated on Lara. Does that count as cheating? That probably doesn't count as cheating unless you're a crazy person.

"Someone outside the speedway had a bottle of rotgut."

"It's okay. I like it."

She likes it. She likes me. *Lara could have danced with any of those boys but she wanted to dance with me.* It was the nicest thought that her mind had ever gifted her, and perhaps the first time that her grandest dreams matched the moment at hand. They got closer and Anna closed her eyes, anticipating the kiss. Instead, Lara put her head against Anna's shoulder and they twirled under the clear black sky. They *became* the stars: two celestial bodies orbiting one another, speeding through the infinite together. Anna took a whiff of Lara's hair. She dug in her nose until it tickled Lara's ear, a prelude to a kiss. Lara looked up at her and when they locked eyes Anna was certain that she hadn't been fooling herself this whole time. This was going to happen.

Then the spell was broken by distinct flashes of gunfire coming from the periphery: PINE agents shooting into the air and clearing a path to the VIP platform. Concertgoers gave them the finger and the lead singer of the band onstage crooned on. The agents ignored all of that and stared at Anna as they drew closer and closer.

"Oh god, they're coming for me," Anna said.

"You gotta leave," Lara told her.

"They're gonna shoot me if I take out my phone."

"No, they won't."

Lara grabbed Anna and kissed her on the lips. It happened. Perhaps not the way Anna envisioned, but they were kissing all the same. Everyone was kissing her too quickly tonight. Anna stepped out of her body and gazed upon the moment in disbelief. The photographers did likewise. They had been dutifully snapping photos of the Kirsch heiress dancing in place before this, and now they were in a frenzy. They shoved their way to the front of the platform to get a good shot off, and happily threw elbows at any PINE agent trying to breach the scrum.

But Anna didn't see their flashes or hear any of their shouting. Once more, everything dropped from the Earth except for the two of them. She closed her eyes and savored this: Lara's buttery lips pressed against hers, a softness Anna couldn't have conceived of until feeling it. The softness was contagious, running through her body and rendering her boneless. The kiss took all her weight away and made her buoyant, floating dreamily through the atmosphere as the sugary taste of Lara's lip gloss slowly seeped into her mouth, sweeter than cheap wine. Up until now, Anna Huff had never experienced joy this pure. But she recognized it now. She felt *wonderful*. She felt like she was being shot out of a confetti cannon. Lara caressed Anna's cheek with a slender hand and that made the moment even hotter. Lara lingered on her mouth. There was a wet crease running across her lips, and Anna sensed that they were jusssssst about to open.

Then Lara pulled away and dragged Anna to the back of the platform as more gunfire rang out from the hill and concertgoers ported out en masse. The band stopped. It was over. The world was back.

"Go," Lara said.

"Lara, I—"

"Go!"

"I'll find you."

Anna was just about to port out when a man grabbed her and yanked her back up next to the dressing kiosk. It was Jason Kirsch, clad in a black t-shirt and khakis, his hair parted down the center of his scalp.

"What the hell is going on here?" Jason asked the two of them. "Lara, why were you kissing this girl? And why are you wearing the dress that *I* picked for you for *my* wedding?"

"Stay away from us," Lara said.

"Little Lara, you've been in the family vault," Jason said menacingly. "What have you done? This bitch you're with is a crazed fugitive. Is she why you friended me a few days ago, hmm? What were you looking for in my history?"

"Leave her alone," Lara told him. "She's just my friend."

Just a friend?

"I don't think so," Jason said. Her grabbed Anna by her hair and brought her down to her knees. The PINE agents below held up to let Jason do his work, turning their guns on any photographer who dared to snap a photo of the scene.

"Where are the notes, you little shit?" he asked Anna.

"I don't know what you're talking about."

Jason Kirsch squeezed her hair until it was tearing away from her scalp. "WHERE ARE THEY?"

"LET HER GO!" screamed Lara.

A second wave of PINE agents climbed the platform and encircled the three, turning their backs and forming a human wall. Anna was out of options.

"The notes are in my bag," she told Jason.

"Give them to me," he said, letting her go.

Anna carefully reached into her handbag for her phone, but when she felt the eyeliner pencil brush against her fingers first, she grabbed it and wrapped it in her fist.

"Here they are." She shoved the pencil into Jason Kirsch's eye. It sank in one inch, then two, then three. His eyeball exploded and he screamed red death.

353

By the time the wall of PINE agents had turned around to see what had happened, Anna had already taken out her PortPhone and zapped away from the greatest and most terrifying moment of her young life. She had been prom queen for a night, but there was no telling if she'd ever get to bask in the glory. PINE wanted her. The Kirsches wanted her. The chase was on.

Mom

Mom?

I'VE BEEN WORRIED SICK. WHERE ARE YOU

Just stay where you are

YOU FRIENDED ME. WHY CAN I NOT SEE WHERE YOU'VE BEEN

Well I might have been porting using a different account. My bad

WHAT IS HAPPENING WHY ARE YOU IN THE NEWS

Turn your caps lock off it's not helping

NO

Just sit tight

YOU ARE GROUNDED, YOUNG LADY

EVERYWHERE

Anna Huff needed a gun. She was now a very famous girl, if her push alerts and WorldGram following were any indication. Already the news had dubbed her the Preppy Psycho. Jason Kirsch was wounded but not dead. Lara Kirsch was nowhere to be found. Anna's WorldGram comments were a toxic stew of death threats from Kirsch loyalists, spam, and vacuous cries of support from thirsty men and women alike. She couldn't stop scrolling through all of them.

There was no telling if PortSys had figured out Anna's latest port ID yet, but she didn't want to be unarmed when they did. She was in Dewey Beach, Delaware, huddled behind a row of townhouses a mile from the water that, shockingly, did not yet have a brick-and-mortar wall surrounding them. Across Route 1, she saw the chilly reflection of a tiny lake and the eaves of shoreline McMansions towering high in the air over their respective barbed wire-topped walls. A seagull circled around the lake and made a throaty whistle.

Snitch.

Only one of the townhomes in Anna's row appeared to be occupied, although when squatters took over a place, they usually kept the lights off anyway. The adrenaline and parched heat from Phoenix had worn off of her and the brutal cold was taking hold. She was more tired than she'd ever been. All she wanted was a bed and the chance to replay her night with Lara over and over and over again. She could still taste Lara's lip gloss on her. She could have eaten a whole tube of it. She took a deep breath, smiled, then hugged herself. *It feels good to be in love. Great, even. God it feels good to admit it.* No shame in the feeling anymore.

Bryce Holton was still awake. Network Z showed him loitering around the railroad crossing in Rockville. Anna chose a pin just out of his range of eyesight: around the corner from an abandoned Army surplus store overlooking the tracks. When she ported to Maryland, she peeked around the corner and saw him handing a dimebag to a kid who couldn't have been older than eleven. She picked up a piece of rebar lying next to a crumbled parking barrier and held it firm. Her hands were developing an affinity for hard weaponry.

Bryce's preteen client ported out. That was Anna's cue. She ran at Bryce with the iron bar and caught him right in the face as he turning around to see who was coming.

"Owwwwww!"

"Remember me?"

"No."

"Yeah well, this is for Sarah."

Anna smashed Bryce's kneecap with the rebar and he let out another howl. This was the fourth man she'd beaten up today, and she was getting a taste for it. She grabbed his gun out of his waistband.

"Hey man, you can't steal that!"

"Sorry not sorry," Anna said. She was gone a second later.

Now she was in Cuernavaca, Mexico, her frigid toes and body gradually warming back up. She walked, without much of a plan, along a darkened and empty street until it opened up into a bustling thoroughfare. She sped past the Baby Rock discoteca and saw all manner of clubbing sleaze—American, European, nouveau riche Chinese—demanding that the bouncer check for their names on the guest list. She hid her face. She was famous for assaulting the prince of porting, and for being a girl who kissed another girl. She knew that few people would take kindly to the former and that certain people out in the free zones, no matter the country, wouldn't take too kindly to the latter either.

PINE agents were so widely despised in Mexico that a gunfight immediately broke out any time they dared to port in, which is why Anna thought it was the best place to enjoy a temporary respite from law enforcement.

She guessed wrong. After three more blocks, she saw an American PINE agent port in ten yards from her and train his rifle on her.

"FREEZE!"

She did as she was told, but the PINE agent didn't count on the plainclothes *Federale* who was waiting in another club line across the street. The *Federale* opened fire and the PINE troop dropped to the ground, blending in with the scattered refuse immediately.

357

Anna ported out of Cuernavaca and onto the wholesale floor of the resurrected Tsukiji Fish Market in Tokyo, where she slithered between hordes of fishermen porting in from the East China Sea and restaurant buyers zipping in from all over the world to snatch up anything fresh from white plastic bins in front of the fish stands: boulders of priceless tuna loin, whole sea cucumbers, crab claws as long as table legs, spiky urchins cracked open to reveal the golden uni custard inside, and the rest of a revitalized marine life bounty. A pair of tourists watched in equal parts anticipation and horror as a fishmonger nailed a fresh horse mackerel to a plank and filleted it for them to eat while it was still alive. They posted a five-star review on WorldGram as they gulped the fish down.

Loading trucks speeding by came within a hair of clipping Anna's ankles on every pass. She stole a towel from behind one fish stand and dried herself off as she snuck by another fishmonger running a mako shark carcass through a bandsaw. She walked at a half-crouch, looking like she was constipated, desperate to remain concealed among the churn of buyers and vendors and insufferable foodies blasting in to shoot port-bys of themselves eating a wriggling octopus tentacle. Near another booth, she caught a glimpse of her face on a tiny, standard-def television sitting on top of one of the coolers.

Shit.

She slipped behind another food stall and snagged a folded white apron off its steel shelving, cinching it around her waist, and around the dress that had made her look so fabulous just an hour earlier. Now was not the time to look fabulous. She opened up her phone and made an old school voice call to Bamert.

"Ahoy ahoy," he said from the other end.

"They know my port ID."

"I can remedy that for you in just a moment. Or, at least, Burton can."

"I don't have a moment."

"Well then, you better make one."

Two PINE agents ported in ten yards away. Anna ducked under a table selling contraband whale meat, then scurried behind a row of giant standalone refrigerators while market security screamed at the troops to go away. She took the gun out of her handbag and gripped it tight as the agents swept through the stalls, overturning storage bins and ignoring angry cries from the vendors. They spotted Anna fleeing behind the massive appliances and held up their rifles, but by then she had already ported to the abandoned passenger terminal of O'Hare Airport in Chicago.

All of the gates and old concession areas of O'Hare were shuttered, never to be reopened. This was strictly a cargo and military aviation hub now. She blew in next at a gate that opened to a jetway to nowhere. The lone vendor in the concourse was a Thai hawker selling fresh noodles to all of the refugees, immigrants, and homeless folk loitering about.

You need a different phone. Anna couldn't keep porting with the one she had, but she still had to be able to port at a moment's notice. She ran, gun in hand, over to a teenage girl sitting next to her sleeping mother on a gate area bench.

"Excuse me, do you like your phone?"

"Huh?" the girl asked.

"Never mind." Anna grabbed the phone out of the girl's hands and gave her the compromised phone as a forced tradeoff.

"Hey!"

"Sorry."

A dozen PINE agents blew in but Anna had them beat once again, porting out with the girl's phone—she didn't have a passcode lock on it—before they could spot her and fire.

She was in the Laotian countryside now, just outside Luang Prabang, consigned to a path littered with signs warning of landmines in the surrounding fields. The constant toggling in and out of daylight was fucking with Anna's equilibrium, like she had left her Eustachian tubes behind while teleporting all around. She could barely keep her balance as she hurried along the path.

The heat wasn't helping. It deadened the air and rendered Anna's drying job in Tokyo pointless. She could smell sweet incense permeating the countryside but couldn't see where, exactly, the smell was coming from. Beat gunfire. A government mosquito control vehicle roared by, its loudspeakers blaring out directives in English to not go near any standing water because of an ongoing malaria epidemic. "GO TO THE HOSPITAL IMMEDIATELY IF YOU HAVE SYMPTOMS," they warned.

Anna called Bamert a second time.

"Who is this?" he asked.

"It's me," she said.

"Your port ID says your name is Marguerita Consuelos de Vallos. That's a gorgeous name."

"Can you help me yet?"

"We're working on it, Marguerita. Just keep moving."

"I wanna die."

"No, you don't. You want to live. Move."

An American couple ported in. When they saw Anna walking along the path in her dress and apron, they double-checked their phones. She had to go again. She was about to zero in on a dead spot in Uganda when, without warning, she felt the shiver.

Someone, somewhere, had selected Anna's pin for her. They chose the center of the 5 expressway in Los Angeles. The wormhole dumped Anna into the passing lane and she had to leap over to the shoulder to avoid a Mack truck whizzing by.

The entire freeway was a truck derby: moving trucks and oil tankers and garbage trucks and cement trucks and wobbly contractor pickups and container trucks that stretched the length of a hockey rink. Funding for street lights in LA was nonexistent, so the trucks barreled down the 5 illuminated only by their own menacing high beams. They drove as fast as possible, except when they were occasionally ramming into one another.

The shoulder was no safer. Another truck came at Anna from the wrong side of the rumble strip and she had to jump on top of a concrete divider that barely kept northbound and southbound traffic separated. She was teetering on the barrier; it was no wider than a balance beam. Mr. Willamy's awful balance training was proving useful once more. She opened up PortMaps again but another hole had already opened up right next to her. She held perfectly still until the wormhole timed out and she was "safe" again, then pinned the row of townhouses in Dewey Beach.

But when she took a step, she found herself on another freeway, directly on top of a moving container truck.

She was not prepared for the wind. Actually, she wasn't prepared for any aspect of her current predicament. Her handbag blew away. The seams in the trailer were digging into her belly as she lay flat against its top. The semi was going 100mph down a long stretch of dilapidated highway, nothing beside it except for filthy snowbanks and tall, thin fir trees that stuck straight out of the snow like hairs standing on end.

Anna saw rusted green exit signs for towns she couldn't recognize: SABATTUS, GARDINER, AUGUSTA, SIDNEY, WATERVILLE. They all drew a blank. All she knew is that she was still in America, and that she was on the verge of freezing to death.

The wind hissed at her. The container truck hit a pothole and her PortPhone flew out of her other hand and landed three feet in front of her.

"OH NO!"

A few more bumps in the road made the phone dance around like it was enchanted. Anna tried to slither forward to grab the phone, but could feel the wind trying to peel her body off the truck and blow her away. She pressed her hands and body down into the roof because gravity and friction were all she had at her disposal to stay alive. The corrugated steel of the container was so cold that any exposed flesh stuck to it.

The truck hit one more big bump. Anna saw her phone hop up, twirl around in the moonlight for just a second, and then fall overboard. She didn't see where it landed. *On the ground? In the snow?* Now Anna had absolutely nothing save for a pair of extraordinarily chafed thighs.

Every second on top of the container made the wind more cruel, like she was being dragged through a field of poisoned nettles. The truck swerved to avoid a pothole and took Anna right along with it, to the edge of the container and nearly off it. She was getting farther and farther away from the phone and without it she was stranded, lost to PortSys but also to the world entire. She may as well have been dead.

Maybe you should jump. After all, what the worst that could happen? Death? Death seemed okay. She had her moment of glory back in Phoenix, but it was clear that she was in way over her head now. Emilia and Jason were toying with her, seizing control of her body and sending it to new and rotten places. She was miles away from the stolen phone, far enough that walking back to it was no longer an option.

But Anna Huff had no other choice. She took a deep breath and prayed for a quick death: the kind where you're already halfway up to the white light before you even know you're bleeding. That was what she wanted if she couldn't have life. If she couldn't have Lara. She wasn't even sad or angry about it at the moment. She had a plan for death and was intent on sticking to it.

Both lanes on the highway shifted over and the truck slowed to a relative crawl at 40mph, past a vacated road work site. She saw a frozen mound of dirt ahead, next to an abandoned excavator. It was her best chance for a soft landing. She rolled off.

Upon closer inspection—like say, hitting it at near terminal velocity—Anna noticed the dirt mound she was aiming for was not soil but rather a pile of hard gravel stones, along with a few razor sharp salt crystals thrown in for good measure. She may as well have jumped onto a mound of porcupines. No death. Not even close. Instead, she hit the top of the mound kidneys-first and rolled down the pile. She spilled onto a patch of dirty asphalt and now every part of her was red and raw: face, neck, back, arms. She was exposed like a shucked clam. God didn't even do her the courtesy of knocking her unconscious. Instead, He had sealed her inside a great chamber of screaming pain. The depth and force of the pain took her breath away. In her mind, she heard a studio audience laughing at her plight.

Please, death. Please, work with us here.

Anna was in so much pain that she couldn't even remember how much she hated everyone at the moment. That hate was vacuum-sealed and preserved for later. Her main motor functions had yet to boot back up. Blood was oozing out from under her body. She picked up her left arm and a flap of skin hung down from it like a sheet from a clothesline.

"Shit."

Every subsequent discovery Anna made about her condition was worse than the last. Her feet were blue. The seams in the truck roof had torn open her belly. Her dress was torn and she mourned it more than her own lacerated skin. She tried to pick the dirt out of her exposed wounds but couldn't get all of it. The cuts were deep and miserable. The rips in her skin had formed strange, glistening polygons. It was like looking at Sarah's scalp after the bullet had done its gruesome handiwork.

Finally, she stood up and crossed the highway. Every step hurt. Every stray pebble and shard of glass found their way into the soles of her new shoes. It was an orchestra of pain inside Anna Huff, with the added degradation of watching each truck barrel down the road and rush past her without giving her a second thought. Most of these trucks were self-driving. They weren't programmed to give a shit.

But then, by the grace of God, one of them stopped. A rickety pickup truck whizzed past Anna and abruptly pulled over. She saw the passenger door open and sprinted toward it, so bone cold that she didn't care what kind of lunatic awaited her.

She was greeted by a Mexican woman in her fifties sitting in the driver's seat. Her son, a chubby little thing, sat beside her.

"Señora?" the woman said.

"Lo siento," Anna said. "Un accidente. Necesito mi PortFono."

"Tienes un PortFono?"

"Sí." She pointed down the highway. "Pero en la carretera. Allá."

"Ven."

There was nowhere to sit. The kid was only seven or eight years old but he was big enough to take up most of the passenger seat. The woman tapped her son, who looked *extremely* reluctant to help.

"Muevete!" she told him.

The boy scooched over in his seat, leaving room for a spare asscheek.

"Ven!" she told Anna again.

"Gracias."

With that, Anna stepped up into the truck and squeezed next to the boy. The seatbelt wouldn't fit around them both. She was bleeding on him. A lot.

This is definitely the worst moment of this boy's life.

The boy reluctantly held out a piece of Trident for Anna. "Gum?"

"No, gracias."

"Cierra la puerta," the woman said. Anna closed the door and they got back on the freeway slowly, the bigger trucks swerving around them with pissy honks.

"Donde estamos?" Anna asked.

"En Maine."

Oh! Maine! This all makes sense now, since there's nothing around. Pretty much exactly how you pictured this state.

After two minutes, Anna saw a PINE agent lingering on the side of the road. She wrested the wheel from the mother and steered the truck directly into the troop. He flopped onto the hood, legs shattered, then fell off to the side as the mother screamed and hit the brakes.

Anna jumped out of the truck and ran over to the agent, who was still alive but blessedly unconscious. Nearby, she saw her phone resting in the snow, the screen still aglow. She grabbed it and went back to the driver and her son, who were now out of the truck and standing over the broken body of the PINE agent. Neither the mom nor the child had passport lanyards.

"I'm really sorry about this," Anna told them. She was expecting the woman to start screaming bloody murder. Instead, she just shrugged.

"Que se joda," she said. *Fuck him.*

Her little boy gave the soldier the bird—the kind of angry finger Anna preferred—and then the two of them walked back to their truck and drove away, leaving Anna bruised and bloody on the side of the frigid highway.

Another truck, with an American flag across its back windshield and two latex truck nutz hanging from its hitch, stopped. The driver got out with a shotgun.

"HEY!" he shouted.

But Anna was gone before he could pump his 12-gauge. She thought she was porting to Dewey Beach, but PortSys had other ideas. After she took a step and felt the shiver, she was two hundred feet in the air and losing altitude quickly.

NORTH ATLANTIC OCEAN

She was falling among the raindrops, frantically reaching out to grab things that weren't there. All she could see was black as the wind toyed with her. She couldn't even hear herself screaming because that same wind was slicing through her eardrums. The stolen PortPhone was still clutched in her right hand, but the water would finish that off quickly.

You're falling and you're gonna die. That much was established. Seeing no light below, she assumed (prayed) that she was over water. So, for the second time in twenty-four hours, Anna Huff executed a flawless dive that Mister Willamy would never see. Gut in. Toes pointed. Arms extended and cleaving through the heavyweight air. The dive of her life and she hadn't even gotten a chance to be in a sanctioned meet this season. 10.0.

She saw the whitecaps and let go of the phone just before hitting the surface. No more Dougie. Before the divorce, the Huffs had a real bulldog that Sarah and Anna doted on. A sweet dog with honest eyes. They would feed Dougie pepperoni and take him for rides in Rhonda even when they had nowhere to go. But Mr. Huff took Dougie with him when he abandoned them for good. That little bulldog cover was a talisman Anna kept close to remember Dougie by. Now it belonged to the Atlantic.

When Anna hit the water, the cold strangled her. *Why won't anyone just let you die?* The frigid seawater gripped her battered body as viciously as Vick had. She went to inhale, but her diaphragm was gone. Massive swells pounded away at Anna and now she could feel the ocean pouring down her throat, spreading death through every corridor of her body.

Do the survival float. Anna had learned it way back in summer camp. You float face down in the water and conserve energy only by moving when you come up for breath. She had to do it for thirty minutes at camp and it was worse than anything Willamy had ever subjected her to. Still, this was the only decent option she had in her maritime arsenal at the moment.

She forgot how to do the survival float.

The salt water ate away at her wounds. The Atlantic was a giant jellyfish, slowly digesting Anna and making her part of its own crystalline body. She was sinking, the cold turning to numbness and rendering her motionless. Her sense of direction was gone in this endless expanse of sea; its surface could have been above her or below her and she wouldn't have been able to tell. It wouldn't be long now. She wasn't gonna beat the ocean, it was clear. Who'd be dumb enough to think they could?

There wasn't time to contemplate. The Atlantic, eternally busy, wouldn't allow for it. Whatever memories Anna wanted to summon—of her mom, of Sarah, and of her beloved Lara—the Atlantic had no time for any of those. Everyone wants to go down swinging, but that isn't how death works. You surrender. You succumb. Death wants your dignity before it takes the rest of you. You don't get to ponder it like some valedictorian asshole.

The only bright side, if it could be called that, was that Anna's death would get to be her own, lousy as it promised to be. This was now exclusively between her and oblivion. An intimate death. No one else could have it. Maybe the bad guys had finally defeated her. Maybe she would soon be encrusted with barnacles and left to rot along the seafloor. But that didn't matter. All of those fuckers would be locked out of her tortured consciousness forever. She wouldn't have to remember a thing about them, and they would never be able to touch her again.

Something grabbed Anna. She didn't think much of it. She didn't think anything. Whatever it was, it was likely to be bad: a trick of the water, a shark, the great sucking pull of a steamship, etc. *Whatever. Let the ocean do what it does. Just go die in peace already.*

She broke through the surface of the water, stunned to be taking in actual oxygen. Then she heard a distinctly Mancunian voice screaming at her.

"GET ON THE MAT, DICKHEAD!"

Anna looked up. There, floating on top of a portable Aerobed, she saw a wad of frizzy hair set against the vast darkness.

"Asmi?"

"GET ON!" Asmi tugged, but Anna was drained past reason. "Anna, you're gonna die if you don't get on!"

A wave hit the mattress and Anna slipped underneath. Asmi hung on but her grip was loosening in the gale. Lethal indifference had set in, and Anna was back to inhaling seawater before she felt a mighty mitt grab her other arm and pull her, with brute force, back to the surface. Before Anna could process anything, she was lying on top of the mattress and saw a tall, hirsute boy jump off of it. A great white shark—one bigger than a fisherman's lies—leapt out of the water to snatch Bamert in midair, but ended up with only a mouthful of rain instead. He had disappeared into the wind as the makeshift raft careened dangerously into the swells.

Asmi reached into a plastic bag and handed Anna a PortPhone. "Hit PORT!"

"Urrrgggghle."

"HIT IT!"

Anna did as she was told. She felt something, perhaps a foot, smash into her ribcage. There was no sensation as Anna rolled off the raft and through a wormhole—feeling a deeper chill than anything hypothermia could unleash upon her—landing face-down on a feather-soft bed of paspalum grass. She vomited up a gallon of seawater while staring out at a snarl of tangerine and lilac glowing on the horizon. A kinder wind carried the sunlight and pressed down gently on her frozen corpus. It felt like the touch of God.

KONA, HI

"Anna!"

Asmi was pressing on Anna's abdomen to get the remaining seawater out of her digestive tract.

"Stop," Anna groaned.

"There still might be water in your lungs, dickhead!"

"STOP."

Asmi quit the CPR. Above Anna was a marquee that read *Kealakehe High School*. They were on a football field, with WAVERIDERS painted in all-caps past one of the end zones. Beyond that were the tranquil waters of the Pacific, filling Anna's soul with joy and relief, one ocean healing her soul almost as quickly as another had destroyed it.

She was a giant bruise, the whole of her skin awash in bluish and greenish splotches. Her insides were waterlogged. She'd never be dry again. Cut her open and she would have exploded like a beached orca. The grass, which looked so pretty at first, was now poking at her raw skin. She could feel her nerve endings come back online but knew that would only bring a new onslaught of radioactive pain.

"Stay right here," Asmi told her.

"I was planning on that."

Three port trips later, Asmi was drying Anna off, cleaning her wounds with iodine and mummifying her in gauze and surgical tape. Everything went from freezing to burning in an instant. Touch any intact part of her skin and it would rip.

"How did you find me?" she asked Asmi. "If they know we're here, we're dead."

"They don't. I'll explain later, but for now, you need to rest."

"Where's Lara?" she asked Asmi.

"Just rest, darling."

"Where is she?"

"We don't know, but we're working on it." Asmi checked her phone. "Okay, it's all ready for you."

"What is?"

"Your bed. I have a pin ready for you."

"Asmi, I can't." She had ported so many times already. Her body and spirit had been pulverized. There were pieces of her still left in Phoenix, and Cuba, and DC, and Cairo, and Tokyo, and Maine (in that case, literally). All that remained on the soft grass of Kealakehe High was a scrap of Anna Huff: the stray piece of a puzzle that would never be put back together again. If she ported one more goddamn time, there'd be nothing left of her.

"You can't stay here," Asmi said. "No one can see you."

Anna began to cry. "I want my mom."

"She's okay. We know where she is and PortSys can't get to her. But now you have to rest, dearie. Please."

"Everyone just leave me alone." *You could have been dead and happy right now. Instead, this.*

The sun was slowly dissolving behind the ocean. Soon, it would abandon her once more and the day would be over here. But what was a day now, anyway? What was time? Anna had pinballed all over the world in such a tight timeframe that she was beyond mere jet lag. She was Anna Huff, but she was also a collection of 37 trillion cells, give or take, that had been meticulously programmed by evolutionary forces to not live this way. Each cell had evolved to adhere to a regimen of nights and days that established the bedrock of her physiology. All of that had now been broken apart, tossed around like a bad salad. Her body was going schizo. Her heart thought it was her liver. Her lungs thought they were her brain. Her feet thought they were her hands. She was less a body than a faint radio signal, flickering in and out as it drifted through the atmosphere.

"Once more," Asmi said. "One more port and then you can rest."

"I've gone insane."

"We all have. Be strong with it." Asmi took Anna's new phone and queued up the pin. "Hit PORT."

Anna took the phone and looked at the location. "You have to be kidding me."

"Okay it's a touch amusing, I'll grant you that. But I promised I wouldn't laugh at your reaction."

"I hate everyone. When this is all over, I'm just gonna watch TV."

She hit PORT and rolled into the wormhole, again feeling an inner cold that went beyond anything the frosty grip of the Atlantic had to offer.

When she opened her eyes, she was in a small dark room, lying on a thin mattress. A male figure loomed over her menacingly. *Fuck. Emilia and Jason ported you somewhere else again.* She expected a butcher knife. She expected Jason Kirsch to use it this time.

It wasn't until she heard the man speak that she realized she was dealing with an entirely different type of annoyance.

"Hey," Burton whispered. "Where's my air mattress?"

GOULD HOUSE

"That air mattress cost me $80!"

"Will you hush? Can you not see that our fair maiden requires silence, mostly from you?"

Bamert was there, too. Just two boys standing over the half-conscious body of a teenage girl and bickering, as if that were a perfectly normal thing to do.

"Where am I?" Anna whispered.

"My room," said Burton. "Keep it down, though. Everyone is looking for you."

"But how do they not know I'm here? How is *he* here?" she asked, limply gesturing to Bamert.

"Oh, Anna Huff." Bamert was trying to whisper but again, even at a low register, his voice could set off seismographs. "No one knows anything. You gave us the secret sauce."

"What do you mean?"

"The recipe. It's everything, Anna."

"The notes! But where are they now?"

"Asmi found a very safe place for them where no one will look, I assure you. Even if they do, Burton copied them to his hard drive. They're ours. I feel like I've grown a comet's tail."

"I don't understand."

"Understand this," Bamert told her. "You're a VIP now. The level under the barracudas. Network Z is garbage. This is everything. I patched that phone of yours. You can port anywhere with that phone and they'll never know. We could go to Area 41 and watch an alien autopsy now OOOOOH."

"But how did you figure this out?"

"I told you I was a physicist. I physicisted it."

"It doesn't matter," Anna told him. "I'm dead if I'm spotted."

"True, true. Everyone is everywhere now. That's very bad. But you do have a bit of an advantage, given that you're dead already."

"What?"

Bamert played her a video clip on the lowest possible volume setting. It was a press conference. The chyron on the bottom of the screen read JASON KIRSCH ALIVE AFTER STABBING;

SUSPECT DEAD AFTER VIOLENT STRUGGLE WITH PINE AGENTS. On the right hand corner of the screen was Anna's dreaded school photo. Standing behind a UCLA hospital lectern were two PINE agents, a neurosurgeon, and Lara and Emilia Kirsch. Lara was still in her prom dress, her skin bleach white and her eyes hollow.

Emilia was the only one talking. "I am extremely grateful to the staff here at UCLA Medical, along with first responders from PINE who acted quickly to protect both my son and my daughter from further harm. Unfortunately, we lost a young PINE agent at the hands of this demented young lady."

"What the fuck?" asked Anna. "I didn't kill anyone."

"So I'm grateful to that brave young troop for the sacrifice he made not just for my family, but for the world as well. I'm also grateful to him and to our other courageous PINE agents for getting Jason the care he needed so quickly," she said. "It's yet another demonstration of the miracle of this porting world."

"Is she cutting a promo right now?" Burton asked. Anna shushed him.

"This girl, this Anna Huff, was obviously extremely disturbed. Tonight we pray for her soul and for her loved ones," Kirsch said. "This has been an extremely difficult night for *my* family as well, and so I ask that you all respect our privacy at this time."

The correspondents who had ported in were not inclined to grant Emilia Kirsch that favor. They shouted every possible question at the two Kirsches as Emilia walked away from the lectern and Lara Kirsch stood there, still in shock. Anna saw the grief in her eyes and felt an extremely strange mix of sorrow and joy. *She's mourning. She's mourning* you. *Maybe she really does love you.* Her heart became a delicate bubble inside her, rising and growing at a pace that the rest of her wilted body—deflated organs, cracked bones, tangled nerves and blood vessels—couldn't accommodate. She wanted Lara to know she was alive. God, if she could only tell her somehow. If she could just clear the world away and get to Lara and look in her eyes, then everything would make sense and love could do the rest. There was only one place Anna wanted to go and yet, even in this miracle world, she couldn't go there. Maybe not ever.

This isn't fair.

"LARA!" someone from the media throng cried. "Why were you kissing Miss Huff?!"

Emilia headed back to the lectern. "You don't have to answer that, Lara. Come along now."

Lara didn't move. Emilia grabbed her by the bare arm, but Lara shook her off. The reporter screamed the question again and the rest of the throng died down, sensing that Lara was poised to answer. She leaned into the microphone as Emilia stared death rays in her direction.

"She was just a friend," Lara said.

The throng rose up again as Emilia pulled Lara away from the lectern and off the stage. A couple of seconds later, two loud portclaps came from off camera and the clip ended. Bamert's phone went dark and Anna stared up at the ceiling, wanting only stillness.

"God almighty, she friend-zoned you posthumously," Bamert said. "The cruelest kindness."

"She's lying," Anna said. "She can't let Emilia know how she really feels."

"You need to be careful with this," Burton warned her. "Don't get blinded."

"You don't understand, Burton."

"That's what everyone says when they're in love."

"I could explain why you're wrong this time around, but it would be easier to just kick your ass instead."

"Okay, okay! Jeez!"

Bamert sat at Anna's bedside, the way her mom used to whenever she was sick as a child. Sandy would make Anna toast, pop open a lukewarm ginger ale, and deliver it all to her on a little tray. Then Sandy would sit and stroke Anna's hair and let her know, even in her misery, that she was still loved.

Now Anna looked up at Bamert and started to cry once more. "I love Lara," she told him. "I love her so much it hurts, Bamert."

"I know," Bamert said. "It's a wild, unkind thing. That first love is always the most epic. It takes you and has its way with you, I know."

"You don't know. No one knows what this is like." She believed this in her soul. No one else knew what it was like to carry this searching, frantic ache. *Love can't be like this for other people, can it? It's good for them, right?* That ache continually impressed its meaningfulness upon her: an insidious way of keeping Anna in its thrall. The fact that she was on a mission to save Lara and the world at large made that ache even more definitive. Who else but Anna Huff could understand this?

"You're wrong," Bamert told her. "You see, this is not the only school I've been expelled from."

"What?"

He pressed down on the mattress to steady himself. "Do you remember that first day we met? When you asked me if I was always like this?"

"Yes."

"I wasn't." He looked down at the ground, the ghost of a much younger boy shining through his garish façade.

"She was a dash of pepper, Jessica. She was sweet and kind and smelled heavenly all the time. And she liked me. That is a hell of a feeling, Anna Huff. To know that a girl could like a million different people out there, but that she likes *you*. It's like finding out you're made of solid gold. We were just ninth graders, and I don't think anyone else thought our love was real but us. I think that's what made it so special, yes I do."

"What happened?" Anna asked.

"It was a Sunday in June, right before school was gonna let out. You weren't supposed to port from Deerbrook but they didn't have a wall, just some stupid honor code they expected you to obey."

"But *you* didn't obey it."

Bamert looked at Anna with a grim smile. He didn't obey the honor code. He got his ass kicked every day at that fucking school. So yeah, Bamert had earned the right to port out when he wanted to.

He and Jessica ported to Branford, Connecticut, overlooking Long Island Sound.

"And we frolicked. Frolicked for hours. People don't frolic anymore, and they should. It was just the loveliest day you could ever hope for. We climbed up this tall cliff and we were making sure it was safe to jump when I heard the owner of that cliff come out his back door hootin' and hollerin'. Well, I'm a Southern boy, so I know what happens when you dare to infringe on another man's property. I took Jessica's hand and we jumped and then…" He looked down at his right hand and opened and closed it. "It's a funny thing. Maybe if I had jumped a little bit farther to the left, or maybe if I had let go sooner she would've drifted more to the right. But no, she landed right where she landed."

"Oh, Bamert."

"I told you that I didn't like heights above water. Anyway, that was three schools ago. Edgar sent me here because he figured the Harkness Wall would keep me penned in. He should've known better."

"I'm so sorry, Bamert."

"Not your fault, Anna Huff. It's my fault. Everything is my fault. I'm sorry you know this about me. If everyone knew everything about everyone, we wouldn't wanna be with anyone."

"That's not true," Anna told him. "I'm glad you told me."

"There I go again, huh? I can't believe I've somehow made even *this* night about me, although I suppose I can." He took a swig of bottled water. "I don't know how people drink this garbage."

"Did you always know this about him?" Anna asked Burton.

"Why do you think I put up with him?" Burton said. "I've known Paul my whole life. My parents are Edgar Bamert's landscapers."

"It's true," Bamert said. "He knows how much I look up to him, yes he does."

"So you started drinking because Jessica died," Anna said.

"No I started drinking because my parents hated me. But Jessica dying didn't help, no. People heard about it, you know. A lotta kids here at Druskin know. That's why they treated me like a freak.

Frankly I'm surprised you didn't know about it. Search my name online and it comes right up."

"I liked you too much to ever Google you."

"That's the kindest thing anyone's ever said to me. But still, ain't it a bitch: The first person who ever loved me, and I killed her."

"We love you, Bamert," Anna said. "*I* love you."

"Thank you." There was no good ol' boy bravado when he said it. He got off the bed and knelt at Anna's side, taking her hand in his piquant mitts. "I love you too, dear friend. And you love Lara Kirsch."

"I do."

"You believe she loves you."

"I do."

"But you don't really *know* if she loves you!" Burton protested.

"Burton," said a weary Anna, "How will anyone love me if I always assume no one does?"

"You believe in this love," Bamert told her. "You would beg for it."

"I would."

"You try to hate that love all you like because it owns you. But deep down, you never want it to stop. You don't want love to listen."

"I don't."

"You believe only the corniest things now—like that boy who climbed the Harkness Wall did—because love has taken root inside you."

"I do and it has."

"And you believe in Lara and she believes in you. True love means you believe in one another."

"Yes."

"True love represents the bones of the soul. You really are a lion, Anna Huff. A true and bold lion. If I do one good thing with this pointless goddamn life of mine, it'll be to wrangle that love for you so that it never gets away. People who fall in love can forget how nice it is to have friends, you know. I'll help. Burton will, too."

"I never agreed to that," Burton said.

Bamert began to furiously dig into his pockets. "Oh my stars, let me just see if I have any fucks left to give." He proudly held up two empty hands. "Why, dear boy, it appears that I have no fucks left to give a'tall!"

"Bamert," said Burton, "We've had this chat already. I am not a garden tool you can grab out of the shed. I have my own life to consider."

"And what higher purpose could that life serve than love?" asked Bamert. "What's more ethical than that?! You can help make true love real! You've already helped in ways that some might categorize as Un-Druskinlike Conduct!" He walked over to Burton, knelt down, and took *his* hand. "Please, Jamie. This isn't me being selfish. This is for fair Anna Huff. She'd do the same for you, because her ethics are good and true. You can grow up the way they tell you to grow up, or you can use the strange and deeply irritating talents the good Lord bestowed upon you to spread His greatest gift of all. You're in."

Burton sighed. "Okay but—"

"Shut up. I said you're in," Bamert said. He walked back to Anna and stood over her, a massive and welcome sentinel.

"We'll get you back to Lara," he told her. "But first, you have to do something."

"What's that?" Anna asked.

"Play dead."

DUCK, NC

Anna slept for fifteen hours, not moving once. When she woke up in Burton's bed, she rolled onto her side and felt a distinct crack, as if her skin were made of wafers. She had bled all over the fitted sheet and that dried blood had fused it to her raw, exposed arm overnight. The bed was now part of her: an extended scab. She had to make a concerted effort to not cry out in pain. Every minor adjustment forced her to bury her agony in a series of strange, throaty gurgles. Anna Huff was the howler monkey now.

Burton had laid out a gym-issued towel, her red sneakers, and a pair of grays, along with a fresh pack of gauze and surgical tape. She got up, unzipped her prom dress and let it fall to the floor. It was so thoroughly stained with grass and dirt and blood as to be tie-dyed, even more so than the shirt she stole from Cairns. The fabric was in tatters, the stitches loose like sutures from a wound that had busted open. She picked up the dress and took a deep whiff, searching for the faint scent of Lara's body wash. The one souvenir Anna had of her night on the VIP stage with Lara, and already it had been destroyed, like the night had never happened. The dress was gone, and now Anna would have to slip into the colorless rags of a Druskin studybot.

She made a quick assessment of her own body. Apart from the endless cuts and scrapes and bruises, everything vital was miraculously intact. The pain was total, the damage minimal. She checked the mirror, fully expecting every stupid teenage insecurity she still harbored to hound her into shame. In the reflection, Anna saw herself bloodied and broken, her head caked in spent plasma and her skin as tender as raw flank steak. Despite everything, the rose pink bangle bracelet had stayed on her wrist.

Actually, you look cool as shit.

Lara's WorldGram profile had no new updates since prom night. She had gone incognito. *Maybe she's dead. Or imprisoned.* Anna's worst fears began their cruel handiwork with glee.

No one was in the Gould House hallway, so she scampered over to the bathroom and showered off. Pieces of her wounds dropped to the tile floor and circled around her feet before sluicing through the drain. She shut the water off. Every ambient sound made her flinch as she wrapped the towel around herself, wrapped a yard of gauze around her poor arm, then whipped on the gray shorts and t-shirt. Bereft of a hefty blanket to muffle her exit, she ducked into Burton's closet. There, packed tight against all of Burton's homemade clothes and gardening kits, she hit PORT and felt the shiver.

Here were the Outer Banks of North Carolina in wintertime: a long spit of sand that carelessly faced the Atlantic, welcoming all of its abuse. There were no tourists on the Outer Banks this time of year, just the usual squatters porting in and taking advantage of the considerable gaps in seasonal residency. Come summer, the beaches would be smothered in humanity, the crowds taking advantage of the lowered sea levels that had widened this spit of land ever so slightly. But now, in January, as the hemispheric drifts sent masses of porting vagabonds closer to the equator, the Banks were home to little more than wind and phantoms.

Anna was standing in a house that was five times larger than any vacation home along the rest of this sandbar. She was in the sun room of this mansion, its coffered ceilings gleaming in wedding cake white paint. The beach outside was frozen in a harsh, corrugated pattern and capped with frost, like a still-life rendering of the adjacent ocean. She was not quite ready to forgive the Atlantic. Pints of it were still circulating through her.

Someone tapped Anna on the shoulder. It was Sandy, who was too shell-shocked to do anything but stare at her daughter in utter incredulity. She was as battered and bruised on the inside as Anna was on the outside.

"Mom."

"What has happened to you? The Internet says you're dead."

"Well, I'm not dead."

"And Lara Kirsch is your *girlfriend*?"

"That part I'm still working on."

"What did you do? Assaulting a dean? Painting hate speech? Attacking the CEO of PortSys?"

"He's not the CEO, he's Chief Creative Officer."

"WHAT DID YOU DO?!"

Anna grabbed Sandy and held her close. The physical contact flicked the pain on immediately, but Anna gutted it out to keep Sandy in her arms. Mrs. Huff still knew her way around a hug.

"I didn't do anything wrong," Anna told her. "I swear to God."

"You're a fugitive now! They're gonna jail you if they find out you're alive, maybe even kill you!"

"Oh, they'll definitely kill me."

Sandy pulled away from Anna. "This isn't funny! God, kids and their jokes. When do you become a *serious* person, Anna? When does the light go on? You show up at my work and drag me out the back, and then you assault a boy, and then your friend tells me I have to hide out here and he gives me a new phone because apparently I'm dead if I use my old one? Do you understand that I already lost a child? Every day it hurts, Anna. Hurts as much today as it did the day it happened. If I so much as hear the name *Sarah* or read it, all I want to do is lay down in a grave somewhere beside her."

"I feel the same way."

"You sure as hell don't act like it. I told you I cannot lose you too, and I meant it. Everything's broken now. I wasn't built to handle this!"

She collapsed on Anna's shoulder as they stood together by a great bay window in the Bamerts' opulent beach house living room. Everything in the house, except for them, was immaculate.

"I'm so sorry, mom," she whispered to Sandy.

"It's too late. What do we do, now, Anna? What do we *do*?"

"Mom, Jason Kirsch killed Sarah."

Sandy let out a scream that shot through Anna like gamma radiation, tearing at her insides. Distending and mutating them. "Everything is broken," her mom wailed. She kept saying it over and over.

"Listen to me, mom: they're after us, but I'm gonna destroy them first. I have a plan."

"No."

"I have something they want and I'm gonna use it against them."

Sandy let go and shook her head.

"No no no no no. You're seventeen. You've thrown everything away."

"I don't have a choice. They've made this world what it is."

"You think *I* want the world to be like this? You think I wouldn't try to burn it all down and start again if I could? I can't, Anna. No one can. There is evil in the world, Anna, and it's its own force of nature. All you can do is build your own life, build your own *good* to keep the evil out. That's what I tried to do but you're gonna let it claim the both of us."

"No, I won't."

"Can you? Look at you. You look like just fell off a cement mixer."

"Actually it was a container truck."

"Always with the goddamn jokes, Anna. Even now, you can't be serious."

"Mom, you have no idea how serious I feel right now."

"You're not ready for this and I'm not ready for you to try. You had all my faith and all of my hope, Anna. Don't you understand that? I trusted you with that hope. I *trusted* you."

"You still can."

"No, I can't. You're a child. You need to accept that and stop this, right now."

"No. Not this time."

Sandy grabbed her arm, squeezing it like a blood pressure monitor sleeve and setting Anna's road rash aflame once more. "No."

"Mom, I have to."

"You're coming with me. This isn't up for debate."

Anyone can rebel against a shitty parent. Whatever open rebellion Anna displayed as a child had been, up until this point, benign in nature. Common. She talked back. She pouted. She wore things Sandy didn't want her to wear. It fell well within the parameters of standard teenage revolt. But Anna had never dared venture beyond such acts in front of Sandy, because Sandy was a good mom and, when it came to vital matters, her authority became supreme and their relationship as mother and daughter came to the forefront with a stunning alacrity.

Like other moms, Sandy also had an appalling knack for being right; for barging into a child's brain and convincing them at the deepest level that a mother's truth is the only truth, no matter how much you fight and claw against it. Anna was only seventeen. It was true. Everyone on Earth knew who Anna Huff was now, and what they knew was probably bad. Any kid could rebel against an indifferent jackass like Edgar Bennett. But it took a certain gall—not necessarily admirable gall, either—to rebel against Sandy. Sandy almost certainly knew better. She had given everything to her children and only had one of them left to show for it. Going against her now would be insensitive, disloyal, and ungrateful.

"I'm not going with you, Mom. Look at me."

Sandy looked. Anna had arresting eyes of her own. Growing up is when you go from faking confidence to having it outright. In Anna's eyes now, there was nothing but the earned confidence and impenetrable resolve of a woman twice her age.

"I have to go away for a little bit. Stay here for now. Paul's family has a house outside of Cleveland that they never use, where you'll be safe. He'll take you there soon."

"I don't wanna go to Cleveland," Sandy told her.

"Few people ever do. Go with Paul and I'll see you again when it's over."

"When *what's* over?"

"You'll see. I have to do this."

"Why?"

"Because I'm not gonna let the world have its way with me. I've got a plan, and no one's gonna get in the way of it. Not even you. Let me go."

"Anna."

"Let me go. You can't hang onto me forever, and you know it."

Sandy did as she was told. "You know, when you and Sarah were young, I always complained that you two never listened. But I guess there comes a time where everything flips and it's the *parent* who never listens."

"Listen to me now," Anna said. "I can do this."

"I just love you so much, honey."

"I love you too, Mom. This won't be the last time you see me. Believe that."

"Okay. But one more hug."

"One."

Sandy took Anna in her arms and squeezed extra tight. When this was over, Anna was gonna hug her mom a lot more than she used to.

"Meantime," Sandy whispered, "Send your mother a postcard, will you?"

"I will."

Anna ported out and left Sandy Huff alone once more, looking out upon a deserted, frozen shore.

FOUR MONTHS LATER

DEAN'S RESIDENCE

Before being accepted to Druskin Academy, Asmi Naru had never gotten in trouble as a student. Despite her predilection for huffing glue and fighting people, she had never been sent to an administrator's office, nor ever been denied privileges, nor ever had a teacher send an angry email to her parents regarding misbehavior. She had never been given detention. She was never tardy. She never faked sick. She was a clever troublemaker. When she was fifteen, a stranger online called her a "whore." Asmi challenged him to meet her in Luton so that she could kick his ass. He agreed, and then she did.

But no one ever caught her. Her permanent record was spotless. Until Anna Huff came along.

The investigation had commenced immediately after Anna disappeared from campus. PINE agents stormed into Room 24 and took everything. They flipped over the mattresses, punched holes in the walls, and pried under floorboards that hadn't been disturbed for over a century. They were no kinder to Asmi's own possessions, manhandling her clothes, rummaging through her supplies and confiscating her Druskin-issued electronics, all of which scanned clean. They never found the notes. PINE was aggressive but sloppy. If only they had thought to examine the other rooms in Sewell.

They never found Anna's doctored PortPhone either, which had its own separate hiding spot. If only they had bothered to raid Gould House. Ah, but Jamie Burton had a pristine reputation among Druskin faculty. Volunteering to walk their dogs only burnished his teacher's pet rep further, plus it gave him access to his resident faculty member's mud room any time he wanted, which was useful for stashing contraband where no one might look.

Asmi didn't get off so easy. During the raid, one PINE agent asked Asmi where she was from. When she told him, "England, you piece of shit," he called her a liar, smacked her, and then spat on her.

Vick was somehow even less kind. He summoned Asmi to his office to hiss and jab at her with his angry finger. He threatened to have her student visa revoked. He demanded to know where Anna had left the notes Lara had given her. Asmi, shaken but unbowed, fiercely maintained her innocence. Vick put her on 'stricts anyway. He summoned other girls to his office to account for Asmi's whereabouts the night she saved Anna from drowning. None of them had a clue about anything. Vick put all of *them* on 'stricts too.

The persecution went on for months. Sometimes PINE agents ported directly into Asmi's room at night. Her parents called Vick to complain about the harassment but Vick, predictably, didn't give a shit.

Finally, consigned to the dean's office for another round of torment, Asmi asked Vick if there was something, *anything* she could do to end the interrogations. All she wanted was to be left alone. The dean, sporting a scar on his back from a nasty puncture wound he suffered at the hands of Anna Huff, was more than happy to take out some of his anger on his assailant's former roommate. Yes, there is something you can do to help remedy the situation, he told her. She was to show up at his residence at 7pm on a Wednesday night, dressed lightly. She was to tell no one.

When the time came, Vick opened the door of his house with that nauseating half-grin and led Asmi down into his foul and dusty basement. He cracked open the vault-like door to his lab and ordered her to stand on the black X on the floor. Brendan McClear labored away in silence nearby. Vick sat at his laptop and banged away at the keys, leaving Asmi to roast in his silence. The way Vick used silence was impressively cruel. The whole room quivered with his unspoken fury. It was not a silence you could trust.

Asmi knew what she was getting into when she agreed to Bamert and Anna's plan, but that didn't make this moment any more pleasant. Anna didn't (couldn't, really) tell Asmi what the experiments felt like, but Asmi had heard enough detail through whispers from other girls, always girls, who had been punished similarly. Everything was going to burn. Asmi had seen a man burning once when she was visiting her grandparents back in Pakistan. One minute she was walking with her grandmother, and the next a living flame was screeching past her. She never forgot his screams. She wondered if she'd scream the same way when Vick did whatever it was he was gonna do to her.

Vick dialed up PortSys headquarters and told Asmi to grab a four-kilogram kettle bell resting on the floor. The familiar voice of Jason Kirsch came over the video call. Asmi listened intently, trying to divine any specific details of Kirsch's location. The Chief Creative Officer didn't *have* to oversee these tests personally, of course. But he often did. If there was a chance to torture someone, even via remote, Jason Kirsch wasn't one to pass on the opportunity.

Vick pointed an external camera at Asmi and opened up the wormhole. She stepped forward and was instantly greeted with scorching pain, the front of her body rendered into hot vapor. Time died off and she was trapped in a quantum hellstate, every particle around her weaponized and digging through her. Then the wormhole spat her out and she fell to the ground, shaking.

"She failed," Vick told Jason.

"We have a year for this, but I don't want to cut it close. I'll be in Singapore next week. Bring her back for testing even if I'm not here."

"Will do." He turned to Asmi, who was clutching at her body in a horrible fright. She was intact but shredded on the inside.

"You can leave," he told her. "Come back next Wednesday."

"And no one will bother me again?"

He said nothing.

Asmi slowly rose to her feet and opened up the lab door. As she walked out, she caught a glimpse of Anna Huff in the corner of the unfinished basement, lying in wait.

Vick, true to character, sat in menacing silence for another twenty minutes, typing up his report summary and firing it back to PortSys headquarters. Then he shed his lab coat and went upstairs with Brendan McClear for a cup of tea, both of them failing to notice Anna along the way. She could have ported in much later to raid the lab, but she still got a twisted thrill from hiding near those two without them realizing it. Part of her prayed Vick would see her behind that door. She had a gun. Nothing would have pleased her more than a chance to use it on him.

Vick had left the lab door open. Anna slipped past its threshold and grabbed the little white camera she had taped to the inside of

Vick's desk lamp the week before, prying the bug off the blazing hot shade and fastening a freshly charged one back into position. She opened up the live stream of the camera on her new, VIP-enabled PortPhone and rolled back through footage it had just taken. The lab Vick was calling into from his laptop was windowless: a long row of technicians sitting at open desks coding away, with Jason Kirsch calling in from a secondary site, his vile face occupying its own little box. Anna scoured the footage for any hint of the lab's location, but there was nothing. Then she plugged in a set of cheap earbuds and listened to the replay again.

I'll be in Singapore next week but you should bring her back for testing even if I'm not here.

Two of the techs in the lab were talking while Jason Kirsch was giving directives, but she couldn't quite make out what they were saying. She closed the soundproofed lab door shut and clapped to Burton's room.

GOULD HOUSE/MINNEAPOLIS

Burton was sitting on his couch crocheting a doggie sweater when Anna blew in.

"You get the footage?" he asked her.

"Yeah, can you help me isolate audio?"

"One moment." Burton kept crocheting.

"I'm gonna stab you with one of those needles."

"I said one moment, please."

She didn't have a moment. She had just spent four months hiding out in an abandoned apartment complex in Minneapolis, rarely porting despite her VIP privileges. ShareSpaces were too dicey. Squatting out in the free zones was the best way for her to remain a dead girl. PortSys didn't know she was alive and couldn't track her, but she kept her guard up.

The news cycle rebooted hundreds of times in the interim. The story of the deranged prep school gal who assaulted the Chief Creative Officer of PortSys had slipped from the collective consciousness. Vanished, just as Anna had. At first, there were a million stories about her online, all of them unfavorable. She didn't want to read them, nor the virulent comments below. But boredom and a lack of willpower caused her to pick those digital scabs routinely. Sometimes the commenters would leave flower emojis to pay their respects to her and to rage at PortSys for framing her, and that would make her smile. Someone even photoshopped SAVE ANNA onto a picture of a water tower, which made her laugh out loud. Another group of commenters espoused a theory that Anna Huff was not dead, but in fact still alive and well and hiding out in Argentina. *Argentina would have been a better idea than Minnesota.* She broke into laughter again when other replies said the theory was absurd.

But so many more comments *celebrated* Anna's death, often in gif form. Those comments left a lasting, insidious sting. The certainty that Anna didn't do anything wrong was little salve to her when she knew so many others—millions, even—*weren't* as certain. You can only laugh so much at all the idiots before you come to realize that they have you vastly outnumbered. At the r/Conquistadors forum, K15 christened the date of her demise as Huff Day to commemorate the occasion. He disappeared online for weeks thereafter, never posting. Maybe *he* was dead.

Good.

Vick sent an email blast to Druskin students and alumni about how the school wouldn't tolerate hate, and the copy made her boil. *She* could tolerate hate plenty right now, especially for him. That was a productive hate. So deep and so right. Hate gave her some semblance of control over that black curtain of depression.

The stories and obits about Anna faded, but she still didn't want too many people spotting her out in the wild. Not for now, at least. She yearned for companionship: if not Lara or Bamert, then her mom, or poor Sarah, or even an imaginary younger sister. But Anna Huff was on her own, left to softly sing herself to sleep at night for company and for comfort.

Her daydreams were her only friend. Honestly, they probably made for better company than actual people. Her imagination had grown a touch kinder now, not as eager to sabotage everything. Her brain was behaving itself. Getting stronger. Doing as it was told. She imagined coming out of hiding to destroy PortSys and then sitting down for an in-depth interview with Katy Wagner about it, mouthing her answers while she tossed and turned at night. In this apartment, she was strangely content to listen to her mind. She had gotten better at that nifty trick, with grudging thanks to Druskin. Her mind was now her ideal sanctuary.

Sandy, hiding out in Cleveland, sent Anna an e-postcard for her 18th birthday. Anna returned the favor by dropping a real postcard of two men ice fishing on Lake Minnetonka—unsigned, with a stamp—into a mailbox for a portcarrier to deliver. Bamert had a full sheet cake delivered to her doorstep, but that was as much "time" with loved ones as Anna got. The best she could do otherwise was to slip into that shadow dimension with her older sister. When Anna was younger and Sandy had to go wash dishes at odd hours, it was Sarah who had to cook Anna dinner, read her bedtime stories, and tuck her in at night. Come morning, it was Sarah who made Anna Bisquick pancakes and walked her to the bus stop, because Sandy Huff was still so exhausted from her night shift. With no one else in the Minneapolis apartment, Anna felt freer to talk to Sarah out loud and not feel self-conscious about it. She told Sarah about Lara and about the terrifying bond between them.

"I'd tell you that I wish you were here, but you are. I know you are. When this is all over, they'll make a movie about it. Maybe it'll premiere at Cannes. Wouldn't that be some shit?"

She maintained a tight radius at all times. Apart from the first daring excursion into Vick's basement toward the end of her stay, she only ported out when she needed a quick charge and/or a computer terminal over at the Minneapolis Central Library, still open and located in the otherwise abandoned Nicollet Mall. The library was a miracle, staffed by a group of elderly women who zealously guarded its stacks, keeping the books locked behind glass to prevent theft. They never recognized Anna, who always popped in with a stolen "Uff Da!" scarf wrapped around her face so that she could tend to her affairs while incognito. No one raised an eye at her keeping the scarf on because the library still let in enough of the Minnesota frost to have its own ambient chill. Everyone at the library was more interested in books than people anyway.

Anna didn't dare step outside otherwise, lest she get spotted by PINE agents or taken down by a stray bullet. Bamert had a port delivery service bring her bottled water, a battery-powered space heater, toilet paper, tampons, a portable generator, top ramen, chili cheese Fritos, energy drinks, and other vital snacks that satisfied her stickiest cravings. He also sent her one of Edgar's handguns along with a deck of cards to shuffle, which she did for hours at a time. No card games. No solitaire. Just swiftly rearranging aces and queens between her busy little fingers. At night, she could hear small bombs going off outside. She was never sure who set them off— Conquistadors, Black Shard copycats, some terrorist sect—but what did it matter? Anyone with a bomb was a bad guy. No one in the free zones was ever safe. She couldn't sleep with earplugs at night because she needed to be able to hear in case someone else ported in, perhaps with bad intentions. Thus, she heard everything: bumps and rattles and every other trick of the night. Even when it was quiet, she couldn't relax because she knew it wouldn't stay that way.

Anna had a plan. It took a while to form, but she hammered it into shape the way she would a critical term paper. At first, she thought about finding the main PortSys switchboard and blowing it to smithereens, un-tethering the company's satellites from their respective orbits and freezing everyone in place: a great reshuffling of humanity that would redraw all borders and give birth to entirely new cultures. Then Bamert reminded her of the number of people who could potentially die from such an audacious act—like if they were, say, hanging out on top of Everest right when she hit the kill switch.

She was forced to reconsider, then drafted a new plan that they both agreed was superior. Sturdy. But it was a plan that required time and an inordinate amount of legwork on Asmi's, Burton's and Bamert's end—work that all of them proved shockingly up for. So she lingered in the frozen heartland and waited there in that dark, decaying apartment as spring clawed its way into existence. She could be patient when she needed to be. This was fine. It wasn't safe, but it was fine. Finer than prison, at least.

Against all odds, Anna Huff was feeling fitter than she ever had. Her wounds healed up. She did yoga in the main living room in the middle of the night. There was a musty piano that the apartment's former owners had been too lazy to move when they fled, so she practiced for hours at a time, never striking the keys fully, instead sounding out ghost notes she could only hear in her mind. Her hands needed the work. Cards only pleased them so much.

Despite dropping out of Druskin, she followed along with the English syllabus Nolan had posted online and did the required reading. Each block of text seemed to eat up a quarter-hour at a time, which served her purposes well. She even typed out mock papers on her phone using the Notes app. After she "died," Druskin shipped all her belongings back to their container in Rockville, which Bamert had a private security guard unpack and store. The school had also sent Sandy a formal letter from trustees explaining why Anna's boarding fees would not be refunded. Dean Glenn did NOT deliver that letter personally.

She slept soundly on a flea-ridden couch in that Minneapolis condo, keeping a gun under the throw pillow. One night, a mangy man ported in and she pointed the gun at him. He cursed at her in Finnish and then ported right back out. Another night, a group of port immigrants blew in, seeking refuge. When they saw Anna, they politely found another spot. She hoped they might stick around so that they could talk and eat canned soup together, but that little sting of loneliness soon faded and she went back to her routine.

It felt good to be dead. In her mind, the longer she stayed dead, the sweeter her reunion with Lara would be. Nothing else mattered. She was more focused and determined now than she had ever been at school. Thanks to the yoga and to her voluntary studies, she was developing a sharper mind and a hard bark around it. She even gave meditation a shot, downloading the MINDFL app and sitting cross-legged on the floor as a calming voice urged her to focus on her breath and her breath alone.

"Listen to the breath going in."

Okay.

"And out."

Got it. Her voice really is *soothing.*

"If your mind wanders, gently nudge it back to the breath. Only the breath."

Move your ass back to the breath, you stupid brain.

"Sometimes we can get so preoccupied with our worries."

Like Lara. Wait, you're not supposed to think about Lara right now. Shit.

"We have so much business to tend to, and so many different concerns about how to invest our money wisely."

What the fuck? Who is this app even for? Did Jason Kirsch write this?

"People beg for our attention and we always feel like we have to indulge them because we know that what we do is just that important. That is the price of ascending to such a lofty position in this world."

Who's "we," lady? She's not talking to you, that's for sure. This app sucks.

Lara Kirsch was still MIA, never posting to WorldGram and never spotted out in the wild. Like the other Kirsches, she remained invisible on Anna's doctored phone. Still, "Lara" remained the preferred keyword search of her renovated imagination, which possessed all the time and space it needed to concoct elaborate daydreams about where Lara was, and what she was doing, and what she was wearing. *That flapper dress. Good god.*

Anna was enjoying the distraction her obsessions provided, perhaps a little too much. She thought about Phoenix, and she thought about that kiss: Lara's lips, her scent, her fingers gently brushing against Anna's cheek. She could have survived for years on just that kiss alone. *Kiss them once and they expect the world.* She was no boy but she expected the world now all the same, yes she did. There was a way to avenge Sarah and get Lara all in one decisive strike. But it required patience. It required Anna to spend months subsisting on little more than dry sandwiches and canned food, unable to ever shower. To live like a bug. But she could do that, and she did.

Now she was back on campus at Druskin, ready to set the grand plan in motion. Yet here was Burton, still knitting a goddamn sweater.

"Can we hurry this along?" she asked him.

"This needs to be done before Friday," Burton told her.

"Or what? Fido gets a cold? You don't even own a dog."

"You know, everybody gives me grief. But the second they need a micro camera, or an inflatable mattress when they're stuck out at sea, or a place to harbor *a technically deceased fugitive*, suddenly I'm a pal again."

"I'm sorry. I didn't mean to be a dick."

"Yes you did," Burton said. "That's why I like being your friend, against my better judgment. But you could at least shower before mouthing off at me."

"Sorry."

"I know I have strange way of doing things, but it's the only way I can do them."

Anna acquiesced and plopped down on Burton's bed as he slowly, painfully, looped the red yarn over and over. She made her fists tight enough to crush stone. Then she spread her fingers wide, reaching her thumbs and pinkies out until her hands were wider than they were long. Like she was back out on the Salton Boathouse dock, stoned out of her brains and watching her metacarpal bones shine through her skin.

"How's Asmi?" she asked Burton.

"Still alive. Less bubbly these days, though. What's it feel like when Vick does the weight test on you?"

"It's the worst feeling in the world. Once you know you can be in that much pain, you can't un-know it. I don't like thinking about it."

"I'm sorry for both of you. That sounds like a really lousy jaunt."

"It's okay. And you? How have you been?" she asked him.

"I'm lonely," Burton said. "Bamert sometimes ports in secretly but I have to chase him out so that I don't get in trouble. He's always taking liberties. I try to stay focused on my future, but sometimes I worry that the world's future and my future aren't exactly compatible."

"You're gonna be fine," Anna told him. "At least you're still here at Druskin."

"Oh, you never liked being at this detention hall of a school anyway."

"I did and I didn't."

Burton set down the sweater and walked over to her.

"Gimme that camera."

She handed it to him and he downloaded it to a homemade PC on his desk that had seventeen separate components. It looked like Burton imported the machine from 1981.

"Ugh, a .wav file," he complained.

"Can you tell what they're saying at the 20-minute mark?"

"Hang on." He banged away at the PC as Anna balled up her fists again. He turned up the speakers to full blast. These were good speakers, much better than they had at the Dunbar welcome mixer. Jason Kirsch was talking about Singapore when a voice came in underneath him. Burton toyed with the clip some more, slowing the voices down and bending them until they sounded drunk. The buried voice was getting clearer.

"We could walk," it slurred, "To Griffith Park."

"That's LA," Burton said. "That's where the lab is. You understand that they'll have surveillance, right? They'll see you in there."

"Will they?" asked Anna. She pointed to the surveillance footage on Burton's laptop. Sitting in the lab was a mousy brunette in a lab coat. Her ID tag was visible. The name read "Victoria Marshall."

"Burton, is there any chance you could give me a haircut?"

LOS ANGELES

It was just after lunch hour Pacific time when J. Paul Bamert ported onto the main stage of the Greek Theater nestled inside Griffith Park. He was dressed in a salmon-colored suit festooned with little fishhooks, custom made for him at the Suitsupply. All of his cherished old Druskin suits—with their geckos and poodles and owls and very small anchors—were now too large for his rapidly slimming frame. He was a lean boy now. This suit was brand new. Bamert would have to break it in at some point, perhaps by running five miles in it. A suit was never fully his until he'd sweated past its pits and subjected its fibers to burning things.

His normally mangy beard had been mowed down into geometrically precise stubble. His hands were freshly manicured, devoid of grease and lingering odors. He wore a wireless earpiece with the mic hugging close to his meticulously groomed cheek. A team of sound men sat behind a console that was seventy-five yards away from him, right behind Section A. The amphitheatre had grown dilapidated over the years now that so many concerts and shows were held at pop-up venues across continents. But the place still had a bigness: a pervasive vibe that a mass of dormant human energy was ready to explode out of it.

Bamert sauntered over to the microphone at the front of the stage and grabbed a bottle of distilled water, drinking it all in a single, rapturous gulp. Behind him was a silver scrim with a logo that read PEGASYS in letters nearly as tall as the Hollywood sign itself. Every seat in the theater was empty, but that wouldn't be the case for long. Two sections of seating were cordoned off with red tape.

The afternoon sun bathed the Santa Monica mountains in warm, thick rays. The sun belonged to California. Always had. It would make for an afternoon of long shadows on this day. Not a trace of smog to ruin it. Bamert wondered to himself why he didn't port to California more often, why he didn't just *live* here. He was free to do as he pleased, after all. He was rich and expelled and his father hated him. But, in a neat twist, Edgar hated Emilia Kirsch even more now that her cronies had burned his mansion down, and the old man wasn't about to let PINE agents harass his son over some crazy girl

Paul was once friends with. After Anna Huff "died," the agency interrogated Bamert for a scant ten minutes before politely fucking off to harass more vulnerable targets.

Signs around Griffith Park warned of mountain lions and rattlesnakes that roamed the small, dusty peaks above. Those were Bamert's people. He would have liked to party with all that messy wildlife. Instead, he stepped up to the mic, cradled it in his paws, and gave a sound check.

"CHECK TWO CHECK TWO CHECK TWO CAN Y'ALL HEAR ME?"

The sound men gave Bamert a thumbs up. He faced stage left.

"Video? Are you guys set to go with the live stream?"

The video crew also gave him the go ahead.

He whispered into his lapel, "Burton? You there, honeysuckle rose?"

"I'm here," Burton told him.

"But?"

"But what?"

"You're not gonna complain to me about something?"

"No," said Burton. He was sitting at his PC back in Gould House, an interactive map of the theater and surrounding parklands displayed on the monitor in front of him. Small blue dots flashed across the map, wandering around before blipping elsewhere. Burton scratched his mouse button like it was a trigger. "I'm set."

"I can't believe it. Truly it is a new day," Bamert said. It was time. Everything was in place. But before Bamert could begin, he had to indulge himself. He crooned into the mic:

> ♫ *These arms of miiiiiiiiiine*
> *They are lonely*
> *Lonely and feeling blue*
> *These arms of miiiiiii-iiiiiine*
> *They are yearning*
> *Yearning from wanting you* ♫

His baritone echoed out and shook the great sycamores ringing the amphitheater. Hikers traversing the dusty paths above stared down at the lonely boy singing and the strange brand emblem behind him.

Bamert usually only sang to have fun, but feeling this song come out of his mouth caught him off guard. He stepped away from the mic, grabbing a pocket square to dab away a couple of fugitive tears. A deep breath and he was right again.

"Okay!" he announced into the microphone. "Let's dance." He took out his phone and held his index finger over the SUMMON button for a few dramatic seconds, like he was about launch a nuclear missile. Then he finally smashed it.

In a blink, 5,000 people appeared in the seats before him. They were mostly older, mostly male. Some of them were still dressed in their work attire. Others had been summoned while in their underwear. They were disoriented, confused, and quite angry. Not all of them had their PortPhones on them.

"Hello!" Bamert cried out to them. "Now you might be asking yourself: what manner of witchery could summon 5,000 of the world's foremost industrialists to a single spot in a single moment? I do apologize for rudely taking you away from your present endeavors, but I assure you that I'll get you back home the second I've finished cutting your port costs in half."

That last piece of information simmered down the crowd. Some of them had clapped back out right away, but Bamert was undeterred.

"My name is J. Paul Bamert and I am an alcoholic," he told the crowd, only confusing them further. "Sorry to mention that off the bat, but it's the first thing I tend to say to large groups of people these days. Force of habit. But I'm not here to wallow in such matters, and neither are you. It's been 130 days since my last drink, but it's only ten seconds until I change the world. For you see, I'm about to introduce something to the porting industry that you've never seen before: COMPETITION."

He ported to a spot beside the great silver scrim. Reporters popped up along the outskirts of the theater, holding up their phones to get footage of this unheralded tech wunderkind.

"This. Is. PEGASYS!" Bamert cried out. The logo on the screen blew up to reveal a graphic of the Earth spinning on its axis, a series of busy satellites orbiting it.

"This is an entirely new port network, and 100% secure. And affordable, too! We're gonna offer unlimited plans to people at less than $40 a month. And we're gonna have even better rates for direct-to-business service. Now isn't that a rainbow?"

"How do we know you can do this?" shouted one man.

"I brought y'all here, didn't I?" asked Bamert.

"How old are you?!" another asked.

"How old are *you*?" Bamert countered. "Don't you know it's uncivilized to make such inquiries?"

Still another. "Why is it called Pegasys?"

"Because I thought of the name myself, and it owns. What I will also disclose to you, the potential investor, is that I am the son of Edgar Bamert. And as they say in the financial business, the word of a Bamert is oak. Isn't that right, father?"

Edgar Bamert had been force-ported into the second row. He was dressed in a suit and bewildered as to how his derelict of a son, who crassly asserted that he could ruin the Kirsches with just a bit of seed money, could remove him from a party that he had been hosting in Savannah just seconds earlier.

"But if y'all need more proof," yelled Bamert, "Here's another trick for you. ALAKAZAM!"

He tapped his prototype phone and now one of the cordoned-off sections was filled with PortSys lab technicians, still in their coats.

"Everyone say hello to the R&D team of PortSys! So glad they could join us. Ah, but that's not all."

He tapped his phone again and the other section filled up with hundreds of young men, women, and children. All of them had been shaved bald. All of them cowered at the sunlight.

"These are the unfortunate souls that the PortSys R&D team uses as guinea pigs. Isn't that right, team?"

Silence from the lab section.

"This may not be music to y'all's capitalistic ears, but I do believe I can offer a more humane network of port travel. I do NOT agree to Portsys's terms and conditions, and neither should anyone else. Instead, I do believe that I will never let the Kirsch family, nor any of you fine people here today, lay a goddamn finger on these men, women, and children ever again. Nor will I be selling anyone's porting information to anyone else. I can guarantee you that much. Pegasys will have ETHICS."

Down the mountain from the theater, a tinge of acrid smoke came on faintly: a black wisp that tickled noses in the crowd until it grew beyond mere suspicion. Something was burning down that hill. Something industrial. Something toxic. The California natives in the audience knew the bitter char of a standard wildfire all too well. Wingnuts often liked to port in during dry seasons and start them as a form of soft terrorism. But whatever was burning down there was feasting on more than just trees and shrubs.

One of the technicians cried out, "THE PORTSYS LAB IS BURNING!" and the displaced crowd rumbled. PINE agents materialized in the aisles.

"Ah, PINE agents! You're just in time, and looking appropriately formidable."

The PINE agents slowly advanced.

"I thought you might do that. Before you get un-gentlemanly with me, let me show you fine officers one thing."

He tapped his phone again, but nothing happened.

Oh shit.

Now Bamert was breaking in that suit. Here came the sweat, mixing with his natural musk and infecting the Egyptian cotton with a Bamertness that would never wash out. Sweat gladdened Bamert. It was his closest ally. He never felt himself when he was fully dry.

He whispered into his lapel, "Burton."

"One second," Burton relayed back from Gould House.

"Seconds are at a premium, dear friend."

"Almost got them all pinned."

"There's no time for almost." Bamert addressed the crowd again. "Sorry for the momentary technical delay, everyone. Startups, am I right?"

He tapped his phone again. This time, every PINE agent surrounding the theater disappeared. The crowd gasped.

"Ah! There," said Bamert. "You know, I'm glad PortSys solved our little global warming problem, but I will say that such a feat will make the North Pole far less hospitable to those fine agents than it might have been in prior years. Now, we have business to discuss, don't we? You see, PortSys may have the recipe for teleportation, but only *I* have the spice. I have transformed the ingredients, and I'm ready to serve you, the entrepreneurial community. Who wants some spice?"

The venture capitalists in attendance shouted offers at Bamert: first $20 million, then $50 million, then $300 million. It was an auction without end.

"Oh, I see you were positively famished for my business. Well, that is sweeter than clover honey to me. But as you can see, PortSys doesn't care to have their monopoly disturbed, so I must be going. You have the URL: pegasys.com. I'll have all of you naked folks home just as swiftly as I can be troubled to do so. Now, before I bid you good day, I'd just like to say CLEMSON FOOTBALL RULES."

And then Bamert was gone, along with all of the port runaways sitting in the second cordoned-off section of the theater. The surrounding hillside grew thick with black smoke as PortSys's main testing lab turned to ash.

SINGAPORE/MANHATTAN

At 3am Singapore time, the reception desk of Tower One at the Marina Bay Sands Hotel received a frantic call from an elderly American woman staying in one of the Premier suites on the top floor.

"Someone was in my room!" she screamed at the clerk.

"Ma'am, I assure you that our system of smartwalls is the finest in the world," the clerk assured her. "No one can get past it."

"I heard the clap!"

"Let me send security up to sweep the room for you, and I apologize for the disturbance."

As soon as the clerk hung up, he got another frantic call from upstairs. Then another. And another. Now complaints were coming down to the reception desks in Towers Two and Three as well. The late night revelers and port tourists staggering through the mammoth, trapezoidal lobbies were blissfully unaware of the crisis rippling through the hotel until guests ported down to the desks in their bathrobes, screaming at any staffers they could hunt down. The clerks, collectively desperate to keep the situation quiet, politely refused to issue a widespread alert. They insisted that everything was fine.

Anna Huff had ported into two dozen other rooms before arriving inside the Chairman Suite on the top floor. She felt terrible about breaking in on all those other guests. One guy was drunk and naked and coming out of the shower when Anna ported in. He let out a noise that she had never heard a grown man make. Like a rooster being choked. The rest of the guests she barged in on were asleep, but not for long after she rudely clapped out.

She stood in the center of this suite's main living room, the sexy glow of the city skyline outside providing the room's only light. The plate glass windows had snuffed out the noise coming from the fully pedestrianized, and always bustling, city streets below. In the flashing neon, Anna could make out a baby grand piano and hard-edged, modernist furniture. A vase of perfectly cut and arranged orchids changed colors with the shifting lights outside, from deep purple to rose to clementine. She moved toward the bedroom with a lightness, as if approaching the end of a diving board. She was fluid, moving in lockstep with the air circulating through the room.

There was a man in the bedroom, clad in khakis in a black t-shirt, staring at the PortSys lab burning on television and screaming into a wireless headset nestled in his greasy hair. He was sitting at the edge of the bed, facing away from Anna.

"WELL, WHERE IS HE? WHAT DO YOU MEAN, YOU CAN'T FIND HIM? He burned down my lab! Why do I even have you on contract if you can't find him? This is all my bitch/slut/whore of a sister's doing. I'll fucking kill her *right now*."

Jason Kirsch hung up and opened PortMaps. But then he felt a presence. Someone was lingering in the room like a faint scent. He turned around and saw nothing. Anna Huff pressed hard against the living room wall, hoping to melt into it. Oh, how awful it was to be in the same room as Jason Kirsch. She remembered the night he blew into Room 24, seeing him loom large over her bed, consuming the room and thickening its air like a noxious cloud. She could feel that cloud billowing again, choking everything in acid vapor.

Jason shook off the odd vibe and clapped out. Anna made a video call to Burton.

"He was in the Chairman's Suite. You got him?"

"I got him," said Burton. "Don't port yourself. I can send you using thermal recognition."

She hit MUTE on the phone, clipped the phone to her pants without hanging up, and then stepped forward and felt the shiver.

Now she was in the darkened pantry of a lavish apartment, surrounded by luxurious non-perishables: bags of dried pasta from Italy, jars of oil-slicked Marcona almonds, canned Portuguese sardines, German butter cookies, vacuum-sealed packages of mullet roe. Jason Kirsch was in the next room over. His voice was pure spittle.

"What did you *do*, Lara?" he said.

"Stay away from me." It was the first time Anna had heard Lara's voice in months and it charged through her like an espresso shot. She gripped her gun tightly.

"I'm asking you a question, you little sack of shit. No more delays out of you. Mother isn't pleased with you and neither am I."

"You're both sick."

"She was right about you, Lara. She was right about how substandard you are. You're nothing more than an average child."

"Average children are gonna save this world," she spat back at him.

"I already saved it. You're only in the way of me saving it further. You should kill yourself."

"Stop it. It's never worked and it never will, you bastard."

"You should kill yourself now because you're not gonna like the way *I* kill you. Do you understand? I was *born* to hate you. Now tell me where the fuck those notes are."

"Go to hell."

Jason lunged at Lara. She let out a half-scream before he covered her mouth with an iron hand. Over a year ago, Jason Kirsch was one room over from Anna Huff, and Anna had done nothing about it. She had slept as soundly as any child that night, only stirring when it was far too late.

But not on this night. Tonight, Anna Huff was wide awake. She slipped out of the pantry and into the Kirsch family living room. They'd only see her shadow first.

Lara was handcuffed to the wrought iron frame of a daybed. Bruises and welts all over her arms and legs. No more bangle bracelets. She was dressed in a white camisole and red skirt, and looked like she hadn't been allowed to change clothing in weeks. She looked thinner too, a mere phantom of the Lara that had exercised lasting dominion over Anna's mind. She looked like she had been chained to that daybed for days on end, abused and malnourished. Her normally razor-sharp bob had been reduced to tangles, like it had been brushed with an egg beater. Jason had carved the Conquistadors logo into her upper arm—opposite her adorable Point B tattoo—with his butcher knife. The symbol bubbled up from her arm in the form of a crude scar, looking like a small animal had burrowed under her skin and made a tunnel in that shape.

Jason gripped Lara's jet black hair with his free hand—apparently, he had been doing this a lot over the past few weeks—and pressed firmly against her mouth with the other.

Anna spotted an upright piano along the south wall of the room. Sitting on top of the piano were dozens of framed photographs, mostly of Emilia and Jason Kirsch posing with industry titans, celebrities, and heads of state. Anna spotted a lone photo of Lara cuddling with a tiny bulldog. There was no trace of that bulldog anywhere in this apartment. She snuck over to the piano and bashed out the opening notes of Beethoven's Fifth as loudly as she could.

BUM-BUM-BUM BUMMMMMMMMM.

Lara's eyes went wide at the sight of her Roomie. Jason Kirsch turned around and stared fiercely at Anna, an eyepatch adorning his face. Anna aimed her gun at the patch.

"Get your hands off of her," she told Jason.

"You," he said. "Still alive, huh?"

"I am. Hello, Jason. How's the eye?"

"I have one good eye and that's all I need to finish you off."

"ARRGGHH ye sure?"

"Fucking *bitch.*"

Jason Kirsch took out his PortPhone and disappeared again. Anna stared at Lara. The noxious cloud receded from the room and Anna felt nothing but hot, spiky light. Lara's lip gloss was smeared and her cheeks were blood red. She was too stunned to move. Too stunned at her brother's vicious assault. Too stunned at the sight of Anna Huff alive and well (and armed!). Too stunned at everything. Finally, she spoke.

"You're alive!"

"Fuck yeah, I am," said Anna. "How do I uncuff you?"

"The key is over there on the buffet."

Anna grabbed the key and freed Lara from the daybed. There were welts on Lara's wrists where bracelets of a different sort had dug in, grinding her skin down nearly to the arteries.

"You got a haircut," Lara told her.

"It was for an assignment," Anna said. "I had to burn your mom's lab to the ground."

"So that *was* you."

"*They can try to tell us what to do, but that doesn't mean we have to listen.* You said so yourself."

"Well, your hair looks great."

"Thanks. Are you okay?"

"I've been better."

"I wanna take you with me but I don't think you're in any shape to tag along right now. I need you to rest."

"Okay. But where are you going?" Lara asked.

Burton chirped at Anna over speakerphone. "He's back in Singapore."

Anna looked at Lara. They were alone again: all her hyperactive imagination had ever wanted. The last thing she wanted to do was leave, and yet…

"I have to go get him."

At that, Lara's face turned dark and she flashed a wicked grin.

"Then go get him," she told Anna. Her voice was lower when she said it, even more seductive. Like talking to a crush on the phone. That voice made it harder for Anna to leave.

"I'll be back," she told Lara.

"I know you will."

Anna stepped forward and Burton ported her back to the suite in Singapore. Alarm bells were going off throughout the hotel: loud PINGS that would make a dog's head explode. Epileptic emergency strobe lights inside battled with the flashing neon outside.

Anna wasn't as sly about her entrance this time. Jason Kirsch saw her and made himself huge as a bear.

"How did you find me?" he asked.

"You should be a lot more careful about what you post on WorldGram," she lied. "You give yourself away so easily when you post pictures of yourself at conferences and what not."

"What do you want?"

"You're gonna tell me why you killed my sister."

"Maybe you should confess to murdering one of our PINE agents in cold blood first, sweetheart. He was so, so young."

"I never killed anyone," said Anna. "You made that up, just like you made up that story about me being a neo-Nazi."

"Don't you understand who we are, Miss Whatsyourface?" Jason asked.

"It's Anna. I took your eye, hotshot. You know my name. Get it right."

"Okay then, *Anna*. We make the truths here. Not you. If we say you're a murderer, then you're a murderer. And if we say you're a neo-Nazi, then you're a neo-Nazi."

"When the world finds out you killed my sister, people won't be so eager to buy all of your bullshit lies."

"Sure they will," Jason insisted.

"They won't. I have proof that you were in our house that night."

"Ooooh, Lara give you that, too? I can make proof that says otherwise. It would take *nothing*. I gave the world porting. I gave it elevated civilization. I made this world and I can break it. I can break *you*. What have you ever given the world? What good is there in believing the word of a preppy psycho over us? Your loser of a sister killed herself. That's all there is. She did it because she was selfish and worthless, just like you. You weren't even awake to save her. You're a failure." Jason didn't have a knife on him, but it was clear that he believed his lethal silver tongue was all he needed to dispatch Anna.

"Why do you do this to people? Why do you troll them to death?"

"It's my greatest experiment, but explaining it to a girl as common as you would be a waste of time," Jason told her. Then he made sarcastic puppy eyes, put his hands up in mock innocence, and said in a singsong voice, "I wasn't even *in* your sister's room that night, little angel. I can proooove it."

"You were there. And now I'm here."

"So? Who the hell do you think *you* are?"

"I am war."

Anna brought the butt of her gun down on the bridge of Jason's nose, blood gushing out of his nose so quickly that it audibly babbled. This pleased her greatly. She grabbed Jason's PortPhone and threw it to the ground, digging her heel into the gorilla glass until it cracked and the phone's guts spilled out.

He rolled his eyes. "You know I can get another one of those, yes?"

"Why did you kill my sister?" she asked him.

"If anyone killed her, it was *you*. Glomming onto her like a needy child and making her life miserable."

"You know nothing about Sarah."

"I know she was a whore."

"Fuck you."

"Jesus, you girls and your weak feelings. Your good intentions lie to you. You wanna know why I made your sister die? Because I could. I am the strong and people like your sister are the weak. *You're* weak, too. I can see it in your eyes, little piggy. It's why your daddy left you."

"You know nothing about my father."

"Oh, but I do know about Arthur Huff. Like I know that he died. Did *you* know that? Shot to death by a hooker in Trieste just a couple months ago. Isn't that fantastic? It's fun to know things about you, Anna. Don't you think? I know your father was glad to spend his final years without you or your pathetic loser of a sister dragging him down."

He's lying. If dad had died, you would have known. "Fuck you."

"You didn't know, did you? Does that news bother you? Did you know he was a member of the Conquistadors? I believe K15 was his handle."

HE'S LYING.

Arthur Huff was an unremarkable man. Whatever money he made as a restaurant accountant he recklessly spent on anything except his own family: booze, hookers, hands of blackjack at the MGM Grand, everything. At home, he did nothing except fight with Sandy and then stare at either his phone or the wall. Her whole life, Anna got the impression that her dad would rather be anywhere else than with her. He constantly reminded all the Huff women that he was a "great man," though they never saw any evidence of it.

Every time Mr. Huff left the house in a snit, she and her sister prayed it was for good. They begged Sandy to leave him. But Sandy, ever the misguided saint, assured them both that their father had a good side. That he meant well. He was gone for good before Sarah or Anna ever saw proof of those claims. Once Arthur left the house permanently, Anna couldn't allow herself to feel relieved because she remained terrified that he would pop back into their lives one day. Sometimes she felt guilty even though she knew she shouldn't. Arthur Huff swore to his daughters that if he ever deserted them, it would be all their fault. Anna hated believing him. Also, he took the goddamn bulldog with him. It was the surest sign he wouldn't be coming back, but also the worst one.

"You're lying again," she told Jason. "*You're* K15."

"I'm a trillionaire. The most powerful man in the world. Why would I spend *any* time hanging out online?"

"Because your mommy can't boss you around there."

"You're really too stupid to believe that your father was one of us, huh? I'm shocked you can even make it through the day, you're such a delicate little flower. How do you think I found your sister, hmm? Your father said she'd be perfect for me. Do you know he sent me a DM after I made her die? Know what it said? It said, 'ell-oh-ell.' *Classic.*"

Jason laughed out loud. It was such an awful thing to live in a world where laughter was a telltale sign of cruelty. Anna became fire.

"Jason," she said, "I'm gonna kill you, and I'm gonna be rude about it."

"Did Lara put you up to all this?" he asked her. "I bet you think Lara loooooooves you."

"Shut up."

"Everyone thinks Lara loves them. It's her talent. I admire it. Did she promise you that you'd both run away together if you just got rid of her nasty mom and brother? She promise you Lily Beach? Was that what she sold you when she gave you trade secrets?"

"She didn't sell me anything. I'm here on my own."

"Then you're an even bigger sucker than the puds she usually ropes in. Do you see her here now, coming to your aid? No. She sent you to do all her dirty work for her, so she could steal this company out from under my mother and me without ever lifting a finger. You think you're so special because you discovered love. The only thing love is useful for is betrayal."

"Maybe in your hands."

"What do you think happens after this, you dumb hog? You destroy this family and this company, and then you and my sister live happily ever after? You think you're gonna change the world? You want the world and you want my sister, but you're not gonna get either one."

"I'm gonna get both," Anna told him. "But first I get to watch you die with a whimper."

"You got hoodwinked."

"Shut up."

He took a deep breath and grew even bigger. He was a skyscraper. His breath rendered the surrounding air unstable at a molecular level. Anna had a gun in her hand and yet she felt as if she were playing defense. All that confidence she had earned over the year was being steadily pulled from her soul.

"You're being used," he told her. "When this is all over, it'll come crashing down on you. You'll never see Lara again. She won't give a shit about you, because she never did to begin with. No one cares about you and no one ever has. You'll be a fugitive and a pariah, and the world will hate you, as it should."

"Shut up," Anna said. Her wit wasn't fast enough to keep up. She was the hottest, messiest mess right now.

"Not so funny anymore, huh? Take that gun and kill yourself," he said. "Oh wait, I'm sorry. Let me rephrase that. Take that gun and *die by suicide*, as you so daintily put it."

"Lara never listened to you and neither will I."

"Do it. You won't remember a thing about any of this. You won't be here. You'll have ported somewhere new and wonderful and permanent. *We are such stuff as dreams are made on, and our little life is rounded with a sleep.*"

414

Her hands were shaking. Hacked. Anna's mind was toying with her as well, right when she thought she had it well-domesticated. Killing this man should have taken nothing at all. Oh, but Jason Kirsch had a lethal knack for disrupting all that certainty. *What would it really be like to destroy PortSys and make the world more chaotic than it already is? Will the rest of the world resent you for it forever? Behold Anna Huff: Queen of the Trolls, a child too stupid to know how childish she was being. An unremarkable girl undone by love, like so many other unremarkable girls and boys. Being dead right now would be a relief, wouldn't it? No wonder your daddy FUCKING STOP IT RIGHT NOW BRAIN.*

She thought about that night she and Sandy opened Sarah's bedroom door and found her, slumped against her own bed, a gaping hole in her throat. Sarah left no note, nor any clues as to who had been tormenting her. Anna saw the body of her sister and it didn't feel like it was her sister at all. Sarah was gone already, leaving only a piece of meat behind. That would be Anna's fate too. One day she would die, and there'd only be a limp mess to remember her by. She should have been dead already.

She could feel her wrist turning the gun on herself. Or was that just her mind fucking with her? This was Jason Kirsch's uncanny power. He could hijack your brain waves and make his inner voice your own. *He's lying about Dad, or is he? After all, why you do think* you *like being a dick to people? Where do you think that comes from, Anna?*

"You really are good at this," she admitted.

"Thank you," he told her. "If I were feeling merciful I'd tell you to take 10 Benadryl and a bottle of Tylenol to make it painless."

"But you never feel merciful."

"Never." In fact, Jason told her, he kept what he called a "living graveyard" for certain victims. It was a five-acre plot of arable land he owned outside of Moroni, Comoros. The plot was surrounded by a brick wall twenty feet high and a smartwall that was so advanced as to be impenetrable. Within these walls, he had workers dig rows of graves and then had them lower a padlocked coffin—each one outfitted with an internal camera and loudspeaker—into every hole.

415

When Jason felt the urge, he would port victims, including the occasional child, into a coffin. His workers would fill the hole, and then he would open up his phone to watch them asphyxiate. Using the loudspeaker, he sometimes cheered them on, although not in terribly good faith, as they desperately attempted to claw their way out. *Just scratch a little bit harder. You'll get out. Your coffin isn't even underground! Aw man, you look like you're losing steam. Don't give up!*

"I had one plot marked out just for you," Jason told Anna. "But Mother thought it would be more fun to put you through the paces. See if you could escape from our little maze. So I went along with her. And frankly, sometimes I prefer watching people die face-to-face. It's just not the same over a conference call. Watching your sister die, that was a good one. She knew how to die with flair."

"How many people have you killed?"

He laughed. "I don't count, little piggy. It doesn't matter. You don't matter."

"But why do you do this?"

Jason sensed his big moment and went into speech mode. "If you could feel the power I've felt, you wouldn't ask such a naïve and stupid question. You will never know the thrill of exercising total dominion over another human. You see, *I* get to decide who should live and who should excuse themselves from this earth. My mother and I designed an entirely new stage of humanity. All of the world's real estate is now *our* estate. And the reason this is so is because we were bold enough to not pretend to care about others."

"You didn't design anything. You stole the recipe from Dr. Stokes."

"Actually, *you* stole it from *me*. And for what? Whiny bitches like you like to think you can change people with your limp compassion. With *empathy*. The bold ones are the ones who know empathy is a grand lie. You cry and gnash your teeth and go crazy when all the BAD things happen, but really you're as selfish as anyone else. That's why your cunt of a big sister is dead. That's why it was so much fun to watch her die, to see that look in her eye when she realized she wasn't tough enough to hack it. They always look so surprised to die. I see that surprise in your face right now."

He took a step toward Anna. She moved back. He took another step, chewing up more available space for her to backtrack.

"Do it," he commanded.

Remember what Lara said. Staying alive and happy is the best way you can make him miserable.

"No."

"DO IT!!!!"

Jason charged at Anna. She shut her eyes and fired at him, missing wildly and shattering the porcelain lamp on the nightstand. He tackled her and grabbed her waist, digging his long fingernails into her already tender skin. Then he grabbed her arm and smashed it against the hard walnut bench at the end of the hotel room bed. The gun fell to the floor and Jason straddled her. She struggled to be free but it was no use. He casually swiped the gun off the floor and tucked it into his waistband.

There was a knock on the door to the suite. "You okay, sir?" a burly voice asked from outside. "They're evacuating the hotel."

"I'm fine!" Jason Kirsch shouted. He loomed over Anna, a heavy fog. He placed a thick hand to her throat. His hand was so strong, she was aghast; she never realized that she could feel that much pressure bearing down on her larynx.

"I'm gonna kill you," he told her, smiling. "Then I'm going to find Lara and I'm going cut off her happy little head. It'll look so perfect mounted on my wall."

Anna tugged at Jason's sleeve, frantically trying to tell him one last thing before he sent her into the void. He could sense she was desperate, so he let up for a second. This was the fun part for him.

"You were saying?" he asked her.

Her wit didn't fail her this time. "Look up."

Jason Kirsch raised his head just in time to see the silver gleam of an aluminum baseball bat come speeding toward his face. He slumped to the ground: his jaw shattered, his teeth pulverized. Looming in the doorway was a girl with a towering frizz of curly black hair alongside a mountain of a boy.

Asmi held the bat up. "I've never swung one of these before," she told Anna. "I'm mad for it. Hold him up so I can do it again."

"My dear, you are a natural," Bamert told her.

They helped Anna up as she gasped for air. Jason had choked her so hard, it felt like the sides of her windpipe had been welded together. Now he was curled up on the floor, clutching at his face, the carpet barely muffling his screams. Bamert grabbed the gun and pointed it at Jason's soggy lump to hold him in check.

Anna grabbed her phone. She was still on the line with Burton. "Did you get all that on video?" she squeaked.

"Yeah, although you were awfully herky-jerky with the camera."

"Burton, not now."

"I can edit the footage. It'll be on WorldGram within an hour."

"My goodness," said Bamert. "Did you hear that, Jason Kirsch? Your confession to manslaughter will be on the Internet within an hour! We get to make the truths this time! The ability to continually shoot video while porting really *is* a gamechanger. I'll have to make sure Pegasys incorporates that little technological miracle. Oh, and I'll definitely have one of my people visit Comoros with a news crew to dig up everyone you buried alive."

Kirsch was less than pleased. "You fucking pigs!"

"We have to leave, darling," Asmi said to Anna.

"There's something I have to finish." Anna told them. "As long as Jason lives, he can lie."

"But you *can't*."

Anna looked at Bamert. "Give me the gun."

"I dare say I shouldn't," Bamert told her.

"Give me the gun, and then both of you leave."

"Anna," he said soberly, "this isn't you."

"It's about to be. Leave."

Bamert twirled the gun in his hand and handed it to Anna, butt first.

"Here you go," said Bamert. "But when we leave, think very hard about whether or not you want to be this sort of person. All right?"

Bamert and Asmi ported out together in a single clap. Whoever was stationed outside Jason Kirsch's room wasn't bothered by the noise. Jason Kirsch had always told members of his inner circle, security included, that they were to do nothing without him saying so.

Anna kicked him in his broken face, and then aimed the gun at him. "How do I look to you now, Jason Kirsch? You think I can hack it? You think I can exert *total dominion* over your sorry ass?"

"No."

"You don't look so good yourself, Jason. I don't think you'd pass my naked test. You know what's nice about this room is that I already know I won't come back. I won't even have to come back to Singapore. There is nothing about this place or this moment that will ever haunt me. I'll just port out of here and then forget all about it, and about you, because *you* are the weak."

"And Lara? What will you tell her, little piggy?"

Anna took out her phone and queued up the pin for Manhattan. She cocked the gun. "I can't wait to tell Lara what happened to you."

She was about to open fire when two dozen PINE agents ported into the room, rifles pointed directly at her skull. PINE head Robb Caraway arrived with them, eager to exact vengeance on behalf of an officer of his that got run over in Maine, and on behalf of another officer that Anna had "murdered" in a fit of passion.

"Drop it!" one agent shouted at Anna.

You got too greedy, girl.

She dropped the gun.

"Drop your phone too," the team leader commanded her.

She took the phone out of the clip and dropped it. A port doctor, one far better than Dr. Fisher, tended to the wounded Jason Kirsch. Emilia Kirsch ported into the room, along with a rigid and angry Dean Vick dragging Lara Kirsch with him. The suite became fully swollen with menace.

"Ah, good," Emilia Kirsch said to the PINE agents. They were entirely under her control, less human beings than vestigial tentacles that Emilia could use to grab what she needed. She turned her x-ray eyes on her own daughter. "You found Anna Huff. I believe this is

419

the young lady who disguised herself as a PortSys employee and burned down my lab, is that correct? Thank you, Lara dear. Thank you so much for helping us find this terrorist."

Anna looked at Lara, whose face was still ragged from trauma. Gave her the feline stare. "You told them?"

"I didn't say a word, I swear." Lara told her, frightened at Anna's burgeoning fury. "Emilia is lying to you. Jason pinged them all. They're gonna kill us both."

"You know," said Emilia, "This might be the very first time you've made an actual impression on me, Lara. You knew this girl had feelings for you, and you used her to lash out at me and your poor, poor brother. I like that. You might have a future in this company after all."

"I hate you, Mom," Lara said quietly.

"Good," said Emilia. "It's good to hate. Hate is the primary fuel of ambition. It's just so sad that you're still pretending to care about this nothing girl, when you don't." She turned to Anna. "I'm sorry, but she doesn't care about you. She won't die for you. I barely had to lay a finger on her to get you to give her up."

"She's lying!" Lara screamed. As punishment, Vick put her ragged arm in a chicken wing, nearly dislocating her shoulder.

Anna looked into Lara's green eyes, dying to see the truth. Everything would have been just fine if Anna Huff had just kept all her love and all her anger to herself. If she had just been a quiet, unintrusive roommate to Lara Kirsch; if she had never jumped off that bridge with her; if they had never made plans for Lily Beach and elsewhere; if she had never told her about Sarah; if she had never resolved to chase Lara once she was gone; if she had tended to her studies and her extracurriculars and not tried to right every wrong and avenge every wronged soul, she could have been all right. She could have survived in this world. She had this love inside her and it felt so real and so good and she wasn't ready—at all—to reckon with the idea that everyone else found that love to be so disposable. She had doomed herself and she was the only one who couldn't see it coming a mile away.

"What happens now?" Anna asked Emilia.

"What happens now is that Lara watches you die. I'm afraid that four months locked up in our New York penthouse wasn't quite enough to give her the edge she needs to compete in this world. So she'll watch us kill you, and then she'll watch as we track down your friends and kill them, too. Your friend's silly Pegasys caper will be stillborn. Dead on delivery. There's no hope for you, Anna Huff."

Emilia motioned to a PINE agent. The agent offered Anna a handgun.

"Take that gun," ordered Emilia, "and shoot yourself. Right now. Do it or we find your mother and kill her in front of you."

"When you get to hell," Jason told her, "Say hi to your little bulldog for me. It's dead now."

Anna had a gun in her hand, but no matter where she fired it, she would end up dead. Her brain was sputtering; who knew if it remembered how to pull a trigger anyway. Lara was screaming at the agents, all hot wails and smudged blue eyeshadow. Anna put the gun to her own chin, wondering what it would make Lara's eyes do. Lara stopped screaming and stared at Anna. It was just them now. No Emilia. No Jason. No Vick. No PINE. Just Anna and Lara, locked in each other's gravitational pull. No place for the truth to hide.

"Lara," Anna said.

"Yes?"

And then Anna Huff noticed something out of the corner of her eye. It was her phone, on the ground. Still on. She had never ended the video call with Burton. He was still on the line, back in Gould House, frantically mouthing the words STEP FORWARD to her. Charles Vick had loosened his grip on Lara, but was still right behind her, ready to strong-arm her at a moment's notice like the brainless stooge he was.

It was time to find out if Lara Kirsch was worth loving so much.

"Lara," said Anna, "This is me, risking it all, asking you to risk it all."

"What?" asked Lara.

"I'm gonna need you to step forward."

"I don't understand."

"Oh for god's sake," shouted Emilia, "*Shoot them both!*"

421

"LARA STEP FORWARD RIGHT NOW!!!!!" Anna screamed.

They stepped forward in tandem and disappeared, leaping together like two girls jumping off a stone bridge and into a midnight river. One second later, a hundred Guardians of Ararat were force-ported, by Burton, into the suite. They were surprised by their new surroundings. None of them had stepped out off of Armenian soil in their respective lifetimes. But they were all conveniently armed with now-standard carbon fiber rifles that each weighed under three kilograms. And they were quite pleased, at long last, to encounter Emilia and Jason Kirsch in person.

SEWELL HALL

Lara and Anna reappeared in the tiny inner bedroom of Room 24. It was, against all odds, unoccupied by a new student. A girl named Aubrey Jackson took Anna's place at school for second semester (Anna had been put up in absentia and expelled in a tidy five minutes), but got booted in mid-March for snorting cocaine off a classroom table. It was too deep into the school year to replace Aubrey with a fifth occupant. This room, other Sewell girls whispered, was now cursed. Anna and Lara sat on the bare mattress, staring at the yellowed walls while Asmi and Bamert covered them with blankets and handed them fresh water to drink.

"Do either of you need a doctor?" he asked the two of them.

"No," they said in unison.

"Hey," Lara said, looking around, "This is my room."

"Actually," said Bamert, "This is now Anna's room."

"Yeah I took it over so I could whip up some meth, remember?" Anna joked.

"It's no one's room," said Asmi.

"Maybe it oughtta be *my* room," said Bamert, cocking an eyebrow toward Asmi. "I could use new sleeping quarters." Asmi blushed.

"Anything is better than being stuck in that apartment," Lara told them. She suddenly freaked out. "Emilia and Jason are still at the hotel! They're gonna find us!"

"I don't believe that to be the case," said Bamert.

"What do you mean?" asked Lara. "They can get past the wall here. How'd *I* get past the wall? How did I port here with no phone? How did *Anna* port here with no phone? Who are you two people? You, in the suit: aren't you Edgar Bamert's kid? The Pegasys guy? Is this who you gave the recipe to, Anna? You really *are* wild."

"We can address all your inquiries in due course," said Bamert, "But allow me to make a phone call first, won't you?"

He called Burton and the three girls listened raptly as he rattled off a series of loud, staccato replies: "Burton, it's me… They're back here in Sewell… They did?… Are you sure?… And the apartment they were in? Still clear?… Good. Well, 'good' is relative here so

I'll just say *better*. What about the Guardians? Did you port them back home?… Send me the video. You've done exemplary work here. Go Tigers."

He ended the call and the girls stared at him. Just to be Bamert, he let the silence hang around a bit. He even checked his watch for a flourish. Anna grew testy.

"What'd he say?" she asked him.

"Ah, right! You're both safe."

"And Emilia?" Lara asked. "Jason? That asshole Dean Vick? Where are they?" No one else in the room could tell if she was full of hope or dread.

Bamert was trapped in an awkward spot now. He had never delivered news like this to anyone. He didn't have to tell Edgar that his house burned down because the old man's surveillance apps did that job for him. But he wasn't gonna be able to wriggle out of similar duties now. For the first time in weeks, he felt the pull of drinking and pictured, in his humid mind, a splash of whiskey inside a crystal tumbler. No two cocktails ever looked the same. They were gorgeous that way. Bamert scratched his mop of hair and let out a grandstanding sigh before mustering up the bravery to tell them all.

"They're not here anymore," he told Lara. "Burton saw everything happen in the suite after he ported you out."

"What do you mean?" Lara asked. "Are they dead?"

"Yes," Bamert told them.

"How?" she asked.

"What's important is that both of you are safe now," Bamert said, "and that they can't hurt you anymore."

"You don't understand," said Lara. "That was my family."

"We're so sorry, love," Asmi told her.

"No no no, not that. What's your name again?" Lara asked Bamert.

"J. Paul Bamert, scourge to all Yankees and, it's true, CEO of Pegasys Industries."

"Bamert! You were on the bridge that night! Bamert, you told me they can't hurt me anymore, but do you understand the hurt that my family can do?"

424

"I might," Bamert said.

"It doesn't go away. It doesn't stop hurting. Those two lived their lives to hurt people. Look at what they did to me."

Anna, Asmi and Bamert beheld the shattered, battered body of the girl they had saved. Lara Kirsch was just a remnant of a human being. This was trauma. This was the gauntlet Lara had to pass through before coming out the other side more of an adult than when she began. Whether that adult would be good or evil was still a mystery, even to Lara herself. She shook with fright at the notion.

"Promise me that they're gone," Lara told Bamert. "I need proof. I never wanna look over my shoulder again. You asked this Burton guy to send you a video, yeah?"

"I did."

"Play it for me."

"You really wanna see it? Are you sure?"

"Yes."

Bamert looked at Anna, who gave him a humble nod. He queued up video of the massacre in Singapore. "You want the sound on?" he asked Lara.

"My eyes are all I need for this."

Bamert handed the phone over. Lara watched the video. Everyone else in the room watched her face as it first went numb and then cracked open. Her body trembled, like a demon was being expelled from it. Then Lara Kirsch took in a mighty breath: her first taste of air as a free woman.

"They're finally gone."

"You're gonna be all right," Anna told her.

"You don't mean that," Lara said back.

"I don't."

"It's okay. You didn't have to."

"You didn't rat me out this time, huh?"

"Never. He chained me to that bed and held that knife over my head for months but I never broke. Every time I thought I might, I thought myself, 'What would Anna do?'"

"I don't know the answer to that," Anna laughed.

"I do. I saw it with my own eyes in that hotel room. I'm sorry for everything Jason and Emilia did to you. What *I* did to you."

She's apologizing. She loves you enough to need your approval. If she only knew how scared shitless you are, all the time.

They joined hands. Lara's skin remained as soft as cotton.

"You sure you don't need a doctor?" Asmi asked them.

"No doctor," said Lara. "But I do need clothes. And we do need money."

"I have that," said Bamert. "I had to kill off our dear friends the Bumlees, but I think we have a new kitty to pull from over at my burgeoning conglomerate."

"I think I'd rather use my Mommie Dearest's money instead, don't you think?"

"If it pleases you," Bamert said. "But you have no wallet on you, dear."

"In my bedroom in the New York apartment, you'll find my phone, clean clothes, plus a porting belt with money and my ID it in. Jason's is in his bedroom. You can loot that for extra cash. Keep your head down when you go. There are cameras all over the place."

"Oh we know that," said Bamert. "We may have tinkered with that system a hair. Are you sure you want me to go back?"

Lara snorted up her tears and stiffened her spine. There was plenty of ambition still in her. She wasn't afraid of using that ambition, especially not now. You can disown your blood but you can't fake it. "Go. When you get back, I'll send you the PDF of Emilia's propaganda guidelines, and you can make that public, too."

Bamert looked up the apartment on his PortPhone.

"Bamert, wait," said Anna.

"What?"

Ask him. Ask him if Arthur is dead. Ask if Arthur was K15. He and Burton heard what Jason told you.

"Be careful," she said instead. "Be safe."

Bamert winked at the girls and then popped out, the clap flowing out the window, over Sewell Beach and across the quad. None of the girls in the room gave a damn.

"The notes," Lara said. "Where are the notes?"

426

"Can you move at all, dearie?" Asmi asked her.

"I can. Who are you?"

"Oh! Oh, fucking Christ. I'm Asmi. I'm the new roommate, the one that Anna doesn't"—she caught herself—"uh, have to rescue from time to time, yes! That's the difference! Anyway, let's visit the toilet."

"What?"

Anna sprung up and, together with Asmi, helped a disheveled Lara to her feet. They staggered up to the Sewell bathroom, which was blessedly unoccupied. Anna kicked open the stall door and grabbed the Shit Memoirs off the floor. There, taped to the back of the book, was the second half of the recipe for teleportation. Someone had scrawled THE FUCK IS THIS? over the formula with a Sharpie.

"PINE can be lazy in spots," Anna told Lara. "We figured they'd never look in here, and they didn't."

"But the notes are ruined," Lara said.

"Oh, Burton copied them. They're on a hard drive."

"So these are worthless now?"

"Worthless? Those notes saved you," Anna insisted. "They saved me. They saved *everything*. And you gave them to me, even though you knew you'd suffer for it."

"I guess."

"Maybe you're stronger than you realize."

Lara's face crinkled into a smile. The two of them were dancing once more. Asmi stepped back because she could sense a moment forming.

Now get a laugh out of her.

But before Anna could get that laugh, Jubilee stormed into the bathroom to brush her teeth. When she saw the three other girls perusing through the Shit Memoirs, her eyes went black.

"What the FUCK are you girls doing here?" she demanded to know.

"I don't know," Lara said. "What the fuck are *you* doing here?" She and Anna giggled at Jubilee. *At* her. *So this is what it's like to troll people by being happy.*

427

"Yeah. Piss off, Jujyfruit," Asmi told her.

Jubilee was the odd girl out in that bathroom. Jubilee was not used to being the odd girl out. She screamed "Assholes!" at them and then stormed out without bothering to brush.

The three other girls laughed their way back to Room 24. Seconds later, a soft wind blew in and Bamert held up the goods.

"Jackpot!" he cried out. He handed Lara a wad of fresh clothes, along with the belt. She tore apart the Velcro and inside the belt were so many thousand-dollar bills that Anna audibly gasped. A good and healthy gasp. Lara squeezed Anna's hand tightly. During first semester, Anna had learned about atoms in Mr. Polycronis' chemistry class. She got an A in that class, but the things she learned nagged at her. She wondered if anyone ever truly touched anything, or if there was an insidious buffer of foreign hydrogen atoms or nitrogen atoms or even smaller particles—particles the size of nonexistence—preventing two bodies from ever coming into actual contact.

That thought didn't nag her at the moment. Their hands were *touching*, the way they touched before Lara and Anna leapt off that bridge the first night of school.

"Shit," Lara told Bamert. "My bracelets were on that dresser, too. I should have asked you to grab them." She wrapped her right hand around her left wrist to soothe the cuff welts.

"I can go back," he said. "It's fun breaking into places. This has all been *very* educational."

"Don't go back," Anna said. She took off the rose pink bracelet and offered it to Lara. "Take this," she told her.

"Anna, I can't. That's yours."

"You gave it to me," Anna insisted.

"It was always yours, Roomie. Always."

Anna slipped it back on and felt strong again.

"We have to disappear," Lara told Anna. "We can't port. We can't go near crowds or public spaces. We have to be gone for a while, do you understand?"

"Aren't you sick of being gone yet?" Anna asked back.

"All the time, but I'm not a fool."

428

"What about PortSys? I think you own it now."

"I don't think I'm legally old enough to run a trillion-dollar company. I'm seventeen. I get to be irresponsible. Let's get irresponsible. It'll take the lawyers a zillion years to figure out who gets what and who runs what anyway. In the meantime, we have to get away. Somewhere quiet and deserted. Someplace where no one would ever bother to port, so that we can go in and out without anyone laying eyes on us."

For once in Anna's life, she had the right idea, the right mood, and the right line ready all at the right time. "Oh, I know where to get away. *And* I know how."

Two minutes later, they knocked on Mrs. Ludwig's door. She opened it up, still clad in a pink terrycloth robe and snacking on a handful of peanuts. Two cats ran out into the lobby and then ran back in. Mr. Nolan was in the living room of the apartment, his wheelchair parked next to the rarely seen Mr. Ludwig, both men sipping tea and munching on fresh pretzels. When Mrs. Ludwig saw Lara and Anna, she went bug-eyed.

"What the shit?" she said. "You two don't go here anymore. One of you is dead, even!"

"Fooled you there," said Anna. "I'm not dead, and I'm not a Nazi."

"Well, I am relieved to hear this. These Nazis, they are very bad."

"I knew you'd be a quick learner, Anna Huff," said Nolan, beaming with pride. "I just knew it."

"Mrs. Ludwig," Anna asked, "Can we buy your Cobra?"

"It's not for sale," Mrs. Ludwig said, staring at the floor and shaking her head. "It's not for sale. It's not for sale... How much?"

THE OPEN ROAD

Lara Kirsch paid $20,000 in cash for the Cobra. After Mrs. Ludwig gave Lara and Anna the title and registration, they ported from Sewell Hall to the parking lot outside of school and watched from afar as U.S. armed forces—none of them PINE—stormed through Druskin Gate to seize all vital documents and administrators connected to Emilia and Jason Kirsch.

The two girls stood next to a trash bin and held the two PortPhones Bamert had given them over it. No more porting for a while. They had both deleted their WorldGram accounts as well. They were about to be as free digitally as they were physically, no longer living a life that was all destinations and no journeys. The rest of the world couldn't have them anymore. The Internet couldn't, either.

"You ready?" Lara asked Anna.

"I'm ready."

Neither girl moved. They both broke down in laughter.

"We have to do this," Anna said.

"This reminds me of our first day here."

"We still gotta do it."

"I know, I know. You first."

"Let's do it together."

"Together, then. 1, 2, 3…"

Into the trash the phones went.

"Let's get out of here," Lara said.

They sauntered over to their new car. Anna was tempted to slide across its hood like she was an undercover cop rushing to chase down some bad guys, but she demurred. Mrs. Ludwig walked over to personally oversee preparations for their maiden voyage, offering Anna tips (nagging, really) on how to drive the Cobra, how to maintain it, and how to keep it running for years. She even helped snap the cloth top over the car, lingering well past the tolerance.

"Now you need to fill it with 93 octane gas," she chided both of them. "This is the highest quality of fuel, yeah?"

"Got it," said Anna.

"And watch out for these trucks. They do not see you there in the mirror. Sometimes they are asleep or taking God knows what pills. The self-driving ones, they are even *more* shit."

"Got it."

"And read the owner's manual in full before you set off. This is important."

"Got it." Anna had no such plans to.

"And take my driving gloves!" Mrs. Ludwig insisted, handing them over.

"Thanks."

Mrs. Ludwig unlatched the passenger door and helped a fragile Lara Kirsch into the low-slung seat, a gleaming chrome roll hoop towering behind it. Anna buckled Lara's seat harness, brushing her hands against Lara's waist and feeling her own cheeks get hot to the touch.

"Do you need iced tea?" Mrs. Ludwig asked Lara and Anna. "I get you some iced tea, maybe some cookies."

"No!" they said together.

"Do you want earplugs?"

"No!" *Wait, maybe you do?*

"Do you want my driving goggles?"

"No!"

"Oh, okay then. I'll tell everyone you said hello, yeah?" Lara and Anna were about to scream at Mrs. Ludwig when she broke down laughing. "It's a joke! I never saw you. *Auf wiedersehen,* Lara Kirsch! *Auf wiedersehen,* Anna Hoof!"

Mrs. Ludwig didn't abide by her own goodbye. She stayed on the decaying curb, still in her robe, watching intently. She might have even been crying.

"Do you need a driver's license to drive this thing?" Lara asked Anna.

"No one has a driver's license anymore. Why? You got one?"

"I have a fake ID that says I'm twenty-six, but I've never needed to use it."

"Oh. Well anyway, I don't need a license," Anna said, although now she was worried they'd get pulled over and the cops would check her passport card, currently tucked inside her shirt to prevent the wind from grabbing hold of it. She slid into the driver's seat, took off the Club, and playfully tugged on the black leather driving gloves. Her hands loved them. She felt like she could shoot fireballs out of her palms. They even had little peek-a-boo holes for her knuckles that made her hands look far more lethal than they actually were.

"Wait!" Anna cried. She leapt back out of the car.

"What are you doing?" asked Lara.

"What the shit?" said Ludwig.

Anna ran over to the trash bin, fished out the two discarded phones, and then tucked each one firmly under a front tire. Lara was cracking up as Anna slid back into position.

"You're really gonna drive over them?" Lara asked.

"I sure as hell will."

"Do you *know* how to drive?"

"Only one way to find out, *Roomie*."

She punched the ignition on the left-hand side of the wheel and the engine thundered to life. One turn of the key and the world became hard, grunting, hot noise. Anna was irritated that Mrs. Ludwig kept hanging around, observing them like zoo animals, but the noise quickly obliterated that angst. Now the only thing Anna could think of was the battalion of greased pistons under that glossy hood, churning at a sickening rate, the Cobra itching to take them away from Druskin as fast as possible. This car was 85% engine.

Anna smiled at a tired Lara, mashed down on the clutch, shifted to first gear, and then the car lurched two inches before stopping. Now it was parked on top of the two phones, crushing them under its wheels. Anna gave Lara a kidding shrug. The racket inside the car had already reduced them to a form of ad hoc sign language, and would do so for the rest of the drive. But the past few months had conditioned both girls well for extensive periods of boredom.

Anna shifted again, praying the car would get moving on this attempt. It did not. The Cobra lurched forward violently and then stopped, like it had crashed into something. The gears ground together and made a sickening noise, enough to make Mrs. Ludwig wince. Anna gave another kidding shrug to Lara, but she knew the cutesiness was wearing off. Mrs. Ludwig was still there, barely able to keep from shaking her head. The gearshift was sticky. Anna had to put real English into maneuvering it, which was a lot to ask given what she had just endured.

A few more false starts and the roadster finally succumbed to Anna's charms, rumbling down the street. She let out the clutch and eased the Cobra onto Route 101. It was like riding a buzzsaw. Lackadaisical trucks barreled past them at terrifying speeds. Anna rolled down her window for a second and the wind battered her and Lara from all sides, their seats humming with the Cobra's insides. They settled in and drove through a perfect April late afternoon, with the trees budding larger and larger leaves as they joined I-95 and progressed farther south. The cerulean blue sky overhead was lined with flat, fan-shaped clouds that shone like mother-of-pearl but somehow consistently avoided blocking out a welcoming, drowsy sun. A small flock of double-crested cormorants migrating north flew close overhead, perhaps headed for a peaceful river to call home for the spring.

Though she was now driving on 95 instead of lying half-dead on it, Anna couldn't drive through the American free zones with the furious abandon she enjoyed down in Cuba. She had to keep tabs on a manual transmission this time, and she had Lara in the bucket seat next to her. There were also the armed convoys rolling down the freeway to consider. Perhaps they would take note of such a conspicuous, downright sexy car passing them by. Also: horses.

Anna kept her left hand gripped tight on the wheel, stealing a glance at Lara's legs only when she knew Lara had her eyes shut. She was getting the hang of the stick shift now, working the clutch like a piano pedal and feeling the engine become an extension of her own body, one that made her stronger, faster, and meaner as she picked up the rhythm of shifting gears. The cold steel gearshift— God, she was so sick of cold things—gave her right hand something to do, which was good because all it really wanted to do was reach out and touch Lara: squeeze her leg, brush against her cheek, twirl her hair. *Gimme you.* Anna was filled with a pure want that blocked out all other needs and desires. She needed this car to distract her from all that want. Anna was finally alone with Lara Kirsch, but the Cobra made for a loud and abrasive third wheel.

She was far too aware of how she looked driving, as if she were being filmed while doing it. She was scared of all the trucks, of getting stopped by PINE, of Lara's judgment, of everything. It was too loud to talk or to listen to music or to do much of anything productive. All the girls could do was trade puzzled glances and point out zombified pickup trucks sitting on the shoulder as they coasted through long stretches of open nothingness.

Anna calmed herself by focusing on the chipped freeway paint and thinking only about *tonight*. Eventually they would stop somewhere and have this night together. Anna was leaden with fatigue, but still hardly able to contain herself at the thought. She was at just the right age to have the idea of *tonight* be loaded with magic. It was the hope—no, the *confidence*—that this particular tonight would be a personal landmark, that it would be indelible. Lara wanted them to get away together. Just them. There's magic in someone saying *let's get out of here* to you. They wanna get away from everyone else, with you, because only you matter. You. They want *you*. Anna ditched her willpower and dreamed about the night ahead on a loop with Lara sitting right next to her, possibly none the wiser. She dreamed faster than the Cobra could speed down an open straightaway. Tonight. Anna was going to get her tonight this night. Every night with Lara was an event, and this would be the biggest one of them all.

You've been thinking three steps ahead since you and Lara first met. You just helped kill her family. Maybe she was high as balls when she kissed you. "Lara Kush," remember? Maybe stop going so fast?

Fuck off, brain.

She looked down at the speedometer. They were going 93. She bumped it up to 110. Life had just made them shit white. No point in slowing down now.

A convoy of classic cars staging a gumball rally whizzed by them at even greater speeds, honking hello to the Cobra. Anna did not honk hello back.

Somewhere in Massachusetts, they stopped for gas and food at a roadside Fermona Mart, one of a smattering of highway rest stops that hadn't been shuttered. Anna, disguising herself in Mrs. Ludwig's driving goggles and a white driving scarf wrapped around her face—scarves were handy like that—flipped around her passport tag so that the ID was facing her stomach, then politely asked an attendant to pump the gas for her because she had no clue how to do it herself. She went into the mart and bought an old-school road atlas, cheap sunglasses, a bulldog face magnet to adorn the lunchbox-sized trunk of the Cobra, and a dozen neon bangle bracelets: bright red, violet, emerald green, sunflower yellow, rose pink, and every other color. Lara squealed with delight when she saw them. They were on her wrists in an instant, turning her weakened arms into a bright, happy spectrum. Lara could be Lara again.

"You feel better?" Anna asked her.

"I feel crazy," said Lara. "But in a good way. It's just been intense, Anna."

"Well, now we get to be bored out of our minds on this goddamn road."

"There's no one I'd rather be bored with. But I still need to know: how'd you get past the Harkness Wall?"

"Climbed it."

"*You* climbed it?"

"AHAHAHAHA, no. I let Bamert climb it. I'm not an idiot."

As they drove on, Lara spent her time in the passenger seat paging through the atlas, studying the curious circulatory system of the dilapidated American highway system. She unzipped a side curtain for air and the pages flapped and tore in the wind. Apart from staring at the mighty air scoop bulging out from the Cobra's hood, the atlas was all they had in the way of entertaining themselves. The daylight receded and Anna thought of all those nights back when she was a kid when her sister drove her to the movies, the two of them always pushing forward and never looking back.

435

She'd be so proud of you right now. Also she'd want you to get lucky.

She and Lara had been on the road for three hours, crossing Connecticut on I-84 to avoid driving through Manhattan, when Anna noticed Lara was sobbing in the passenger seat. She found an open spot along a debris-ridden shoulder and cut the engine. The booming trucks and surly horns passing by offered little relief from the noise pollution. Anna placed a gentle hand on Lara's shoulder, desperate to mask the thrill she got from it. She wanted to kiss Lara all over, and she wanted to spend the rest of her life protecting her from harm.

Love. Love is dominion, not power.

"Are you okay?" Anna asked Lara.

"I'm fine," Lara insisted.

"We can stop for the night."

"I don't wanna stop."

"Do you want to drive the car?"

"Well, I did pay for it. Technically it's *my* car."

"It is. Do you want to drive it?"

Lara shook her head and smiled warmly. She reached for Anna's hand on her shoulder and the world felt much more calm and quiet.

"I'm just messing with you, Roomie," said Lara. "This is *our* car."

"Oh."

"Keep driving me. Please."

So Anna did. After enduring an inexplicable traffic jam just outside Danbury, they crossed the lower wedge of New York state into Pennsylvania, where the trucks grew even more aggressive and reckless. The Cobra plowed through a sea of burger wrappers as they passed deserted housing developments and endless graveyards, where porters breezed in to visit the headstones and leave flowers for the departed before clapping out and rendering the dead forgotten once more.

She couldn't drive anymore. Her hands and her back and her psyche were spent. Her arm was a piece of wet string after all that hard shifting, and the Cobra's pedals were just far enough away from her feet to make reaching them a strain. The sun was getting drowsy and they were closing in on 300 miles: far beyond the car's desired joyriding distance. Their getaway was now officially a tedious road trip, and they still had 350 miles plus to go until they reached Cleveland.

Anna pulled off of I-81 and into the parking lot of a Redford Suites—a real hotel, not a dumb ShareSpace—less than a mile from the shuttered, moldering Wyoming Valley Mall in Wilkes-Barre. She cut the engine for a final time and there, with the Cobra asleep, there was something approximating silence for Lara and Anna to bask in. They were free now to share their trusted souls with one another. The air turned still and the retiring sun burst through the windshield to coddle them in springtime. They had both been traumatized. Trauma is an infection. It stays around far beyond your expectations. But they were still in the strange grace period of shock, with trauma gaining on them but still lagging behind. It would pull even with them soon enough. But for now, there was the sun.

They stared at the hotel lobby. It was empty save for a single, bored clerk. There were no front doors they could enter. Take a photo of the place and it would have fit right in as part of Anna's old WorldGram gallery.

"Guess we'll have to knock," said Lara.

"Why did you step forward?" Anna asked her.

"What?"

"When we were surrounded by all those PINE assholes. Why did you listen to me?"

Lara took Anna's hand and held it tight. Real touching, once more.

"Because I knew," Lara said. "Isn't it obvious? I knew you were looking out for me, Roomie. You stayed real. And I owed you."

"No, you didn't. You stayed real, too."

"Jason tried to tell me you were worthless. He said he'd seen all of your online history and that you were just a weird troll who would post rants about lemonade over at GizPo."

Oh fuck.

"But I actually can't stand lemonade, so I thought those rants sounded funny as shit."

Oh, thank God. Wait, she hates lemonade? Really?

"You're not worthless, Anna. My family killed your sister and tried to kill you, too. You didn't deserve that."

"They tried to kill you, too."

"I've spent my whole life expecting they would." Lara held up a forearm and the bracelets slid down to reveal one of her chafed, infected wrists. One day the cuts would heal, but the cutaneous evidence of them would never disappear. "But they're gone now. I've been terrified of them for so long, I don't know what to do with myself now that I don't have to be."

Anna reached out and ran her fingers along the Conquistadors logo that Jason had cut into Lara's arm. It rose out of her skin, embossed there forever. Another insult of a scar. Anna thought that touching it might help make it disappear. Even if not, she still got to lay a hand on her girl. The logo was sickening but touching Lara was anything but. Lara giggled as Anna felt around it. There were more normal ways to flirt, but again, normal was a delusion in 2031.

"I know how to fix this goddamn scar," Lara said.

"How?" Anna asked.

"I have a plan."

"You and your plans."

"Haven't failed me yet!"

"I'm sorry about what they did to you," Anna said.

"Don't be sorry."

"I still am."

"Like I said: don't be. You saved me from them. I owe you."

"Whatever you owe me, you already gave to me."

"And I'm sorry I kissed you," Lara added.

She's sorry she kissed you. It was like Anna was back on that field in Kona, feeling a pair of hands pressing the vital organs out of her body. "What?"

"I'm sorry I kissed you. You probably didn't see that coming." If only she knew how many times Anna had indeed envisioned it coming, and in every conceivable permutation.

"*Um…*" *Blargh.* "It's fine. *You* saved *me* when you did that. I didn't mind." *Keep it at that.*

438

"That's so sweet of you."

Ugh, *sweet*. A fucking head-pat of a word. Anna tried not to wince.

Lara looked around. "How far are we from Cleveland?"

"Far," Anna said.

"Like, how many more hours?"

"I don't know. I've never driven this far to begin with."

"Well, you drove well. That's for sure."

Anna locked the Club in place on the steering wheel. Then she and Lara unlatched the doors to the Cobra and got out, reaching as high as they could to awaken their muscles and take in the springtime air. Both of them still felt phantom vibrations from sitting in a voracious, speeding hot rod from hours on end. Their ears would ring for hours afterward, but that would only serve as a pleasant reminder that they had gotten away. The two girls smiled at each other again. They were free now to leave all potential consequences of their actions unpondered.

Anna grew worried. "We have nothing," she told Lara.

"What do you mean?" Lara asked.

"We have no food apart from rest stop crap. We have no change of clothes. I don't even have a fucking toothbrush."

"Oh, and I left my vape pen at the apartment, too."

"Well yeah, there's that. But I meant necessities."

"I *need* that." Lara said. "But whatever. We can have port delivery come."

"Lara."

"Right!" Lara yelled. "We have no phones! Wow, we really are empty-handed."

"Yeah. But we still believe in each other. Bamert said we had to have that."

"He said what?"

"Never mind."

"We'll figure it out. Let's just get a room."

They walked across the decaying pavement. Anna, hiding behind her faux fashion mogul shades from the rest stop, rapped on the lobby window. Lara waited behind a shockingly violet bush of fist-sized peonies, careful to not be spotted from inside. Bereft of PortPhones, the two girls couldn't just book a room and port into it online. They had to do things the old-fashioned way.

The clerk was startled by the knocking, then gave Anna a helpless shrug, the same shrug Anna gave Lara when she botched shifting gears. The clerk took out a PortPhone and mimicked using it. Anna pantomimed emptying her pockets to tell the clerk she had no phone. The clerk grew even more perplexed. A couple ported to the front of the desk from their room and commandeered her attention.

Anna turned her back to the glass and sighed. "Well, this sucks."

"We can try another hotel," Lara said.

"Eh, their clerk will be just as worthless. Plus: I love that car, but I don't wanna get back in it."

"Me either."

"You ever been to Pennsylvania?" Anna asked her.

"Yup."

"I lived next to this state my whole life and somehow never stepped foot in it. Is it all like this?"

"Most of it, yeah," Lara said. "Sometimes you get to see a mountain. Like, a small one. I think I know how to get a room. Is the clerk still there?"

The couple was still arguing with the clerk. Finally, they ported out of the lobby with a rude clap. Anna rapped on the window again. The clerk looked pissed and mouthed the word POLICE for her to read clearly. Anna pressed a thousand-dollar bill against the glass and that wiped the snarl off the clerk's face right away.

She gave Anna the best room at the hotel. She and Lara had to climb five flights of stairs to get to it, seeing as how elevators were now extinct. One more endless staircase to ascend. But once they were on the fifth floor, they found themselves inside a two-room suite with a working portwall and a scenic view of both the mall and a pool that was covered in an old mesh tarp. The tarp itself had been ravaged by both winter and by countless birds looking for a place to relieve themselves. The hotel room in Singapore was far nicer.

Neither Lara nor Anna cared. Lara bolted for the king bed—the only bed—and made a snow angel on top of the bedspread. Anna grabbed a water bottle and drank it all in one gulp as Lara propped herself up on her elbows and made a mock angry face.

"They charge for that water, you know," she told Anna.

"Oh they do? Shit. Sorry."

Lara laughed. "I think we can afford it, girl. No more *sorry*s. Toss me one of those."

Anna grabbed a second bottle from the bar table and lobbed it onto the bed. Management had also left the girls a bottle of Pinot Noir to drink. Anna picked up the wine and gave Lara a sly look.

"Actually," said Lara, "Gimme the corkscrew."

"For real?"

"Yeah."

Anna set the bottle down and handed Lara the wine key corkscrew that the staff had left next to the Pinot: the kind of corkscrew that wouldn't have been out of place in the apron of a waiter at Sandy's old steakhouse. Lara flipped open the foil cutter at the end of it: a nasty fingernail of a blade that could cut you with the lightest touch. She gave the corkscrew back to Anna and traced a line on her arm, connecting the end points of the C in the Conquistadors logo together.

"No," said Anna.

"Told you I had a plan."

"I'm not gonna hurt you."

"You never could. Do it. Fix this for me."

Anna put a bath towel under them and held the foil cutter to Lara's arm, trying not to throw up at the thought of cutting her as Jason had, and in nearly the same spot. This was not the tonight she had envisioned.

"I really don't know if I can do this," she told Lara.

"I'm a big girl," Lara said. "You know it'll look better."

"Do you need, like, anesthetic?"

"No. I know pain. This is easy pain."

"How deep do I cut?"

"Deep enough for it to last."

Anna dug the foil cutter into Lara's skin, feeling her heart bleed in tandem with it. She brought it down an inch, re-fashioning the logo into a standard Mars symbol. Lara didn't make a sound as the blood cascaded down her arm and spattered the formerly pristine towel. Instead, she traced a small plus sign at the bottom of the newly minted circle for Anna to carve, to complete a hybrid Mars/Venus symbol.

"Seriously?" Anna asked.

"It'll look corny, but I don't mind corny things now."

"Me either."

She hacked the crisscross into Lara's arm, as instructed. It was hard digging because Lara's skin—soft as it was—was tough underneath, and because all her blood made everything slick.

God, please don't fuck this job up.

When Anna finished, she rushed to the bathroom to grab a washcloth and some tastefully packaged supplies of gauze and bandages adorning the sink, and then cleaned the wound. It was a gruesome sight, but at least it wasn't that dreaded logo anymore. She had stanched the bleeding, but that made her slightly worried she hadn't cut deep enough. Once she finished wrapping up Lara's arm, she rubbed it gently to help spur some extra healing. Lara kissed her on the cheek in gratitude.

"Thank you," she told Anna.

"I feel like you should cut something into me to make it even," Anna offered.

"We *are* even."

"That's good because I didn't actually want you to do that. Are you okay?"

"Not really."

"You need that wine now?"

"I think I'd rather just sleep tonight," said Lara.

She just wants to sleep. She just wants nothing. Shit.

Anna popped open the minibar fridge, grabbed a precious energy drink, and slurped it down.

"How are you gonna sleep if you drink that?" Lara asked her.

442

"I dunno. I never worried about that before." Anna looked out past the mall to a strip of shops and restaurants that were still open. "I guess we could go out to eat?"

"We can't be seen, Roomie."

"Right."

"You're still not quite used to being infamous yet. It shows."

"Gimme time! We need dinner, man!"

"Check the minibar," Lara suggested.

Anna did. All it had to offer was a cursory assortment of candy bars, kettle chips, overpriced artisanal beef jerky, and top ramen. Anna had just spent four months alone with top ramen yet still loved it dearly. She held up the Styrofoam cup of noodles.

"Ramen?" she asked Lara.

Lara nodded. "Ramen."

Anna filled the cup to the line, stuck it in the microwave, and jabbed at the buttons. Nothing. "The fucking microwave is busted."

"Do you want me to call down to the lobby?" asked Lara. They had bribed the clerk into keeping her mouth shut about their presence at the hotel. She was theirs to boss around.

"No. I have a much worse idea." Anna drained the cup and filled it back up with tap water as hot as she could get it from the faucet. She set it on the table as Lara went to the bathroom, showered off the ordeal, redressed her arm, popped some complimentary ibuprofen, and came back out in a short terrycloth robe. Anna did likewise. Clad in their robes, they stared at the ramen cup. The noodles were still a brick, steeping in the water like bad tea.

"How long you think it needs to soak before we can eat it?" asked Lara.

"I don't know. I'd say sorry about this, but—"

"No more *sorry*s."

"Right. I guess we'll just poke at it."

"Let's watch some TV while we wait." Lara walked over to the plate glass window to pull the shades closed. They screeched with every inch, like they had never been closed before.

Anna stood there watching. Maybe the tonight she wanted would have to wait. Ah, but Anna didn't save the world just to wait for what she wanted. Not this time. She risked it all, and she won. The rest of the world—hell, the rest of *time*—could jolly well wait right now instead.

Let's get irresponsible.

"Lara," she said quietly.

Lara paused drawing the blinds. "What?"

"Lara, I don't know if we can be roommates right now. Even tonight."

"Why not?" Lara asked.

"Because I wanna touch you."

"I wanna touch you, too."

Every step they took toward one another was as quick as a shiver. Suddenly they weren't so tired anymore. The two of them met in the center of the suite, where Lara wrapped her arms around Anna and opened her own lips. It was effortless, their mouths fit together so perfectly. Anna wanted to live inside this kiss. *This is the tonight.* She smelled the hotel's aromatherapy conditioner in Lara's hair and heard the heavenly clickety-clack of Lara's neon bangle bracelets jangling as the two of them kissed and made each other whole. *First hands, now lips. Soon, bodies.*

Lara nipped at Anna's ear and then, in a fragile whisper, told her, "Anna, I love you."

"I love you, too."

"I've *always* loved you."

"Promise me you're not lying."

"Look at me."

Anna slipped back, but not far. Their noses were still touching, their faces occupying each other's entire field of vision. Lara didn't have to say a word. Love was all over her. They kissed so hard they couldn't breathe.

Lara pulled away for a moment but Anna wasn't ready to let go, ever. She wanted more.

"Lemme close the blinds all the way," Lara insisted.

"I can't wait that long," Anna told her.

"I can't either."

Lara hurried to draw the white curtain shut as Anna walked over to the bed and sat down, gamely trying to stay cool but restless with joy. She was operating on euphoric autopilot, living outside her body and astonished at her current good fortune. Anna could have rocketed to the outer planets on adrenaline alone. This beat daydreams. No Lily Beach or piano serenades or ski lodges or shadow dimensions required. She never wanted to stop hearing Lara Kirsch say *I love you*. All the places in the world that she'd been and it was here, in a shit hotel on the way to Cleveland, where love made good on all of its outlandish promises. For the first time, Anna was exactly where she wanted to be. She was home. All of her senses were reborn.

The curtain was closed now. No one would see them. They were alone and ready for each other. Lara plucked a yellow silk tulip out of a welcome vase and held it out for Anna.

"Three feet on the floor?" Anna joked.

"No one will see us in the dark," Lara said, her fingers grazing the light switch. Her voice had gone low again. Soft as her lips.

"Who said I wanted it to be dark when I touch you?" Anna shot back playfully.

Lara Kirsch flashed another devilish grin.

"Do you think I would just run away from you again, Roomie? Don't you worry…"

She flicked the light off.

"I'm not going anywhere."

THE END

ACKNOWLEDGMENTS

You've read this far, so I may as well subject you to one last story while you're still here. First of all, as you might have surmised, there is no Druskin Academy. At least, not that I know of. There is only Joe Druskin, my old jayvee football coach in Minnesota, who introduced me to Hüsker Dü and to Cyberball and who was kinder to me than I ever deserved at that age.

There is also no Sewell Hall. There is only Soule (pronounced *sole*) Hall, the dorm in which I resided when I went to a haughty dipshit prep school—one not-so-coincidentally similar to the haughty dipshit prep school depicted in this very book—back in the early 1990s. Why yes, that dorm DID have its own Shit Memoirs resting on the floor of the upstairs toilet. One time I cracked it open and was both honored and horrified to see that someone had made a list entitled, "Top Ten Things Drew Always Says." One of those things was "The Saints are my dark horse team this year." It was true. I did always say that, even though I'm not a Saints fan and even though this was back when they never won anything.

Anyway, the story. Back in April of 1992, Jerry Seinfeld hosted an episode of *Saturday Night Live*. This episode is probably best remembered for the immortal "Stand Up And Win" sketch where Adam Sandler answers, "Who are the ad wizards who came up with this one?!" for every clue. A couple of my dorm-mates attended that taping live at Studio 8H. When Seinfeld came out to do his monologue, they cried out "YEAH SOULE!" from the balcony. At least, it sounded like "YEAH SOULE!" to them and to those of us watching with elation back in the common room. To the rest of the audience watching in New York and at home, and to Jerry Seinfeld himself, it sounded very much like they were screaming ASSHOLE at him. Seinfeld pointed up to the balcony with a smile, gave an ironic "Thank *you*," and then carried on. That part of his monologue was cut from subsequent reruns of that episode, but I swear it happened.

I was only able to write this book thanks to the formative years I spent living in that dorm, and to the friends I made at school while I was there. Those friends include but are not limited to Howard

448

Spector, Jesse Johnston, Steve Martyak, James Fisher, Winthrop Short, Robin Mahapatra, Matt Breuer, Scott Mitchell, Joe Urban, Ameet Thakkar, Moses Sabina, Enrique Smith, John Crisostomo, Virginia Corpus, Sam Brooks, Matt Addesa, Izzy Lawal, Sid Brown, Xander Hargrave, Josh Panas, Josh Dapice, Ettrick Campbell, Brooke Killheffer, Vivek Masson, Chris Sandeman, Scott Iason, Grant Whitmer, Brook Katzen, Ashwin Mehta, Anna Hochstedler, Linda Jenkins, and many, many others. Hoo boy, that's a big list. Frankly, it makes me sound WAY more popular than I actually was.

That list also includes the actual Paul Bamert, who has nothing in common with the Paul Bamert you just met in these pages, except that he's a great dude AND that he enjoys Clemson footbaw. So thanks to the real Bamert for letting me swipe his name for this. I owe you an Edible Arrangement for your trouble.

This book hopscotches all over the world, so I'm also deeply grateful to all the family members, friends, and colleagues who gave me loose field reports from many of their travels beyond the horizon. Is it time for me to list off another bunch of names? Dear reader, it is. My eyes and ears around the globe included my wife, my parents, and my brother and sister, plus Megan Greenwell, Laura Wagner, Patrick Redford, Barry Petchesky, Giri Nathan, Libby Watson, Steve Czaban, Howard Spector, Erica Wishnow, and Spencer Hall. One day I hope to go to all of the places that these people have gone to. For now, they remain pleasant dreamscapes: out of reach but not despairingly so.

We're not done here yet. This book is based on what is, charitably speaking, a scientifically implausible premise. I toil in a real world where hoverboards for sale don't even hover. It's total bullshit. Despite science's miserly ways, I did rely on an actual physicist, Matt Bellis, to physicist this book and to give me a rudimentary course in quantum mechanics that IMMEDIATELY sailed over my head. You have Matt to thank for the idea of portclaps, portwinds, and other phenomena in this book that are not coming to your future but at least sound like they could be. Science is MAGIC.

There is some car shit in here and since I'm not a car guy, I wanna thank all the car people in my life—my in-laws, my brother-in-law Greg, and Patrick George—who chipped in to make sure that other car people wouldn't throw their ratchets at me over the mechanics detailed herein. I'm sure I still got some things wrong but I swear I did the best I could. Your cover and interior design come courtesy of the fabulous Dennis Padua. I can write a zillion words but it's the art that pumps fresh oxygen into everything, so thanks to Dennis for that.

While Anna Huff is NOT based on my 14-year-old daughter, both girls are avid divers. So thanks to my kid for giving me a vital lesson in diving technique when all I know how to do off the board is an underwhelming cannonball. Furthermore, no characters in this book are based on my two sons, which is for the best since no fictional character could ever do those boys justice.

I also need to thank everyone who gave me notes, in particular Kelsey McKinney, Jesse Johnston, and Mary Pender. Bonus feedback and inspiration came from Mari Uyehara, Tim Marchman, Tim Burke, my mother-in-law, Matt Ufford, Justin Halpern, Byrd Leavell, David Roth, Chris Gayomali, Lauren Theisen, Rob Harvilla, Luis Paez-Pumar, Rob Grabill, and many more. I was only able to write this book because Megan and Susie Banakarim gave me a sabbatical from Deadspin in 2018 to go finish it, so I thank them both for the time and also for so much more beyond that.

Finally, about my wife: I spent the majority of my time writing this book remembering what it was like to be a lovesick teenager. I was *desperate* for a girlfriend back then. That was all I ever wanted and all I ever thought about. And lo and behold, I found my wife. I love her and she loves me, and that remains impossibly fucking cool. We've been married seventeen years and have three kids. Our marriage is, itself, a teenager. That is also impossibly fucking cool. If I sound like every cornyass dad on Twitter when I say all that, so be it. I don't mind corny things now. I never want to forget how lucky it is to be loved. It's the fucking greatest. I may get old but being in love never will.

And to Byrd: Thanks for the lift.

ABOUT THE AUTHOR

Drew Magary is the author of *The Postmortal*, *Someone Could Get Hurt*, and *The Hike*. This is his third novel. He lives in Maryland with his wife, three kids, and a dog. In a past life, he was a writer/flamethrower for Deadspin and GQ. Nowadays, he's an in-house columnist for GEN magazine. He also won *Chopped* once and will never let you fucking forget it.

Printed in Great Britain
by Amazon